O. MURRAY CARR

O. MURRAY CARR

A Novel

Neil Rolde

Tilbury House Publishers
Gardiner, Maine

Tilbury House, Publishers
103 Brunswick Avenue
Gardiner, Maine 04345
800–582–1899 • www.tilburyhouse.com

First paperback edition: July 2010
10 9 8 7 6 5 4 3 2 1

Library of Congress Cataloging-in-Publication Data
Rolde, Neil, 1931-
  O. Murray Carr : a novel / Neil Rolde. -- 1st pbk. ed.
     p. cm.
  ISBN 978-0-88448-332-8 (pbk. : alk. paper)
  1. Legislators--United States--Fiction. 2. Assassination--United States--Fiction. 3. National Governors' Conference--Fiction. 4. United States--Politics and government--Fiction. I. Title.
  PS3618.O543O3 2010
  813'.6--dc22
                                  2010018919

Cover photograph by Nancy P. McGinnis (www.communicado.us)
Cover design by Geraldine Millham, Westport, Massachusetts
Copyedited by Genie Dailey, FinePoints Editorial Services, Jefferson, Maine
Printed and bound by Versa Press, Spring Point, Illinois

for
America the Beautiful

I

THOSE TWO GUNSHOTS in almost split-second succession woke me from my dream. They were reality—actual history, you might say. I sat up in bed and found myself shivering. All around me was darkness. Whatever fantasy my subconscious flashed to me had vanished. *Go back to sleep, Jonathan*, I thought. *Don't even turn on the light. What else did you expect?*

This sort of thing would happen during the wee hours whenever I needed to make a trip to our state capital. I no longer worked there, no longer was a member of the legislature, either, but occasional tasks summoned me hither to spend time in the Statehouse. Why do I always feel so skittish, hear fatal shots in my sleep, before every visit to my old stomping grounds?

Silly boy. You know the answer: political murder. The sound of assassination—a pistol *pop* followed by the *blam* of a service revolver. The sight remains in your mind, too, Jonathan, but you've utterly repressed that. It all happened so long ago and so far away.

You might think, Jonathan Jackson, that you could blot *every* part of this shocking memory from your being. But no—scolding has never ended such moments of panic. Except on this particular day in mid-December, just weeks after the recent presidential election, I hadn't the slightest inkling that my latest return to the capital city would finally goad me into exorcising my ghosts.

I'd been invited—in my capacity as an academic historian, an ex-legislator, and, earlier, a gubernatorial assistant—to participate in a little-known ceremony that takes place every four years in our Statehouse. Not many Americans are aware that the electoral votes they hear so much about during a presidential campaign actually consist of marked paper ballots dropped into a ballot box. Presidential electors, persons designated by their political parties, do this actual voting—that is, the winners do. In our state we have four electors, and since my party, the Democrats, won here, we continued our tradition of holding a little celebration, and it was my job to present a mini-history of the electoral college—how it came to be and how it has resisted serious change from its inauguration in the Constitution and now has fifty states conducting these same votes simultaneously on a certain appointed day in December. The results are then sent to Washington, D.C., counted by Congress, and pronounced official.

Enough of my pedantry. Before I knew it, I was up, shaved, showered, dressed, at breakfast with my wife, Jill, and soon on the road, a drive of fifty to seventy-five minutes, depending on traffic conditions and whether I felt like speeding or dawdling.

Both modes were employed today—the dawdling especially, once I caught sight of the Statehouse dome.

I have seen a few other Statehouse domes in my travels and I am always impressed by the majesty they seem to convey. They don't have to be tall. In the old days, when I lived in New York City and went home to New England by train, Providence, Rhode Island, provided a perfect example. In the midst of the city's downtown was a rather small building housing the state government, its dome gray, seemingly made of stone, yet full of quiet dignity amid a cacophony of structures. I don't suppose I have to tell anyone about the capitol in Washington, D.C. It's on a "hill," of course. Forget about what happens inside; its exterior is sublime and commands immediate respect. Boston's—on another hill, Beacon Hill—has a golden dome, beaming like an inspirational searchlight. And so I am led, in our state, to the fortress-like, thick granite of the approaching edifice, already in view beyond my windshield, about which I want to say a few things.

At this distance, I'm on the east side of the river that runs through our capital city. The Statehouse dome on the west side of the river is like a smear of murky green—or, in the sardonic words of my one-time mentor, the late Honorable Representative Matthew X. Drew, "diarrhea verdancy." Its metal sheathing is weathered to an unpleasant hue, and although I still couldn't see it clearly, I caught a glimpse of the statue of a robed female goddess with an upraised arm, also of the same ghastly color, atop the dome.

Nevertheless, our dome has dignity, too, despite such shortcomings.

A legislature is a place that is always trying to change matters and, if possible, make improvements. That baneful green above us had been a target in the past, according to Matt Drew, but bills even to *paint it* something else had never so much as gotten out of committee. A waste of taxpayers' money, a large majority had invariably agreed.

Then, in my time, along had come the Honorable Representative Helen Bailey Pratt, among the ditsiest of our members, a sweet, aged, archconservative lady Republican who had a better idea. Gild it, with donations from everyone in the state—send in worn, obsolete wedding rings, no-longer-fashionable jewelry, and—who knows—perhaps unwanted gold teeth, the whole lot to be melted down and slathered by bucketfuls over the offending surface. Mrs. Pratt had been to Boston and was a great admirer of the Bay State's glittering dome.

Inevitably, then and there, a familiar memory would fill my mind, an incident from my freshman year as an elected official.

Prior to this milestone in my life, I had also worked in the Statehouse as a special assistant to Governor Richard N. Ellery, a period I will detail later on.

For the moment then, regarding our dome, a bunch of us first-time Democratic Representatives were clustered in the Members' Retiring Lounge about the portly figure of the Honorable Matthew X. Drew (an understatement since he weighed close to 300 pounds), listening to him after he'd held up and read aloud from a news clipping announcing Helen Pratt's quixotic plan to beautify the Statehouse dome.

"I've got a better idea," Matt finally declared in his blustery voice. "Let's gild the gentle lady herself. In place of the statue up there, we'll set down dear Helen, all bright and golden and stiff. And that will be excruciatingly appropriate. Do any of you know why?"

We all looked blankly at each other and at Matt.

In those days, you could smoke in the lounge and we were in the smoking section. Matt flicked the ashes of his dark brown cigarillo and said to me, "Jonathan, you're the historian. Whose statue is on top of the dome?"

I did know the answer. But one of our fellows piped up ahead of me, "Some Roman broad."

"Yeah, that's right, Minerva," I was quick to get in my licks.

"The Roman goddess of what?" Matt demanded.

Another of the guys beat me to the answer. "Wisdom," he replied.

"To guide us," I volunteered. "That was their original intent, when the state's founding fathers built this place. They wanted an image overhead—it's actually written in the records—to inspire the debates that would occur inside."

"So what more fitting exchange could we institute?" Matt asked with a wicked grin. "Helen for Minerva. The failed Goddess of Wisdom displaced at last by our rightful tutelary grande dame, Helen Pratt, the Goddess of Stupidity."

Matt's words carried, Helen was within earshot, and we all cringed. I, for one, remember that exchange every time I spy the

Statehouse, although now more than two decades have passed. On this present occasion, I was still four or five blocks away. It was midmorning and the rising sun had hit the dome and everything up there was still a dull, sickly green.

But no sooner did I reflect about the famous moment in the lounge than I sought to rebut Matt's cynicism and focus my gaze on a certain row of windows along the second story of the edifice ahead of me, where in my time the governor's suite of offices was located. Why do I stare? Because in my innermost depths, I always want to give the lie to Matt's implied charge that no one was ever wise in the Statehouse. Perhaps they were clever or knowing or fiercely dedicated like he was, but farseeing, principled, selfless, Minerva-guided—never, in his eyes. So, in mine, I needed to conjure up my old boss, the late Governor Ellery, the "Duke," as everyone called him, and on our bumper stickers just plain DUKE. His image would flash into my mind: a six-footer, sandy-haired, obviously Anglo-Saxon, Harvardian, with his movie-star good looks, but kindly mien, infectious smile, and displaying instant charisma simply by walking into any room.

There. I always douse myself with those two contrasting memories. I don't make the drive much anymore, now that I'm retired, so to speak. Once in a while, I'll attend a Reunion Day, which is when we old-timers from the legislature mingle with all the young pups who are presently being elected and we have a bit of a bash—lots of nostalgia followed by a pretty good free lunch, courtesy of the taxpayers. As for governor's office sentimentality, the staff today doesn't have the time, even if it had the inclination, to want to meet in a reunion mode, never mind celebrate, with its predecessors in those top executive department political jobs.

There'd been a shift in the weather, a January thaw, except it was not quite yet mid-December. We'd had three solid weeks of winter from the end of November and now the early snow had gone—temporarily, to be sure—and, as always, I found myself rooting for the white stuff at Christmas. Two weeks after that, the legislators would be coming in to their opening session. "Idiot birds, flocking north when they should be flying south." Guess whose wisecrack? Matt Drew's, of course. He'd stand on the third-floor balcony, out in the cold, and point with his cigarillo at the vehicles with special license plates, blue for the house and yellow for the senate, pulling into our reserved spaces, and every January he'd make his sarcastic bon mot. Until death took him, right on that very same balcony, he'd been elected for twenty-one consecutive terms—almost forty-two years.

The maples and oaks on the last stretch to the capital complex were leafless and sad. It was a down time, a slack season before the holidays, and following the November elections for the legislature as well as the presidency this year, slack time for the legislature, too. The legislative leadership and the new freshmen would have already been here for orientation sessions, but full attendance by the entire elected body, plus the crowds that flocked to sessions and hearings, was a full month away.

Nevertheless, I told myself, *it's still gonna be hell to find a parking space.*

Lots of years have passed since I had those special blue license plates on my car, ever since I went back to being a peon again. When Rachel Antonioni, the chair of the Democratic State Committee, called and invited me to participate in this shindig, I couldn't ask her for a parking pass, could I? Some Republican might squawk that I was taking up an official parking spot while hardly on state business. See, I always think like a pol. Timid, though, I'm really not.

Underlying any serious angst was also a question of ethics. How I used to howl when I saw non-legislators violating our privileged space, denying some of us an earned perk. But the capital police explained they could merely ticket; the law gave them no authority to tow. "Sorry, Representative Jackson. We guess the theory is those folks are taxpayers and voters and would holler like mad."

Since I'd made such a fuss in those days—I myself put in a bill to give our cops the right to tow until I was "persuaded" by the leadership to withdraw it—I was fearful of being labeled a hypocrite if my car were ever found in a legislator's spot to which it was not entitled. *Who'd remember?* the devil in me teased, as it often did. *A matter of principle*, I'd insist, and conjure an image in my thoughts of Duke Ellery.

Within sight of the entrance to the parking area, I turned left at the traffic light and then turned left again. There were no gates, no guards: an open welcome to the public, who paid the bills. That's how we ran things in our state.

The serried ranks of automobiles, vans, SUVs, pickup trucks, etc., seemed impenetrable at first glance, so my inner debate continued. As I drove between the rows, I pondered in my usually intellectual way: *Could my appearance here arguably be interpreted as state business?*

That subject was good for a host of speculations. Admittedly, on the surface, the newspapers would dub our ceremony a political party event: "Democrats assemble." Something of that sort. But whoa! It's held in the chamber of the house of representatives—on state-owned property, inside the Statehouse itself. Then again, the results of the actions taken are to be sent to Washington, D.C.—to the Congress of the United States of America. It is directly by the instructions of the Constitution of these same United States that said activity *must* be undertaken. Federal mandate. Should the party fail to comply, poor Rachel Antonioni could possibly end up in Leavenworth Prison.

Wearing my professor's hat, I might want to point out to my students the amazing concurrence of state, federal, and nongovernmental aspects of American life in a single act—

and explain how consequential and inconsequential this act was at one and the same time.

There was a lot more to it than just the physical effort of putting ballots in a box. In one respect, the entire stability of our republic rested upon the same enactment in all fifty states in each state capital on the same day. Yet, simultaneously, it was a total anticlimax, since there was no real suspense because the outcome was already public knowledge.

My role today was not as an elector, but as a pedagogue, assigned to discuss the whys and wherefores of our frankly bizarre method of confirming our national chief executives. Who knows exactly how it works? To gauge your state's number of electoral votes, count up your congressmen and congresswomen, add them to your two senators, and that's the number. As I've already said, in our small state, population-wise, it's four.

Next, let's turn to the actual electors themselves. How are they chosen? But before I get into such details, you all know that whichever presidential candidate wins the popular vote in a state, he (or someday, she) gains *all* its electoral votes (and here, in academia, I would probably waste time on a footnote, drawing attention to an exception in several states, where the winner within a congressional district can receive an electoral vote, although losing the rest of the state).

A common inquiry at this juncture is: Do the electors have to vote for the candidates to whom they're pledged? The answer seems to be no. Can they vote for themselves? The answer seems to be yes.

I was happily into this inner dialogue of mine, cruising the vast parking scene without any luck, when I was damn near hit by another car.

A big cream-colored Lincoln came at me down an alleyway in which there was barely room for the two of us. I admit I wasn't paying the attention I should have been and had unconsciously crowded over onto his side. He screeched to a halt. I swerved, backed away, and also stopped. My driver's window had lined up nearly opposite his, and initially, I thought we would start yelling at each other.

My window went down. So did his. But before I could speak, the other guy called out, "The honorable former representative Jonathan Jackson! I haven't seen you in ages!"

Prior to our near collision, I had glimpsed a masculine face, a man with dark hair and a full dark mustache, otherwise blurred in the tension of the moment. I squinted across now and distorted, "Meyer Fishman! Mike. Good God, Mike Fishman, it's you!"

Thus it was that an odd conjunction of circumstances threw the two of us together early on, and let this figure from my political past, whom I knew only tangentially, spend some moments chatting with me. Mike was Jewish, as you may have guessed. That was neither here nor there, except in my experience he had always been a kvetch, a Yiddish word my childhood buddy Gerry Margolis taught me—a pest. But he was a very determined and effective kvetch. He got things done. And all at once, I remembered why *he* was here and why he was one of the party's four honored electors.

"Sure, it's me. I have to be here. I didn't see you at the last state convention. They voted me an elector again. And you're here to talk about history, right?" A stream of words came from the other driver's seat. I would have responded, except right then a car was coming behind him and he had to move. "Let's catch up," I heard Mike yell, and he gunned his motor and was gone.

Not far away, though. The son of a gun pulled straight into the legislative parking section, which was about half-empty.

I was sorely itching to follow him, noting that he, a total civilian, as we elected guys would say, had no qualms about parking inside the forbidden zone. Maybe if I hadn't had to turn around to do so. Or maybe if my parking karma, to use my wife's expression, wasn't working. I had barely driven another ten yards when I saw an opening the size of a car and immediately pulled into it.

The walk to the Statehouse steps took about five minutes. Mike stood waiting for me on the top landing. Neither of us wore a topcoat, although it was a tad chilly, and Mike had a maroon wool scarf draped rakishly around his neck. We shook hands.

"Professor Jackson, you're a shitty driver," he said.

"Sorry, Mike." I sort of hung my head. "Absentmindedness. I'm approaching my dotage."

"A statement I doubt," he countered. "You were always one of the smartest ones. It was a pleasure to listen to you in the house. And at the state conventions, when you spoke. On the platform committee—yeah, especially. And you helped me. I never forgot how you helped me."

Well, Mike was off and running at the mouth, chattering all the way to the elevator, up to the third floor, then down the corridor toward the speaker's office, which was adjacent to the house chamber. This practically ceaseless monologue, interrupted by me with no more than an occasional "Yes," "Sure," or "I remember," harked back to what he always made seem the greatest moment of his life and the reason, in his words, that "a poor schmuck haberdasher like me, the son of immigrants, has the pleasure today to cast one-quarter of this state's presidential vote. . . ."

Usually his speech, as I remembered, ended with *God bless America.* Today he was too busy recounting, as he did every time we met, the battle we had fought in the state Democratic Party to change its rules on presidential electors. They used to be named by the party leaders and strictly reserved for party big shots. Thanks to Mike, who raised the issue and braved ridicule and hostility, with a few allies like myself, we changed that long ago. Now, you run for it at our state convention and are elected democratically by your peers.

Since then, Mike Fishman, the trailblazer, had never failed to run and be elevated to one of the four spots, available every four years whether our national candidate won or lost the White House, as long as we nailed the state.

There was a small crowd ahead of us, milling outside the speaker's office. I noticed Rachel Antonioni. But suddenly, Mike stopped still, bringing me to a halt, too.

"Hey, you know, Jonathan, I knew I had something to ask you," he said, eyeing me dramatically.

"Shoot," I said, not even speculating on his intent.

"You know, I never so much as asked you how the missus was, and the kids."

A hint of vagueness in his expression told me this wasn't *the* question. Blithely, I answered anyway, "Jill's fine and we have but the one son, Ritchie—or Richard. He's in Los Angeles, has a nice job, not married yet, and like these kids nowadays, living in sin with a girl. And you. How's the store? Your kids are in business with you, if I remember. Business okay?"

Mike shrugged his shoulders, smiled to himself, and replied, "There's an old Jewish joke. One businessman says to another, 'Ask me how's business.' The other says, 'All right, how's business?' The first guy says, 'Don't ask.'"

We both laughed a bit. Yet I could see by his furrowed brow that he was still trying to get around to mentioning something else. "Jonathan," he started, cleared his throat, got my attention. "What about your book?"

Plainly puzzled, I retorted, "Which book?"

"The one you were going to write," he said.

"About what?"

"Um. . . ." Mike Fishman was never at a loss for words. With those dark brown button eyes of his, he glanced in a direction that seemed to indicate a nearby staircase, and only after he spoke did I realize he was referring to another floor. "About the guv. You once told me you had it in mind."

"Oh, a book on Duke's life." I finally grasped his meaning.

"If it came out, I didn't see it."

"Never finished the writing," I admitted sheepishly. "Started, quit, started over again. I have a lot of research. His years in Congress. His record here. Some stuff on his childhood, prep school, Harvard—"

"You sound like you still could write it," Mike interrupted. "You really should."

"I know." Once more, I sort of hung my head.

"If you do, I have an idea for you," Mike volunteered.

"Frankly, Mike," I said, "I'm happy to listen to your idea. But I have to tell you, I've never had such trouble with a project. Aside from the fact it won't ever get published. He was an important person for us. He might have been important, very important, for the whole country, and he *was* a congressman. Even so, it's not an academic book, and as a trade biography, it wouldn't sell, either. Too 'narrow'—that's what they like to tell you in the publishing world."

"Do it for yourself, Jonathan."

I looked at him. He nodded.

"Do yourself some good," Mike continued. "The whole thing's been eating at you for years. Me, too. And you were a lot, lot closer to him. I always told you he could've been another Harry Truman. That's my idea. Make him into another Harry Truman."

True enough, I remembered, I'd heard such expressions from Mike before. We'd had a fairly extended, liquor-lubricated argument one night in a hospitality suite at one of our conventions. Everyone said Duke was Kennedyesque. Maybe FDRish. We all admired Harry Truman, but the style was so different.

With a chuckle, right there in the Statehouse corridor, I told Mike, "Let's save that discussion for another time, my friend. We should go join the others." And I pointed to the group in the distance. Some of them were beginning to enter the house chamber.

"The human touch," Mike went on, as if he hadn't heard me. "They both had the human touch. Why do you think I love Truman—because he was a haberdasher? Duke, he saw into people. And that's how you should write about him. From your point of view. Tell it like a story. But like it was. Like all this is." He waved his arms to take in our surroundings, the diminishing crowd at the end of the hall, the polished doors of the debating chambers, house and senate at either end, the walls full of framed photographs, the statues, the old flags in glass cases, and overhead, the hollowed interior of the dome stretching up and up to an unseen Minerva.

Real life. The *inside* story. I didn't think Mike Fishman meant one of those *True* magazines, or whatever you call them, that sensationalize celebrities in the public eye with a lot of salacious crap. Nor a "tell-all" biography posturing as scholarly work. In academe itself, the history stuff we put out is all too frequently dry and lifeless, strangled by footnotes and suffocated by an overload of detail, but at least it's fairly accurate. As much as it can be—for how can an author stuff in every last detail? When you're playing God, you still have to pick and choose.

It was Matt Drew, again, who came to mind on this score. He once told me that his idea of the most diabolical torture any human being could undergo was to be tied in a chair and forced to watch, unrolling before your very eyes, second by second, the entire life you had lived up until then. "All the boredom, can you imagine, the horrible monotony, the bits of shame, puking, sleeping, defecating, moments of rejection, pain, pure hell, watching the triumphs, too, no matter how fleeting and inconsequential. . . ." Those words of Matt's, suddenly revived in the Statehouse, stuck with me throughout the electoral college ceremony, particularly as I sat and waited for my turn to speak.

Everything began with a bit of pageantry, a color guard, loaned by the National Guard, marching in, solemn-faced, uniformed young men and women holding flagstaffs, showing the state flag, the Stars and Stripes, the banner of their own outfit, wheeling smartly at the command of an officer wielding a sword. The counties were represented by several deputy sheriffs in full police regalia, one of whom would serve us as sergeant-at-arms. The house speaker presided. The four electors, following an established organizational procedure, selected a spokesperson (in this case, a young woman) to go through a formulaic rigmarole that led eventually to the climactic instant in which each of the quartet ascended the dais and inserted their already Xed ballots through the slit in a wooden box prettily decorated in red, white, and blue.

Was there any suspense? Of course not. The presidential winner, as we spoke, was preparing to govern for the next four years. The so-called election here today, even had we been the most populous state in the Union, could change nothing. Entirely symbolic though it was, we drew a pretty good crowd, much to my surprise.

Family members, party stalwarts, some state employees, a few tourists on a tour of the state capitol, a minimum of a dozen or more legislators taking time out from other duties—all these folks nearly filled the empty seats and desks of the hundred-plus house members. People stood in the back of the hall, too, most peeking in, watching a bit, and leaving.

It must have been close to an hour before my performance began. It happened prior to the actual voting. They had me up with the other dignitaries on the dais, in one of those big winged chairs to either side of the speaker's rostrum. The microphone system had been turned on. We had prayers, as we did every morning at the commencement of a house session. A singing group, a chorale of teenaged boys and girls, serenaded us, and a band stationed up in the gallery performed loudly and often. In between were school-kid declamations and some political speechifying (but scrupulously nonpartisan). For this electoral college stint, the musical theme was strictly patriotic. In addition to the National Anthem, we had "God Bless America," "America the Beautiful," "This Land is My Land," and "The Battle Hymn of the Republic."

The four electors were in the center of the front row. I was conscious that my gaze would stray especially to Mike Fishman, watching him sing or mouth the words to those heart-stirring songs as they were played. He had tears on his cheeks. I couldn't help but feel for him. The other three electors had their families with them. He was alone. His moment to shine and no one of his flesh and blood around for a witness. His Estelle had died of breast cancer maybe six years ago, and of the boys, neither had wanted to come or they had to stay home with the business, or both. I saw that Rachel Antonioni was sitting nearby. I hoped she had arranged a photographer to snap Mike's picture.

One more signal remembrance of the period was when "America the Beautiful" was played and sung. I've always loved that tune. Like many other Americans, I wouldn't mind seeing it substituted for "The Star-Spangled Banner." Naturally, I found myself singing along. And on the refrain "America! America!" I suddenly, so to speak, woke up—and, to a drum roll almost, those sounds were humming "Ohmuhricar, Ohmuhricar," and then, like a stab of pain, I remembered a cute boyhood thought of mine, expressed to a certain pal, about how I had twisted the lyric in my mind into someone's name: *O. Murray Carr*—a Mr. O. Murray Carr.

My talk to the audience, which eventually did follow, need not be elaborated here in great detail. I may well have bored them at the outset with allusions to Rome and her republic, the etymology of the distinction between capital (the seat of government) and capitol (the building housing it) and Minerva as our tutelary goddess. Soon, I went on to the electoral college, allegedly modeled on the Holy Roman Empire, and then brought up Aaron Burr and Jefferson and their tied electoral vote in 1800, which led to the end of separate voting for the vice president. Citations of Article 2, Section 1, of the Constitution, the 12th Amendment, the Electoral Count Act of 1887 following the messy presidential election and recounts in 1876, were my oral footnotes. I tried not to be too erudite in explaining why we had stuck with the electoral college despite recent attempts to change the practice under Nixon and Carter that indicated, if nothing else, a wholesale dissatisfaction with this (and I didn't use the word) cockamamie arrangement.

Before long, we were done. Another public spectacle, such as it was, had transpired and been swept into the invisible memory bank of the house chamber, the Statehouse, the capit*ol*, and capit*al*. Some official pieces of paper would go to D.C. for their archives, plus our memory bank on the state level, over in the state archives building, might receive a few papers from today, probably including the printed program. And we could all go home.

A reception on a minor scale—cookies and coffee and tea—in the speaker's office would not keep me for long. Now, if there'd been Scotch. . . . But booze was a no-no in the Statehouse. Openly and officially, I mean. After all, we did have lockers, we did have drawers in our desks, not to mention the amount some of the members carried back in their stomachs from lunch. And thinking about that, who should pop up in my mind for a third time? Matt Drew, who not only smoked those foul brown cigarillos of his like a chimney, but drank like a you-know-what. Some early mornings, when I sat next to him in the house, I could smell that he had already had a nip or two. But I never saw Matt drunk, unsteady on his feet, or with a slur in his speech and, in the course of a session, he was on his feet far more than the rest of us, offering wisdom—and often it genuinely *was* wisdom—on any number of legislative subjects.

When I left the speaker's office, following a minimal amount of schmoozing, I didn't go straight to the stairs or the elevator. I opened the doors to the third floor balcony and stepped outside, moving to the balustrade, gauging the section of railing where Matt used to stand and make remarks. I had always assumed, since I wasn't present the moment he died, that the massive heart attack he'd suffered had felled him in the same approximate location. I was around the complex that day, but his body had been removed by the time I had learned about his death and had rushed upstairs.

Thus, gazing down at an expanse of concrete flooring on which in the past you might have seen a few cigarette butts, over-flows from the sand buckets put out there for ashtrays, I was as reverent as if I stood at a gravesite. *Matt left no trace,* I couldn't help thinking. *He was here forty-two years and like a puff of smoke, like one of his coffin-nail exhales, he was gone.* It occurred to me to add: *No one leaves a memorial to a mere state rep, to a plain old infantry grunt. You gotta be a governor or U.S. senator, at least, to get your portrait painted and hung in this place.*

Then, it occurred to me also: Duke had his portrait hanging downstairs in the Hall of Portraits. Thus I bade a silent good-bye to invisible Matt and went to peer at the visible Honorable Richard N. Ellery, governor of the state and ex-congressman, noting on the plaque below the painting the dates of his terms of service in both venues, including the truncated last one.

The artist had worked from a photograph, needless to say, since Duke was dead by the time they selected a portraitist, and you never posed while you were in office. His death had been as sudden as Matt's, but it wasn't something I wanted to think about then. Simply pay my respects, staring up at the canvas, my hands clasped. I didn't like the picture much. He was behind his elegant desk. You didn't see his tall, athletic frame, that sense of permanent youthfulness. I would rather he'd been in his tennis clothes, standing, instead of seated formally as he was in this image, wearing the traditional governor's garb, a dark gray worsted business suit (for him, Brooks Brothers), white dress shirt, and red "power" tie. I knew that Madge, his widow, had picked out the photo, and Madge and I, you should know, do not always see eye to eye, which is an understatement.

Another reason for my writer's block, for my reluctance to go ahead with any project attempting to memorialize Duke, creating anything beyond the approved square of canvas before me, would be Madge's potential displeasure. Hardly the number one objection, however.

I felt someone coming up from behind, and a moment later, Mike Fishman was standing alongside me. We both silently studied the handsome blondish, blue-eyed man on the wall.

"What could have been, huh, Jonathan?" Mike finally commented. "What could have been."

My thought was: *Yeah, for me especially.* Only I wasn't going to say that to Mike. "The country's loss," I said.

Mike nodded several times. "We'll never know," he said, giving me that full-faced, full-mustached, direct, browbeating look of his. "Jonathan, you owe it to yourself to do the book. You owe it to the world," he insisted.

"That's a big order," I said.

"Do it. Do us all a favor. Do it."

We left the Statehouse together without saying much more to each other. A few pleasantries: I kidded him about his car in the legislative lot—how he was an outlaw—and he told me to go take driving lessons and say hi to the missus, and God willing we'd all meet at the next state convention, and, in keeping with his natural, friendly garrulousness, he had to have the last word.

"Remember, Jonathan. The book. Reveal Duke. Immortalize him. Don't forget."

2

MY COMMUTE, when I was a legislator, was 52.5 miles from portal to portal. Many a night I stayed in the capital in a motel. We bought our house, Jill and I, while I was still working in the governor's office, although it was after Duke's death, under his successor—same party, but I could no longer stand the guy—and Jill was pregnant and fed up with her job. So "we went to the seashore," a place named Swanstown (I'll describe it later), ten minutes from the college where I'd landed a teaching post in the history department. My run for office came afterward, unexpectedly, and I'll explain that later, too.

An hour at the most today on the road and I would be home, providing the weather held up and the traffic wasn't too bad. Rush hour could be problem, the main blockage being the fairly recently renamed Ellery Bridge to the Cross-State Parkway. Midafternoon though, no problem. So I was outta there, following the electoral college affair, without any danger of finding a fuming wife at home because I'd delayed her dinner.

Unfortunately, it was a little too early for the public radio news. Not that I didn't have plenty of music CDs to fill the quiet of my car interior with rhythmic or syncopated melodies. Anything to avoid deep thinking en route in such perfect silence. Damn you, Meyer Fishman. You had certainly opened a can of mental and emotional worms.

Moreover, didn't I have to watch my driving, according to Mike? Too much cogitating and I might end up in a ditch.

The CDs were in reach of the driver's seat, in a compartment

I could open and still keep my eyes glued to the scene beyond my windshield. I just had to grab blindly, bring the plastic case over, and—for a fraction of a second—scan the title.

Would you believe it? The winner on this occasion was *America's Songs*. I laughed out loud. "There is a God," I said out loud. *Call Him Chance or Coincidence.* I let this last unspoken thought hang silently, not daring to philosophize any further. Besides, I was simply too tickled by the serendipity of random selection. I decided: *Okay, I'll listen to some of the stuff I already just heard,* and I slipped the thin disc into its niche and pressed the *On* button.

I might have swerved wildly if "America the Beautiful" had come on right then. Instead I heard "The Stars and Stripes Forever," "Anchors Away," "Dixie," "Yankee Doodle," and, coming fifth on the disc, finally, "America the Beautiful."

"O. Murray Carr," it left me muttering to myself. "O. Murray Carr." And I pressed the *On* button to make it go *Off.*

In defense of my odd behavior, an elaborate explanation can no longer be deferred. Something uncanny *was* at work. Two dead friends—Duke Ellery and Gerry Margolis—had already entered my thoughts. Now a third seemed insistent on intruding. He was Mr. O. Murray Carr himself, alias Miles Monahan, alias the second grader I'd told about my fantasy whenever singing "America the Beautiful," and—so help me this is not fiction—he was to use it as a stage name when he pursued an acting career in Hollywood, or rather, he did in the latter years of his spectacularly unsuccessful venture in Tinsel Town. It also occurred to me that this whole freaky O. Murray Carr business, which I would re-create in my mind, had to have a commanding place in the book Mike Fishman had urged me to write.

Therefore, driving along in my car, I mused on how I might write about them.

TRY TO IMAGINE, PLEASE, the Los Angeles Airport, LAX. You know the old joke about us Easterners when we arrive on the West Coast—saying we notice something different immediately. The ocean is on the wrong side! Following a maiden voyage of mine to those parts, three thousand miles from my New York City base, I was heading back to Manhattan. I'd stayed in LA a week. On business, as well as a lot of pleasure. I'd bunked in with Miles Monahan, my grammar-school chum, then an aspiring film actor, partly to save money, although I was returning a lot flusher than when I'd left.

My father had died about four months earlier. My mother had predeceased him, so I was officially an orphan and, as an only child, the sole heir. Dad, in his youth, bumming around the country but from a substantial family, had bought several plots of land in what then were the outskirts of Los Angeles. "Was drunk," he once told me. "Forgot I had 'em. Now they're worth a fortune." They sure were, since they were right near where LAX is today. He hung onto those acres, positive they would rise still more. I suppose I ought to have done the same after they were left to me. But I didn't want to be bothered, so I took vacation time and hiked myself out to the Coast, had a ball with Miles and his cohorts, including a few sexy starlets, and made a bundle on the sale.

The American Dream. Financial independence. Big money in a bank account to add to a not inconsiderable inheritance, and it would let me tell my cockamamie boss in New York to go do something expressive to himself. What a turbulent, oddball, liberating period of my life these four months had been, capped by the maddest, most implausible yet defining moment of them all: an encounter with a certain stranger on the jet ride east.

That stranger was Governor Richard Nathaniel Ellery.

I had a window seat. Still too new to owning any kind of

money, I was flying coach. That a governor would do the same, accompanied by his state police bodyguard in civvies, was something I understood only when I entered politics, i.e., the importance of *image,* being penurious with the people's taxes, especially while on state business. To me, they were just two guys sharing our row of three, the tall guy inexplicably squeezing into the middle seat, next to me, while the husky, shorter guy sat on the aisle.

Executive types, I thought to myself. They had briefcases. From my own carry-on, before I stuck it under the seat in front of me, I took out a book, propped it in the seat pocket, and turned away to stare out the window.

Did I mention this round trip had been my first transcontinental airplane ride? Yes, but not how I stared bug-eyed on the way out from New York at the panorama below whenever any ground was visible. I found it truly amazing that you could see so much from a high-flying jet. Superbly vivid were the mountains all through the West—the Rockies, the Sierras—and for contrast, that incredible moment earlier when the pilot announced, "The Grand Canyon to your right," and a collective tremor and vocal "Ah" surged amid the passengers while we viewed this ultimate sandstone landscape in its pleasing hues of layered red and yellow and tan. During other parts of the trip, when clouds obliterated all vision, I had my nose mostly buried in a book.

Why should the return flight and such fitful gawking have been altered? I had psyched myself first to be ready for the high scenery immediately beyond Los Angeles, where the vast valley the city occupied seemed to end. Then onward, backwards, to the East Coast we would go, as if reversing American history, the flow going the *wrong way,* yet still a spectacle of magnificence in geography, if nothing else. But I hadn't counted on attracting the attention of my new seatmate, the tall guy to my left. Rather, it was my book that caught his interest. The top half, with the title showing, stuck up above the edge of the seat pocket.

"Are you an American history major?" he asked me suddenly, pointing toward the thick volume.

All you could actually see was the upper lettering: *Democracy in America.*

We were airborne by then, I remember. LA's cookie-cutter blocks of houses stretched endlessly below, punctuated by occasional palm trees and, here and there, ribbon-like freeways. I must have turned away momentarily from that uninteresting scene and our eyes had met.

"Oh, gosh, no," I said, a bit flustered. "I mean, I was. I'm through with college. Well, I have my master's in history—American history, you're right."

"Are you teaching?"

My CV was pretty much laid out well before I even knew who he might be. To account for my not teaching, my job in New York was revealed, how I was on the staff of a certain prestigious magazine, but being honest, admitting I was merely a lowly checker of facts for the nonfiction pieces they published. I did, on occasion, do some freelance writing and had had a couple of articles on American history accepted in some fairly glitzy magazines, I added. As a response, after nodding understandingly, my new newfound conversation partner pointed to my book cover and said admiringly, "Then for you, de Tocqueville is merely light reading. I'm impressed."

Blushing, I replied, "I'm trying to catch up on America's nineteenth century. I figured the Frenchman was good to start with. Up until now, in college and grad school, I was focused nearly exclusively on the U.S. before it became the U.S."

"What d'you know, my favorite period, too," the man next to me said enthusiastically. "Colonial settlement, particularly in the 1600s. Early Massachusetts. Early Virginia. My own major undergraduate paper was on Nathaniel Bacon and his rebellion."

I must have looked startled, gave off a whistle, and, grinning, said, "Believe it or not, that was my master's thesis."

Such an astounding coincidence made us like instant old friends. Moreover, I soon added a cementing memory. It came to me in an image of research I'd done, a pile of papers, footnotes, and attributions. "Hey, I used an undergraduate paper, I now remember," I told him. "A guy from Harvard. Really good stuff. And his name was—I cited it enough—wait, yes—R. N. Ellery."

"That's me," he said.

"I don't believe it."

"I don't, either."

The gush of disbelief from both of us caused his companion, who appeared so taciturn and close-mouthed, to turn in our direction. "Tim, how's this for incredible luck?" he was informed, with a full mention of the million-to-one odds of this chance encounter. The other man's dark eyes, almost black in color, showed no expression. "Real fantastic, Governor," he commented finally, without any emotional timbre whatsoever.

In our rush to compare notes and exchange knowledge on Bacon's Rebellion, we continued to chat away and I only belatedly picked up on the word "Governor," uttered by Sergeant Tim Lavery, his bodyguard, who at the time I had seen as a business associate of this engaging man beside me. I was not a political junkie. I kept current by reading the *New York Times,* as did most of my peers in the city. Still, we were mostly into literature and the arts. The governor, and prior to that, congressman from an obscure state, wouldn't have caught my attention, notwithstanding the surname Ellery had I seen it in print.

On our plane ride, what really brought the political matter to the fore was a woman passenger, coming back from the toilet, who glanced again at the handsome man she'd passed and decided she had, indeed, recognized him. She was a constituent, she had voted for him, and she introduced herself after she'd stopped, said, "Aren't you Governor Ellery?" and he acknowledged he was.

By then, he and I had had a running discussion of pre-Revolutionary American history, interspersed with several other delvings into my personal life, such as the fact that I was planning to quit my job within the next few days, now that I possessed a decent nest egg, and was possibly considering more graduate school, going on for a Ph.D. and conceivably a career in academia.

The revelation that R. N. Ellery was actually the governor of a state quietly embarrassed me. Shouldn't I have known it? Shouldn't I have said something to show I'd seen his picture? Instead, I had shown only ignorance.

Overhearing him talk to his female fan, I learned a bit more. He'd been on a trade mission to California, seeking business for the state, and had some appointments in New York on the way back. He'd be staying overnight in Manhattan. There'd been some promising leads and some good news he'd announce at home in a few days. He said he was glad she'd made herself known to him. As they discussed acquaintances they had in common, I took advantage of their tête-à-tête to open de Tocqueville where I'd left him and read on.

Not long afterward, he tapped my shoulder and said, "Excuse me for interrupting your *light* reading, but while I think of it, I wanted to give you a way to reach me if you're ever in our state capital or, for that matter, anywhere else, if you'd like to contact me." A super-fancy business card was handed over, capped by the state seal embossed in gold. Then, he asked, "Do you have a card, in case I have some hot new information on the seventeenth century to impart?"

Needless to say, a lowly young wanna-be in New York City, like me, didn't have business cards printed for him, but I wrote out an address and phone number (my apartment, not the magazine) on a slip of paper. Nor did I think much about his invitation of future contact. Pure politeness, probably. That he might have had an ulterior (but honorable) motive never in this world occurred to me.

Until we landed, we talked only sporadically. He had a bunch of papers in his briefcase to handle and I had the impression he was sensitive to letting me concentrate on reading my book. Since there wasn't anything to be seen below before we practically reached New York, I spent a lot of time with de Tocqueville. We all three shook hands, the governor and Tim and myself, prior to deplaning, and I figured—our exchange of info notwithstanding—that I would never see those guys again. Back in my apartment, I stuck the governor's card onto a bulletin board in my front hall, quietly showing off to any visitors—usually female—that I knew someone in a high place, a real VIP.

Not more than four days later, following my departure from my job, I was puttering around my apartment when the phone rang. An operator asked if she had Jonathan Jackson on the line. Somewhat curt, thinking maybe this was a sales pitch, I said it was.

"Please hold for Governor Ellery," she continued.

I suppose there have been stranger moments in my life. But none quite so decisive. Before that surprise conversation was ended, my life had utterly changed. He offered me a job on his staff. And without much hesitation, although he told me I should take all the time I needed, I accepted.

"It doesn't pay very well," he warned me. "It's solely guaranteed until the end of my term. And I know it means uprooting yourself. On the other hand, I took you for an adventurous young man, free to relocate, and at a temporary juncture in your career. You'd be entering a whole new world and yet doing a lot of what you like to do—historic research."

My title would be special assistant to the governor. How

grandiose it sounded to me. The research part was to help him with a book he was writing, dealing heavily with American history. There were other things to do, too, some of it scut work, but mainly interesting stuff. He said he knew he was taking a long shot in asking someone he had just briefly met, but I was exactly the type of person he was looking for.

"You know, we never discussed politics," he said, after I'd agreed. "I haven't a clue to which party, if any, you might belong."

"I'm a registered Democrat," I said.

"I hoped you would be. Thought you might be. Good. It isn't essential, but will keep the rest of the family happy."

Had Ellery been a Republican, would I have gone to work for him? The question is not inconsequential. Was I acting out of a core of integrity or plain old-fashioned opportunism? Actually, I had cheated a bit; in the interim, out of sheer curiosity, I'd gone to the New York Public Library to look up Richard N. Ellery in the *Congressional Record*, newspaper files, etc. (this was before the advent of computers), and had noted, with silent approval, his party affiliation. That he would ever call me, as he did, was the furthest thing from my mind. Except in fantasy. I do remember one far-fetched daydream I experienced at the time.

From the main branch of the New York Public Library at 42nd Street to the beginning of Times Square was but a few long blocks. I had done my research on R. N. Ellery and thoughts of him remained in my mind while I walked. This was the second day of my liberation from a job I loathed, yet I was already restless. Aside from those several hours with the files concerning my "airplane buddy," I had nothing else to do. Technically, until I made a move, probably to start enquiring about a Ph.D. program, my future was in limbo.

Beholding the Grand Canyon of neon lights, traffic, pedestrian flow, billboards, and seeming excitement that constituted

Times Square, allegedly the crossroads of the world, the acme of success and tawdriness (in that era) side by side, my thoughts skipped about; far be it from me to create here a James Joycean stream of consciousness—I have no such talent—but to the best of my memory, a series of cogitations went as follows, leading up to a vision which sailed off into Lala Land, an upwardly mobile ambitious young American male's idea of glory.

Wow! The Great White Way in the afternoon. If Miles were with me, he'd be chewing my ear off about having his name blazing on one of those marquees. Who knows? It could happen. He's already had some parts, even a speaking role, out there in Hollywood. A talented actor, maybe not a leading man, but. . . . So what about you, Jonathan? Just another ant. Look at all those people. So you got money. Unearned, but who cares? Buys security. Freedom to do what you want. No abyss for you. Look at these low-life losers hanging around this place, too. Porn shop heaven on 42nd Street. Hustlers, druggies, hookers, dregs. One side of a coin and the other. There but for the grace of God go I, no kidding. Christ, am I already really thinking I oughta get a job fast? No, I want to rise like that guy Ellery—way, way up. . . .

And capping off this mind-meandering of the well-dressed preppyish youth in the midst of a sidewalk throng, one of many thousands, was the fleshed-out concept of enormous power, of standing somehow above and bestride all this mass of humanity and activity, raising arms in command and having every bit of movement jolt to a screeching halt.

I wondered afterward if anyone around me had noticed this young fellow, not even into his thirties, still with an occasional zit on his face, laughing quietly at his own silliness.

New York—Manhattan—did such things to you, I remember thinking. One winter night on 59th Street, I had watched a man I took to have been driven crazy by the city, stripped to the waist, barefoot in 10-degree weather, rushing down the built-up side of that broad thoroughfare, opposite Central Park, tipping over trash barrels put out by the hotels and apartments, screaming obscenities all the while, oblivious to the astonished stares he attracted.

So it was hardly amazing that, when Governor Ellery phoned two days later like a bolt out of the blue, I decided to leave the Big Apple and try to take another route to the top.

One final incident in the great metropolis I departed is worth mentioning. I had a date—my last—with a girl named Louise I'd been seeing casually (pretty much exclusively for sex). I'd buy her dinner, say goodbye, promise to write and maybe visit, and enjoy a climactic roll in the hay at her place downtown.

Habit from my pre-inheritance days, more than stinginess, had me take the subway to her apartment, and so I was standing in a crowded IRT car, holding onto a strap, when a perhaps typically urban ruckus started. The sliding door of an adjoining car was suddenly snapped open and in strode two uniformed cops, guns and billies at their belts. They stood, gazed around for a minute, until one pointed and yelled, "There's the little bastard!" We were jammed in fairly tight. A surge went through the standees as a teenaged kid, probably Hispanic, sought to move fast. He banged into me, making me cry, "Hey!" I instinctively reached to grab him, but the cops were right behind and I got pushed hard aside, fell into an old lady's lap, and all I knew when I struggled back up was that the quarry had been caught and the train had stopped at a station and the cops were hustling their prisoner onto the platform.

My shoulder still hurt when I picked up Louise and, at dinner, I regaled her with my story of that abrupt spurt of violence underground, embellishing it greatly. The next morning, I bought a tabloid, but saw nothing related to the incident. What had the kid done?

So what does this have to do with Duke Ellery? Nothing

directly, except the idea of sudden, unexpected, ostensibly inexplicable violence in our society. On another level, a reference to the females in my life—all the Louises and Margos and Audreys from high school to Manhattan—preparing me for my one major, lasting flame, my wife, and how my ultimate encounter with the fairer sex could never have happened if it hadn't been for my chance encounter with "the guv," as we on the staff would refer to him among ourselves.

Jill, the lady now waiting for me in our large house near the water in Swanstown, had first appeared in my consciousness when I was six months into my new job with Duke. On television. I was having a drink in a popular capital city bar with my immediate boss, Harry DeWitt, Duke's administrative assistant, and the evening news came on the screen. It was a local station delivering state news and we stopped our conversation to watch and see if it concerned us.

One segment did. Rather, it was about one of our departments, the usual sniping over some governmental miscue. What wasn't usual: the coverage was narrated by an absolute knockout of a young woman I had never before seen on the tube.

"Wow, she's new, isn't she?" I exclaimed to Harry, as soon as the story ended.

"Just started, and rather attractive," Harry said. "I'm looking forward to having her interview me."

"See what you can do for *me*," I shot back jokingly.

"Well, she'll be around. She's been assigned the political beat, among other things."

"What's her name? I didn't catch it on the broadcast."

"Jill Something. Jill McSomething."

"Doesn't matter. You can bet I'll be watching tomorrow night."

The moment she was off the air, however, this quick flash of masculine posturing petered out quickly enough. Harry, in any case, was married—happily—merely having a slug of booze before going home. Truthfully, I didn't bother to tune in the evening news the following day. Just another fantasy, a weakness to which I was especially prone in my youth. Like dreams of dating a movie star. I was jealous of Miles, who *had* done that, actually. Quite frankly, it was some time before I learned the TV beauty's name was Jill McKenzie, much longer before I saw her in the flesh (clothed attractively, to be sure) entering Duke's office with a cameraman one day, and months until I happened to catch her attention and say hi. As for conversation between us, that's a tale that lies ahead in the narrative.

HAVING THIS REVERIE in my car, which I did think of as preliminary "work" on my proposed book, it rather naturally followed that I realized the public radio news might be on by now. That program would last throughout the drive to Swanstown and my motive for curtailing these remembrances of the distant past was that the very, very immediate past—i.e., the electoral college event—might be chronicled when the statewide segment ran.

My timing was lucky, and I hadn't more than a minute to wait for a local broadcast of the day's happenings in our state. But we weren't mentioned—not one word, as I listened right to the end. Too bad, I thought, and not because I had a personal stake, possibly hearing my name mentioned; it would have been a nice little feature, I genuinely felt, full of human interest, educational, a touch of true Americana. How much those hard-nosed newsies missed! Maybe at supper, I reflected mischievously, I would argue the point with Jill, who still always, or at least generally, stood up for her old profession.

After the exit for Swanstown, I tuned out my radio. If the state capital has merited a few illustrative pen strokes, so, certainly, should my adopted home community of the previous several decades. From the Parkway turnoff to the ocean shore where we lived, I'd clocked an exact 3.5 miles, all within the municipal limits. A lightly populated country road accounted for the first two of those miles. A few trim, working dairy farms still existed out there and a commercial apple orchard. I passed the family homestead of my first legislative opponent, the late Earl Johnson. That good ol' boy's people had been inhabitants here since the late 1600s. Yet I'd won the support of most of his neighbors, which said a lot about what kind of rapscallion Earl was. Beyond Johnson's Corner, where Earl had his country store, gas station, and real estate business, the "suburbs," as opposed to the "exurbs," began, with a small housing project of split-level homes. Our full-service shopping center wasn't much farther away. That touch of modernism had been added since Jill and I had arrived. Handy, but not much loved. Downtown was our historic district, the waterfront, offices of lawyers, doctors, insurance agents, etc., antique stores, retail shops, churches—nothing out of the ordinary. The country club was not on the route I followed, but I passed right by the posh home and adjacent law office of its longtime president, Ronald A. Gordon. Talk about Democracy in America. Ron, the redhead, my buddy, my campaign manager, head of the Democratic Town Committee, was Jewish, a transplanted New Yorker, and the Swanstown gentry had made him the number one poo-bah of the most hoity-toity of their establishments and kept him running it for umpteen years.

The official Historic District was something I had been involved with well prior to my maiden election. Those dozen or so eighteenth-century houses were now protected from intrusion (such as a McDonald's next door), demolition, or any disfiguring outside renovation. I was particularly proud that I not only could get the oldest structure in the town under its sheltering legal wing, but that I had also helped persuade its owner to donate it to the local historical society and be opened for the public. This was the Jonathan Weeks Garrison House dating back to the Indian wars of the seventeenth century, its dark, somber, aged wood exterior literally pockmarked with arrow holes. Situated next to a fairly modern-looking yellow brick Roman Catholic church, it provided a piquant contrast, if you knew our local history, since the Catholic-hating Yankees of the original settlement who had flocked to hide and fight behind its heavily timbered front had been repelling hostile Natives goaded on by French Catholic missionaries and royal Gallic officers. This formerly fortified colonial dwelling had previously been the property of my late friend, the Wall Street big shot and U.S. diplomat—i.e., troubleshooter—Norman Page.

Two blocks farther east and one block from the ocean, Jill and I resided in our empty nest. A three-story former summer home, built around 1900, long since winterized, it had been too large for us even when Ritchie was growing up; but plainly and simply, we've been too comfy in our ways to want to move.

At Chez Jackson, Christmas lights were already aglow, sedate single crimson bulbs in each of our windows. Toasty warm inside my car with the heater working, I stepped out into crisp, chilly darkness, pausing to put on my topcoat before heading inside. I didn't need a scolding from Jill. *Yeah, sure*, I thought, *I could instead only wrap a scarf around my neck like Mike Fishman.* Finally, bundled up, without deciding what I would tell Jill about how Mike's words were bugging me, I prepared to face my darling wife, whom I could already see beyond the back-door window glass, bustling about the kitchen.

3

ROUTINELY, I WOULD HAVE gone straight into the house from the driveway (we never had a garage). How many thousands of times had I come home like this, most often from the capital? Nor was Jill always here ahead of me. When Ritchie was in school, she did part-time work at a community TV station in the nearby shire town; once he was off to college, she became its full-time manager; now my lovely wife was a golfer and a club-woman, heading up the women's auxiliary at the hospital and performing other good works.

So we led a bourgeois life—we were comfortable, as the saying goes. Smug, too? Up to a point, maybe yes, in that the fires of youth and ambition had all but died down, that one saw a straight and generally smooth path ahead, to be interrupted one inevitable day by death, that we had settled in, had friends, ate out frequently, traveled, still participated politically to an extent. I had my book projects, Jill had her interests.

But this particular early evening, I did something weird. I got back in my car, the motor off, lights out, and watched her for about five minutes, as her figure came in and out of my view. Should or shouldn't I tell her about Mike Fishman? I wanted to make a decision and knew I'd get questioned when I went inside. *What were you doing in the car so long?* My immediate instinct was to fib, say I was listening to the end of a program on the radio. The journalist in her might bore in, though. *What program? Tell me about it. Describe it.*

Yet why bother? The day's events had put me in a mood not

to sweat the petty stuff. I decided I'd tell her right away about Mike Fishman and his touching my nerve by reminding me about the book on Duke I'd never really started. Yes, sure, I *was* thinking about that—and if the truth be known—also studying Jill, her looks, her movements, since she now had become, shall we say, "matronly" (she's gonna kill me), and remembering her as a gorgeous creature when our paths had crossed and the miracle it had seemed to me of our mutual attraction for each other. Putting all of this together would be necessary, I realized, the merging of *our* merging with the story of Governor Richard N. Ellery. In such an undertaking, I'd not only want her approval but her advice.

I could have sat longer in the car, moving on mentally from the moment in the bar with Harry DeWitt and Jill on television to the first time I saw Miss McKenzie in person at the Statehouse or, for instance, the much more complicated business of our traveling together to a national governors conference, but if I stayed much longer, Jill could think I'd had a heart attack or that something else was wrong and come rushing out, all upset, or as upset as that generally *cool* cookie ever got.

How cool, exactly, I was to witness later the same evening. But first, we had dinner, the two of us, preceded by our habitual cocktails; a Scotch and soda for me, a gin martini for Jill. Except for the theme of the conversation, it was a typical evening at the Jacksons'.

True to my intent, I did not need a cue—no *Did your speech go over well, Dear,* for an opening—to unburden myself. Once I had my Scotch made and she'd finished mixing her martini, I sank into a living room armchair and said, "Do you remember Mike Fishman—Meyer Fishman?"

Sometimes, we wouldn't say anything during this pre-evening ritual, but simply watch the television news. Since she knew I now had preempted such a possibility by speaking, she was sensitive enough to realize I wanted to talk.

"Fishman, the pest," she replied to me. "Naturally, he would have been there today."

"Yes, they made him an elector again. The third or fourth time, because of his initiative, remember, at one of our conventions in the past."

"Why mention Fishman?"

My wife has stunning blue eyes—Scottish eyes, I suspect—and they stab you with a cutting directness that may be ancestral. Nor does she mince words in getting to a point.

But she also listens. I had the floor for a monologue of about fifteen minutes. In a loosey-goosey style, picked up in the legislature, I rambled from my meeting Fishman in the parking lot to our exit together from the capitol building, threw in descriptions of the electoral college voting and ceremony, then focused on the two of us standing beneath Duke's portrait and Mike nagging me about the book I'd unfortunately told him I had planned to write.

"So you still aren't finished with your writer's block yet—is that what you're trying to tell me?" Jill said archly.

"I don't know," I said. "I *am* thinking about making another stab at it."

"Do you want me to talk you out of it?"

That not-wholly serious riposte (although she was poker-faced) drew a short laugh from me. "God, no."

"I'll hold your hand," Jill said. "And read the manuscript, as I always do."

"And refresh my memory when necessary?"

"Naturally."

"Then, you really think I should do it?"

"You poor dear. I know it's hard to chase away your demons. But writing about them is cheaper than psychotherapy. Otherwise, you may be forever restless."

I put my hand tenderly on hers, a gesture I hadn't done for a long time.

For a minute or two we sat hand on hand, side by side, as if we were back more than several decades earlier. At the same time, I was scared and, paradoxically, a trifle angry. *Now, goddamn it, I have to write the goddamn thing.* It was a relief, truly, when she said, "All right, drink up, we need to eat."

Post-supper, I didn't think I should sit down again in the living room and watch TV with Jill. We had a three-story house and my office (and library) was on the second floor. At our stage in life, we had separate bedrooms—also on the second floor; I'd moved into Ritchie's room now that he was gone. The third floor was pretty much unused. It had a spectacular view of the ocean, well above any intervening roofs. During daylight hours, I would sometimes sit in a rocking chair upstairs, my eyes on the scene beyond our harbor, clear out to the dim Barnacle Rock lighthouse and beyond, and clear my mind and concentrate and muse creatively before descending, in preparation for whatever I was planning to write.

To do so at night made no sense. Consequently, I went straight to my office, taking with me the manila folder containing my electoral college notes and research, which I'd lugged back and forth to the state capital.

I had a filing system, three metal cabinets filled to the brim with folders of varying size, depending on the subject matter. Some were very stuffed, like the one on Duke Ellery. After putting away ELECTORAL COLLEGE, I saw ELLERY right next to it.

Strange I hadn't noticed this side-by-side connection earlier.

Or had a link, meaningless as it might be, been made subliminally?

To lift out the ELLERY file, I would need both hands, it was so thick. Speeches, news clippings, letters, position papers, campaign material, photos, official publications, even brochures for hotels where we'd stayed on official travels, magazine articles—everything was in there—*except a book,* was my thought, because no one had written any. Before I hefted that mass of paper out to begin sorting through it, I wondered, as I had in the past, about a title. The one that always had leapt to mind was "A President Manqué." But the bit with the French accent had always been rejected by me as too literary and well over the heads of the general public. Others I'd thought of were far ickier: "Richard N. Ellery, Unsung American," or just plain "Duke."

You don't need a title, Jonathan, until you write the book, I told myself, finally and firmly grabbing hold of what I knew was the heaviest collection of material in my metal drawers and placing it on top of my desk, to the left of my computer. Then I went for the next fattest load. It was under MONAHAN and not in the same place. Soon, lying next to ELLERY was that piled-up folder, Miles Monahan's, about half the size of Duke's folio. Contemplating both research troves, I asked myself, *Should I stop here for now?*

My three cabinets were labeled on top: 1. PERSONAL AND POLITICAL; 2. AMERICAN HISTORY; 3. MISCELLANEOUS. All my life I've had the instincts of a packrat, and this appearance of an orderly mind in the arrangement of decades of accumulation is somewhat deceiving. While stuff did not go into files willy-nilly, I knew that there were many other places I had to search, besides pawing through the two major folders on my desk. In addition, there were framed photos on my walls. True, I had removed any trace of an image of Miles Monahan. My family (Ritchie, Jill, my parents, etc.) figured in about two-thirds of these pictures, but certain shots evocative of the Duke era, and pictures of me later on in the legislature, produced a conviction that this subsequent period of my life was, if anything, more important in explaining the aftermath.

All right, Jonathan, the aftermath of what?

Very well, here we need to start talking about *political murder*. Of course, I can also mean *assassination*. Open the top drawer of my AMERICAN HISTORY cabinet and you will find a pretty large folder under the A*s* of ASSASSINATIONS and a plethora of writings about those that took place in the United States. Killings of foreign officials, the few I thought of interest, can be found in MISCELLANEOUS. Anyway, I've gathered a slew of details about Lincoln and John Wilkes Booth, Garfield and Charles Guiteau, McKinley and Leon Czolgocz, Kennedy and Lee Harvey Oswald, and all the ancillary horrors and attempts, Robert Kennedy, Martin Luther King (although never elected), the potshots at Reagan, Ford, FDR, (killing Chicago Mayor Anton Cermak, instead), Teddy Roosevelt, all the way to U.S. senators slain like Huey Long, governors like Frank Steunenberg in Idaho and our own Duke Ellery, shot down in LA, and even a city councilor like Harvey Milk in San Francisco, slain with Mayor George Moscone, or an ex-congressman like Allard Lowenstein. These shocks to our political nervous system come and go in this country; we briefly wonder why, but get momentarily shocked again the next time it happens.

That is, if we're not as close to one as I was.

For who else in the USA had ties to both the victim and the perpetrator, which an ineluctable Fate seemed to have dictated? More about such Greek-style irony will be revealed in due course. Not many readers, but some, may remember that Miles Monahan was the real (not stagey) name of that wacko who murdered that governor in Los Angeles and, in turn, was cut down on the spot by the guv's plainclothes state police bodyguard. Practically no one knows that the assassin, Miles Monahan, had been my best friend (or so we'd dubbed ourselves) since the second grade.

Out came the folder on ASSASSINATIONS to join the line-up on my desk. But immediately afterward, I turned back to the cabinet marked PERSONAL AND POLITICAL. Not far from the large vacancy where MONAHAN had been, I quickly located MARGOLIS. Without hesitation, I placed Gerry Margolis's file next to Miles's. Within moments, a third joined the other two: JACKSON with (JONATHAN) added to differentiate it from any others having my common surname.

Okay, gang, we're all together again, I remarked silently, simultaneously entertaining the memory of us as a trio of pals from fifth grade through high school. We didn't call ourselves "The Three Musketeers." We might have done so had not Margolis, a transplant from Manhattan and far more sophisticated than us two suburban bumpkins, presented a more original suggestion. We would be, among ourselves, "The All-American Patrol." It was a takeoff on war movies: one WASP Congregationalist, one Irish Roman Catholic, one Reform Jew. In retrospect, we all would agree it was the best we could do in that zeitgeist. There wasn't a single African American, Asian, or Muslim in our neighborhood.

But where should I start? Peruse which folder first? Or, more basic still, *how* should I start? Thumbing through the research? Beginning from scratch again? I had some stuff I'd already written and rejected. It was in the MISCELLANEOUS cabinet—typewritten sheets, pre-word processor, yellowing with age. I suppose I could retrieve them, but not now. Why not sit still for an hour or so, keep pad and pen in front of me to jot notes, and, as the phrase goes, collect my thoughts.

To be quiet for a whole hour, not disturbed, in modern America, sylvan as Swanstown is, might have been asking too much. Five minutes into my meditation, the phone rang.

Sheer habit, an unconscious reflex, led me to reach for the receiver of the communications apparatus on my desk. Half its bells and whistles I know nothing about, but I have no trouble with the good old-fashioned telephone part. Whatever was forming in my mind at that precise instant went right smack out of it and has never been recovered. Worst luck, too, the call was for Jill. Because I'd answered first, she wouldn't answer, so I had to get up, leave the office, go down the corridor to the head of the stairs and yell, "Honey, it's for you!"

A voice from below responded, "Who is it?"

"Hell, I don't know. Some club woman."

At last I heard Jill's footsteps—my signal to return to my lair, hang up, and resume pondering.

Good Christ, if the phone didn't ring again, maybe six minutes later. This time, I let it ring and ring. Had to be for her, I decided.

If Jill didn't move her butt, we'd still probably receive a recording from whoever it was. No big deal. Besides, after four rings, I didn't hear a fifth, following which on our answering machine a voiced invitation to "leave a brief message" would activate.

So Jill *had* picked up the call.

In the interim, my mind had been wandering irresponsibly. That is to say, I hadn't been able to concentrate directly on the Duke Ellery project. Periodically, I kept urging myself: *Get back to work, Jonathan.*

To a certain degree, I did so right after the second phone call. It was Duke, after all, who had gotten me thinking about the *chaos/order conundrum.*

One of the reasons he hired me, I believe, was to provide him an outlet for talk that was not just political, practical, goal-oriented, glib, or superficially clever, as so much of the badinage in our political world tended to be. At home, I don't believe he had much opportunity for weightier conversation, either—Madge, his wife, was certainly bright enough, college-educated, but hardly intellectual. I guess I made the best sounding board for ideas of his only tangentially connected to the intricacies of government and public affairs.

This trend was over and above our discussions on American history, which he also enjoyed. We both had taken philosophy courses. When he dropped a word about Hegel's *dialectic,* he knew that I knew—or had a concept—about what he meant. Invariably, we would be by ourselves in his office or on a trip in the back of the state limousine when these discussions spontaneously erupted. The first time he started in on the dialectic that he called his chaos/order conundrum, I remember we got talking so enthusiastically in his inner office that Sally Armstrong, who ran his reception operation, had to come in and remind him he was already twenty minutes late for his next appointment and a passel of hot-shot businessmen had been cooling their heels in the waiting room all that time.

"Back to work, alas," the governor told me with a rueful smile as I scooted out a side exit, clutching my bundle of papers—containing the original reason for my summons to confer with him.

I hadn't taken any notes on what he had said about chaos and order—not on that occasion, anyway. Here, umpty-ump years later, I realized I could dig into the massive file I had on Duke and might eventually discover some notations. But suspecting such a task could take me hours and would not be—as we used to say in the legislature—*germane* to the issue, I sat back at my desk and sought to recall the philosophic point Duke had been seeking to make.

Dialectic means opposites which clash and, in turn, morph together into a *synthesis.* Hegel gave the idea to Marx. And because Marx had put it into play in politics, I remembered this notion pretty well from college. Feudalism saw the breakdown between the aristocracy and the peasantry creating the *bourgeoisie,* the business middle class—and they triumphed. But they, in turn, created the *proletariat,* the working people—and the latter would triumph—and for Marx, that's where all these iron laws of history would end.

"It comes out of our very nature as a species," I remember Duke saying. "We're individuals, yet we also need to be a herd in order to survive." Not the kind of talk you usually hear from a governor. His job, of course, was to maintain order. But merely doing that—maintaining the status quo—could get you in trouble with—and here he threw another un-gubernatorial word at me—*entropy*—the tendency of things to start deteriorating. Not acting could lead to chaos. So could taking action.

"Don't think I've got the key," he warned me.

He said it, I now recalled, with a deprecating smile, genuine in its modesty, yet still somehow making me believe in his superior knowledge and leadership, the sense he exuded of being ahead of all of us. Good God, with the burdens of his office, a million day-to-day practicalities facing him, and here he was, right up there with Hegel and Marx, for crying out loud. What might have . . . !

I know it's melodramatic to have an interruption cutting off a thought, but my wife never knocks when she comes to my office. I was too engrossed to notice her footsteps on the stairs or in the corridor. Thus, when I turned my head somehow instinctively, Jill was in the open doorway.

"Do you want to talk to our son?" she asked me.

"That second call was Ritchie?" was my somewhat surprised response.

She nodded.

"Kind of early out there," I said. "Is everything okay?"

Equally silent, she shrugged and made a very strange face.

I immediately grabbed for the phone on my desk.

Panic has a character all its own. With me, the attack commences in the shoulders, a tingling, a weakening of the muscles, but a tightening-up stomach. The dread of the unknown feeds it. As soon as I heard Ritchie's voice, I knew he was drunk. But why—in the late California afternoon, quite possibly when he still should have been at work?

Very drunk. He'd obviously been boozing for several hours.

After I said, "Hello, Ritchie," my own voice full of parental apprehension, he mumbled, "I'm on m' cell phone, Jonathan. How the fuck are you?"

I never like to see bad language in print, but I've left in the f-word, exactly as pronounced, in token of the shock value it had for me. That a son, especially one as well brought up as ours, should speak to his father like that, right off the bat, was a startling indication that *order* had broken down. How far away was some descent into real *chaos*?

Not too far off, it seemed. In language I am not going to reproduce, Ritchie soon let me know, in a slurred diatribe, that he had upped and quit his blankety-blank job that very same day, had told his unprintable boss what to do with their unprintable company, the same more or less expletive-not-deleted language to his unprintable girlfriend when she, uptight Irene, had protested, then his storming out of their unprintable apartment and taking to the streets (and a succession of bars, it was evident). Moreover, you could take this unprintable country and its unprintable way of life and blow the whole f—— craporoony to smithereens, for all he cared. "It's time for a [further expletive deleted] revolution!" he exclaimed into his cell phone, then added, "Hey, didn't you tell me that a *revolution*—it's one complete turn? Start everything over. And you quoted Jefferson about watering it with blood. Careful, Jonathan, careful. We might just do that. And who's we? My generation, and Jonathan, Dad. You old guys. . . . Oh, what the hell."

I think my immediate response was, "Ritchie, are you by yourself? And you're not driving, are you?"

But he merely said, "That dumb broad. Doesn't understand squat. Marry her and actually settle down. Yeah, you and Mom

❖   45   ❖

would love grand——" Whereupon the gadget began to crackle and fill with static and, shortly afterward, died completely.

I had his number, dialed it frantically. The thing rang, but Ritchie either couldn't or wouldn't answer.

Jill was still in my doorway. The awful silence, as we looked at each other, lasted about a minute.

"Great. Just great," I said. "I can't reach him. What if he doesn't ring back?"

The best Jill offered me in reply was another shrug.

"Should I phone Irene?"

This time, Jill did speak. "Let sleeping dogs lie," she said mysteriously.

"What does that mean?" I fairly shouted, plainly wrought up.

"Good night, Irene," she said, with a broad, pleased smile. It was no secret to me, even if Ritchie hadn't sensed it, that my wife felt her son could do better.

"I'm absolutely overwhelmed," I said. "He's kept all this negative stuff bottled up inside him."

"When he sobers up," Jill said, "my only fear is he might go back to her."

"Goddamn it, why doesn't he call?" I screamed out, not at Jill, but at a nearby wall.

"What a hangover my poor baby's going to have tomorrow," commented my wife with a half smile.

"What a heart attack he's giving me!" I complained vehemently.

"Go back to work," Jill said. "Ritchie'll be fine. And . . ." she hesitated, "and maybe now, he'll *really* find himself."

"Yeah, sure," I snapped.

I had not left my swivel chair during all these proceedings. So, swinging myself around to face the pile of folders on my desk, I turned away from Jill. I heard her step into the corridor a few moments later. *Back to work,* I silently commanded myself.

Hopefully this would blot out the worry that every moment of passing silence made ever more acute.

4

INSOMNIA, AFTER A TRAUMATIC ASSAULT on one's deepest inner fears, was not unexpected. I slept hardly at all, continually bugged by a lack of any contact from Ritchie and trying to overcome my queasiness by reading material in Duke Ellery's file—that is, until I went to a bedroom bookshelf, found the driest history by the biggest bore academic writer I knew of, and took this ho-hummer to pore over while lying down. Yet my eyes never drooped, tired as I was.

It was not so much the fading romance of established marriage that had put Jill and me in different beds; instead, different habits, like her inability to fall asleep without the television blaring and my inability to slumber with the idiot box on. You should hear us wrangle when we go on vacation and have to share a single hotel room. So at the best of times, I'm the more neurasthenic type and sleep lightly to boot, subject to dreams whose grotesqueness will wake me, as you've seen, and often keep me awake.

My alarm clock showed it was 4:56 A.M. when, having tossed and turned for maybe two hours, I'd dozed off for good, only to come out of a dream in which I was seven or eight years old and on a baseball diamond, unable to move, my spikes caught in the straps attached to the bag at first base, and bearing down increasingly in my direction was the ride-around mower used for cutting the infield in big-league games, with no one on the seat guiding it. Seeing that I couldn't run, couldn't escape, was about to be mangled, my subconscious did the next best thing: once again, it roused me to reenter reality.

Which was: a hint of roseate color in the grayness of my windows that faced east. Otherwise, an inky darkness predominated until I flipped on the bed lamp, checked my clock, groaned inwardly, and prepared to return, if possible, to sleep, but not, I hoped, to the awful dream and its still-fresh memory.

I am no Sigmund Freud and wouldn't *dream* of interpreting any dream. Not in his style, anyway. All those flashing blades, coming to cut me up, possibly in my most private parts. Wouldn't old Sig have had a field day with me? But to argue my case, I had a real-time example of why my defenseless ego or id, or whatever makes us dream, chose that subject matter. It had to be because of Miles Monahan—an incident out of our childhood, an actual event. After Ritchie's call, I deliberately hadn't looked into his (Miles's) big file, concentrating on Duke's instead. However, the sneaky Irish rascal had gotten into my psyche all the same.

The second-grade encounter between us (to which I have been up to now obliquely referring) took place on the playground of the Edward W. Foster Elementary School. In later years, Miles and I played baseball on its diamond; indeed, white, puffy, strapped-down bags *were* on the bases, but the time we first collided, as we did, we were too young during recess to do much more than run around. Miles always wanted to fight, but I wouldn't put up my fists. Therefore, he ignored me for the better part of a school year. Then, one day in the spring, this feisty little pug-nosed, freckled towhead ran at me screeching, "I'm gonna split your noggin!"

I suppose I knew what his slang word for "skull" meant. The amazing fact was my composure. I never moved. Until the last instant, I admit. Stepping deftly aside, I stuck out my foot and tripped the bullying bugger (another slang word we used without, thank goodness, having the slightest idea of what it meant). Miles went sprawling in the dust. When he stood up, though, it wasn't to punch me. He walked over to shake my hand.

From then on, we became best pals.

All of which was preamble to a flood of reminiscences. None of them, unless I'd specifically written down their accounts, could have been found in Miles's folder. Nevertheless, they were all potential grist for this project.

An example: Miles played John Wilkes Booth in our eighth-grade class play about the assassination of Abraham Lincoln. He played Lincoln, too, a short, stocky, thirteen-year-old with sandy hair somehow appearing stovepipe tall, gaunt, black-bearded, and black-haired. And he wrote the script. Miss Havemeyer, the drama teacher, directed. She had wanted *me* to be Lincoln. I was fairly tall, certainly dark-haired, and thin enough in those days. However, Miles rigged himself with makeup and elevator shoes in the most astonishing fashion and he really *was* Lincoln. In my pre-political years, I showed no acting talent so he got the part. His extraordinary segue into playing both the martyred president and his slayer almost simultaneously was because Duffy Turnbaugh, initially cast as Booth, kept flubbing his all-important line, the Latin cry of *"Sic semper tyrannis"* shouted by Booth upon firing his shots and before leaping from Lincoln's theater box and breaking his leg on the stage at Ford's Theater. Miles, as John Wilkes Booth, too, couldn't have been more realistic in an assassin's role.

Portent of events—one actor, both Lincoln and Booth, but ending up like Booth, the real-life killer, in a hideous moment at the Los Angeles Airport.

Why?

It wasn't just a roll of the dice. This guy whom I was so close to, a freaky, talented, charming, off-the-wall, ambitious SOB, had seemingly inexplicably turned murderous. He shot and killed my boss for no ostensible reason. I sometimes consider Miles my *Secret Sharer* (apologies to Joseph Conrad), or "I have a little shadow that goes in and out with me" (apologies to Robert Louis Stevenson): the dark side, in other words, existing in all of us.

Finally, though, I got maybe another hour of sleep and was up in time to see that the sun had just risen. Still listening anxiously for the phone to ring, I lay in bed for a few more minutes. I had no place to go this morning. I could laze around, doze if I liked, for hours longer. Jill was only too happy to let me make my own breakfast. Instead, the whim struck me to go upstairs to the third floor and gaze out at the ocean in the growing morning light.

A grayish sea stretched away to Portugal. Before my eyes, the wintry Atlantic lapped against its northwestern margin in a panorama of attractive coastal scenery. I beheld evergreens by the water's edge, rocky headlands, various mansions on shore, and a tawny beach tracing a crescent upon the rim of land, followed by our harbor and its marina, now almost entirely bereft of boats. A few working craft were still anchored in plain sight, those of intrepid lobstermen who ventured out year-round and a small dragger or trawler or whatever catches cod—or is it groundfish her owners go after? A sailor who knows his ships, I ain't.

But I'm ever the historian. My thoughts, as soon as I settled into the old rocking chair, carried me far away into the vast expanse of icy-looking, undulating liquid, past the dim silhouette of historic Barnacle Rock Lighthouse and the even dimmer outlines of stony, rockweed-draped ledges or tiny islands whose place in the nation's past was actually very important. At this moment, I wasn't so much thinking about the USA as I was reconstructing mentally the dawning in the past of a new age for this continent of ours. Right then and there, I was literally off to medieval Portugal in my thoughts.

I envisioned a place called Sagres. Upon a promontory on the other side of the Atlantic, it remains (I've visited it) almost directly opposite (and 3,000 miles away) from our portion of what was once undiscovered America. There, a brainy, half-English, devoutly Roman Catholic local prince named Henry (Henrique) established a school of navigation. To spread the glory of Christ and Christianity, he sent ships all around the globe, to India, Africa, the Azores—and Europe was on its way, too, imperializing, until the Europeans had pretty much conquered the world. The sight of prosperous Swanstown— more acutely so in the summer when the yachts were plentiful— attested to the navigator's ultimate success. Also, the wind from the European coast, blowing east to west, provided an incentive to explore for the countrymen of Henrique's mother (the daughter of John O'Gaunt of Shakespeare fame), who eventually sailed their Anglo-Saxon butts across the wide ocean. Out on those islets, just barely in my view, big hairy guys speaking probably like Cockneys, had set up fishing stations in the 1500s; not exactly civilization, but incipient capitalism, at least.

By closing my eyes to the present, I could summon the multitudinous, unbroken forest that was the sole major land feature of the area then. Oh, look at the small clearings through the foliage where the Indians have planted corn and beans and squash. In the late spring/summer season, they have come to sow and harvest and frolic on the beach like today's tourists; big white shell middens have attested to their feasts of clams. Before winter, they were gone inland, hunting game, no doubt leaving here during the season we are now experiencing in December, prior to a big snowfall, but after the hardwood leaves have dropped.

Thus did I ponder Swanstown's past. Flat, shallow thoughts, available in any standard history text. We know so much now about the early contact period, germs included, spreading unperceived from white strangers into the ranks of the defenseless Natives—smallpox, plague, measles, *their* worst nightmares— although these invisible mites never entered their rich, monster-infested tribal stories and dreams. When respectable families of English colonists arrived in the 1630s, supplanting those cod-chasing galoots out on the shoals, the Indians hereabouts had already perished en masse—of natural causes, imported diseases, silent horrors their shamans could never exorcise.

Their Algonquian distant cousins came back later in warfare, but that is another tale.

Or is it? I suddenly had scenes of violence in my head. I'm rocking back and forth. What image should pop up cerebrally if not Jack Kennedy in his rocking chair? A slain president again. Assassination again. Then murder, pure and simple. Los Angeles, you can be sure, due to Ritchie's phone call last night, had a prominent place in my near consciousness. The sprawling Pacific metropolis materialized in gory thoughts of Charles Manson, the Sharon Tate murders and—with them—a natural transition to political crimes. Didn't one of that crazy, bloodthirsty, chaos-creating gang—a female called "Squeaky"—try to shoot President Ford? And how could I forget? Bobby Kennedy on the convention hall floor!

Meanwhile, my son, my only offspring, drunk and angry, was currently roaming LA's deadly environs, bent on who-knew-what.

Whence all this rage? Was it in the water we drank, the air we breathed, the product of our genes? The Indians, amid their placid Eden for thousands of years before we Europeans interfered, were not exempt. They slaughtered each other, most cruelly, too. Just around the corner from this nineteenth-century house of mine and Jill's, *our* one-sided white man's history records the hideous death of Jotham Weeks two hundred years earlier during the siege of the colonial garrison that bears his name on a plaque. The revenge extracted by his immediate descendants, the scalping of Indian women and kids, is also known, yet never graphically described in the state's annals.

Why do I keep coming back to Ritchie from these lugubrious

meanderings? My son has his mother's fierce blue eyes and a strain of her stubborn Scottish intensity. As well, he has my dark, almost black hair, and he's tall and, until his surprise outburst, easygoing, like political me, always able to get along with most folks and situations.

He certainly looks nothing like Miles Monahan. Admittedly, this fair, Celtic Mick childhood friend of mine was a master of disguises, could pass for anyone, even a woman, with the proper makeup and costuming, so maybe it wasn't totally unnatural for me to confound my wayward boy and the killer of my old boss. What had Ritchie said? Something like: *Blow up the whole she-bang?* Rather—the whole *craporoony*—where did he dig up that word? How different was such ranting from Miles's intent—the *real* Miles unmasked, so to speak, yellowish eyebrows and freckle-faced, no putty, no dye—with a black pistol in his hand in the LAX airport lobby?

To relax my tension, erase those contrapuntal visions— worse, that of Ritchie's possibly going underground, committing felonies, atrocities—I needed to think of an engrossing subject. No fantasy would hold me—nothing soft, nothing easy—at least, not as long as I wanted to stay here, gawking at the sea.

Then a brainstorm hit me. I'd write. The very act of compos-ing words would douse those fires of fear in my brain, distract a poor, heartsick, bourgeois father, could bring as much numbing forgetfulness as a pint of downed whiskey or a shot of dope (a sensation I didn't know firsthand and could only hope Ritchie didn't, either).

That was that. The only question remaining: Should I retrieve a pad of paper and pen downstairs in my office and return back up here to my rocker and ocean view? Otherwise, I could peck away on my computer.

Fool! A more basic question was: What would I write?

It will be the start of the book about Duke, I abruptly answered myself—commencing with the fatal trip to the National Governors Conference in Los Angeles from its beginning to its tragic end.

Immediately, I grew excited. A spurt of ideas ensued. Reconstruct the whole five days, although they wouldn't necessarily *have to* constitute the book's opening chapter. Hang everything else off them. For example, Duke's shocking death occurred on the final day of the trip, although the murder in no way represented a climactic finish to my story about him. Likewise, it was during this cross-country flight and our attendance at the conference that Jill and I—she as a journalist, me as a staffer—became, shall we say, *an item*. In terms of what Miles Monahan might have called "movie production values," one could add the vast sweep of scenery—America from east to west, mirroring our history. And the conclave itself, what a spectacle: fifty governors from fifty states, all crammed into a single superhotel and its gated grounds in view of the Pacific. Plus, to round out so much pageantry and politics, a presidential visit. For an unexpected encore, too, we had Miles's farewell performance, his own *Sic semper tyrannis.*

I stopped rocking. Would I need to see the ocean again for inspiration? I wondered, but only briefly, before tiptoeing downstairs to my office.

Jill was still sleeping, I figured. If I woke her by accident, she'd be sure to question me closely. *Interrogate,* I mean, draw out of yours truly all his silly dread, his inability to sleep, and then smirk at me without openly smirking, except in her tone of voice.

You can be sure I decided to stay in my office with the door closed. Should she catch me typing so early, I could plead an onset of irresistible inspiration.

As a consequence, once I had the computer humming, lit-up, softwared into a writing mode, my fingers had to get busy. No chance to fuss about tense or style. Since this protracted event I was going to write about happened more than thirty years ago, the verbs should not denote the present, although that is a technique some writers like to use, myself included.

What I really wanted to do, did attempt, only to erase, was setting the stage as follows: *Dawn. Heading east toward the Atlantic. Smell of salt air. Old guffer, sitting on a porch this early; yard full of lobster traps. Passing me, the governor's black limo. License plate 1. They wave. I wave—Duke, Harry DeWitt—Mrs. E. (Madge) in the front seat. Ditto, Tim Lavery in mufti, a uniformed state trooper driving. Ahead, the entrance to the airbase. . . .*

Back to the blank screen. Another tack, which I'm folding into this present narrative, now follows:

It was Harry DeWitt's idea for us to take an Air National Guard plane to Los Angeles. Their cargo aircraft had to do so many training flights (paid for by Uncle Sam) and they *were* equipped (somewhat rudely) for passengers. I knew this syndrome from experience—Harry's public penny-pinching of state funds—because if Duke flew commercial on our nickel, he always flew coach. The state owned a twin-engine four-seater plane of its own, but it was doubtful it could safely reach Minnesota, never mind California. In addition, this being a potentially newsworthy trip, we had local media we could accommodate by flying them free to the National Governors Conference, where they'd also have a chance to hear the president speak—a genuine opportunity for an underfinanced provincial press corps. Out of Harry's offer, we picked up three print reporters from the three leading state dailies and one television team. Until our entire group had gathered inside the hangar with our Air National Guard head, General Bill Thompson (he would also pilot the transport and was wearing a jumpsuit), I had no idea the lovely Miss Jill McKenzie was the anchor of the TV pair. Sly old Harry DeWitt had kept that secret to himself. Or hadn't bothered to remember how the most junior member of the governor's entourage might have been interested.

Anyway, I had to be grateful I was being taken along. No doubt Harry had discussed our staff roster with Duke. I had been helpful in researching a resolution the guv was planning to propose to his forty-nine other colleagues for presentation to the Feds. I'd had a hand in writing its text, also. Maybe I was invited as backup, in case any rewrites were necessary. From what I'd heard from veteran staffers, there wasn't a lot of work done at these annual parleys. *Junket.* That word surfaced easily in the discussion. I was plain lucky, for someone so junior, to have been included so early in my employment. I was sure I detected envy among my colleagues, but frankly, I didn't care.

One of the first things I did, as soon as Harry broke the news to me of my inclusion, was to telephone Miles in LA. He had an answering service—an absolute necessity for an aspiring actor—and I left a message about my impending arrival in his city in a month's time and—here is the tricky, ambiguous part—adding a rather triumphant boast that I, his old buddy, would be attending *the National Governors Conference*—as *an aide to a governor.* This was surely *success* in American terms, solid, boastable success to flaunt in the face of a pal who was having a less than successful period in *his* career.

As the word "American" became converted to print on the computer screen, it was natural for me to think: *Omurraycarr.* I saw no image of Miles Monahan in the lighted space before me. Rather, using digital magic, I retreated from the document I was haphazardly framing and retrieved a previous entry, an electronic file dubbed—what else?—O. MURRAY CARR, and soon was staring at the full-color facsimile of a business card. On it was embossed a miniature red-white-and-blue–costumed Uncle Sam, wispy beard, star-spangled cutaway, striped trousers, and all, with tri-hued lettering to match:

FOR ALL PATRIOTIC OCCASIONS

Mr. O. MURRAY CARR

(Alias Uncle Sam)

Impersonator of the Great Beloved Symbol of America

All-American Stories, Songs, Laughs, and Dances

In the lower right-hand corner was a phone number to call and the terse advertisement: "Clean-Cut Entertainment Available Anytime, Anyplace."

It was maybe five months before we flew to the National Governors Conference that I received this artifact from Miles's own hand. Had we been in Hollywood, I would probably have thought nothing of it. But in this case, we were on my turf in my state capital. Indulge me a brief flashback within a flashback. It had all started with a surprise phone call from Miles.

"Hey, Jonathan, I'm in New York. Lots o' good stuff happening, but I'll tell you about it when I see you tomorrow."

Just as if we'd talked the previous night.

"See me? Here? Jesus, Miles, I'm up to my eyeballs in work."

"Tomorrow morning, sweetheart, I land on your doorstep. At the Statehouse, right? In the governor's office, right? Very, very impressive."

"Holy shit!"

Anyway, to make a long story short, out of nowhere, in the middle of the week, my stubborn boyhood pal did arrive. It was late springtime and his precipitous appearance, no doubt carefully calculated, was timed so that he would stay with me until Friday evening, whereupon, at his absolute insistence, we were to drive up to our old fishing, camping, canoe-trip stomping grounds on Lake Edgeremet near the Canadian border and spend the weekend. He hadn't changed: Miles Monahan was as unpredictable and demanding as ever, and I admit I nearly died a thousand deaths awaiting the moment this eccentric Hollywood hipster would appear at the governor's office requesting to see me.

Would he behave himself? Would he be overawed, which was what I really hoped? Truthfully, underneath my outward angst, I was expecting he would acknowledge to *himself,* if not to me, how his old schoolmate had come up in the world.

Summoned eventually by the governor's receptionist to the outer office for my visitor, I could not believe my eyes. Standing inside the executive suite, there was Miles, talking to the governor, to Duke, my boss, as if they were bosom friends.

They'd had a chance meeting, I learned. Duke was on his way out, Miles on his way in—the patrician natural-born politician, who always had a gracious, friendly word for everyone, and the garrulous actor. By the time I joined them, they were deep in conversation started by the crazy business card of Miles's, handed by him to Duke (and another later to me). The whole thing was bizarre. They were cooking up a "deal," the two of them.

It seemed that the following day Duke was scheduled to have several busloads of school kids to entertain. In return for Miles putting on his Uncle Sam performance (did he have his costume with him?—of course), the guv would allow *me* Monday off from work so that the two of us could have an extended trip up in the North Woods. My fate, apparently, had been settled well before I'd come upon the scene.

If my boss was happy, so was I. And so was everybody who attended Miles's show. The kids were absolutely enthralled. How Miles did it, on hidden stilts, prancing around, loading the audience up on bits of American history, getting everyone to sing patriotic songs, was something to behold. I was standing near Duke and Harry DeWitt and they were both telling each other, "He's great," and at the end, Duke remarked to me, "You should bring him here more often. Good work, Jonathan."

5

Driving toward the military airport in the early dawn light to catch our transport to LA, I had noticed the old guy on a porch and his wispy beard and gaunt features, like Uncle Sam, which had set me remembering. Thoughts about Miles flooded in and out, particularly of the message I'd left the night before on his machine. Had I made a mistake? Why did I feel disturbed, when everything else was ostensibly going so swimmingly?

I know for a fact that if the airfield hadn't been so close to me by then, if I hadn't had to turn in at the gate, following not far behind the governor's vehicle, having to respond to the guards by the entrance, be checked off, etc., I would have started mulling over my trip to Lake Edgeremet with Miles, analyzing why I still felt uneasy. *Oh, hell,* I thought, *there'll be plenty of time during the flight for that.*

What do the French say? *Cherchez la femme.* "The lady is the cause of everything." I hadn't counted on the physical presence of anchorwoman Jill McKenzie.

Inside the hangar, where we all assembled, it was chilly. Coffee was provided, and I went to get a cup. So did Jill. Far be it from me to have seen anything but coincidence in this timing. I had noticed her upon entering—how could I not, in her fetching Prussian blue cloth coat and dress to match—but she was deep in conversation with George Everoff, Duke's press person, and so we didn't get to exchange our usual "Hi" and quick smile of the Statehouse corridors. Since I had reached the urn first, I poured for her. "I guess you're interviewing the governor before he leaves," I said, acutely aware this was the first real sentence I'd spoken to this beautiful lady and that it was a rather vapid one.

"Interesting atmosphere here," she answered, indicating with her glance the high-ceilinged aerodrome structure around us. "The governor, I'm told, will say a few words, which we'll get on film." Jill warmed her hands on the filled styrofoam cup, sipped her drink, and added, "Well, you ought to know, too, that we're going to be traveling companions."

With awkward little laughs and grins, she and I introduced ourselves, although we obviously knew each other's names. That I hadn't been shown the roster in advance wasn't surprising. Harry controlled it. Besides, George Everoff ran the press operation and *his* territory was off-limits to me.

But needless to say, I was pleased she was coming, even if I had no real reason to expect anything.

Before introducing the group that was going to California, let me comment on our "interesting atmosphere." We were in a federal facility. The guards who had checked me in were U.S. Marines. The interface between our state governments and Washington was most pronounced in our uniquely American National Guard mechanism: fifty separate militaries, financed to a large extent by the Feds, yet led and staffed by the recipients. Duke was the commander-in-chief of the "air force" that would be flying us.

That said, those traveling were Duke, his wife Madge, their friends the Leavitts (invited along, I learned, because they were such good tennis partners), us staffers (myself, Harry, George, Sergeant Tim Lavery), Jill and Charley Fischer, her cameraman, and three print reporters whose names I have long since forgotten (those underpaid fledglings come and go like sparrows in the small-market journalism of our state).

If the addition of the Leavitts with their tennis rackets spoke perhaps of the junket nature of this excursion, it had to be offset by the discomfort we would face on such a long trip in bucket seats, with no flight stewards or stewardesses except a couple of non-com National Guard airmen. Also, George Everoff explained in prepping us, once we gathered to hear the governor's comments, that there would be several stops along the way—in Iowa and Colorado—including a business opportunity Duke was pursuing in the hinterland, a possible industry seeking to expand in the East and might be induced to choose a location in our state, thanks to Duke's persuasiveness.

Thus, here was the "spin," as they say. His comments would be augmented through the footage Charley Fischer was shooting. I watched him panning around the hangar as well as focusing on Duke while he was speaking, producing what our constituents presently would be seeing, reinforcing subliminally the notion that their governor was always at work for them and trying to cut down on expenses wherever possible.

Jill, the cynical one, believed it her job to try to puncture this aura. Smoking out hidden agendas was her specialty, or at least her passion.

"I'll be happy to answer any questions in the short time before takeoff," Duke said, after some opening remarks, which had begun with, "How fortuitous" (he used big words so naturally, so unabashedly). He'd gone on to state that it was the Guard's training flight schedule that allowed for this trip and—with a wink—that Harry DeWitt's innate *penuriousness* had led him "cat-like, to pounce upon this particularly opportune mouse of a free ride" (laughs and smiling leers at Harry all around). And then, seriously, he made a few observations about the annual ritual when the fifty governors of the nation assembled. "Is it useful?" he asked, as if anticipating the first of the media's queries. His rhetorical response was, "I think so. The governors have been doing it, I believe, since the 1920s, first gathering at a resort in a place called Baden, Indiana. Starting a dialogue among themselves, they framed a consensus message to take from this state level of government to the federal government—a single voice on agreed-upon issues—instead of just disparate moans and groans and pleas and protests. Lots of positive ideas, too. And, as is the case again this year, we will have the president's ear, in person."

Listening, I invisibly smirked because the Baden, Indiana, touch was *my* research. I dug it up and included the factoid in my memo to Duke, although warning I couldn't prove absolutely it had been the *first* NGC get-together. Would I be contradicted in the Q and A? Fat chance, with those three newsroom tyros who tossed puffball inquiries at the guv like, "How does the organization interact with the federal government?" "Who is the current chairman?" "Will you run for chairman?" I was still unscathed when Jill's hand finally went up and I knew she would have bigger fish to fry than correcting me, if necessary, on Baden, Indiana.

"Miss McKenzie?" Duke recognized her.

"Why Iowa, Governor? Is there any special significance there?"

Her beauteous face couldn't quite ever be grim, only stern and determined. Charley had his camera on a tripod now, aimed at Duke. Jill wouldn't be seen, but would do commentary later.

Duke, on the other hand, looked mischievous. He scuffed his shoes like a school kid. "It's true," he said. "Some people would have me running for president and others for chairman of the National Governors Conference. It's hard to make up my mind between those two. In other words, I'm still undecided about both, or either."

Tongue-in-cheek stuff. Jill knew it, yet didn't crack a smile.

"Surely your experience in Washington, Governor, as a congressman all those years, must have given you some exposure to the presidency and its duties," was Jill's arch reply.

"Enough, Miss McKenzie, to make me doubt I would ever want to go back that way to D.C. However, a good politician never rules out anything."

This jousting might have continued had not General Bill Thompson announced it was time to start getting ready to board. A trip to the restrooms was recommended, although there were facilities on the plane. En route back and forth to the men's W.C., I caught snatches of Jill doing her spiel for Charley's camera, heard her say the governor seemed to be in a "playful" mood regarding rumors of his future ambitions. That tape, I understood from her later, would be picked up at the airbase by a studio messenger (we were, you can see, still in the semi-dark ages of television technology).

How it happened that Jill and I ended up in bucket seats next to each other once on the plane has never been adequately explained. These portable units had been arranged commercial-style, aisle and window. Since I got on first and had looked forward to a lot of scenery viewing since we'd be flying at low altitudes, I plunked myself down by one of the porthole-shaped openings. Having stowed all my luggage except a book (Francis Parkman's *The Conspiracy of Pontiac*), I settled in, preparing myself mentally for the practically day-long trip ahead of us. The scent of Jill's perfume preceded her when at last she boarded and moved in my direction. There were other empty places. What could I read into the fact that she stopped alongside me?

I actually stood up (as my parents had taught me to do, whenever a female joined my company). Jill later told me she found that "cute." I offered her the window. She graciously refused. The book caught her eye.

"What are you reading?" she asked.

It was an old copy of Parkman from the state library, printed in the 1890s, with a drab hard cover, not a paperback reissue. "Francis Parkman, a great American historian," I responded.

"This one's about the Indian chief Pontiac's rebellion against the British. A two-volume work. This is part two."

She later also told me she found my somewhat flustered seriousness cute, as well. The only *Pontiac* she knew, she said, with a gorgeous smile, was one her father had owned and drove the family around in when she was a kid. So what was all this actually about?

By now, you surely have noted a real pedagogic streak in my makeup. I never set out to be a teacher, never mind a college professor, but it's no big surprise given my innate tendencies toward didactic explanations. However, I apparently didn't bore Jill. Like Desdemona, wooed by Othello's tales of his exploits, she seemed interested in my knowledge of and willingness to impart American history.

My talk about Pontiac, his assault on Detroit in 1763 (thus, connecting to the brand name of her father's automobile), and the subject of Indian warfare in general, led her finally to ask me a question that put me instantly on my guard.

"Is it true," she wanted to know, "that Governor Ellery has some red-hot resolution on Indians he'd going to present to the governors conference?"

Aha, she's pumping me, I thought. *Now I know why she sat down here, the sly wench.*

I tried not to seem hostile in my answer. "Did George mention anything to you?" I asked casually. As press secretary, Everoff had full control of any such disclosures, although I'd worked on drafting the resolution.

"He said you would know about it."

I hope my squirming was likewise cute. Immediately, I went back to Pontiac, the importance of this eighteenth-century warfare to the future of today's Middle West, on states such as Pennsylvania, Virginia, and Maryland in their frontier regions, and I threw in the story of the Paxton Boys, who massacred the

Conestoga Indians—a gush of obfuscating detail that sought to throw her off the track without answering her inquiry.

By then, we were airborne. I noticed that she had appeared suddenly tense—an apparent fear of flying—holding on to the arms of her seat tightly during takeoff and afterward. A gentle, reassuring pat on the arm from me brought a wan look of partial gratitude, as I whispered, "We're gonna be safe, don't worry," and then to divert her, I said, "Hey, there's something interesting down there to see!"

In such fashion did I get her to lean as close to me as she could, buckled in, and showed her, as we were circling and literally heading east to make a wide turn, a group of barren islands on the dark blue, enamel-like surface of the Atlantic below. "In the 1600s," I said to Jill, "whole villages of English fishermen lived on those rocks. Our country, you could honestly say, was born on those outcroppings." Aware of her nearness, her fragrance, her hair brushing against my cheek, I regaled this beautiful woman with tales of early colonization. Later, she confessed that this was the most unusual "line" she'd ever gotten from a guy and, yes, that it was cute, too.

Soon, naturally, General Bill Thompson had us flying in the right direction—due west—and up to our cruising altitude so we could walk around and stretch. Yet Jill and I, for the longest while, sat and talked.

So much for scenery. So much for reading. The adventures of Pontiac faded from my mind while Jill and I jabbered on, discovering each other, at least on a verbal level. We were both children of the suburbs, both offspring of families that were "comfortable," both college graduates, both ambitious. Our fathers had both been professional men and had provided no businesses for us to inherit. Unlike myself, Jill had siblings—three brothers— and both her parents were still alive.

We shared nostalgia, stories of our growing up, high school, college, what we'd been doing since. Here's one tale she told me, which I always remember. Why, should be evident once you've heard it.

Jill said, "I'd been riding horses since I was six years old. Probably since that age, I'd been pestering my parents to buy me a horse. We even had an unused barn on our property. You know about young girls and horses, I suppose. It's a sex thing, the attraction, they say. . . ." She made a funny, skeptical face, which made me laugh. "One night, totally out of the blue, my dad comes home and says he's getting me a horse. I was fourteen at the time. Knowing him, I wasn't surprised he'd found some kind of bargain in horseflesh he couldn't resist. But surprise, surprise, I didn't jump up and down with joy. You see, I'd simply lost my interest in horses. I'd found it in boys, one in particular, my first beau."

"Tell me about him," I interjected.

"Allen Phillips. Our little infatuation lasted about six months. What a disappointment." She leaned close to me and whispered, "He turned out to be as fussy and full of himself, although a lot better looking, than your friend Georgie Everoff." Instinctively, we both turned in the direction of the plump young press secretary, sitting by himself a few rows away.

"My *colleague*," I corrected her, then added, "And consequently, you went back to horses."

With a very sexy expression, she patted my hand and said, "Hardly, my dear."

There, we now had each touched the other. It was the dawning in my consciousness of the thought, in the language of men's locker rooms, that maybe—just maybe—on this trip, I might get lucky.

Prurient ambitions aside, I found I really enjoyed conversing with Jill. On TV, she came across as cool and hard—a *sapphire,* in her blue outfit—but she had plainly shown me her feminine side, softness and vulnerability, which proved quite endearing in concert with her toughness, stark beauty, and quick intelligence.

How did I come across to her? Brainy, "cute," destined for big things, husband material? All these years together, I've only gotten hints of what her secret feelings were. A grain of single-minded stubbornness revealed itself when the subject turned to my boss, to Governor Duke. I forget the exact context wherein our conversation veered back to the morning's impromptu press conference. The exchange between us, though, has remained clear.

"Are you ever thinking of running for office?" Jill suddenly asked me, apropos of nothing.

"God, no, I haven't thought of it," I finally answered truthfully. "What made you ask?"

"Some people think so," she answered. Long since, I've learned you must never ask a journalist for his or her sources. But then I was entirely green.

"Some people?" I responded quizzically. "Who?"

Her smile was inscrutable and she shrugged her shoulders. "Some people."

I caught her gist: don't probe. So I replied, "You know, honestly, I've never had the slightest thought about running for office. Honestly, I don't think it's something for me."

The double use of *honestly* made me seem like a liar, Jill later confessed. Yet honestly, really, I had spoken the absolute truth. Paradoxically, I learned, this obvious slickness on my part positively enhanced my image as a potential political "swinger."

As Jill saw things, I had the wherewithal to "really go places." This was in line with her unshakeable belief that Duke intended to run for president.

Pointing around at the interior of the military transport plane, she said, "This is all camouflage. Gives him a chance to make some early key campaign stops. Iowa, for heaven's sake."

"Okay," I responded. "I admit my boss would make a great presidential candidate. God knows our party could use him. But I don't think it's going to happen."

"Why not?" Those probing blue eyes demanded proof.

"I don't think he likes Washington," I answered lamely.

Jill laughed. Once again, she patted my hand. "Poor boy, you certainly do seem innocent," she said.

Rather than resent her condescension, I just silently savored the touch of her fingers. "You hear a lot of rumors about Duke," I spoke up at last. "You should discount most of them."

"Wanna bet?"

"Bet what?"

"That in Iowa, we visit one of the state's leading Democrats, a certain major heavy hitter on the national scene, someone very rich and powerful who can thoroughly influence Iowa's caucuses."

"You sound like you know who it is."

"Just guessing." She wore a cat/canary smile. "Do you dare to bet?"

"What about Colorado?"

"Same drill. Another campaign stop."

It would have been useless to tell her I was totally in the dark about these prearranged landings. Admittedly, I could have bet against her, to establish my innocence. But I expected she might be right and told her so. Besides, why shouldn't I want to believe her? President Ellery! What a scary, wonderful idea!

How long after this bit of conversation did we reach Iowa? The first indication was the Mississippi River. "There's the Big Muddy," I suddenly announced to Jill. A lull in our chitchat had let me glance out the window and note an extraordinarily wide expanse of water running a north-south swath perpendicular to the plane's east-west trajectory. Why hadn't I thought of announcing scenic landmarks more forcefully before this? My seatmate had to lean straight across me to take a peek. While I luxuriated in the prolonged feeling of her soft body against mine, we passed from one riverbank to the other. "That's Illinois, I'm pretty sure," I said, pointing to the near side, and "Here's Iowa!" I proclaimed like a TV host a few seconds later. "Davenport is the city down there, if I'm not mistaken." Anyway, my words kept Jill gazing a tad longer, oh, so close and silky. *Hot shot,* I was thinking to myself. *Impress her with more erudition.*

Alas, nothing jelled immediately. Jill moved back to her regular sitting position. When an inspiration finally appeared to me within a few moments, I must have smiled, for she asked, "What's so funny, Jonathan?"

I loved having her call me by my name. Maybe it worked the other way, too, I thought. "Jill," I said, "seeing the Mississippi made me think of something humorous, but apparently true."

I was name-dropping from history again, but now it was about La Salle—René-Robert Cavelier, Sieur de La Salle—who discovered the Mississippi. But before he did, I told Jill, La Salle was in a birchbark canoe with a bunch of eastern Indians as his guides on one of the Great Lakes. "What's that land I see ahead of us?" the Frenchman asked his companions. Places were being named then in a North American genesis, mostly Indian names or how they sounded to European ears. Of the Indian response identifying the looming lakeshore, a grunted "Michigan," stuck in La Salle's mind.

"And the good chevalier went to his grave," I said, "never knowing the meaning of "Michigan" in the tongue of those Abenaki guys from New England."

"My grandmother lived in Troy, Michigan," said Jill.

"Then maybe I shouldn't tell you what the word really stands for," I added coyly.

"I can take it," she said, with mock bravery.

"Shit," I said. "Feces. Kaka. The Indians were pulling La Salle's leg."

"Poor Grandma," Jill moaned, and we burst out laughing.

I saw George Everoff turn his head to glance at us. Most likely, others were also noting our conviviality. Harry DeWitt, certainly. Although my administrative assistant boss sat up front with Duke and the VIP group, he was pretty peripatetic once the plane had leveled off at its cruising altitude and we passengers were allowed to move about the transport's interior. He caught my eye more than once and winked when Jill wasn't looking. But he didn't interrupt us.

In fact, she and I had flown all the way to the Mississippi in an intimate tête-à-tête. The time had whizzed by. The geography, too. I never had a chance to check the flight plan, to learn the states we actually flew over, and which were a distance away, as Michigan was, I'm sure.

It wasn't long before Harry DeWitt passed by again. "Are you guys hungry?" He stopped now to talk to us. Harry, the owlish political guru, was making an announcement. We were landing soon. That's why they'd held off feeding us on board. If we felt faint, he had crackers.

"Aren't we there yet, Daddy?" Jill wisecracked.

"Patience, my child. Patience." Harry joked back.

"And Mr. Waggoner's having us all in to lunch, right?" Jill continued.

"Ooh, you have classified information, Miss McKenzie. Has George . . . ?"

Jill vigorously shook her head. "No, Georgie is guiltless. And you know, I never reveal my sources."

"And Jonathan, obviously, couldn't be your informant." Harry picked up in that same joshing, good-natured style. "Look how befuddled he looks."

As usual, an exaggeration. But I was glad to be acquitted of treason to the Duke Ellery forces. No one had said a word to me about Waggoner—or that our stop in Iowa would be at

Waggoner Industries. The "Refrigerator King." Horace Waggoner III. To be sure, even I'd heard of that dude.

Once Harry left to go back to his seat, I said to Jill, "Do you really believe I'm as dumb as I look? That I don't know who Waggoner is?"

Smiling and nodding, Jill answered jocularly, "Yes, dumb—but cute."

Our conversation halted temporarily as we were told to re-attach our seatbelts. Jill was white-knuckled again, once the aircraft began its descent. All the way starting down, my left hand rested comfortingly on her right hand.

Out of the clouds we emerged and below was the Waggoner industrial complex and the town of the same name adjacent to it, spreading into view, and the nearby airfield not far from the factories we were approaching, with its fleet of small private planes and a corporate jet visible, and a football stadium over toward the town, all seemingly plunked amid the flattest farmland I'd ever seen. Passing over the equally flat roofs of the manufacturing units, I could read the advertising message laboriously painted on their surfaces, telling the aerial world about "WAGGONER OF WAGGONER, THE BEST REFRIGERATOR MAKERS IN THE UNIVERSE."

Not anxious to peer vertically at anything, Jill didn't lean into me, but did grab my hand and, squeezing, gripped it while we flew lower and lower. I tried to distract her fear by commenting on the roofs—their flatness, wondering aloud how the Waggoner Company dealt with snow here, since surely they must have blizzards in Iowa. I doubt that Jill heard anything I said until we were on the ground.

WHOOSH. THAT LONG-AGO IMAGE abruptly vanished. Jill was suddenly standing in the open doorway of my study. The "blue sapphire" of dreamy recall was the matron of today—

but by God, she was still one attractive broad, all gussied up in a handsome beige suit.

"Wow, you look great! Where are you going?" I asked.

It's said that women dress for other women. "Meeting with my business girlfriends," she replied. "Then getting my hair done. And some food shopping."

"Yes. Right. Your investment group. Okay, make us tons of money, dear." I got up from my desk to go over and give her a peck on the cheek.

After I did, she said, "In case you've forgotten, dinner tonight with Ron and Mitzi at the country club."

My response was, "Six-thirty for drinks, I didn't forget."

Jill was actually out in the hallway before she told me, "Oh, by the way, Ritchie's back with Irene."

Was she kidding? "How do you know?" I blurted.

But she had already turned and was heading away from me.

"How do you know?" My second demand was more of a shout, and almost frenzied, too.

"I just called her," she shouted back, without turning around. And she was not only angry but disgusted in her tone.

I also had two emotions: relieved and damn puzzled.

6

IF I HAD BEEN A PHILOSOPHER, rather than a part-time historian, my quandary regarding Ritchie might have led me to a speculation like: *Does Man have too much freedom?* With an adjustment for political correctness, changing *Man* to *Human Race* or something else gender-neutral, the question would have been prompted by my having too many choices. What should I do next? Call Ritchie on his cell phone? Call their apartment and speak to Irene, presuming Ritchie was sleeping off his drunk? Send them an e-mail, asking them—nay, commanding them— to call me? Do nothing? Worry in silence about my son's future? Moon airily on the nature of American society, as I've been doing in the formulating of this book about Duke? Or would that track have me philosophizing too much and ultimately becoming a bore?

Yet Duke himself often waxed philosophic. All his stuff about chaos and order. Even the public utterances of this governor were not immune from a deep thoughtfulness rare among his colleagues. I remember standing in the rear of an old Grange hall (yes, we still have them in our state) when Duke addressed a local crowd and overhearing one farmer say to another at the end of his talk, "I ain't none too certain what he said, but I sure do like the way he sounded."

The thought of which conspired to unveil my *feelings*—they weren't really rational deliberations—about the notion of the *abyss*. Duke had introduced it in another speech (before a more sophisticated audience than at the Grange hall) to illustrate the need for a caring government. In our form of economy here in America, he argued, the prevailing rule seemed to be "sink or swim." Sinking into what? Some people held an image of being in a lake or on the ocean and submerging underwater after a vain struggle to stay afloat. Duke saw the danger as an *abyss* into which so many Americans would fall, wiped out financially, poverty-stricken, disappearing, unless—and here I can recall the approximate words of how he put it—the metaphor, at least, which he borrowed from the famous Scottish economist-philosopher Adam Smith—the Edinburgh sage's concept of "the Invisible Hand." Conservatives have abused it ever since the eighteenth century to justify laissez-faire free enterprise. "No need to regulate anything, boys. There's a mysterious force that keeps business healthy, if only you leave us corporate guys alone." Who else but Duke would give the notion a humanitarian twist? He stated defiantly, "The real 'Invisible Hand' is a government that cares. It keeps the abyss from opening up beneath your feet. It levels the playing field. It's the referee who ensures the game is fair and honest. A government *truly* of the people, by the people, and for the people must exist in tandem with the capitalist system. Otherwise, the latter becomes the handmaiden of a monopolizing few."

In that regard, I couldn't help but reflect moments later on the Waggoner industrial empire so recently in my memory. That company still existed. Horace III "Hank" Waggoner was still alive, still flying around the country, no doubt, in his personal jet. Was there a disconnect between Duke's professed ideals and his hobnobbing with this *Prince of Capitalism,* who had inherited the Waggoner fortune and expanded upon it greatly? "Hypocrisy," those to the left of me might mutter. Verily, an arguable point.

I realized I needed to make a decision. My narrative of our trip to the National Governors Conference, having enjoyed its pause, should it continue? Or, instead of picking up my pen, I pondered another direction. Into the abyss perhaps? A detour would be to start writing about, or at least thinking about, Miles Monahan. Chronologically, the idea even made sense, although again I'd have to flash back from within a flashback. Well, why not?

But the abyss made me conscious once more of Ritchie. Pick up the phone first, Jonathan, before you do anything else, I urged myself.

Momentarily paralyzed between choices, as I often had been during my political days, I did what a good politician will often do: none of the above. I'd go and have breakfast and put off any decision.

Laissez-faire, no less.

While I squeezed orange juice, cooked an omelet, toasted two slices of bread, made myself a cup of instant coffee, I wondered about—what else?—free will. At my advancing age, how much did past decisions and accidents still hedge in my movements? Was I like some anguished Greek hero stuck with some fatal course no matter how hard I struggled? Or could I, as soon as I'd finished my meal, depart impulsively on some untoward adventure, off to a war front or an uncharted jungle? Oh, sure I could, as long as I was prepared to take a year's supply of my most necessary pills with me.

I'll tell you where I was headed with this sloppy, juvenile reverie. It wasn't pure maundering. Weirdly enough, it was related to our dinner date tonight with Ron and Mitzi Gordon. In the back of my mind, a question—no, a suspicion—had been nagging me. What did Ron have up his sleeve? We were his *invitees*—the country club was a big deal. Was this a full court press? Was he softening me up for something?

It was chutzpah on my part, I knew, but my former campaign manager, my political guru, was still active in state Democratic affairs, still chair of the town committee, still on the county committee. We were going to need a candidate for state senate in the next election. Could he have his eyes on me?

You had to know Ron. His style. Otherwise, you might wonder: Why didn't he just pick up the phone and ask? We were close personal friends, had been since my very first campaign for office. The Jacksons and Gordons took trips together, often dined together, went to the theater, ballgames, etc. My redheaded pal was never frontal. "Too subtle and legalistic ever to offer myself as a candidate," he once admitted. What he didn't say was that *running for* and *serving in* state office would cost him money. Yet he spent hundreds of billable hours pro bono directing campaigns from the background. The *eminence grise* type.

What should I say to him, if he asked me to throw my hat in the ring? How about, *Yes, if you can guarantee me the nomination?*

A no-brainer. Ron could instantly give me a dozen reasons why the party would clear the path for me.

What if I then said, *Can you guarantee me I won't win the general election and save me the commute to the capital?*

I can hear him laugh and say, *Sure, no problem.*

Such a fantasy in the breakfast nook was fun.

Less amusing, when I'd finished eating, was the knowledge I still had to wrestle with the Ritchie dilemma. Well, so he was back with Irene. Did he really quit his job or was his outburst simply some hyperbole, some dream of glory and revenge against a stupid boss, followed by a binge of general rebelliousness, alcohol-fueled, which would end in a hangover and back to same-old, same-old?

About to return upstairs to my writing again, I realized I still needed to face an earlier truly deadly rebellion of someone close to me—today, if I chose, but eventually, in any case—that of Miles Monahan's wild behavior.

Actually, I had thought of Miles while preparing breakfast. It was he who had taught me the trick of using a fork to pin back edges of an omelet to let all of the liquidy egg flow out of the center until you had everything firm and could add cheese or ham or whatever filling before you folded it over. This lesson occurred on one of our fishing trips up north. The first night, we would always stay in a rented cabin, which had a kitchen, at Edgeremet Landing. From there, by canoe, we would go camping and fishing all the way to the Canadian border.

We kids started vacationing at Lake Edgeremet while we were still in high school. Those times, Gerry Margolis was with us. Our first years in college, too. Nothing of note occurred initially. More than a few fish lost their lives, a lot of beer got consumed, bawdy stories were told, mosquitoes and blackflies were swatted, etc. Gerry was killed in an auto crash our junior year. The first especially strange trip I remember happened five or six years afterward.

The American patriot, Uncle Sam, Mr. O. Murray Carr, whom Miles later became, was utterly wacko about Ireland in that younger period of his life. I always joked how he was secretly a member of the most terroristic branch of the IRA. One year, he painted his car the colors of the Irish Free State flag—emerald green, white, and orange. Anti-British slogans were stenciled on its sides. When I flew home from New York City and he picked me up in this weird-looking jalopy so we could go on our northern excursion, I said right off the bat, "You gotta be kidding, Miles."

The guy had a way of making his eyes gleam. "We're driving it into Canada," he declared.

The historian in me replied, "Oh, I see. The new Fenian invasion."

"Don't be a smartass," he warned. "You know the violent streak I have in me. Just get your stuff in the car and shut up. And practice shouting: 'Oop the Rebels!'"

"Oop something else," I retorted. "Like oop yours."

Admittedly, this was the good-natured banter of fairly recent, as yet unsettled, college grads. Nor did we get into any trouble, although we could have had a disastrous ending to our adventure. We snuck into Canada illegally by foot in the middle of the night, carrying cans of green paint, daubing "IRA," "BRITS OUT," "UNITE IRELAND," on any appropriate surface before we scooted back across the line. Why I went along was part of a bargain. Miles's original plan had been to leave this graffiti behind us and *then* try to drive back into Canada.

"You're doubly insane," I told him. "I'm not going on either of those mad excursions."

I'll delete the expletives as we argued. We were setting up camp early in the evening. The fire was crackling. Miles literally threatened to throw me into it. I reminded him of a bloody nose I'd given him when we were kids.

"Okay, humor me," he finally said. "Come with me tonight in the canoe and I'll scrub the drive into Canada."

"The whole thing is crazy," I still argued.

"Humor me," he insisted again. "Do we have a deal?"

"Will you shake on it?" At grammar school, a sealing of hands was sacred.

"On my Irish honor."

Thus, by touch, like blood brothers, we became co-conspirators during what—at the time—seemed not much more than a college prank. Miles kept his word. Back at Edgeremet Landing, he made no attempt to turn north when we exited. Happy I didn't have to battle him, I merely reflected—and I resurrect my exact wording now with a dose of irony—*At any rate, he's harmless.*

I figured he had an overwhelming urge to role-play, the born actor's drive always to be someone else. When I was faced with further aberrant behavior from him on yet another camping trip, the one we took following his gangbusters performance as Uncle Sam in the Statehouse, and before the National Governors Conference flight, I plainly was a bit more troubled. *Not enough at the time,* some people might claim. *All too true,* has been my own thought.

Okay, rather than continue being cryptic, I'll plunge right on, go straight to the lake with Miles in his California car the day after his triumph with the kids visiting Duke. The night before our departure, he'd stayed with me at my bachelor pad in the capital, a night of heavy drinking, lots of laughs, and nostalgia. In other words, I wasn't on my guard.

Miles's Uncle Sam schtik had struck me as eccentric, even overwrought, but sort of a rationally desperate reaction to his failure to set Hollywood afire. He had found a gimmick. Rather than waiting on table between fewer and fewer acting jobs, he could earn a couple of bucks entertaining children or propping up patriotic dinners and other events, and still enjoy the limelight of performing. While prepared to be embarrassed (he'd arrived in our state capital in a jalopy now painted red, white, and blue), I was actually pleased with the outcome of the "favor" he did for Duke and my boss's approbation of this colorful friend of one of his junior assistants.

In a perfectly good mood, then, I started off for Lake Edgeremet with Miles in his funky automobile, gradually getting used to the reactions of bystanders, people pointing from the roadsides, drivers gawking as they passed us. Outwardly, Miles seemed impervious to this attention, although I knew he craved it—all the more, I thought rather smugly, *now that his career has tanked.* This was my own projection, I have to confess, based on a sense I tried to conceal of *my own career having taken off.*

By working hard not to be patronizing, did I upset him further? Increase his boastfulness, his prevarications? Or had the Hollywood bug already infected him thoroughly before he'd begun this trip east?

Why had he come to see me? How much of it really had anything to do with the guns? That's right—guns, genuine weapons.

He'd brought two rifles and two small pistols, wrapped in canvas, lying amid the clutter on the floor in the back of his tired old secondhand sedan.

"For target practice out in the boonies," he told me, saying we'd wait until we'd isolated ourselves out among the far-off islands of Lake Edgeremet.

What nonsense. Yet I couldn't believe he was set to murder me and let my body rot in the *williwogs,* where it would be forever undisturbed. Too much like a bad movie. Aside from the obvious fact too many witnesses had seen us together, he'd also transported four weapons, two for him, two for me, or so he said, and it seemed equally obvious he didn't intend for us to have a shoot-out.

There was also his own explanation for this odd behavior, which had a certain plausibility. We were spending our first night in our usual shoreside cabin when he opened up after dinner, which was a steak he cooked, complemented by wine, not beer, as our beverage (being now mature adults, not undergraduates).

"I've got a secret to share with you," Miles said to me, pouring himself another glass of the Sonoma red he'd contributed to our supplies.

At this point, I didn't know about the guns and was feeling pretty mellow. "Your secret will remain inviolate," I said sententiously. "Go ahead. Shoot."

I hadn't expected him to laugh. "Precisely," he said. "Shoot. Precisely."

I know I looked baffled. "Okay," I said. "You have my full attention. I'm waiting. Are you sober enough to make sense?"

"I'm going to become a star," he announced, "by playing a presidential assassin in a new movie."

"John Wilkes Booth again," I countered.

"Not exactly."

The whole story, at least as Miles told it, was soon unveiled. It was bizarre enough, but believable because of its very oddball, show-biz nature. Did I remember a movie in which Frank Sinatra played one of a group of marksmen hired to shoot the president of the United States? The entire action took place in a room where the killers were hiding out, ready to ambush the official motorcade.

"That film came out only several months, I think, before Kennedy was shot," Miles said.

"Yes, I saw it," I said enthusiastically. "Sinatra was terrific."

"It revived his career," Miles went on. "Seriously. Until then, he couldn't get himself arrested, and the buzz he got out of that single performance propelled him right back up to the top in our business. One break is all you need."

"And you're getting yours?"

While I said this, I wasn't sounding skeptical. I really did want to see him successful, much as I relished silently lording it over him at the moment. The guy had talent—a bit crazy, but certainly talented. Gerry Margolis had called him a *meschugener* years ago. You had to be, to get ahead in *that* business. Plus *lucky.*

To hear Miles tell it, his luck had turned. It all had to do with a script and a producer he'd met at a cocktail party. "Six months ago," he said, "my life changed. This guy—his name is Jerry M—Jeremy, and not Gerald, like Margolis—but I can't tell you his last name—had a terrific story and backing but no one to play the most important part . . . not the leading man but the heavy, the murderer, or, in this case, the assassin . . . like Frankie Sinatra, a type who aims to blow away the U.S. president, except he's a loner, a psycho and—yes, sir—an outsized American patriot. He's Uncle Sam, in other words, an Uncle Sam impersonator!"

His presentation of this key premise was done with a *tah-dah!* flourish, the full drama of a Miles Monahan gesture in that rude cabin by the lake. Hollywood, although immensely far away, seemed close, enveloping both of us while the aspiring actor wove a most unlikely story that magically held together, as might happen on the screen. "My job," Miles continued, "was to convince Jerry M that I could play the Uncle Sam character. Don't ask me how I did it, but I did. Of course, these projects take time to get rolling, raising the money, assembling the cast, obtaining distribution, so meanwhile I've got myself a little sideline, doing gigs, making myself a little name for myself—that is, O. Murray Carr, which I'm planning to keep for the film credits, too. Smart, huh?"

Miles was nothing if not persuasive. Yours truly had drunk too much wine to attempt to critique his tale. So instead, I ragged him a bit. "Hey, I always thought—which you used to say, too—Miles Monahan is a perfect stage name, made for Tinsel Town."

"Yeah, well. . . ." He shrugged. "Time marches on . . . ," and the subject soon faded into other lubricated channels amid our alcoholic haze.

Until the next morning, the moment I had my first genuine inkling of the weaponry he'd brought. Before we loaded our canoe, we paid a visit to the general store at the landing to see if there were any last minute supplies we required. As I searched around in the food and patent-medicine areas, Miles stood at the counter, talking with the proprietor. This old-fashioned emporium, I should add, sold firearms and ammunition, which were kept behind the counter. To my astonishment, I discovered Miles had bought several boxes of bullets. When we were outside, I asked why, and he just said, "For target practice out in the boonies."

I was woefully puzzled by his remark until he opened the back door of his car, reached down for a longish, innocuous, canvas-wrapped bundle on the floor, and briefly slid it open to show me one fast glimpse of the contents inside.

"What the hell are those?" I sputtered.

Once more, he repeated his terse dictum, "For target practice in the boonies." Then, he lifted the awkward burden and started for the canoe.

I forget what I was carrying. Walking alongside him, I expressed my dismay. "Jesus, Miles. We have gun laws in this state. What if some game warden hears us shooting, thinks we're hunting? Christ, the newspapers will have a field day. A member of the governor's staff—"

"They're legal," he snapped, obviously contemptuous of my cowardice and selfishness. "Don't get your panties in an uproar. I've got permits."

Cowing me, I suppose, from continuing to fight him on this issue, was my anxiety that I might never come back. What a thing to think about my oldest friend, notwithstanding his dysfunctional behavior. Almost immediately, too, as we paddled away from the wharf—Miles in the stern, me in the bow—he seemed to sense my uneasiness and sought to assuage it.

"Look, Jonathan, look," he commenced, "I had no thought of getting you in trouble. Target practice isn't against the law. Gun ownership isn't either, thank God. The problem for me was where could I do practice shooting in and around LA? The cops are too nervous, too many gangs. I tried a private range, but—"

"Anyway, why do you have to do target practice?" I interrupted. "You're in a movie role. You don't have to do it for real."

"Au contraire," Miles replied. "Haven't you ever heard of method acting? Immersing yourself right inside the authenticity of the part?"

"Wacko," I commented.

"Humor me, old buddy."

I shut up. Perhaps the peacefulness of the lake's ambiance was taking hold the farther away from shore we glided. Already, within twenty minutes, we were beyond sight of any human habitation. The islands no longer had camps on them, only here and there an isolated open campsite. We were headed for the farthest north of them. This was evergreen country, towering pines and spruce, mostly, and at this time of year, at this latitude, the few hardwoods were only starting to leaf. It wasn't so long ago the ice had gone out. We were not likely to encounter many other hardy fishermen and it wasn't anywhere near hunting season. So we pretty much had the upper lake entirely to ourselves.

Miles was in an expansive mood. Coming close to one of our favorite fishing spots, he suddenly rose from his seat (damn near upsetting us), waving his paddle in the air, shouting (howling, actually), "I'm a different person out here! I'm a different person! Yahoo! Wahoo!"

His echo boomed across the tea-dark waters, confirming, it appeared, how utterly alone we were. No sound but his own reverberation ensued. That is, except a few moments later, we heard a loon. The cry was the epitome of the North Woods for both of us, we had many years before agreed.

"God, how I love that eerie noise," Miles exulted. "It's worth the trip."

"Your fellow loony," I joked.

"Loony is right," he said, in a tone soft, satisfied, and yet somehow sad.

We didn't catch much in the way of fish—much too early in the season. We did use up the bullets he'd bought, popping away at improvised targets with his rifles and pistols. Miles was particularly insistent about needing to know how to fire a handgun. Hold it with both hands? Squeeze the trigger with one hand and use the other to steady your aim? According to him, a final script had not been done for the movie and no ultimate decision made on the choice of weapon for the Uncle Sam assassin. I joined in these fusillades, too, my paranoia eventually evaporating.

I have to say that last camping trip, in the main, ended up as quite enjoyable. In parting, we were still buddies.

However, during the next six months, before my trip west with Duke, et al., we were not much in contact. One letter had come from Miles, slightly disturbing to me. He was doing a lot of historical research, he wrote, looking up presidential assassins. "Interesting stuff. This guy Guiteau, who shot Garfield—what a character. Wouldn't I like to play him someday. Hey, I'd have a lifelong career. So I'm type-cast. As long as I'm working, right?" This all seemed benign enough, normal enough, if you ignored the subject matter. But there was also this phrase: "I can sympathize with those guys." Followed by another: "Poor squirts who never would amount to anything, making a name in history, immortalizing themselves." The rather chilling kicker was a P.S.: "What do you know about anarchists, bomb-throwers, random acts of violence aimed at the ideals of America? Name some publications for me, you bookworm."

Okay, again, I "humored" him. I went to the state library and spent one whole lunch break cataloguing tomes that might fit his request. Homegrown terrorism, conspiracies—both theoretical and real, *undergrounds*—the hidden, bad-Janus face of the American polity. The image of Janus, the god with two sides to him, also entered my perturbed thoughts about Miles. I felt he was slipping. In my metaphor, Miles and I, who had been on the same level, were now being separated; he was turning the evil side of his visage to me.

Despite such lugubrious thinking, I mailed off my research to him and subsequently waited in vain for a reply. It never occurred to me to research a movie producer named Jeremy M, nor explore somehow whether Miles's cover story might prove just that—a cover story, but for what?

Not surprisingly, the question of why I phoned Miles as soon as I knew I was going to Los Angeles has haunted me ever since.

I once wrote about it in the form of rather sophomoric dialogue drama, of which an excerpt follows:

The Prosecutor: "Jackson's motive: Hubris. Pride. Showing off."

The Defense: "Jackson's natural desire to connect with an old friend about whom he was worried."

The Prosecutor: "Had the contact not been made, there might never have been the tragedy resulting from it."

The Defense: "Nonsense. The news of the National Governors Conference and the president's attendance was in the Los Angeles newspapers, on TV, radio, etc. Monahan's actions would have been no different without that phone call."

The Prosecutor: "I leave it to the jury to decide if a connection did not exist, a conspiracy one might even assume—since it's known Jackson took part in their target practice."

The Defense: "Oh, bullshit!"

Obviously, this stuff still bothers me. I may take its sting, its doubt, its twistable paths of logic and illogic to my grave. Exorcise your demons by expiating them on paper? The result is this silly prosecutor-defense exchange. Too tame. I need a full-fledged juju man or shaman to pour sacred smudge smoke, or some cool priest, hidden in a confessional, so I can arise, purified of recriminations.

I was back in the present as I experienced this last insight. Back in my study. Back at my desktop instrument with its screen inviting further prose.

But I still wasn't ready to turn back to the big flashback.

7

OSTENSIBLY, MY SUDDEN DECISION to take a break from all this cerebral activity and walk into town to the drugstore was as much to clear my mind and fill my lungs with fresh air as it was to add to a depleted supply of a certain over-the-counter pill. Yet my sojourn through the local scene appropriately continued the political trail I had been traveling. How could it not?

"All politics is local," the famed Speaker of the U.S. House, Thomas P. "Tip" O'Neill had opined, purportedly lifting the phrase from his father, who had been a city councilor and superintendent of sewers in their home community of Cambridge, Massachusetts. The remark had followed Tip's defeat for his own Cambridge City Council seat because he had taken for granted the ward in which he lived and hadn't campaigned there—his first run for office having been made when he was still a senior at Boston College. Eventually, he did get himself elected to the Cambridge School Board, followed by a career in the Massachusetts General Court (their legislature), rising to speaker of the house beneath the Commonwealth's golden dome before moving on to the D.C. capitol.

Then he spent many distinguished years in the U.S. Congress: an electoral gamut from the streets of Cambridge, that gritty home of immigrants (mostly Irish and Italian at the time) and Harvard, to the broader avenues of national power, but never forgetting where he came from—famous, too, for his constant visits to the local emporiums of power, a Chinese laundry, a certain Italian restaurant, a Star Market shopping center, and, most certainly, more than a few favorite Irish drinking spots.

We had no such exotic locales in Swanstown. The drugstore wasn't really a hangout—no soda fountain. But several buildings away was Ken's, where coffee and sandwiches, burgers and fries, newspapers and sundries could be purchased. At any hour (they also served breakfast), a "gang," meaning a couple or more of the local population, could be encountered inside.

Question to myself: Having bought my box of tablets and chatted pleasantly with Bart Roberts, the druggist, should I drop in next door at Ken's?

Three considerations led me to say *yes*. During the entire five-block stroll from my house, I'd begun projecting some airy, professorial ruminations on the *local* content of our federal political system—i.e., trying to illustrate Tip O'Neill's dictum with concrete examples. Nor was there absent from my calculation the vague, if flattering, conjecture of how Ron Gordon might ask me tonight to run for state senate. I had no answer whether I would or not, but figured it wouldn't hurt to practice a little shmoozing at Ken's. And the third goal? I was thirsty and wanted a Diet Coke.

"Lookie, lookie, who just blew in. Hello, stranger!" was the ironic yet friendly welcome boomed out by Hartley Young, one of a trio of men in the closest booth as I entered. "Come sit with us, Jonathan," he added.

I had always had Hartley's vote, principally because he'd hated my first opponent, Earl Johnson, his neighbor out on the Farm Road, and afterward, his gratitude for a number of favors I'd done him. He was still a Republican, I knew, and enjoyed telling people I was the only Democrat he'd never voted against.

Such had been our little joke, spawning this interchange. *But did you really put an X next to my name? Hell, yes; I held my nose and did, too, you damn communist.*

Good ol' boy Hartley. The other two guys with him were

good ol' boys as well. They weren't exactly farmers, although they did grow truck garden plants. None of them had ever held steady jobs. Jacks of all trades. Hunters and fishermen, too, you bet. And don't ever talk to them about gun control, unless you planned to lambaste the idea. By doing so, I had always had them in my corner.

"Now you just sit yourself right down here, Jonathan. What are you drinking?"

"Diet Coke," I said.

"Nothing stronger?"

"Okay, champagne," I said.

They found my wisecrack wicked funny. Ken himself came to the booth to take my order, and also to say hello and hang around a bit, to listen to our chatter and add his two cents. Since I had been the resident politician for all those years, they wanted to know my opinion of certain goings-on, not only in the state capital, but also in town.

"Christ, I wish you was up there again in the funny farm, Jonathan," Hartley led off.

"You know, I was actually there yesterday," I said. "You can't imagine why, either. Something you fellas probably never thought about."

Having gotten their attention, I kept them spellbound for the next five minutes, describing yesterday's electoral college ceremony.

"Jeezum," said one of my tablemates, "I had no idea they *actually* voted."

"There's lots you don't learn in school," I commented.

"Hell, school was too long ago, anyhow," Hartley said. "Kids today—do they really learn anything?"

For the next ten minutes, we discussed education, primarily a local issue, but with the state supplying a big chunk of the money and the Feds, despite only a tiny investment, trying to call many of the shots. Those guys, if they couldn't articulate the fine points, still had opinions. One of them (I knew him solely as "Rusty") was not as pessimistic as the others about the youth of today. "My grandkids—they're gettin' a helluva better set o' opportunities than we had," he insisted. "Now, you take Joanna, my Amy's oldest—guess where she's goin' on a school trip. Saved up her money from waitressin'. Them kids are travelin' to Paris, France, can you believe it?" His pride wouldn't permit any rebuttal.

Hartley turned to me and asked sincerely, "What do you think, Jonathan? We spend a lot o' money on our schools. Is much of it wasted?"

"Probably some, Hartley," I said. "But have you ever seen the bumper sticker, 'IF YOU THINK EDUCATION IS EXPENSIVE, TRY IGNORANCE'?"

The nods affirming my words showed this cliché was hitting home. Then the third old-timer, whose name was Forrest Henderson, asked, "Do you think there'll ever be another move to take away our guns, Jonathan?"

"God, I hope not," I said. "You all know I wouldn't support registration of guns, fought it hard. Well, what about Chad—he's okay, isn't he?"

Chadwick Bannister was the present state representative from Swanstown. A Republican.

"Chad Bannister is about as useful," said Hartley laconically, "as a pair o' tits on a bull."

"You never see him," said Rusty.

"Not like you was when you was in, Jonathan," said Forrest Henderson.

If I could have canned their exchange and broadcast it on the air, I thought, I could certainly tell Ron Gordon tonight I would be a candidate. It was as if I were back at my old stand. Moreover, while I drank my Coke and bazooed with these old guffers, other people dropped by the booth and we had a high old time, laughing and kidding and yet touching on serious matters, even of international import, like what was happening in China and the Middle East.

That Diet Coke took me more than an hour and a half to consume.

In addition, before I left Ken's, I made the rounds of other booths and also talked to people I knew seated at the counter. As a foretaste of full-scale campaigning, this would have been my lunch break. How many hundreds of times had it been this way in the past! Foot-slogging all morning, knocking on people's doors, talking, talking, whenever anybody was home and would let me in, drinking a gazillion cups of coffee or tea—and after an unrelaxing hiatus at Ken's or similar local eating place—plunging back out onto the streets in the different neighborhoods until dark, greeting whoever opened a door, if I didn't know them, with my invariable, "Hi. I'm Jonathan Jackson, running for state rep, visiting voters today to see if you have any questions or anything I can help you with."

Oh, there were a few varieties in my opening spiel. In later years, it would begin, "Hi. I'm Representative Jonathan Jackson, running for reelection . . ." or, since I was often no longer a stranger, "Here I am again. It's that time of year. How you been?" (This used only among solid supporters after one man had snapped, "Yeah, and we only see you at election time.") As my incumbency grew, I wouldn't need to say anything, because they might gush, "Jonathan Jackson, you come right in here, boy. Mary's just made some cookies. Mary, look who's here!"

Stepping into the sunlight, leaving Ken's late in the morning, I glanced tentatively at the array of storefronts in sight. At some point in a campaign, you had to *do Main Street*. I never much liked interrupting a flow of business, fearing the owners could resent it, yet visiting retail establishments was an expected and time-honored ritual. The more daring or partisan of the proprietors would let you leave your material—palm cards, flyers, buttons, bumper stickers—by their cash registers and even stick signs in their windows. My eyes now sought out those shops near Ken's where I'd been received so warmly. Should I go say hello? Just in case tonight, Ron . . . ?

Inwardly, I laughed at my temerity—and, could I call it cowardice?—any excuse not to have to go back to the computer, to writing, to hard remembering. No, what I was doing was *loitering,* simply deciding to saunter along toward the waterfront, regarding a landscape of memory where practically every building, every side street, every corner, every tree almost, evoked connections to my experiences in the town.

There was one house, for example, which I could never pass without smiling. It was here on Elm Street where I customarily started my campaigns. Ron Gordon had counseled me, "People driving by on the main drag will see you," he said. "'Who's the young guy walking around, going to all the houses?' they'll ask. 'It's that Jackson,' someone'll answer, 'looks like he's working his tail off.' Later, you can do Elm Street again. 'There's Jackson, still at it,' folks'll tell each other. 'That kid really wants the job.'"

Anyway, about this one house: It was maybe on my third day covering Elm Street. I was still, as they say, green as grass, as yet still slightly terrified after ringing each bell, banging each knocker, wondering what to expect. Talk about suspense. Fear of hostility was then an acute factor. Remember, I was a Democrat starting out in a Republican town.

Ever wonder about this divide in American political allegiances? It almost seems foreordained. Admittedly, the amount of rationality in these preferences is limited, more gut feeling and family heritage than a few soupçons of reasoning—and those predilections are often on shifting sands, malleable, responding to an individual issue or personality. Nowadays, we have umpty-ump "Independents." Many of them, in proudly announcing the fact, actually believe they belong to a party.

Even then, in the distant past, due to Ron Gordon's instructions, I didn't have my party affiliation listed on my handout material. Until I reached this one particular Cape Cod–style saltbox that these days always draws my mirth, no one had commented on the absence. But here, after opening the door to me, stood a stern-faced, dark-haired, muscular fellow of about forty, wearing a woodsman's black-and-red-checked flannel shirt, who took my card and kept me standing outside while he perused every word of it on both sides.

Finally, he spoke. "What are you?" he rudely demanded.

Mute for at least half a minute, I felt the hard, gimlet eyes of Mr. A. Gregory Veilleux (pronounced *Vayoo*) rake me from head to toe. The "sorehead voter," alienated from both parties, was a phenomenon Ron Gordon had told me to expect. *Exhibit A of the species,* I told myself, as I stalled, struggling to come up with the right response (by the way, his use of *A. Gregory,* one of his neighbors later informed me, was to disguise his real first name of Adolf—no brush mustache, however, but bushy sideburns).

I managed ultimately to mutter, "Well, I assume you mean which party label. Well, I know a lot of the voters here, a majority, have traditionally—"

"Are you a Republican?" he interrupted brusquely.

Okay, here it comes, both barrels, I said to myself, then thinking, *Frig it. I'll be honest.*

"No, sir," I answered. But I couldn't bring myself to say the D word. "I'm of the opposite party."

"Are you a damn Democrat?"

"Yes, sir."

"Good. Because I'd as soon shit myself as vote for any goddamn Republican."

And with that, he handed me back my card and shut the door.

I didn't know whether to exult or laugh out loud. Shaking my head, I proceeded to his next-door neighbors' house. Two nicer elderly people never lived—Charles and Mary (yes, Mary of the cookies).

"Mr. Jackson, please come in," I was greeted. "We're Democrats, too."

On the same score, I had one more surprise coming. My very first tasting of Mary's "latest batch, fresh from the oven" was accompanied not only by great coffee but also a lot of friendly talk, as if we'd known each other for ages. In the conversation, at one point, the political makeup of the district became a subject, particularly the minority status of our party.

We were all shaking our heads over this sad state of affairs when I said, quite innocently, "But at least your next-door neighbor seems to be one of us."

Charles, his kindly eyes widening, looked incredulous. "Who, Gregsy?"

I then related my recent experience with the quirky gentleman, taking pains to soften the language of his final, unexpected blast against the GOP.

Both Charles and Mary were amused. In the course of their telling me why, I learned that, appearances notwithstanding, I couldn't count on Mr. Veilleux's vote.

"Why not?" I asked. "Is he just a two-faced guy?"

By this time, over the cookies and coffee, Charles was already calling me by my first name. "I'm afraid, Jonathan, Gregsy doesn't vote here."

"Are you sure?"

"Unless they've changed the immigration laws."

For A. Gregory Veilleux, it turned out, was a Canadian.

Charles's eyes twinkled now. "If you ever want to hear him really swear, ask him why he's never become a citizen. He's been here for years."

Oddly enough, I did later induce Gregsy to tell me, once I got to know him and win his confidence. He'd actually come to me with a minor immigration problem and I'd gotten the staff of our Democratic U.S. senator at the time to straighten it out (more cross-fertilization of our layers of government). Since he was effusive (in his surly style) in thanking me, I asked him, on an impulse, why he *hadn't* become an American and then remembered I should expect a profanity-laced tirade. Instead, he seemed sheepish at first. "It's the health care," he finally admitted, whereupon the floodgates of his rage did pour out, and in blue language, infused with at least one bad French word I knew—*merde*—he lambasted the lack of any system in the U.S. that could keep you from going bankrupt if you got seriously ill.

Sounding sheepish myself, and defensive, I replied, "Well, some of us in American government would like to do something about it." I got a glower in response.

Indeed, Gregsy went back to Ontario once he had treatable heart trouble, sold his house, and never returned, not even for a visit. Charles and Mary are gone, too, dying within a year of each other, but saved from total financial ruin by Medicare. I attended both funerals and comforted Charles when Mary died ahead of him, often looking in on the old fellow until he had to be moved to a nursing home. The house was sold by their kids to help pay for his final care.

With strangers in them, those two homes, side by side, didn't appear quite the same, despite the grin on my lips whenever I passed by. At the end of Gregsy's driveway, I noticed, the new owner had put up a basketball hoop on the garage wall. Children, too, next door at Charles and Mary's: a tricycle left out on the lawn and a cut-out Santa Claus hung over the front door.

Should I ever run again, I warned myself, it could be like starting all over from scratch. A glance farther on down a side street at the façade of our town hall confirmed the thought. Yet another layer of government, which had impinged frequently on my work in the state apparatus. Most, if not all, of my buddies there—the council members, the clerk's office staff, the police chief, the planning department, etc., were different now. A tickling urge tempted me to direct my steps toward that venerable building, last renovated in 1910 (the good citizens of Swanstown, since I'd been among them, had twice voted to defeat a more modern replacement). A little subtle pre-campaigning wouldn't hurt. Schmooze a bit. Certainly, I might find someone I knew in one of the town offices to tell me what was going on, maybe even introduce me around unobtrusively.

If I hesitated to put this silly plan into effect, it was not only because it was silly, or, shall we say, *premature*. My attention span came into play, too. When my glance across the street fell upon the Jotham Weeks Garrison House, I wanted for the next few moments to think about Norman Page.

Norm, too, buried like Charles and Mary, was buried in the First Parish Cemetery, alongside his crippled granddaughter Agnes, who had shared his home in his retirement and had preceded him in death.

An instant flash to my brain was a reminder of how Norm Page had gone to Harvard, like Duke Ellery. Moreover, that Norm's son John, Agnes's father, had been Duke's classmate and fellow resident of Leverett House. Finally still, that I was a horse's ass in thinking about another campaign at my age, or could see it as pure escapism, since I had a book to write and was writhing about to side-step the responsibility and its really excruciating exercise in self-examination and unearthing of long-buried emotions.

On top of this revelation, a new distraction attacked me.

Christ, I had totally forgotten about making a phone call to Ritchie, as I'd intended. Shocked by such absentmindedness, the immediate instinct I had was to rush right home, since I'd neglected to bring my cell phone with me.

But I didn't retreat to our house. I kept on walking slowly along the main drag—oceanward—and instead of veering right, at the turnoff to my domicile, went left toward the local beach adjacent to the harbor. I had decided to pace on the sand first, an old habit of mine when struggling with a problem.

Ritchie had given me a good scare. Did I want to bawl him out? Did I want to pretend nothing had happened? Or did I plan to ignore him completely? Let Ritchie call me? Stepping across a high-tide-line boundary of crunchy dried seaweed, I began wrestling with these options.

This being December, I expected to have the whole strand entirely to myself. For the first few dozen yards, my eyes were concentrated exclusively on my feet while my leather shoes trod across the brittle wrack, missed stepping on a couple of blue mussel valves and a broken whelk shell, and finally skipped over some piled kelp to reach a smooth, tan-gray surface of hard-packed sand leading to the water's edge. Only then did I look around me.

The Atlantic, with its complaisantly rolling, green-gray waves, lapped the cold shore. In the distance, Barnacle Rock was a smudge on the horizon, showing a barely perceptible lighthouse tower. No boat traffic in this wintry seascape. No lobster pots bobbing at this time of year. Utter emptiness. Except from the far end of the beach, a couple strode toward me.

It turned out to be a pair of adventurous tourists. Their surprise appearance had interrupted my inner debate over the Ritchie question. And instinctively I knew they would stop to talk.

"'Morning," they both said.

"'Morning," I replied.

"We're from Oklahoma," the man, a beanpole-tall, friendly type of person volunteered. "Can you believe, until this moment we'd never seen the ocean?"

"It's the main reason we've come to New England," said the woman, who was as fresh-complexioned as a country apple.

"And to see the historic old houses," the male added.

These folks (they were the Blanchards, Mark and Pauline) had pinpointed Swanstown as their first destination via the Internet. A picturesque place to stay on the coast was one motive, but the prime attraction, it seemed, had been our colonial past and architecture, especially those extant remnants of the eighteenth-century buildings we (the historical society) had preserved. Most of these, already decorated with Christmas lights, were open for the holiday season and the Blanchards, both of whom were retired elementary-school teachers, had plans to visit them. Having done their homework, they knew a lot about our community and its extensive heritage.

"Did you folks teach American history?" I asked, once our conversation developed on the beach.

Mark grinned. "No, I taught mainly math and science and Pauline home economics. It's just sort of been a hobby for us, a passion to know the country in its earliest days. Oklahoma, you realize, wasn't even a state until 1907."

I nodded and said, "I'm a history buff, too. Have taught it myself. But I'm afraid I'm quite ignorant about Oklahoma. You call yourselves Sooners, right? Learned that from being a college football fan. Red and white, those are your colors. No, actually, red and cream."

"Good start," Mark said appreciatively, "but that's the university. We both went to Oklahoma State, orange and black."

I should have known better.

"Sorry." And we all three laughed.

The rest of the talk had aspects of a travelogue on my part, lasting about twenty minutes. Its guidebook essence began almost at once when Mark pointed out to sea and asked if an island and lighthouse were what they had observed and Pauline said she had been sure it was and I confirmed their supposition. "We call it Barnacle Rock," I told them, "home to shipwrecks and rumors of pirate treasure, and the site of one of the first U.S. government lighthouses ever erected, dating back to President Washington's reign." *Your federal tax dollars at work,* I was going to inform these Oklahomans, but thought this sounded too flip, so I merely added that the Coast Guard continued to maintain the beacon.

Waxing eloquent, I then went on to talk about those islets they couldn't see at all on this misty morning, which I'd pointed out to Jill at the start of our California flight. One thing I said drew a raised eyebrow from Mark, I noticed. My words about those earliest English settlers out there were, "You might say they started the peopling of this continent," adding, "but the Revolution forced them to evacuate to the mainland, due to their fear of raids by the British Royal Navy."

"Fascinating stuff," said Mark, "although I think our Indians in Oklahoma would give you an argument about the first peopling of the continent."

"So would those in our state," I agreed. Since we were mentioning Indians, and I knew Oklahoma was originally Indian Country, I wondered if they were Native Americans themselves. No high cheekbones, though, but it made for a slightly dicey bit of conversation when Mark Blanchard expressed his and Pauline's special interest in the Jotham Weeks Garrison House.

"That's the major one of the old homes we want to visit," he told me. "Can you tell us much about it?"

I hesitated in my answer. Did I want to describe, if these people *were* Native Americans, how the fortress-like edifice's builder and first owner, poor Jotham Weeks, had been tortured to death by Indians who were calling to the colonists huddled inside to spare him his agony by surrendering—all this during one of the French and Indian Wars. Or should I talk about Norm Page and

Agnes and how I helped steer my friend to will the historical society the property? Or just feign a lack of knowledge, which was hardly credible?

"Don't miss the tour this afternoon," I told them. "It's the only garrison left in this part of the State and we're the oldest section. You know what garrisons were—fortified homes, rather like bomb shelters, to which everyone in town rushed when an alarm sounded and . . . ," I took a deep breath, "there was an Indian attack, or the threat of one."

I waited to see whether or not I had touched an ethnic nerve.

It didn't seem so. Mark switched to another local topic—the wild swans—a pair allegedly on hand to greet the initial settlers of Swanstown who'd rowed ashore in the 1600s—magnificent birds never since seen again. Is that true, the Oklahoman wanted to know.

All I could reply was, "I haven't spotted any."

We talked a while longer, mostly about what especially good area restaurants I could recommend. Before we parted, they thanked me profusely for adding to the enjoyment of their trip.

Right afterwards, I wasted no more time on the beach. I ceased trying to think about Ritchie. It was unlikely he was going to run amok, emulate Miles Monahan, or concoct any such horror. I was suddenly eager to hurry home and research a matter—yes, connected with the Duke book—pertaining to Norman Page, a matter I'd plumb forgotten.

8

WHERE HAD I PUT NORM'S LETTER, the one that began "Today we buried dear, sweet Agnes . . ."? I didn't think it was in the folder I had kept of memorabilia connected with Norman Page: correspondence, newspaper clippings, personal reflections (mine), notes on the Jotham Weeks Garrison House he owned, etc. I would search the file anyhow. But before I did, I'd rummage through the various Duke Ellery collections I had amassed: GOVERNORSHIP, PERSONAL, EARLY CAREER, GENERAL BIO, etc., and also one of my insertions about myself under LEGIS-LATIVE CAREER, namely CAMPAIGNING.

Starting with the latter, I found no entry relating to Norman Page among the various documents. Nor, as I pretty much expected, had I put his letter there. But I had certain memories. Closing my eyes, shutting out the piles of material I'd assembled on the desk in front of me, I proceeded to remember my very first visit inside the restored and (internally) modernized Jotham Weeks Garrison House.

This unusual building bears further description. For one thing, the Weeks Garrison was painted a deep, dark red, with shutters to match, unlike all of the other colonial dwellings in town, which were white with either dark green or black shutters. Norm himself was responsible for such a break with local con-formity because, he said, "The Puritans had colorful house exteri-ors and white paint hadn't yet been invented in the 1680s." His will, I should add, stipulated that the "authentic hue," as he put it, must be retained.

No exterior changes, of course, would be permitted. The plaque he had erected by the front gate remained JOTHAM WEEKS GARRISON, BUILT 1687, ATTACKED, 1691," but the society could also add its own interpretive placard. On it, besides the gruesome story of the siege, during which Weeks, out hunting, had been captured by the marauders and killed in front of the horrified but unmovable settlers, were explanations of the garrison's architecture, its overhung second floor, the rifle slots, extra water supply, escape boards from the attic, and so on. More politically correct than other narratives about our "massacre" in Swanstown, the wording contains a slap at the seventeenth-century French military for inciting the Natives, and ends with the oft-told tale of captive women and children marched to Canada and sold into servitude to the *Quebecois* or ransomed.

To get back to my first campaign, however, I could never walk past the garrison without reminding myself I was running against a descendant of one of those redeemed prisoners. Earl Johnson's family had been here that long.

Nor did I have any intention of approaching its blackish wooden front door, pockmarked, as I knew, with arrowhead holes and bearing Goody Weeks's original pineapple-shaped metal knocker. This tropical fruit, an expensive delicacy at the time, symbolized hospitality in colonial New England.

Why did I shun the Weeks habitation? Did not its owner, Mr. Norman Page, vote? "Only a straight Republican ticket," Ron Gordon had assured me. "Don't waste your breath, even to say hello. For Christ's sake, he's worked for two GOP presidents!"

In my case, possibly compounding the difficulty, was Norman Page's feud at the time with our historical society, or rather, with its board chairman, Thomas Morgan Meiklejohn, another retired Wall Street biggie and longtime summer resident. Ron Gordon characterized their spat, allegedly over the design of the plaque Norm had erected, as "a spitting contest between two

Park Avenue Super-WASPs." How did I figure in this hoo-ha? Simple—if, Ron's caution notwithstanding, I elected to try to see Mr. Norman Page anyway, I was not only a damn Democrat but an active, out-front member of a group he currently loathed.

Therefore, I must have been in one big feisty mood or feeling ultra-mischievous and devil-may-care when, toward the end of a certain campaign day in late October, I impulsively decided I was going to make my last stop at the Jotham Weeks Garrison. I walked past its rock wall, paused, turned around, went back and tested to see if the gate was locked. It wasn't. Telling myself silently, *Every vote counts. No stone unturned,* and only slightly scared, I headed toward the intimidatng reception I expected as soon as I banged the brassy golden clapper I could see in the gloomy entrance ahead of me.

I certainly wasn't prepared for Agnes. The door was slowly opened after maybe half a minute, seemingly by no one. Shadowed by the fast-approaching darkness, backlit from the hall, Norm's granddaughter's short female form in her shapeless dress was almost impossible to discern at first. It was as if a disembodied voice could be heard—and not the cackle of an old crone from a haunted mansion tale. When Agnes spoke, there was a musical quality and refinement to her pronunciation, redolent of finishing school, and hints of the accent my upper-crust college friends would teasingly accuse each other of having: a Park Avenue brogue.

I noticed her eyes next, how beautifully soft and lustrous and brown they were, how simply lovely. As for the rest of her, unfortunately Nature had been most unkind to Miss Agnes Page.

Her clubfoot was only one of a series of disabilities. The second major birth defect she had suffered concerned her spine, producing the twisted-over appearance of a hunchback, but without the hump. Short, squat, quite heavy, she obviously could never enjoy much exercise. Inside the hallway, where pewter sconces gave off sufficient illumination, I thought I could also note the slightest traces of Down's syndrome in her facial features, including those beautiful limpid eyes.

For, to my utter surprise, Agnes had invited me in. Shyness was her style in every aspect of her demeanor, yet as soon as she'd seen me standing at their threshold, before I could even introduce myself, start to make my campaign pitch, she stated rather boldly, "You're Mr. Jackson. You must want to visit my grandfather. He's in the library."

Agnes's age, despite the childlike quality she exuded, struck me as thirty or thereabouts. I held up one of my palm cards for her to observe and said, "Well, since I'm running for office and I want every vote, I need to ask *you*, too, to consider my candidacy," whereupon I handed her the piece of propaganda with my picture, CV, and platform.

I fully expected she might say, *Oh, I don't vote.*

Instead, she beamed and her smile was just as pretty as her eyes. "Thank you, Mr. Jackson," she said. "Thank you." Then, in a lower voice, "And don't tell grandfather, he's so-o-o Republican." In a real whisper, she added, "I'm for you. I'll vote for you."

These unexpected surprises often occur in campaigns, some good, like this one, others not so pleasant. While I was silently happy to chalk up one vote I hadn't counted on, I was still a bit leery of what might transpire once I reached the library, toward which Agnes was soon conducting me. I spent the time en route inspecting the pine-paneled interior of the garrison, both in the corridor and through glances at the side rooms I passed, which gave off a sense of authentic pioneer sparseness, although I guessed much of the décor had been redone by Mr. Page. In the days of Jotham Weeks, the library certainly hadn't existed with so many bookshelves and books. Moreover, the walls were now papered in a flowery colonial pattern that seemed to me more eighteenth than seventeenth century, and the furniture—mostly leather-bound—quite conducive to the Harvard Club in Boston I'd once visited with Duke Ellery. Indeed, I noticed as I passed a desk an accompanying wing chair, a handsome reproduction, bearing the seal of that august university in Cambridge, Massachusetts.

Norman Page sat in one of his leather armchairs. He had been reading under the very modern fluorescent lighting of a floor lamp. Before I got to him, this elderly but nonetheless erect and dignified gentleman pointed to the Harvard chair and said, "Bring it over and sit by me, Mr. Jackson."

After I did, he asked if I might stay long enough to join him in a cup of tea, to be accompanied by Agnes's special cookies, which she had baked that morning. How could I refuse, with Agnes standing in the entry and staring at me so hopefully, particularly considering what she had revealed about her voting intentions. Once I eagerly acquiesced, she brightened, then limped off and soon was limping back with trays for us both.

In the interim, I learned from Norm—er, Mr. Page at the start—how Agnes had spied me from their front window campaigning in the neighborhood and how her interest in my candidacy stemmed from the tie between her late father and my late employer, Governor Ellery. "Believe me," said her grandfather, "she is so delighted you have paid us a visit, I can't tell you how pleased she is."

One thing I'd soon learned in people's homes was the rarity of political issues being discussed. It might seem odd in the midst of an election. Although a state representative contest wasn't exactly front-page news in the major media, the *Swanstown Weekly* did cover my race well. At least the editors printed my press releases verbatim, since the Honorable Earl Johnson, despite having all the power of incumbency, never sent them any material. The most we heard about Earl were a few letters in print, signed by one or another of his cronies, urging his reelection and mostly praising him for his votes against "unnecessary spending" and "keeping down taxes."

In a previous issue of this local paper, our side had developed the theme of "penny-wise, pound-foolish" into an oblique attack against the present officeholder. An op-ed piece by Ron Gordon had listed Earl's attempted cuts and zeroed in on something deemed "utterly unconscionable," a barely minimal increase of funds in a program supporting people with mental and physical disabilities.

Ron described his strategy as a "jab"—his offering on the editorial page—followed by my statement—an "uppercut"—the candidate speaking, *news,* in other words, for the front page. JACKSON WILL SEEK MORE FUNDING FOR RETARDED AND DISABLED was the head, and I didn't mention Earl Johnson, not even to knock him. Since then—and it had been three weeks—I'd received a fair number of favorable comments on my stand but still nary a word from my opponent, who had never really been challenged in any of his previous runs.

I won't get into writing yet about Willy Bretherton, our previous perennial Democrat loser in the Swanstown District's state rep contests—later, he *will* figure in this narrative. But right now, my memory has me at a moment of tension, having finished my third cookie, sipped most of my tea, waiting for Norman Page to initiate a real conversation.

Although he was dressed informally, wearing slacks and sports jacket and expensive loafers, his clothing was nevertheless unmistakably Ivy League. He seemed a man who obviously had taken very good care of himself over the years. There wasn't an ounce of fat on him. His ramrod carriage, I learned, came from a stint as a Marine Corps officer, and eventually I noted the pin in his lapel tastefully displaying the Corps' insignia. Yet he was slightly bantam in size, physically diminished even more by his age—at the time, he was in his middle seventies. Norm was quite bald, with a reddish, healthy-looking pate, surrounded by carefully tended grayish hair, cut close.

"You may as well know, Mr. Jackson, I am a lifelong Republican—a black Republican, in every sense of the term." With such a blunt warning from Norman, our discussion of substantive matters commenced. His patrician tones, I had been noting, contained the merest tinge of a New York accent in the pronunciation of certain words. I nodded understandingly, and. wholly sincere, asked, "Does 'black Republican' mean, as I think it does, the same thing as 'dyed-in-the-wool'? I've never heard the expression before."

His answer was, "My grandfather always spoke of himself as a 'black Republican'—very proudly—since it was a slur the Southerners had used against the advocates of Abolition in our party. In my day, it had come to mean strict loyalty to the GOP, vote the straight ticket, even if you needs must hold your nose to do it for particular candidates."

Feeling he might be talking about Earl Johnson, I said, "Nowadays, that's actually pretty rare. Most of the folks I've talked to here are choosing to vote for the person, not the party."

"I'm aware of the trend," my host replied, "yet can't help but fear the results. All political discipline lost. Yes, as you might have expected, I'm old-fashioned and stiff-necked." His warm smile completely took the chill out of this last statement.

"I wouldn't want it any other way," I countered and we both chuckled.

This beginning rapport between two dire opposites in party allegiance perhaps underscored the confusion, if not irrationality, of the American political structure, for we soon discovered we shared a number of values. Norm congratulated me on my position, which he'd seen printed in the *Weekly,* vis-à-vis funding for people with disabilities. Through his experiences with Agnes, he had come to appreciate the need for government help to those so afflicted—not in his own case—he'd had the financial where-withal to assist his granddaughter—but for families without suffi-cient means to support their loved ones. "I've watched good people wiped out, reduced to desperation, and due to no fault of their own, just a bad hand fate dealt them." I eagerly agreed. Still, I couldn't refrain from saying silently to myself, *But he's going to vote for Earl Johnson.*

Norm hadn't said so in so many words. The train of events which led to his *ultimate* support for me, to our subsequent, enduring friendship, to "Norm" and "Jonathan" instead of "Mr. Page" and "Mr. Jackson," went well beyond the confines of the cozy library room inside the old garrison during this campaign's final week.

Agnes appeared once more. She had already come in with her cookies and tea, standing by, blushing furiously while obviously pleased when I praised her baking, then slipping out like the quiet mouse she was. All of a sudden, maybe a minute later, she was once more in the entryway, simply standing there, holding something. Norm, catching sight of her, instantly said, "What is it, my dear? It looks like you want to show Mr. Jackson your picture?"

The answer, whether it was voiced or not, had to be yes, and soon I was looking at a framed photograph I myself might have taken had the timing been different. I mean to say, it had been shot in Governor Duke Ellery's office, but before my time, using the same bulky reflex camera I had been trained to operate among my other duties on the staff. It was standard procedure for Duke to call one of us special assistants in at the end of a visit and we would pose him with his guest or guests, get the film developed and printed, with the end product (suitable for fram-ing) autographed and mailed to the right parties. "No better way to nail down a vote," Harry DeWitt had admonished in assign-ing me my share in that somewhat irksome task.

Duke always dated his autographs. The one Agnes showed of herself and the governor side by side had been taken during the visit she and Norm had made to the Statehouse midway in Duke's first four-year term, well prior to my arrival on the scene.

I remember, too, how Agnes particularly urged me to read the inscription. By now, since the photo has been in my possession for some time, I can recite his wording by heart: "Dear Agnes, the 'dearest Agnes' of my dear, dear friend and classmate Whitney Prescott Page and his wonderful wife Carole, at whose wedding I was an usher—thank you so much for coming to see me. We had a super time, didn't we, except too short a visit. Let's do it again. Governors need to have good fun some of the time."

If necessary, I could check myself out for the accuracy of the quote since the framed picture is in plain view on one of my office shelves. Yet more immediate still was finding the cover letter Norm had sent me after Agnes's death, entrusting me *forever* with what he called his granddaughter's "most prized possession," or, as I also seem to recall he put it, "a memento of possibly the most thrilling moment of poor sweet Agnes's short life, meeting a governor, *her* governor." I could remember some of Norm's other lines, too, like: "Governor Ellery was her idol, although she only met him once. . . . You were her link to him. . . . Her parents, who died when their private plane crashed, were but a wisp of memory to her, she was so young."

The human twists and turns of a campaign were a particular lesson I learned this first time out as a candidate. All the fine theoretical theorems pumped into us about political science in our college classrooms and textbooks on how government works had already been challenged throughout the time I worked in the governor's office. However, the real lessons were to come once I got onto the hustings myself, "into the streets," inside voters' homes. In our business, as I've already shown, you never knew what lurked behind a closed door.

Nor, drinking tea with Norm, admiring Agnes's photograph and cookies, immersed in the clubby, bookish, pine-boarded, spare, quintessential pre-Revolution American atmosphere, did I have the faintest inkling this was anything except another door-to-door campaign call. To be sure, I'd become aware of a vote I didn't know I'd had and of another I could never get, no matter how chummy I ended up with the aged Harvardian gentleman in the leather armchair beside me.

Once Agnes left us finally, Norm and I talked a good deal longer. Who can remember all the topics? I think even foreign policy was among them. Certainly we spoke about Duke Ellery. No, Norm hadn't ever voted for him, either, he made plain, much as he would have liked to do so.

"Richard Ellery—my son Whit always called him Richard, never Dick, nor, as most persons apparently did, Duke," began the one of Norm's statements I recall most clearly, "was, in my mind, the finest example of what an American politician should be."

A flitting, cat-like grin accompanied this tribute. "How often I mourned his unfortunate choice of parties," my Republican soon-to-be friend continued. Following which, I received a searching stare from behind his wire-rimmed spectacles, professorial-like, as if we were engaged in a rather friendly oral exam. "Did you ever believe the rumors Richard was planning to run for president or, since, in a manner of speaking, I have the horse's mouth right here, do you have any inside information you care to impart?"

My answer was at first calculated, as if Duke were still alive, still in the public eye. "It was never discussed in the office, really," I said.

"What's your personal opinion?" Norm pressed me.

I remained cagey. "I believe he would have made a great president," I responded.

"I agree," said Norm. "But what's your *personal* opinion about his intentions?"

Again, I started to fudge. "Well, my wife—at the time, well, before we were married, when we were both going to the National Governors Conference in Los Angeles, where—well, right afterward, is where the killing happened—she was a working journalist and absolutely convinced he *was* running. *Honi soit qui mal y pense.* They—the news people—are a cynical bunch, you know." My aside drew a knowing, appreciative smile and I went on, "Heading out west, we did stop in Iowa, met with Hank Waggoner, the Waggoner of Waggoner, big heavy hitter in the Democratic Party, and at another political stop in Colorado—"

"So what is *your* personal opinion?" Norm bore down on me. It was later that I learned he'd been a top troubleshooting negotiator for the U.S. State Department at various foreign conclaves, not to mention his years of business experience.

These skills aside, I decided to be ruthlessly honest. What did I, or Duke, for that matter, already dead and buried, have to lose?

"Yes, I believed Duke—Governor Ellery—was planning a run for the presidency. In fact, you could call it wishful thinking on my part. I prayed he would include me in the staff he took to D.C." Pausing, I noted the elderly gentleman's look of interest, a sense that I had impressed him with my forthrightness, which caused me to wax a bit eloquent. "Of course, it was never to be," I continued. "I've often thought—you know the Greeks—Icarus. One flies too high toward the sun—hubris—angering the gods. I can't help but regard the tragedy of Duke Ellery in a similar classic fashion."

"Interesting answer," Norm commented. "Good answer."

Ever since I'd first mentioned Jill, I'd been meaning to glance at my watch to see what time it was. We had supper at a certain hour, campaign or no campaign. Our house was practically around the corner; therefore when I saw that I had only five more minutes, I stood up, told Norm why I had to leave, how much I'd enjoyed meeting the two of them, etc., etc. Agnes saw me out after I got my coat from the hall closet. We shook hands and her pudgy face was somehow aglow and full of shy pleasure.

I departed the Jotham Weeks Garrison House with no sense of impending trouble, my hands in my pockets, whistling on the path, feeling pretty good, half-convinced that if Norman Page wouldn't vote for me, he might not vote for Earl Johnson, either, but leave the space blank. Chalk one up for Jackson, then.

Earlier, I had left my automobile parked on Elm Street, not far from the garrison. Thus, I was obliged to drive the short distance to my home. Hardly could I imagine the political nightmare I was about to encounter when I reached the Jackson abode just minutes later.

9

LITTLE RITCHIE WAS OLD ENOUGH at the time to rush to the back door once he spotted my car pulling into the driveway. More than a minute ahead of my "curfew," I entered the kitchen. "Daddy home, Daddy home," I could hear his shrill voice announcing to Jill, whose back was to me as she continued to do something at the stove. But the instant she turned, I immediately caught the hint of trouble in those gorgeous blue eyes.

"Call Ron," she said (or rather, barked).

Ritchie had jumped up into my arms and was clinging to my neck. Without dislodging him, without showing my fright, I said inquiringly, "Something bad happen?"

"Horrible bad," Jill said. "The bastards."

Swearing, particularly in front of Ritchie, meant she wasn't kidding. I put our son down; his entreaties of "Les p'ay, Daddy— p'ay 'chase me'" were answered with a softly curt "Later, pal," while I stared at his mother, obviously seeking further information. Jill jerked her thumb toward the adjacent parlor. "I put today's *Swanstown Weekly* next to the phone so you could look at Chadwick Bannister's letter while you're talking to Ron," she said, the anger in her voice plainly palpable. I hurried on, but mindful and more than somewhat resentful that Ritchie had begun whimpering at this tense juncture.

Exhibit A. The incompatablity of participatory politics and a smooth family life.

The actual news clip of Chad's communication is in my files. What I don't have in print is his confession to me, years later, that he never wrote it, only signed it. Who put him up to it? That, he wouldn't tell me. It undoubtedly wasn't Earl Johnson. Ron thought the mastermind was Martin Carter in the GOP state committee headquarters, who handled local races.

"It's Marty's MO," said my redheaded campaign manager, once we were on the phone with each other. "Hit 'em hard at the very umpteenth hour. I've been expecting an October surprise, but never this unbelievable, dishonest crap."

Here was brilliant dirty politics—the dirtiest anyone could imagine. If you read Chad's missive to the *Weekly*'s editor thoroughly, you might very well believe I'd had a hand in murdering Duke Ellery.

Pure innuendo. Stuff like: "Strange coincidence. The acknowledged assassin of Governor Richard N. Ellery was a boyhood friend of Jonathan Jackson's. And Jackson was present in the Los Angeles airport with the governor when the shooting took place. The assassin was shot down before he could be questioned. These are matters on which Jackson has maintained complete silence. Should his silence not be a consideration for the people of Swanstown and District Nine to consider, since he's asking for their votes?"

Until then, Chadwick Bannister had been primarily a dabbler in Swanstown's local politics—a term on the school board, a term on the town council, a voice often raised at town meeting. "The genial bubblehead," Ron Gordon called him. It was the Bannister name, everyone agreed, which gave him prominence enough to get elected or shoot off his mouth. Malcolm J. Bannister, Chad's uncle, *ran* Swanstown, or so the mantra of conventional wisdom went. Like much of the buzz in public affairs, whether in Swanstown, statewide or nationally, the reality was less exaggerated than the remark. But Malcolm was a *power*, and particularly in the Republican Party, a point Ron reinforced to me as soon as we both finished venting our indignation over the phone.

"One thing's strange, though," Ron said. "Malcolm's a gentleman. God knows I've fought him enough, but this isn't his style. Marty and Earl probably got Chad drunk and he never bothered to seek Malcolm's okay."

"Whatever," I said impatiently. "But what's our best thing to do now?" I was literally shaking, and in no mood for Ron's professional, lawyerly analysis.

"I've been giving it a lot of thought," he said. "Either do nothing or . . . ," a long pause.

"Or do what, for Christ's sake?"

Panic time. Ron had warned me it would be coming. In fact, the whole last month of a campaign, he said, had been likened to the last month of a woman's pregnancy when—and I took this to be facetiousness on his part, hardly a legal opinion—she could not be held responsible under the law for her emotional actions. I had been kept from such a frenzy until now due solely to the procrastination of my opponents, Ron would later say. But first, he tried answering my frantic question.

"We've got the *Daily* until this coming Monday, right before election, in which to respond directly to them, and the weekend edition, if we choose to. Or, best of all, we'll find someone else to answer for you. Not me. I'm too close, too obviously prejudiced, and I've been too prolix already."

"Okay, but what about me? Or Jill?"

"Wouldn't you sound defensive, like you're guilty? I'm sure they're hoping you *will* get into this idiocy and give it credibility. That goes for Jill, too."

"Great, I should just stay cool, calm, and collected, ignore this outrageous—what would you call such shit—a *smear?*"

"Maybe—maybe. Let me think some more. Now go have a good stiff drink, enjoy your dinner, get a good night's sleep, go out and pound the pavements tomorrow, and we'll confer again after I nose around."

Putting down the phone, I was still trembling. I didn't go right back into the kitchen. I just stood there, cogitating. No longer was I simply a first-time political candidate hit with an unexpected blow, seeing my future, all my hard work for months and months possibly going up in smoke. My pain was much deeper than any thwarted ambition. The most hideous few moments of my life were being thrust back at me after I had considered them safely buried. Those seconds of gunfire in the LAX airport had been catastrophic enough. The aftermath—the investigation, the funeral—had been a sheer nightmare, days of chaos almost, imposed upon a once orderly, secure, and—having met Jill—most propitious-looking life. I was never a suspect in any fashion. Hell, I had tipped off the authorities to Miles's odd behavior ahead of time. Even the dumbest of cops wouldn't have tried to make a case. I had nothing to be guilty about—and now these bastards, with their insinuations, guilt-by-association, off-the-wall accusations of *nothing,* actually, that some voters would interpret as *something* where there's smoke, there's fire, a tarnish, a blot, unworthy of the knight in shining armor you were supposed to be as their proxy in government.

"What did Ron propose?" Jill eagerly asked the moment I came back from the phone call.

"For me to keep cool," I answered. "He's going to think about the right response."

"Screw that!" my feisty wife objected. "Go after Earl. Take off your gloves and tell the world what a whoremaster he is—how he spends his time in the capital chasing low-life women—all those broads he's seen going in and out of hotels with—a married man, a father, even a *grandfather.* Blow the whistle on the fat pig."

Ritchie was nearby, no longer sniveling, and gave me an excuse to be evasive. I picked him up and, instead of replying directly to Jill, said, "I'm going to go down to the playroom with my son and ask him his advice."

"*Our* son, you chickenshit," Jill spat at me, but the tension was broken, at least temporarily.

After dinner, when I did take my good stiff drink (two Scotches, in truth), and Jill joined me in the living room once *our son* had been put to bed, I discussed her idea in a more dispassionate manner. I agreed to call Ron again with her suggestion and returned to say that he thought it had merit and would try to figure out the best way to proceed.

Frankly, a ham-fisted approach made me pretty nervous. Sure, this was politics—the tough stuff—slugging it out in the trenches—but not really my cup of tea.

While Ron Gordon and I were dithering, weighing the pros and cons of Jill's idea—to go on the offensive using Earl's not exactly secret reputation for (to put it more delicately than my wife did) *sexual athleticism,* the clock was ticking ominously. The enemy had timed it to be too late to respond in the *Weekly*, whose next issue wouldn't appear until the following Wednesday, right after Election Day, Tuesday. To get in the *Daily's* weekend edition, the pressroom would need copy before Friday evening. And Friday afternoon was the time of our big rally, which Ron was striving mightily to pull together. The event was set at 1:00 P.M. precisely for the scheduled arrival of a "Victory Cavalcade" arranged by the Democratic County Committee and consisting of a contingent of party VIPs in a caravan of vehicles, wending from key municipality to key municipality, where knots of enthusiastic supporters would turn out to greet them. In Swanstown, they were to stop at the temporary headquarters we had rigged up in a rented storefront on Elm Street.

What a time for a bombshell to explode! But Ron had an idea.

"Let's hold off a decision until noon Friday. We'll have the whole town committee at the headquarters and time to bat it all around before the shindig starts, and an hour or more later, after we're done, we can rush a statement to the editors. If we're too late, they'll run it on Monday, anyway. With luck, they'll run it twice."

Very professional, I thought, but also, sourly: *Delaying a decision.*

Friday's event was a big, big deal for us, incidentally. In the past, the Democratic Cavalcade had only paused in Swansville long enough for a few handshakes. But, lo and behold, now the powers-that-be in the county had decreed our once almost moribund town committee could host a full-scale wingding, as if we were a Democratic stronghold! Would wonders never cease!

My candidacy, indeed, had sparked some noted excitement among the Swanstown D*s,* so used to being outnumbered and heavily outvoted, particularly in the state representative race. Ron Gordon told me we had never won it, at least since prior to the Civil War. Helping level the odds presently was the energy exhibited in our having a storefront headquarters—and right in the center of town, no less! It was manned—actually swarming with volunteers, plastered with signs, piled with brochures and buttons and stickers to hand out. We even had a phone bank at work.

Ron, the long-suffering chair of the Democratic town committee, had become a happy man. Six previous elections running (since he'd assumed his thankless duties), he'd been stuck with "Witless Willy," aka Bretherton, Willis R., as the Democrat name on the ballot for the district house seat. No others would offer themselves, and Ron wouldn't leave his law practice to run himself. Willy always insisted on running and could easily procure the twenty-plus signatures needed to qualify; no one wanted to hurt his feelings and tell him how crazy he was when he perennially boasted how each time he had it all figured out, the foolproof strategy that would lead him to win. No one wanted to work for Willy, either, and no one ever did.

We only got him to step aside for me by endorsing his run for state senate against the very popular Peg McEntee, of whom it was said "Jesus Christ might poll 40 percent against her." We all helped Willy gather signatures in the various towns, not because we needed or much wanted a "sacrificial lamb" against Peg; we merely sought to keep the guy from launching any childish outburst against me for *stealing* his chance for "certain victory" on his umpteenth try for rep.

Perennials like Willy are an amazing phenomenon in American politics. They crop up even in presidential races. Nothing discourages them. No hint of reality penetrates their oblivious layers of ego. They're like rubber dummies, rising up from the mat again and again to get knocked right back down—over and over again. In his twisted, bizarre approach to the world, his utter self-absorption, thirst for attention, constant fantasizing about success, Willy Bretherton reminded me, odd as it may seem, of Miles Monahan.

However, Willy was indisputably harmless, despite an occasional tantrum. Ron had a piquant description of him that became a classic joke in Swanstown, unbeknownst to poor Willy. "If that klutz were walking through an immense field," I'd heard my political mentor pronounce, "and somewhere in the huge pasture lay one single isolated cow turd, he would surely step on it."

All right. At noon Friday we were in a back room of the headquarters' suite of offices, the half dozen members of the town committee and myself, expecting Ron, who'd called to say he had been delayed a few minutes.

While awaiting him, our leaderless discussion was not on the subject at hand, the scurrilous "October surprise" attack, but a kind of banter appropriate to these occasions—nervous chatter, witticisms, shop talk, trying to show confidence and dispel all sense of worry and gloom.

When at last Ron entered the room (by the way, in those days, it had elements of being smoke-filled), his florid, freckled, vaguely Semitic visage was hard to read. Grim, he certainly seemed. We quieted down as he stared at each of us in turn. But once we appeared properly cowed, his expression changed, lightened up into what I could think of only as a foxy smile.

Reaching inside the neckline of the expensive sweater he was wearing, he took a folded paper from his breast pocket and waved it in the air until we all saw what looked like a cut-out newspaper article.

"Who has read this letter to the editor, which was in today's morning edition?" he demanded to know.

Silence. A few of us shook our heads.

"Okay, I'll read it to you," Ron continued.

Alas, my personal archives do not contain a copy of that critical document. At the time, in the heat and confusion of the moment, who would have thought of collecting it for posterity? The *Daily* in question went out of business a good many years ago. No back numbers were saved or microfilmed. Ever since, I've advertised (in successor publications) asking if folks had some of the old numbers in their attics or cellars, but without a single bite. And the original of the letter, whose printed version Ron was displaying to us, never has been found.

Agnes Page, who had written it in my defense and hand-carried the typed page to the *Daily* for the Friday morning paper, had never made a carbon.

Using my memory, recalling to the best of my ability the words Ron recited in our smoky quarters, I have produced a facsimile. As to Ron's own copy of the clipping, he could never find it in his files. Most likely, along with other records we might have had, all the stuff went to the trash pile when the headquarters was shut.

"A recent letter in your paper and the *Weekly* from Chadwick

Bannister makes no sense," let's say it began, or very similar wording from Agnes, and the next few sentences, I'm sure, are equally close to the original. "I know Chadwick Bannister," Agnes went on. "His uncle is a dear friend of my grandfather's. We were brought up together. I don't believe he wrote that awful letter claiming Jonathan Jackson was somehow involved in the death of Governor Ellery. How ridiculous. How cruel. What rotten politics. Who put my friend Chad up to it? Mr. Jackson stands for all Governor Ellery stood for, everything good in government. Shame on you, whoever made Chad write his bad letter. I'm voting for Jonathan Jackson."

Following Ron's reading, I remember, we were briefly speechless. The first to comment was one of our most irascible old Democrats, Michael Connors, and Mike simply asked, "Who the hell is Agnes Page?"

An immediate reply was provided by another elderly member of the group, the non-irascible old Vance Macy, a white-haired, kindly farmer from the back country. "She's that poor crippled girl I see in church from time to time," he said. "Sickly lots o' the time. Very sweet. Poor thing."

Ron spoke next, offering a political perspective. "Keep in mind," he said, "her grandfather, Norman Page, with whom she is living, is arguably the most rock-ribbed Republican in this town. Or possibly next to Mal Bannister, he is."

As Ron pronounced the name of Swanstown's ultra-arch Republican, I saw the change in his expression. Again, the look of the fox, the clicking mind, and perhaps a hint of secret knowledge. *For God's sake* I wanted to cry, *tell us what you're thinking! Tell* me, *at least.*

Unprodded, Ron finally supplied an answer. He was already exhibiting a certain style of his, arrogant, confident, the attorney-in-charge. "Miss Page has said all we need to say," he declared. "If you guys agree, I'll just shit-can a statement I was planning to draw up for Jonathan to put in Monday's paper."

"You're the boss, Red," said Mike Connors, who always called Ron that.

A perceptible snicker—or was it a wince?—showed the lawyer's distaste for the nickname. But no one tried to put down Mike Connors, despite his seeming amiability at the moment. I myself did not venture a comment. The nods of agreement around the room thereby gave Ron full license to let Agnes Page's letter stand as our reply.

Once the meeting began breaking up, Ron signaled me to stay behind.

"You didn't say anything," he said after the others had gone.

"You're the boss, Red."

The reaction I elicited was a humble shrug, followed by a piercing prosecutorial glare straight at me. "But you think maybe Jill's right? Cut off Earl's you-know-whats? Expose the prick?"

"Not if you think Agnes's letter's strong enough. Is it, by itself?"

"Let me tell you why I think it is."

My barrister friend and mentor thereupon proceeded to present the political version of a legal brief. Points 1, 2, and 3—laid out methodically, their drama underplayed. 1) Thanks to my disobedience, Norman Page was now—get this—planning to vote for me, open about it, had called to say so and to say that he, Ron, could say so publicly; 2) Malcolm Bannister was involved, as well. He was furious about his nephew's letter and felt Chad had been duped; and 3) I was to hold onto my hat—at the conclusion of today's festivities, we were both to go visit Mr. Malcolm Bannister, invited by him to his manorial home!

"He wants to meet you in person, Jonathan," Ron finished.

"All because of Agnes's letter?"

"Ripple effect," Ron nodded. "Backlash time. Toss a pebble into a pond. You never know what concatenations may follow."

Whether Ron had any more secret knowledge to impart suddenly became moot. A noise of honking motorcars out front told us the Democratic County Committee's Victory Cavalcade, or at least the advance guard of its parade, had arrived. We needed to leave the back room and greet them.

Old-fashioned hullabaloo was the intention of the cortege that flowed down Elm Street toward our site. The automobiles and trucks reminded me of Miles's patriotic Uncle Sam jalopy, except the omnipresent red, white, and blue wasn't in their paint jobs but in bunting, posters, and flags. The idea was also to make as much noise as possible wherever you drove, circle through a town, and bring out people who gawked (and a few who cursed and shook their fists). Then you'd end up, in our case, parked in long lines on Elm Street and rushing up the stairs of our headquarters to stand, listen to a bunch of speeches, munch some refreshments, then rush back off and transport yourselves to another destination.

But this year there was a new wrinkle that even Ron, the veteran, admitted he had never witnessed. They had brought a live donkey with them. The trailer in which they hauled the beast, decorated in stars and stripes galore, was parked across from our entrance and to great fanfare from a sound system, they unloaded the gray, furry ass amid loud cheering. They coaxed him (it was plainly a male) to our side of Elm Street, but not before—groans were heard—he'd deposited a placid plop of defecation on the roadway, tethered him to a lamppost, and let hordes of excited children pet him and feed him hay and carrots. Stationary at the spot, hung with red-white-and-blue blanketing that declared VOTE DEMOCRAT, the patient, bony animal was a living billboard for passing motorists to ogle. More than one saluted him with the blast of a horn.

Now, speaking of asses. . . . While Ron and I stood outside the headquarters front door greeting the flow of county loyalists who trooped into our offices, we noticed none other than Willy Bretherton hurrying down the opposite sidewalk. Actually, he was slouching along, which was *hurrying* for Willy, since someone had once told him that all important office-seekers, office-holders, and politicos were always late. Our guests were inside, already helping themselves to coffee, doughnuts, and other goodies, and Ron and I were about to join them. I turned, but Ron held me back. "Wait a minute," he said, "let's watch this," and he directed my attention to the blob of fresh donkey excrement directly in Willy's path as he was about to cross Swanstown's main drag.

"Let's see if he steps in it," Ron said.

"You don't really think so?" I said incredulously.

"One buck says he does."

"Your prediction about him can't possibly come true," I added.

"One dollar, yes or no?"

"You're on."

We were both fascinated, transfixed, breathlessly observing Willy as he stepped off the curb. "No yelling to warn him," Ron whispered in my ear. In pantomime, I showed sealed lips. My resultant guffaw when I saw Willy plunk first one shoe and then the other into the mushy dung was all the more of an explosive burst. "Oh, my God!" I exclaimed. Blithe spirit that Willy was, our state senate contender neither noticed nor heard anything, but lumbered right on, the soles of his footwear spreading brown imprints on the tarred surface. Doubled-over, Ron was howling but as muffled as could be, his hand clasped over his mouth, and making signs for me to pay off the bet, which I promptly and gaily did. With a bit more decorum, when Witless Willy finally arrived, we shook hands with our hero, who smugly commented, "I guess I'm late again."

Inside, all was Democratic conviviality. When the speech-making began, Ron and I had to avoid catching each other's eye, or Willy's, for fear of roaring again. My composure returned in time, however, for a rah-rah, fighting speech, which was all about victory and a veiled illusion to Republican dirty tricks we would overcome. Less than an hour after it started, the rally was over, the donkey was rebundled into his van, and the tumultuous visitors were dispatched on their noisy exit from Swanstown, off to the next stop.

God knows, I've been through plenty of these events. Why we still do them in an age of television advertising and the Internet is a bit of a mystery. If we involved a hundred people in Swanstown that Friday, I'd be astonished. *Ripple effect,* okay, possibly four or five hundred. Big deal. Thus, here is a mystical aspect of American politics. Hokum of this sort does fire up the troops, the party pundits tell us, and the absence of any activity kills you. The message our community got for so long was: "You Dems are dead." And your own people, your own voters, mysteriously stay home. Irrational? Utterly. In Swanstown, afterward on Friday, all our people were aglow. Willy Bretherton kept telling everyone, "I know I'm gonna take it this time. I know I'm gonna. . . ." Hypocritically, we all nodded, straight-faced.

While the diehard committee members were happily cleaning up, Ron and I snuck out—en route in secret to confer with Mal Bannister.

Honestly, some moments of a campaign are really sublime. Ensconced in Ron's Cadillac (much more appropriate for visiting the upper crust than my Chevy, and besides, my big-time lawyer friend never puts on bumper stickers or other paraphernalia of partisanship), the drive to the Bannister estate was unforgettable. It was a combination of factors: the excited suspense we felt, the intimation that a turning point was in the offing, and the giddy mood we were in, continuing to giggle like schoolboys over "Witless Willy Dip-Shit's" literal dip-in-the-shit, and pumped up by the turnout at the headquarters and the ineffable feeling in the air of momentum going our way.

Then, too, the scenery was mostly radiant with the colors of fall. The incredibly long, winding driveway through Mal's property was bordered by flaming maples, the majority in crimson leafage, or if not, at least bright orange and yellow, glazed by brilliant sunshine. You could almost *see* the crispness in the air. The massive Federal-style red-brick building at the end of our journey was the closest thing to a New England castle I had ever viewed. *Awesome,* my son would have said in his teens, and actually more than once did when he became a friend of Mal's grandson and stayed overnight there. But this was America and no footmen, no butler, appeared to take our car and usher us in. Ron merely pulled up behind Mal's station wagon and parked.

Pausing before we went to ring the bell, standing in the shadow of an elaborate, ivy-ringed entrance, before the pruned bushes, the old gaslight fixtures, the towering, metal-studded oak door, we two Democrats, somewhat young and rather cocky, were momentarily reverent in the presence of so much wealth. "Okay, buddy, let us go forth," Ron finally snapped to me and, once we moved forward in tandem, our unorthodox adventure began as soon as our host himself answered the ring.

10

MALCOLM BANNISTER WAS AN IMPOSING FIGURE. He had to
be six-three or -four and had played basketball for the state university when that now diminutive height meant something.
Pictures of him in his uniform were part of the gallery of photos
spread out on bookshelves and tables in his living room. Ron,
who knew him well, had done legal work for him and, having
been in the house before, was quick to point out a group pose
of guys wearing similar shorts and skimpy jerseys, but with
a younger-looking Mal on an obviously different team from
State U.

"See the banner back of 'em?" Ron said. "Swanstown High
School, Class B State Champs. The very first time we won it, but
hardly our last, thanks to Mr. Number One hoop booster here."
Mal beamed. Handsome in an Anglo-Saxon way, once blond,
now gray, well-tanned and outdoorsy-looking, he was dressed
informally in a sport shirt, jeans, and probably very expensive
sneakers.

He was more than gracious in meeting me, saying how
pleased he was to have a bright young man move to town and
take an interest in public matters, albeit from a standpoint with
which he occasionally had a small quarrel, prompting a timed
(and no doubt expected) quip from Ron of *Occasionally? Small?*
and we all laughed congenially. In the same pleasant vein, Mal
proceeded to show us key images of his other "prides and joys,"
namely his wife, his daughter (especially the wedding pictures),
and, *pièce de résistance,* the same young woman, her husband,

and their offspring, his "first grandchild—a grandson," who appeared to be the same tender age as my Ritchie. When I commented on this fact, his response was prophetic.

"They'll bring Todd to visit us in the summers and perhaps we'll see these two tykes on the beach, building sand castles together." Which is exactly what came to pass.

"I'd like that," I said.

Presently, following the serving of various libations, we got down to business.

By then, we were on a "Jonathan" and "Mal" basis. I sipped my Scotch and soda as our host spoke. Ron also listened quietly and neither of us commented, unless we were asked a question. The gist of his opening statement was about *good taste* in politics. He congratulated me on having run a "clean, issue-oriented race." I nodded appreciatively, hanging on his every word. "Unfortunately, I can't say the same for your opponent," he continued, but this time I didn't nod or show any reaction, glass down, erectly attentive, waiting—waiting—for a denouement. "Earl Johnson is not a favorite of mine," he said. I remained poker-faced.

Quite candidly, Mal detailed his fellow Republican's faults. "Earl's behavior in the capital is scandalous and an open secret to everyone but his long-suffering wife. I like my cocktail as well as the next man, but Earl is well on his way to being a lush. He fills a seat up there, nothing more. And his foul mouth. . . ." I well remember Mal's pause. What followed next was the nub of the reason we had been invited.

Earl had said something—said it privately, yet the word had gotten back—a remark so crude and so cruel that it had become a "final straw" for a man as upright as Mal Bannister. It had come from my opponent in reaction to Agnes Page's letter on my behalf and referred graphically to her poor misshapen anatomy and to some unspeakable acts he would like to perform on it—all stated before witnesses in the raunchiest of gutter language. Mal's nephew, Chad, none too bright as always, had "blabbed," and Earl's language had somehow reached Norman Page who, terribly upset, had called his dear friend Malcolm.

"That fine man, a thorough gentleman at all times, literally cried with rage when he protested to me," Mal stated, adding, "This time, Earl Johnson has gone too far, been inexcusably boorish. It's time he was taught a lesson."

But beyond this last statement of his, the Republican leader did not provide any specifics about what he intended to do— like, we hoped, coming out publicly for me in these few days before the election. Nor did Ron and I dare to make such a request. Instead of even asking how he intended to punish my opponent, we just listened as Mal carried on about the stupidity of the attack into which his nephew had been sucked. "Trying to link you, Jonathan, with the horrible killing in Los Angeles, when you yourself could have been shot. I remember all the newspaper accounts. You've been smart to ignore garbage like that. Governor Ellery was a great loss. I obviously never supported him and certainly didn't want to see him as president, but I had great respect for the man, obviously a complete gentleman, through and through."

Later, our interview over, back in the Cadillac, I commented to Ron on Mal's language. "I thought he was for real," I said, "until he began repeating the 'complete gentleman' stuff."

Ron laughed and said, "It used to be 'Christian gentleman.' Now he edits when I'm around. It's his manner of speaking, a touch of the old WASP past, not necessarily a sign of phoniness, although he can be tricky."

"So what was this all about? Why did he bother to have us meet?"

Ron's explanation, as we drove back to town, was like a graduate course in the byzantine subtleties of politics, which existed no less on a local scale than in the big time. What Ron saw happening was that Mal: 1) had been genuinely turned off by Earl's behavior; 2) had heard my campaign was going well and wanted to be on my good side in the unlikely (but possible) event that I won; and 3) would like to see Earl significantly weakened, so he'd be vulnerable the next time around in a Republican primary.

"Mal's lining up Chad to run," Ron explained. "All this nonsense gives them a perfect chance to undermine Earl. Not enough to defeat him this time, just shave his victory margin. The argument can then be made that the Honorable Earl Johnson is over the hill and should be replaced, especially if a tough opponent like you goes after him again."

"Suppose I mess up those plans by being inconsiderate enough to win," I said rather peevishly.

"It could happen," Ron answered. "I've seen it in both parties when they went overboard on trying to teach a guy a lesson."

"Okay," I said, " I'll still have to win it on my own, which suits me fine."

"Mal's contribution won't hurt," Ron offered.

I detected the slightest note of pique in the redheaded lawyer's voice and thought I understood why. "Or most especially your help," I hastened to say. "Win or lose, I'd be nowhere without your support. Hell, I wouldn't have run."

"Maybe," Ron said, hiding his pleasure at my praise, "because I do believe you've caught the bug."

Election Day wasn't the first time I'd stood at the polls. It was merely my first time as a candidate rather than as a worker handing out materials. What a difference. Particularly the attention you got. It's a longstanding local tradition in Swanstown that candidates are allowed to remain outside the polling place and greet voters. State law forbids asking for their vote, but wearing a name badge is kosher, or even sporting a campaign button. I always chose the former as more dignified and less political-seeming. To my surprise, when the polls opened at 8:00 A.M., there was no sign of Earl Johnson and, except for the short time he showed up to vote himself, he didn't bother to hang around, shake hands, say "hi" to everyone, and trade pleasantries.

Does such schmoozing win votes? I doubt any serious political scientist would take it into account. Assuredly, if you're running for a major office, the personal touch can't be a major factor. And yet, I can remember times when I was traveling around the state with Duke and someone would come up to him and say something like, "Governor, I shook your hand at the Milford Fair and we had a nice talk and you remembered my Aunt Clara and I've been for you ever since. . . ." and Duke, God rest his soul, I'd been with him dozen of times when he would draw on his incredible memory and respond, "You're right. And I can recall right where we were. You had prize sheep and we talked wool prices and I praised your Aunt Clara's quilts . . ." and not only this guy, but people around us would be flabbergasted and, if not already converts, would be swayed on the spot and the story would go around.

Now, I was never in Duke's league. I wasn't bad at remembering names and attaching them to faces, and even without much practice, I found myself, my first Election Day, recognizing people whose homes I'd been to, plus snippets of what we'd talked about, a reference to one guy's interest in woodworking, or a couple whose kid played football for the high school, etc.

Those visits, I learned, had the famous "ripple effect," as well.

"You went to my brother Jim's house and I didn't meet you, but I'm going to vote for you." The voice was that of a young woman who stopped to talk to me on her way into the middle-school gym, where voting is done in Swanstown. With her was her husband, and on his back in a baby carrier their little son, maybe a year and a half or two years old. A pretty smile accompanied her cheery remark, and gesturing to her companion, she added, "And Mitch is going to vote for you, too."

"Great! Thanks ever so much," I blurted effusively. But because of my euphoria, I actually went further. Pointing to the sleeping child, I jokingly asked, "And what about him?"

The wife caught my playful mood and replied in kind, "Oh dear, we forgot to get him registered."

In the good-humored, spontaneous laughter of the three of us, there was, so to speak, a reward—momentary and fragmentary though it might be—for all of the drudgery of a campaign. You could get high on hearing people say you were their choice. Not many folks openly told you their preference. But you could see it in the buttons they wore or, negatively, in their steely eyes and the brisk way they brushed past you, pretending to be in too big a hurry to shake your hand.

On the wide plaza where we candidates were allowed to stand, little fluid knots of supporters, friends, the curious, the sociable, formed and re-formed around the day's political stars, as the stream of voters came and went. I wasn't the only glad-hander. We never usually enticed any of the real big shots (Democrats, that is) to stop by Swanstown, but that Election Day—maybe because he heard I was running a strong race, our guy for Congress in the district, Peter Warner, put in an appearance. I introduced him to some folks, conceivably won him a few votes and, *whoosh,* he was gone, having stayed about fifteen minutes. Another multi-town contestant to arrive, yet who remained much longer, was the local Republican state senate incumbent, Peg McEntee. She gave me an uncomfortable few hours, since her sheer presence seemed to lure the GOP like a light attracts moths. Blonde, vivacious, intelligent, what a charmer! Almost the first thing she did was rush over to give me a hug (we knew each other from my days on Duke's staff), and we had a pleasant, laugh-filled chat. I would like to have believed her open show of friendliness to me sent a signal to her fellow party members that

I was okay, only I knew this was pure fantasy. She was here to bring out the Republican vote—all the more so seeing she absolutely had no opposition in Witless Willy Bretherton. It was equally necessary, I suppose, since Earl wasn't on hand to help himself or the rest of the ticket.

You could clearly start to see some activity was going on, invisibly fomented by the Republican town "machine," which meant a bunch of volunteers on the phones at their headquarters or in their own homes, calling the faithful, using the "win lists" painstakingly prepared beforehand. We had a similar operation—for, no kidding, the first time in the town's history—at a *Democratic* headquarters. Like our well-organized foes, we, too, were using "checkers"—people who stood by the polling stations, taking down the names of those who arrived to vote. The idea was at a certain late afternoon hour to remind the laggards on our win list to go to the polls before 8:00 P.M. Amazingly, even inveterate voters could forget it was Election Day.

In any event, Peg's presence and the flood of vehicles bearing visible Republican insignia showed unmistakably how, valiant as our efforts were, we remained a distinct minority. So, despite spurts of optimism, my stomach stayed in knots while the day wore on—especially when Peg was in the vicinity.

Once she left, a strange thing happened. Sporadically, one of those obviously Republican types (a couple of them actually wearing Earl Johnson buttons) would saunter past me and quietly semi-whisper encouragement—phrases I remember like "Jackson, I think you're gonna do all right," and "Mr. Bannister said some nice things about you."

One badgeless person told me, "I'm a black Republican like Norman Page, but I always did put in an X for Governor Ellery and you'll get mine, too." It was a game of emotional Ping-Pong, with your emotions batted back and forth continually, amid the ceaseless comings and goings of your fellow townspeople, most of whom, despite months of trying to reach them personally, remained perfect strangers to you.

Unexpected, if not weird, stuff happened. Most memorable, I believe, was an incident initiated by a middle-aged woman who accosted me on her way back to her car after voting. I had noticed her earlier because of her henna-dyed hair, equally colorful and brassy clothing, and the big high-five she gave me as she sashayed on by. *Oh, well, I'll take my votes wherever I can get them,* I silently said to myself.

Her payback for my mental snobbery was to dart away from the bald, pockmarked man with whom she was walking, reach my side, interrupt a conversation I was having, and say loudly, "You're Johnson, aren't you?"

Collecting myself finally, I replied, "No, Ma'am," pointing to the identification tag pinned on my coat, reminding her that I was *Jonathan* Jackson.

"Oh, God, I made a mistake," she gasped. "I meant to vote for Johnson."

Inwardly, I smirked and thought: *Too bad, tough shit, lady.*

Then, when her companion, who was wearing a pro football team jacket and a pro baseball team cap, belatedly approached, she immediately shouted to him, "I've got to go back inside, Rex, and tell them I made a mistake. I need to vote again. I meant to vote for Johnson."

"They won't let you vote again," the bald man said. "And you're crazy. You told me you wanted to vote for Jackson."

"No, Jonathan Johnson," she insisted.

"You nit. It's *Jonathan Jackson.* And it's Earl *Johnson.*"

"Well, I didn't vote for Earl, that's for sure."

"Okay, you voted for Jonathan Jackson."

"I'll bet *you* voted for Earl."

"No, I didn't. You know who I voted for."

"You didn't."

At this point, the man with whom I'd been chatting, an old-time Swanstown native, interjected, "Rex, you didn't."

"Damned right I did," Rex said. Whereupon he turned to me and apologetically explained, "No offense, Mr. Jackson, but if I don't know somebody on the ballot and don't like the other guy, I end up writing in. . . ." He paused and the next split second, as a trio, he, the woman, and the native chimed in unison: "Mickey Mouse."

Let the record note that the tally of my state rep contest did include a write-in for the Disney rodent. Also, a single write-in for Abraham Lincoln, another for Napoleon, and, of all people, one preference for Willy Bretherton, his own doing, I was sure, the stinker, while I had loyally checked off his name rather than Peg's, my real preference.

In that era, but no longer, the counting of ballots was done by hand. Pairs of registered Republicans and registered Democrats whom the town clerk chose for their number-crunching skills and their probity, sat opposite each other and examined stacks of paper squares. One read off the votes for each of the races and the other tallied. Then the process was reversed, until both were satisfied the totals were all the same. The whole floor of the gym was covered with tables where everyone worked. It was a tedious job (I had done it prior to becoming a candidate), and you never finished the entire operation until the wee hours of the morning.

But it certainly was democracy in action. Although paid a small stipend, these folks were really volunteers doing a civic duty. But they had fun, too. Coffee and cold drinks and snacks were provided. Lots of good-natured kidding went on, despite the obvious partisan nature of their task. And I remember my own rather "rah-rah America" feelings at the end of these sessions, bleary-eyed, stubbly, yawning, looking around at the basketball hoops, the pushed-aside bleachers, the small crowd listening as the warden of the election read off the results, and thinking, almost incredulously: *Out of all this comes power!*

When it was finally my turn to stand outside the roped-off area away from the counters in order to hear the warden announce my electoral fate, I was the only candidate present. Ron Gordon had stayed with me; Jill would have, except she couldn't get the babysitter to remain beyond midnight; and as for the other competitors, Earl and Willy, they never hung around, I was told. Peg had a bunch of towns and made her home elsewhere in her district. The county and top-of-the-ticket candidates would hardly bother to be in rural Swanstown, but rather would have their campaigns telephone the local warden to pick up their final figures.

This defining moment when the official announcement of numbers would occur was ever so slow to emerge. Our warden, rest his soul, was a local lawyer, a nice guy, much respected, but a stickler for every nicety of nuance in assembling every last little indication of the people's will. Consequently, the world did eventually learn Mickey Mouse had one vote in the state representative race, so did Napoleon Bonaparte, and, of greater significance, Malcolm Bannister had thirty-three. Ron, as in previous elections, muttered about this "pettifogger in charge of the count who, it felt like, had been doing it since the Civil War." I knew he itched to streamline the procedure, but he knew, too, that his minority status—as a Democrat, that is—prevented his ever being selected warden by the town powers-that-be.

While we stood together in the early morning, waiting impatiently, I could feel my redheaded friend and mentor's tension. This time, there was a real chance for some kind of triumph. He had no advance information to go on, only a few smiles and nods when he'd caught the eyes of veteran Democratic counters, yet I detected a distinct buoyancy he exuded. I do also clearly remember our terminating interchange before the finale.

"You really *would* think they'd find a better way to handle three thousand votes," he suddenly, explosively remarked, as if having reached a point of exasperation.

"You told me, but I forgot," I replied. "What, again, was the exact overall count?"

"Marilyn [the town clerk] said 3,127," he replied.

In our few moments of silence following, I had an awful thought: *Jesus, if I lost it by one! One guy, like Rex. . . .*

I turned to Ron and asked, "Has it ever happened that someone lost an election by one vote?"

"Absolutely has, but not often. Witnessed it myself once, working in a recount."

Recount! There was something I hadn't considered. What would trigger one? What numerical disparity out of 3,127?

Only before I could broach the question to Ron, the warden was coming to the front with his sheaf of papers.

His reading of the tabulations commenced with the top of the ticket, except we had no races for governor or U.S. senator in this off-year, so the congressional contest started us off. Incumbent Karl Hoppe, Republican, versus challenger Peter Warner, Democrat. Hoppe, it turned out, had a large plurality and I felt my heart sink, but Ron nudged me and whispered, "Pete made out a lot better than I thought he would here. His visit helped." Still, Warner had lost in Swanstown by almost 500 votes.

Following the warden's infuriating habit of reading off every single congressional write-in, the state senate seat race was reported. Mickey Mouse, I noted, was absent from the string of superfluous names at the tail-end of Peg's landslide win over Willy Bretherton, which led me to surmise Rex had gone for Peg. Willy's total was pathetically microscopic in size, and well before I learned he had written himself in instead of voting for me in the next race, I was having a pang of conscience that I really *had* voted irresponsibly.

Trying to cheer myself up until my fate was announced, I dwelt on a sudden pleasing memory. Earlier in the day, among the good things, was the appearance of Norman Page at the polls, wishing me luck on his way in and hurrying over to me on the way out and confessing, "I have to tell you, young man, I stood inside the booth, after having for the first time in my life voted for a damn Democrat, and expected lightning to flash down and strike me dead for my sin. But since nothing happened, I expect the gods must be smiling on you. Let's hope so."

Before I could thank him, the dignified old gentleman, as if reading my mind, assured me Agnes had already supported my cause. "Unfortunately, she's not been feeling well lately and had to use an absentee ballot this morning," he told me. "Nothing serious, a bad cold, but she has delicate lungs and must be careful." With real delight, then, he described the scene to me: the official whom Marilyn, the town clerk, had sent from her office, presenting the document to Agnes, who sat propped up in bed, wearing one of my campaign buttons on her bathrobe, her treasured photograph with Duke on the night table next to her, and her beatific smile after she completed filling out her choices, sealed the finished entry into the envelope brought for the purpose, and affixed her signature, which was then attested to by the notary public from town hall.

Deep into this reflection, I was nevertheless suddenly aware of a slight commotion in the gym. I felt Ron's hand grasp my elbow and heard him almost shout, "Warden! Mr. Warden, would you repeat those figures for us?"

Now I was paying full attention. I will never forget the sound of the man's rasping, tired voice.

"For state representative," the lawyer intoned, "Jackson, Democrat, 1,591, Johnson, Republican, 1,350." Whereupon, in the same impassive voice, there followed that annoying deliberate listing (also including almost 200 ballots left *blank*), during which I somehow, barely listening, caught Rex's *Mickey Mouse.* I turned to Ron and excitedly stated, "My God, I'm ahead." To underscore my naiveté at the time, I quickly asked, "Will they demand a recount?"

Ron laughed. "They'd be crazy if they did. You can't overturn 241 votes. And Earl won't try, I assure you, 'cause unless he's successful, he'd have to pay for it out of his own pocket."

"So it's final?"

"You bet. You won, Jonathan. You sonofabitch, you broke the mold!"

With his half-heard expletive and a spontaneous bear hug came applause in the background, mostly but not exclusively from the Democratic counters.

We had no cell phones then. Nor was there a pay phone inside the gym. I couldn't call Jill immediately. But I didn't rush out to let her know.

The warden was droning on, announcing the totals from the bottom of the ballot. Sheriff. Register of deeds. Judge of probate. Register of probate. . . . Ron had gotten his coat, preparatory to leaving. "I'm dead on my feet," he told me, shaking hands. "Congratulations again. *Mazel tov!*"

"I'm gonna stay a little while longer," I replied, and indicating the counters, "to thank those folks, ours and theirs, too."

A big grin lit up Ron's freckled face. "Terrific, already you *are* learning on the job, bub," he happily teased me. "Jonathan, you're gonna do all right."

When at last I left the gym, strolling into the morning light of a new day, I really did, indeed, feel different.

II

AH, DEMOCRACY. The Greek, from which the word in English is derived, means: "rule of the people." Then why—at least in Swanstown—was I suddenly a big shot, simply for being thrust out of the crowd to represent their will in the state capital? The term "the Honorable" was put in front of my name. To quote the wise and venerable Representative Matthew X. Drew, "That and thirty-five cents [remember, this was some time ago] will get you a cup of coffee."

It was tempting to take myself seriously. For a young man, as I still was, the inevitable vision, after my election, was of a new steppingstone. Once before, as a gubernatorial assistant, I'd been on the high road to ultra-achievement, American-style. My boss had been heading for the White House, no less. And I was to rise with him. But you can also fall damn fast—as Miles Monahan's crazed single pistol shot taught me.

I would willingly skip over the nasty aftermath of those few horrendous seconds at LAX—that is, the many months I stayed on, working for Duke's successor, lieutenant governor Robert J. "Big Bob" Benton, who automatically and immediately assumed the position of chief executive.

If I have not mentioned Big Bob until now, it is not entirely an accident. Mention of the job of lieutenant governor in our state always brings to mind what "Cactus" Jack Garner said about the vice presidency of the United States when he held it: "Not worth a pitcher of warm spit" (or, more likely, *warm piss* in the original). In other words, Big Bob had precious little to do as

LG, which was fine with Big Bob, who spent a good deal of his time hunting, fishing, hanging out at home, and jawing with the good ol' boys at the general store in his rural community. He was a *conservative* Democrat, whose political antecedents lay in the old Grange movement, and he had seemed a good balance on the ticket to Duke's younger, liberal, more forward-thinking persona. We never had a problem with Big Bob—meek as a lamb despite his bulky size—but assuredly it *was* a problem when he unexpectedly ended up in the governor's chair. More on that later.

Let's see. I was actually going to pontificate a bit about the effect of ambition upon an elected official. No sooner had the people spoken in my favor (in my case, by a plurality of 241 votes), than I began fantasizing about a future dizzying meteoric rise through the ranks. Young whippersnappers like me were akin, I've always thought, to those soldiers in Napoleon's armies of whom the history books say, "Each had a field marshal's baton in his knapsack."

Realistically, of course, I could never contemplate for myself the lofty goal Duke had set *him*self—nothing less than the presidency—the top of the heap, the king of the mountain—at least for Americans—and, by God, it was not inconceivable he could have made it.

Don't take my word as gospel.

In this compendious treasure trove of mine—i.e., the "research collection" stored in innumerable files—I can retrieve an article to bear me out, written by a nationally known Washington, D.C.–based columnist. Here, in the last major interview ever held with Duke Ellery (datelined Los Angeles, two days before he was shot), is a sampling of what the renowned media guru had to say about my former boss:

> This hotel emporium, so full of governors, resembles nothing so much as a racetrack paddock, where you go to

look over the field before the race. But I have to admit that only one has caught my eye. He's a real thorough-bred—governor and ex-congressman Richard N. Ellery, whom everyone calls "Duke." His Harvard pedigree notwithstanding, he is a people's patrician, handsomer than most movie stars, yet utterly down-to-earth, good humored, good-natured, a politician who genuinely con-nects with the average guy and gal. Look up his numbers in his previous races for Congress and the governorship of his state. I did. Wow! Nothing less than 70 percent of the vote. Wait till the country gets a steady diet of him on national TV. He's got an FDR smile, a Kennedy quick-ness of mind, a deep belief in the fundamental decency of the US of A, and a compelling urge, nay a passion, to see it live up to its ideals.

"People tell me you might want to be president" were my first words to him.

After a protracted, searching, almost pixyish look at me, he answered, "Well, I'm old enough now. Over thirty-five."

"That *is* a major qualification," I agreed. "Got any others?"

Again, a glint of mischief was in his deep blue eyes.

"Let's see," he pretended to reflect. "I've got a stun-ning, brainy wife, photogenic children, nice teeth—or so my friends tell me—and . . . and . . . to be serious for a moment, a stout belief in American virtue."

Being a bit of a lexicographer myself, I fastened on his artless use of that archaic term *virtue*. Much in vogue in American politics in the eighteenth century, he informed me. His off-the-cuff knowledge of U.S. history was impressive. *Virtue.* He kept coming back to it as a yard-stick by which the founding fathers meant to measure the government they were creating. Its principles had to mirror those, in Duke's words, "of a just and benevolent God, plus be all-encompassing, enduring yet flexible, and perpetually self-correcting." What politician ever talks to a journalist in such language?

A National Governors Conference is a venue where the guys and gals can strut their stuff and especially for the presidential wannabes, make some noise. Duke's game plan here seems surprisingly modest—a mere resolution that he's gotten his confreres to adopt. It's hardly the stuff of headlines—has to do with Indians—which brought us back, he explained, to the idea of *virtue* in the American system, or the absence thereof, the current status of the tribes standing as a rebuke, the stain on the escutcheon, not only in his state, but everywhere throughout the land these natives once had exclusively occupied.

"Strange issue," I commented.

"A matter of conscience," he replied.

But lest my more cynical readers think Governor Richard N. Ellery is a naïve dreamer, he did make sure I learned that on his flight out here from the east, he had landed in Iowa to visit his pal Hank Waggoner of Waggoner Industries, the quintessential Demo moneyman. And, furthermore, there's a lot of Indians in key western states who vote in Democratic primaries.

No, Duke's no slouch. Worth a parimutual ticket or two.

In toto, this is the article, a piece of yellowing newsprint before me on my desk—primary source material, an original documentation of an objective opinion at the time, from an "informed source," certifying Duke's credibility in a national race. The morning we read it at breakfast in the LA hotel, our staff was ecstatic, for its author was syndicated in at least 150 dailies.

Now, back in my cloister, putting the aged clipping back in its file folder, I was reminded of how much *internalized* history I still needed to relate.

Were I to be writing, say, fifty years from now, with access to my stockpile of information, documents, notes, etc.—in other words, like most historians, a total stranger to the events, personages, circumstances, etc.—what would I be writing at this point? I've had plenty of practice at reconstruction stuff in my previous books, going back through imagination even to seventeenth-century America. Yet I wasn't doing fiction. You can't *invent* irresponsibly. Futuristically, therefore, the objective chronicler of Duke Ellery's life, extrapolating from only a half-century retrospective, might be said to have reached the critically important, climactic National Governors Conference. Assembling those files of mine, a whole box-load of papers painstakingly accumulated, plus secondary sources, books from which to quote snippets underlined previously, one would take a long pause, suck in a deep breath, exhale and commence the agonizing, hair-tearing work of trying to make an entire historic episode come alive.

But, something you already know: *I was on the scene.* I was inside the Air National Guard's funky plane, bringing Duke and Madge, et al., to LA. I made the stop with him in Iowa at Waggoner's and the later one in Colorado, left undepicted by our columnist friend. To continue, I saw Los Angeles, spreading out from the mountainous barricade of barren brown heights on its eastern flanks. I was driven in a van, seated next to Miss Jill McKenzie, through the gated entrance out near Malibu toward a sort of Xanadu hotel, following the escort of California Highway Patrol cars provided by the governor of the Golden State for each arriving potentate and his or her entourage. To have been in a Roman emperor's triumphal procession must have produced a similar feeling.

Enough. I'm getting ahead of myself. Iowa, I'm well aware, was the geographic location where I left off my narrative on the cross-country run we were making by air from the Atlantic coast to the Pacific.

It might not be accurate to claim that at Waggoner's we were right in the middle of the country. I'm not sure how to look up a statistical measurement, which, for population, keeps moving westward. Was it Illinois, over which we had already flown, as the U.S.'s human balancing point, or Nebraska, still lying ahead? I haven't the patience nor the time, really, to chase down such remote pieces of research. And as for the exact, unmovable *geographical* center, equidistant between the two oceans?—who cares, anyway? But in the Hawkeye State (I *must* look up the derivation of their nickname), flat, flat, flat, full of cornfields, you sure felt like you were plumb in the middle.

Symbolically speaking, too. Heartland. Americana. The most memorable reminiscence I retain of Waggoner, Iowa, revolves around *football*. What else is important on a late autumn Saturday afternoon in small-town USA? The Waggoner High School Bobcats were defending a twenty-five-game win streak and a second successive state championship in the size division they were in—the "big game" against the only rival who could beat them—and no greater fan and booster existed than Horace "Hank" Waggoner himself, who had played fullback for the Bobcats and later the Hawkeyes of the University of Iowa, and had built the new Waggoner Stadium in his community.

Duke had played tennis at Harvard—at a time when the Crimson had already de-emphasized football. I never had any idea of what he thought about having his private political tête-à-tête with Hank in the stands in between the moments when our host wasn't on his feet, hollering encouragement to his boys in red and black below. Madge, sitting on the other side of her husband, couldn't have been a happy camper, even though we only stayed for the first half. Scheduling was Harry DeWitt's baili-wick, and I'm sure he took a ration of you-know-what from our generally fussy first lady. Meanwhile, ensconced on the fifty-yard line, I was happy as a clam. For one thing, I like football, not that I was ever much good at playing it. Even in my early post-college years, I weighed a mere 150 pounds, was skinny to boot, and neither tall enough nor fast enough nor shifty enough to excel at end, which was the position I tried to play in high school. Whether it was pro or college or kids like those in Waggoner, Iowa, I always enjoyed watching a game, with or without having a beer in my hand. With a girl snuggling next to me in the brisk midwestern climate, now what could be better? With Jill by my side, it was continually electrifying.

There is a saying that a football game is the one venue where you can get away with being under a blanket with a female in public. Those blankets, by the way, had been supplied by Hank Waggoner, and our whole row had them, producing a sense of innocence in Miss McKenzie's proximity to me. To this day, my wife will attest I was a perfect gentleman—no hands moving where they shouldn't, full of "respect." Of course, we kept jump-ing up and down—the blanket falling off, my re-settling it around her—in response to the excitement on the gridiron and our host's standing enthusiasm, affording numerous opportuni-ties for delicious contact with her soft, warm body. Jill, it turned out, if anything, was as much of a generic pigskin fan as myself. Her three brothers had each been varsity on their respective col-lege elevens.

Love and the gridiron. How can I explain that what may have forever endeared Jill to me was her knowledge of college football? One incident will never leave my memory. It had to do with a discussion I somehow initiated before the game started about the color combinations college teams wore, their uniforms, home and away, "like battle flags," I declaimed, "political symbols almost . . . for who thinks of Alabama as anything but red and white—crimson, really—the Crimson Tide?"

Jill had been listening intently, wide-eyed, following my meaning, I was sure, which pleased me greatly. Except, in reality, the canny little minx was getting ready to spring a surprise. Ever so sweetly, she added, "But aren't you forgetting Auburn in the State of Alabama—orange and blue?" How absolutely fetching Jill looked when she was being earnest. "And like in Kansas, red and blue for the university, purple and white for Kansas State. In Oregon, green and gold as opposed to orange and black for Oregon State. Texas, orange and white, Texas A&M, maroon and white . . ." on and on, she rattled off these disparate match-ups and I listened admiringly and said nothing until ". . . Michigan State, green and white, Michigan, a navy blue and maize."

"Navy blue and what?" I interjected.

"Maize."

"What the hell is mays?"

"Corn, dummy. Corn color. Bright yellow."

"Michigan! Jesus! Yes—they have those funny helmets. Those old-fashioned stripes across the upper part of them."

"Maize on blue. My brother Tom played there."

"You're terrific," I suddenly said. Even more impulsively, I kissed her on the cheek—a mere peck, but an audacious move all the same, since we were out in the Waggoner stadium, awaiting the kick-off. The reward for my boldness was an expression of *her* surprise, not discomfort, and considering subsequent events, I'm sure she had to have been pleased.

The first flowers I ever gave Jill, I should add, once we were in California, were mainly blue with a smattering of yellow that I labeled *maize.*

All this lay ahead of us, *the best of times and the worst of times,* with a nod to Mr. Charles Dickens in *A Tale of Two Cities,* where he applied such a bipolar split to the French Revolution. At a high school football game in Iowa, obviously, one could not imagine anything remotely like social discord or violent head-on-a-pike death. The mayhem was strictly on the field, a territorial war pantomimed by colorful helmeted (and shoulder-padded) warriors, real estate gained and lost by way of an oval ball. Was the "pigskin" really made of the skin of a pig? Even today, the thought does entail for me a whiff of barbarity, like Afghan horsemen tossing a bloated sheep's corpse, or Mongols, perhaps, playing polo with a human head. Games once *were* violence; now, in civilization, they're a substitute for real battle.

I couldn't help but note to myself Hank Waggoner's behavior.

Suave, dignified, engaged in high-level conversation with the governor of a state and a soon-to-be actual aspirant for president, he was right away in the first quarter of the contest nearly frothing at the mouth over a referee's call. Or rather, the lack of an officiating penalty for what Hank screamed was an illegal block. There was one of his Bobcats writhing on the ground and no flag. Then, this lion of industry, whose doings were regularly noted in the *New York Times* and the *Wall Street Journal,* was motioning everyone in the home team stands to rise and applaud the boy being helped to the sidelines and yelling for revenge, which morphed into a noisy vendetta against the opposing quarterback, who was doing an extraordinary job of riddling the Waggoner defense. No. 12—I still remember him, a cool, lanky kid—his passes had pinpoint accuracy; his running, in quarterback sneaks, delayed bucks, optional sweeps, always good for five to ten yards. Hank, seemingly beside himself, shouted orders to his tacklers, "Stop him, Jacky!" "End around, Warren, get to him, get to him!" "Kevin, kill him, break his leg!"—a verbal bloodthirstiness echoed by the crowd all around us. At intervals, when the action slowed, he and Duke could be seen in calmer discussion. I don't recall my boss on his feet, not even when No. 12 hit a receiver in the end zone and Hank was up, protesting,

"Offensive interference!" (and so was I, along with Jill and Harry DeWitt); moments later, again, we were all back standing (including Duke this time), cheering, when the kick for the point after was blocked.

I have seen hundreds of football games at every level, pro, college, high school, even sandlot-type pickup scrimmages. It was not only Jill's nearness and Duke's and Hank Waggoner's presence that made the Iowa contest so unforgettable; the action itself was damn exciting. Once the Bobcats got their offense going, they had a player to equal No. 12's skill. They called him Chicky, a small, African American scatback, who effortlessly ripped off chunks of yardage; only gang-tackles seemed certain to bring him down, and frequently, he slipped those, too—either for additional gain or, eventually, the home team's first score at the start of the second period, an electrifying 45-yard TD run. The kick after was good. Waggoner ahead, seven to six. Hank and the local folk went wild.

But No. 12 was soon right back to work. A pass here, a pass there. They couldn't stop him. Five plays later, a 30-yarder to his tight end put the visitors in the lead, and with a two-point conversion, another pass from No.12, by 14-7.

The Bobcats received. Chicky took the ball at the 11-yard line and proceeded to scamper 89 yards for a touchdown. Pandemonium in the stadium, then gloom, groan, and horror among the Waggoner followers. A clipping penalty nullified the score. Hank's language would have made a longshoreman blush, as he appeared near apoplexy. The Bobcats, however, still drove deep, only to miss a field goal after being stopped on the 18-yard line.

However, No. 12 wasn't quite as awesome on his next possession. After amassing four straight first downs, a blitzing linebacker upset his timing and he threw an interception. Time was ticking away toward the completion of the second period. Hank and others were pleading with the Bobcats to score again before the half. Once more, Chicky complied, with two seconds left. He had slithered and bulled his way into the end zone from eight yards out. The coach then opted to go for two points.

"Oh, no, God help us!" Hank cried. "You shoulda kicked it! You shoulda kicked it! Tie it up!"—and so on—that is, until the maneuver worked, a trick play, fake to Chicky, give the ball to his blocking back, who just stepped into the end zone. *Davis*, I still remember the chunky kid's name—"Davis! Davis!" The cry resounded. Waggoner 15, Visitors 14.

Would you believe I have never been able to find out how the game ended? Harry DeWitt was *our* timekeeper and the Ellery schedule had not contemplated we would stay for the second half. After a brief press conference held underneath the stands, we were whisked back to our plane and airborne before these two teams were back pummeling each other.

Curious as I was at the time to know how the Bobcats made out, subsequent events overwhelmed any urge of mine to investigate. So it was not until years later, as an historian, that I tried. Hank Waggoner couldn't be reached. Several letters to the company (now part of a conglomerate) remained unanswered. Several phone calls were just as futile. The local weekly newspaper couldn't help me out. The principal of Waggoner High School promised to get back to me and never did. The Internet has mountains of information, but not that tidbit.

When it comes right down to the nub of things, what import *does* this entire football episode have? Well, it's not only my feel for the pure Americanism of the experience nor its role as a crucial element in the start of my relationship with Jill, but I would bet dollars to doughnuts had Hank Waggoner's team not been leading when we left our seats, he might well have canceled the press conference we had planned.

I'm serious. According to Harry DeWitt in a much later conversation with me, the idea had come from Duke of a "briefing" for the press he'd brought with him, i.e., Jill and the print reporters. It was something of a reward, giving them an exclusive on the news that the Iowa firm was considering building a major plant in our state. Reportedly, the head of Waggoner Industries had *reluctantly* agreed to Duke's genial yet effective persuasion.

"Honestly, though," Harry told me, "and I was sitting right behind him, as soon as his team scored those two points after and the second period ended, he put his arm around Duke and said, 'Okay, *now* we can tell the world your news.'"

Apparently, the order had already gone out to make the necessary arrangements, and when we were herded into a pavilion-like outbuilding underneath the seating—Hank's private pad—lights were in place to assist Jill's cameraman, microphones available, a portable podium set up, and several rows of folding chairs arranged. The presentation was brief, but definitely journalistic big stuff. Jill had a field day, interviewing these two guys after their announcement. Boy, did she look gorgeous, all lit up and enthusiastic because of the scoop she had been handed. In addition, one of Hank's assistants had taken charge of sending her material back to her station. On the surface, therefore, she was an eminently *happy camper*.

Never one to hold back her true, complete feelings in any prolonged fashion, Jill confided she was having a good time on this trip so far. Otherwise, she confessed, her job had been getting tiresome. The same old monotony at home, local stories played night after night. "I grabbed the chance for this assignment," she said in what to me was a low, sexy, intimate whisper, "hoping it would be like a mini-vacation. If I can do some good work, too, it's a nice bonus."

"A *junket,* in other words," I added somewhat pompously. "Our political term for what we're actually doing."

"You said it, I didn't," she teased, with a flashing white smile.

"My fate is in your hands," I riposted. "But I can always deny I said the J-word. Who believes the media, anyway?"

"Thanks." She stuck out her tongue.

And I had to admit I hadn't seen anything so cute since a pretty little blonde named Molly made the same kind of face at me in the third grade.

Jill, it could be argued, was a dark-haired version of the instinctively fetching young girl who had first stirred my young heart. It was often remarked later by my relatives that Jill has a certain resemblance to my late mother. The Freudian implications, I will leave to someone else. My clearest memory, in effect, of this particular conversation of ours on the Air National Guard plane—we had made our second stop by then, the one in Colorado with a group of Indian leaders, and Jill had gotten another interesting if more of a feature-type story—and were on the last leg of our flight to California, when I responded to her, "Well, my dear, I'm into mini-vacations, myself. What do you say we play hookey in LA whenever we can?"

I can still hardly believe I made that bold suggestion, ambitious, workaholic me. Nor could I believe at the time my inner delight as she smiled and nodded.

The only downside was a sudden thought I kept to myself: *Maybe we'll go see Hollywood, Jill and I.* The prospect of encountering Miles Monahan suddenly arose quite paranoiacally as a possibility. But not if I didn't call him. But damn him, I'd told him when I'd be in town.

A long-forgotten, extended memory began emerging silently.

The third grade. Pretty Molly. As the phrase goes, Miles had "taken her away from me," won her with bright, glassy, prize marbles and a box of colorful jacks. Remembering, amazingly bitter still after all those years, I received a vision of the two tykes hand-in-hand, exiting the classroom under the benevolent gaze of Miss MacPhail.

Next, I was sneaking a glance at Jill, eyeing her in profile while she gazed out our aircraft porthole at the mountain ranges below—the Rockies?—which we had both been admiring.

Why should I even introduce her to Miles?

Screw him. If he calls, I'll just lie, tell him I'm too busy with my work to get together.

Friendship later. Hanky-panky first.

12

I AM GOING TO DON A POLITICIAN'S HAT for the next few paragraphs. At this stage of my life, I obviously don't need to fear the public anger of any organization and if the National Governors Association were to take me to task, so what? Yet I want to be fair. Words like "junket" and "hanky-panky," in conjunction with one of these regular gatherings of the nation's fifty chief state executives, invites a distorted picture, but is far from the whole story. A mountain of work goes into the preparation by the secretariat of this yearly major event. The show in LA was truly *national;* the NGA holds regional get-togethers, as well. Sure, there is partying and folderol, but also purpose, which is to collect the fifty temporary "American kings" (as an author in the 1920s dubbed them) under one roof for a very long weekend and allow them to intermingle, exchange ideas, and, on occasion, despite their diversity, present a solid front to the Feds. The institution doesn't lack weight in being among the various unsung methods through which the USA keeps itself intact and running fifty-one major governments relatively smoothly.

Jill's cynicism was really about all of us pols, from the president on down. For example, regarding the occupant of the White House at the time, she said she had it on good authority that the only reason he had accepted the NGA's invitation to come and speak in LA was that he'd been shacking up with one of the female governors.

"I was told," Jill reported to me, "that he wisecracked, 'They asked me to come and speak, but I plan to speak and come.'"

I did guffaw, but I let Jill know I didn't believe a word of it. More shocking still than such a bit of smut from those lovely lips was her fierce, blue-eyed insistence "they all sleep around," including my own supposedly lily-white boss. Here, tremulously, I drew a line. "No way," I objected, and when she objected to my objection, I offered, like a child, to bet her.

"How would we know who won?" was her sly response. "If you asked him point-blank and he said no, what would that prove?"

"Don't worry, I'll never ask," I rejoined.

"Maybe I should offer to sacrifice myself. . . ." Her slyness now turned into openly sexy provocation.

But I think I made points by being quick on the draw. "Oh, so you're not speaking from knowledge already gained," I shot back.

Again, her stuck-out, pretty pink tongue.

"Okay, no bet," I said. "I just happen to believe Duke is much too square, much too intellectual, actually too ambitious, to screw around. Besides, he knows Madge would kill him if she caught him straying, even glancing. . . ."

"Still, there are rumors."

"Always," I added. "Who in public life isn't a suspect, particularly good-looking guys and also some not-so-good-looking." (Even then, I was aware of Earl Johnson's reputation.)

Jill nodded in agreement. "I know who you mean," she asserted. "From what I hear, it can be like Sodom and Gomorrah up around the Statehouse. Now you, a nice-looking, single guy, don't tell me *you* stay out of trouble."

"Are you kidding? I'm working twelve hours a day, six days a week. And on Sundays, I sleep—completely alone, I assure you."

"Poor soul." A soft hand patted my cheek.

"Furthermore," I went on, "the available pulchritude at the capital complex never lit up my life or libido until a certain newscaster appeared, like a radiant diamond, on my television screen one night."

Flowery, bullshit-sounding as these phrases might have been, they were the honest truth. Jill stared at me in a funny way. Once again, I had the impression she was pleased.

Where did this particular conversation of ours take place? Were we still on the Air National Guard plane, with the flat rooftops and sporadic palm trees of LA stretched below for block after block after block? Or was it in one of the vans taking us from whatever military airfield where we'd landed to our gated hotel spread by the Pacific? I don't think the latter instance, because then we were all crammed together, myself, Jill, her cameraman, Harry DeWitt, George Everoff, the reporters, et al. Duke and his party were ahead of us in a black limo, another van carrying luggage was behind ours, and, leading the cortege, the California Highway Patrol car and its uniformed driver. As we progressed in convoy over the different freeways and coastal routes, drawing glances from motorists, we could feel genuinely regal, privileged, a cocooned elite. My suspicion, therefore, leans to the theory that the slightly salacious talk just reported occur-red in the lobby of the hotel while we were waiting to register. Indeed, in those posh quarters, viewing the hurly-burly atmos-phere of a vast and grand self-importance on parade, never has the average American's cynicism about the upper rungs of our political system seemed so aptly merited.

Security was tight, as befitted a American-style royalty, inevitably objects of envy and perennially plausible targets of cranks and kooks. Gubernatorial bodyguards could logically not protect their employers from the most obvious dangers they faced—political calumny and unspecified accusations of misbe-havior, sexual or otherwise—but these armed guys, usually state police, came with the job. In the delegations in LA, quite a num-ber wore uniforms, the diversity of design and hue (mostly greens and grays and blues and browns), polished boots, gleaming holsters, and so forth, adding yet another touch of "color" to what looked like a perpetual festival crowd, coursing endlessly through the hotel premises. Then, too, there were more discreet governors like Duke, who'd brought only faithful Tim Lavery with him—and in civvies.

Since the president was scheduled, which provided the only real, rational need for so much defensive hardware (how often does a governor ever get attacked?), an advance phalanx of federal Secret Service agents were on hand, and they, too, à la Tim, tried to blend inconspicuously, wearing mufti (except they had little round ceramic badges in their lapels and earphone plugs, and all seemed to have bought their suits from the same unimaginative tailor). I suspected that among the mass of humanity, which always seemed to surround us, they had also sprinkled undercover operatives, totally camouflaged.

The lobby was constantly full of people, but so were the hallways, the elevators, the paths between buildings, the pools, the tennis courts, the gym, you name it. Everyone had to have credentials, wear badges bearing official logos, with your name and state in readable type, color-coded, too, if I remember. Jill's, which stated PRESS, was blue-striped, I think, and mine, STAFF, yellow. In any event, we were legit as long as we sported them, fellow members of an arrogant, intimidating mob of insiders.

Woe to whatever outsiders thought they could crack the wall of security, dent that smugness, breach such ramparts erected around the Establishment, like the uniforms and state seals and state flags, quietly exuding their power.

The place was also an advertising bazaar. Corporate America was out in full force, booming sponsorship of this or that part of the proceedings, a dinner, an entertainment, or reminding us of the products that had been contributed pro bono. The states themselves were big on boosterism. Some had rented stalls, from behind which pretty girls passed out brochures, buttons, souvenirs, anything to emphasize their salient points. We were each given a tote bag stuffed with free goodies, these canvas receptacles themselves emblazoned with the names of Company X or Y. One guy I met, a staffer about my age from Idaho or Montana, some western state, only wanted to talk about the "loot" he was collecting, the "freebies" he kept jamming into his sack, and how was I doing in what he presumed was my equally spirited quest for ever more gewgaws.

Duke didn't believe in spending taxpayers' money on ephemeral promotions of this ilk. In the past, I'd learned, he'd once been criticized editorially for our "lack of presence" at a similar gathering; in response, he publicly invited the accusative newspaper to send one of its reporters to a comparable event to check the trash barrels and see how many of these handouts ended up getting dumped (note: none of the print reporters on our trip were from that scolding publication).

Brand names. Each state had something about itself or some product of its soil and waters it wanted to promote. Kansas advertised with little bags of sunflower seeds; Idaho gave us samples of potato chips; New York had pins in the form of miniature Empire State Buildings; Massachusetts offered the same types of small, cheap broaches shaped as bean pots or codfish, while Maryland touted its crabs. Signage and decoration, being the task of the association staff, not the individual states, had a less entrepreneurial basis. All fifty of us had ourselves included somewhere on the premises; not only in half a hundred labeled scenic prints, but since this was autumn, football became *the* theme—*college* football, because each state had a public university (at least one) and thus an appropriate universality for our fifty jurisdictions.

On this account, they threw in mascot names and school colors, so that there on a wall you might see a placard, orange and white, and the lettering: VOLUNTEERS, and for identification, the legend, *University of Tennessee*. On another wall, HOOSIERS, against a field of bright red and white, *Indiana University*. Those were single shots, in a manner of speaking. A bit more complicated was seeing TIGERS in more than one place and color combination: purple and gold—well, that was *Louisiana State;* black and gold, *University of Missouri;* blue and orange, *Auburn*, a State of Alabama-financed institutionm used by tricky-girl Jill to put me down a notch.

No "foolish consistency" was applied to their gridiron schemata. Thus did I find myself witnessing a red and yellow placard proclaiming TROJANS, over a caption of *University of Southern California,* and seconds later, doing a double-take and saying to myself, *Hey, that's a private institution!* Ditto to THE FIGHTING IRISH of *Notre Dame University* (they had chosen a blue-and-gold background for the South Bend, Indiana, outfit), which was not only private, but *religious.*

The usual American mish-mash, I had to reflect—constantly—throughout the three-day proceedings. Coca-Cola signs were everywhere. Disneyland had posters in prominent spots. There *were* bus trips to Anaheim you could take. To Universal Studios, as well. And cheek by jowl, a pageantry, wherever applicable, to fifty united political subdivisions, formed by history and sustained by tradition and the Civil War, to fuse into a single federal whole represented in those halls—and the closer we got to the president's arrival—by streamers of red-white- and-blue bunting, numerous stars-and-stripes banners, and images of a gaunt, bony, tall, goateed gentleman in spangled cutaway, Uncle Sam, which made me wince the first time I saw one and remembered with guilt my neglected old pal Miles Monahan.

Another sports metaphor had also occurred to me: *major league* and *minor league*. Not all, but most, of the present-day heavy-hitters (governors) had served an apprenticeship in public service, some even at the lowest rung, like a town councilor or a sheriff's deputy—the farm teams, so to speak. Even Duke had begun as a New England-style "selectman." The current president of the U.S., we all knew, had once been a county executive. A few every season escaped the training camps and went straight to the big leagues: a sports personality, an overnight hero, a hot-shot business executive, a popular broadcaster, a successful actor— *exposure* being the name of the game—but the largest number, by far, had toiled upward through the ranks. That politics was hardly rocket science remained a secret we kept to ourselves, yet it required skills and they *could be* honed by experience. During those days among Duke's colleagues, I might wonder: *How did so-and-so, a real clunker, ever get elected governor?* Yet he or she did have something on the ball or, more importantly, a trait or quirk of character that epitomized his or her electorate in an uncanny fashion or, perhaps above all, just good old-fashioned dumb luck.

Cognizant, as I write now, about my own career in electoral politics, most of which lay ahead of me, I've tried to summon what my fairly raw, novice feelings were within that gated hotel hothouse atmosphere. On the one hand, I'd been around enough to be cool, or to think I was savvy; on the other, my eyes *were* swiveling about with a *gee-whiz, wow, look where I am!* glaze to them. On top of it all, I had the faintest inkling of *Christ, maybe I'm falling in love.*

Once we had our room assignments and luggage, there was some momentary milling about among us "ordinary folk." Jill abruptly asked Harry DeWitt, who was acting as our major-domo, "What's the program for the rest of the day? Will I have time to get to the pool?"

It was still sunny; balmy outside, too; California warm. Harry's answer was, "Nothing is on our schedule until the meeting of the Resolutions Sub-committee tomorrow morning where Governor Ellery intends to make his presentation, and the location of this meeting is to be posted on the lobby bulletin board this evening, I understand." A goofy smile then followed from him. "Have fun, kids."

Jill turned to me at once. "Did you bring your bathing suit?"

Caught by surprise, I gulped and made a sort of helpless gesture with my hands. "Who knew . . . ?"

"Well, you could always try going without." There was a wicked but sexy gleam in those gorgeous blue eyes.

Of all people, Tim Lavery, who'd overheard us, rescued me from my embarrassment. The governor's dour state trooper bodyguard and I had been assigned to share a room.

"Jonathan, I've got an extra pair of trunks you can borrow," he said in his usual efficient, expressionless way, engendering a smile of appreciation from Jill and effusive thanks from his bunkmate.

George Everoff, I noticed, was scowling. Even more so when I picked up Jill's suitcase and gallantly offered to escort her to her quarters. As the two of us walked away down a corridor together, I suspected Georgie wasn't jealous—I'd never known him to show any interest in a female—just nervous, afraid I was angling for his press job, as if I didn't have a helluva lot bigger ambitions than hand-holding the fourth estate.

Hand-holding Miss McKenzie—literally—well, that was quite another matter. Impossible at the moment, since I gripped Jill's suitcase in one hand and my own in the other. Jill had a backpack, too, I believe. The little details are a bit fuzzy at my age. But there was a particularly jarring image I can never forget.

It happened after I deposited my honey at her threshold. We had chatted all down the hall, as if we were on our first date. No kiss by the door, however.

"See you at the pool," or something equally brilliant was my parting remark. I went up in a nearby elevator, found my room, entered, and practically the first thing I saw was Tim's service revolver laid out on his bed.

The holster was beside it. A few seconds were needed before I realized my roomie was in the shower, and a few more to spot the plaid bathing suit he had thoughtfully placed on the other bed.

What had he been doing . . . checking the bullets? I wondered, turning back to stare at the weapon, actually mesmerized. The bright metal had the sinister attraction of a coiled reptile. I simply shuddered. Don't ask me if it was a .38 or a .45 or whatever. It was a big mother, oiled and sleek, and so incongruous on the hotel bed. I remember sneaking peeks at the deadly object while hurrying to change into the proper attire for my romp at the pool.

We all know swimming pools mean luxury; they symbolize the wealthy life, conspicuous consumption. This Olympic-sized beauty, a central feature of our hotel's posh offerings, seemed as big as a pond, for God's sake, an oddly shaped, meandering body of water in which several bars had been set up for the convenience of guests who could sit waist-deep and consume their drinks while their lower parts remained refreshed in cooling liquid.

Jill and I were good for two Tequila Sunrises apiece. Equally intoxicating was the sight of Jill in a bathing suit. The minx. She knew I couldn't take my eyes off her. Whichever satiny material that one-piece outfit was made of clung to her body like tight silk, a slightly different blue from the dress she'd worn earlier, verging toward blue-green. She positively shimmered. No bathing cap. Her wet hair, the color of dark honey, hanging down in strings, added a youthful quality to her sexiness, softened the brassy, well-made-up facial patina of a professional television commentator.

My only problem was the mystery of why she was being so friendly to me, letting her hair down, so to speak. Physical attraction? Horny on vacation? Or was the spark genuine (I was beginning to think it might be), as we were jabbering and drinking and snacking on peanuts, telling stories of our childhood and families and adventures at college and what-have-you.

We weren't kids, obviously, with our alcoholic drinks. But there was some reversion. Like a water fight after we swam to the shallow end—raced actually, and stood. She'd started it because I'd beaten her by a stroke. In the melee of flying splashes that erupted, we finished by clinging, wrestling, copping a couple of teenagers' grabs. Our touching was chaste enough, but extraordinarily titillating. I had a devil of a time keeping myself decent in Tim Lavery's shorts. And she knew my plight. It was eventually a blessing that she decided to go up on the diving board and show off her splendid skills. I do believe she was delighted that I turned down the pantomimed invitation to emulate her. One up at last, in the category of strenuous activity.

As for other sports we indulged in—well, I promise a description of the ultimate seduction scene all of this not-so-innocent foreplay was leading up to (and the very same evening, as a matter of fact). There will be no attempt to designate who was the victor in that match—both of us probably. I'm well aware I might be straying from my political theme to bring in sex so openly, but how can you write a book these days without purposefully including at least one vivid roll in the hay—and it will be literally as it happened between Jill and me, and, moreover, in a political context.

Besides, right now isn't opportune for immersing myself in such an intimate segment of memory. I've just heard my wife's car pull into our driveway. She will be expecting her dutiful hubby to come down and see if she needs any help carting in groceries or, noting the hour, having a bite of lunch together or, if neither is the case, the not-really-optional ritual of paying obeisance to her return. Anyway, whether or not I needed an excuse for interrupting myself, I did have a question for her. Plus, I wanted a break from writing—and reminiscing.

13

"I LOVE YOUR HAIR."

Those were the first words out of my mouth in the kitchen. Jill herself had brought in some groceries, in two small plastic sacks, and was putting stuff away in the refrigerator. Mercifully, I remembered she'd been to the hairdresser, as well as to her meeting and the market. Too often, I flub those little details.

For Jill, while no spring chicken, is still an eyeful. She has plenty of feminine pride, despite that steel-trap mind and quick-trigger tendency to cynicism.

"You noticed?" was her tart-enough remark. But her hand fluttered toward the permanent or whatever arrangement of her locks it was, making it hard for me to believe she wasn't secretly gratified by my attention.

In fact, she invited me to have lunch with her. "I've got cold cuts and I'm making a salad," she said. "Want to join me?"

"Super," I said. Taking a seat in the breakfast nook, watching her, I suddenly asked, "Is this thing tonight at the country club with Ron and Mitzi more than just the four of us? Do we have to get really all gussied up?" However, I must add, these questions were *not* exactly what I had in mind to ask her.

"No, my dear, nobody is joining us," Jill replied in a somewhat arch tone. "But it *is* the country club. We do have to look spiffy."

"Yes, I am well aware that I am, or rather was, an important person in our community," I responded with the same air of mock gravity.

My all-important query was held back until we nearly finished eating.

After taking a last forkful of ham and masticating it thoroughly, I asked, "What are we going to do about Ritchie?"

The words actually just popped out, but the thought had literally been dogging me ever since earlier in the day, when I'd heard our son was safe. In other words, I hadn't let go of my original idea that he was capable of exploding, another budding Miles Monahan, or similar nonsense. Conceivably, my plea to Jill was, in truth, *What are we going to do about my nervousness?*

Jill's reply came within a few seconds. "Disown him," she said, absolutely poker-faced.

Hardly the answer I expected. I felt myself frown. "Perfect," I snapped sarcastically. "We can talk to Ron tonight, get him started on the case."

"Good. Threaten Ritchie," Jill rejoined, "unless he dumps that dingbat."

Still poker-faced, serious, Jill never let her now hard blue eyes leave mine.

"Your little boy. So you'd throw him to the wolves."

"No. Scare him." Was there a glint of amusement cracking her stony façade? Hard to tell.

"Will you go to the wedding if they do get married?"

My shot was like a jab in boxing. Sometimes we don't talk; we spar. Jill sounded deflated, nonetheless, in her retort.

"I suppose I would," my wife sighed. "Otherwise—well, no need to give her an excuse not to let me see any grandchildren they might produce."

I had to marvel at my own contradictions. One moment I had Ritchie as a bomb thrower, a *terrorist,* no less, dispensing mayhem out of hate-filled frustration; and next, I had him domesticated, settled down—and even tough, tough Jill had been sparked to think of grandchildren. Here was Duke's dialectic in spades: chaos/order, side by side, and interchangeable.

To get coffee for us, Jill needed to leave the breakfast nook and go back into the kitchen. Lost in my most recent train of speculation, I wasn't aware of how I looked when she returned. "Are you smirking?" she demanded, putting a full mug down in front of me.

What in tarnation had I been mooning about? Chaos/order. How would I explain it?

"Was I unconsciously smiling?" I answered her question with a question.

"Call it smiling," she said sternly. "I call it smirking."

"In Japan," I said, inspired suddenly to be bold and ridiculous, "the *rictus* you saw, the seemingly absent-minded semi-grin, would signal the first sign I had eaten of a fabulously expensive poison blowfish called fugu, not expertly gutted, with instant death and rigor mortis to follow from a bit of deadly intestine unknowingly consumed. Aargh!" I comically grabbed my throat with both hands. "What did you stick in this coffee, lady?"

Okay, I did earn a slight laugh from her, then a shake of her head, then a furrowed brow. "You're always so frigging intellectual," she commented.

"Speaking of intellectual," I released my windpipe, "think back many years ago, before we were married, to a certain evening when you and I and Governor Duke Ellery had coffee, like we're doing now, in a certain coffee shop at a certain California hotel during a certain National Governors Conference—"

"C'mon, what are you driving at?" she impatiently interrupted.

"Dialectic!" I responded brightly, if mysteriously. "Remember Hegel?"

"Get lost," she groused, finishing the rest of her brew and standing up. "I don't have the time for such nonsense now."

"But you do remember?"

"Vaguely."

Turning her back to me, she soon was at one of the kitchen counters, fiddling at something. Thus was I left alone while quaffing the last of my coffee.

The flashback was of an event that happened on the *second* night of the National Governors Conference. Exactly how the three of us—Jill, Duke, and myself—wound up together at the end of the evening still remains hazy. There'd been a welcoming dinner for everyone, some entertainment, and yet more speechifying. Could the food have been skimpy? Jill and I had gone for a late snack and a "java nightcap." Into the coffee shop, likewise, had walked my boss, who joined us. No Madge, nor their friends. Those three had "avoided the pontificating" (Duke's words) and gone to a show in LA. No Tim, either.

I've often wondered what was in Duke's mind when he saw us. *Should I leave those two lovebirds alone?*—or—*Will they think I'm a snob and a big shot if I don't sit with them?* Or was it truly the hint he gave us: what a great relief it was to talk to someone other than a bunch of governors, which he'd been doing until about ten minutes previously. I won't say he'd had a snootful, but I *had* watched him at the head table, having his wine glass refilled and refilled, an antidote to the tedium, I'd figured.

Normally voluble, Duke seemed especially loosened up with us at the table. Jill, as a press person, didn't inhibit him in the least, and "off the record" wasn't uttered at all. We didn't start with philosophy, either, and most of his talk was about politics and history. Since we three were Statehouse regulars back home, the initial chatter developed a nostalgic tinge as we swapped stories about some of our local characters, starting in, I remember, on the incomparable, unforgettable Honorable Matthew X. Drew, who was still very much alive then.

Tales of Matt Drew were told, one even by Jill.

"Did he ever pinch your bottom?" I asked her rather

brazenly, having had a few alcoholic "pops," myself.

"I'm not telling," she said, looking at me coyly.

Duke, I remember, added, "Did you know he's a great dancer? With all his weight, you'd imagine he could only waddle. The man's a paradox in other ways, too. On the surface, a 'professional politician,' hard as nails, cynical to the core, ruthless. Yet he accomplishes more, does more good, more positive stuff, than the other two hundred, including the senators, put together." Duke paused, reflected, grinned, and concluded, "Tell him so, though, and you'll get an argument and maybe a puff of cigar smoke in the face."

"They say he inhales those little stogies," I volunteered.

"Which is why he has a purple face," Jill chimed in, giggling.

It was so pleasant to hear Duke laugh. Long afterward, Jill told me she, too, had been pleased by his appreciation of her joking. He had loosened his tie—a bright red "power" cravat—and the jacket of his expensive gray business suit had been removed and draped on the back of his chair. With his blue shirt (*always* blue, in case you needed to pose before a television camera), plus highly polished black shoes, he was in the uniform of an important candidate, "dressed seriously." How much had Harvard and centuries of Yankee breeding given him an innate formality, regardless of apparel? And his obvious intelligence, sense of leadership, *charisma,* frankly, always shone through,

Whether it was joshing and familiar: "Compare Matthew Drew and Helen Bailey Pratt," Duke started to say. "But no, wait. I mean their *records,* he always *for,* she always *against.* Imagine them together *physically.* Oh my Lord, what an X rating!" (The vision of the almost 300-plus-pound progressive if wily Democrat and the diminutive right-wing if delightfully ditsy Republican as a *performing* couple did wrench guffaws from Jill and me.)

Or analytical. Duke went on: "As if there's a physics to

American politics invariably spawning a Matt and a Helen. I'll wager if you check every legislature everywhere back to its origins, you'll find equivalents of Matt and Helen in each." With a Kennedyesque smile, he added, "Correction. Matt and Mort until 1920."

His oblique reference to woman suffrage did not escape Jill. "Hooray for the long-overdue change," she felt comfortable enough to add.

I had been coming to the conclusion that Jill didn't really like Duke. Watching her in action in an interview with him, one had the impression of a hard-assed bitch on her best behavior. Behind the outward professional politeness seemed to lie contempt. To her, he was simply another pol, despite his sleek good looks, Ivy League polish, and patently brilliant mind.

Possibly, that late evening, I brought out Jill's best behavior. Had she already set her sights on me as a future mate? It would never do to diss her boyfriend's employer. Or her lover's. For the previous evening—well, I'm still going to get into detail on our initial coupling. . . . But back to the character of Governor Richard N. Ellery.

"Has either of you ever read *The Education of Henry Adams?*" Duke commenced after Jill's plug of applause for the ladies. With simultaneous negative shakes of our heads, we acknowledged neither of us had. "Before Adams taught at Harvard in the 1870s, he studied in Germany," Duke's expository sequence began. "This Massachusetts Brahmin, the great-grandson and grandson of presidents, admitted reading Karl Marx. In *The Education,* Adams states his political creed is that of a 'conservative Christian anarchist.' His anguish about our democracy, the way it seeps out in this quirky autobiography, is something I understand, being a Harvardian and born of the same Puritan stock. The America of the Gilded Age right after the Civil War was running off course. With the slave power vanquished, New Englanders thought New

England ethical values would again prevail in our unified nation. But our body politic, instead, became all muzzy—corrupt bosses, dirty industry, greed, poverty, exploitation of labor, KKK racist terror, and the last gasp of Indians in the Dakotas. Hemispheric contradictions—that Hegelian dialectic I've talked about to you, Jonathan—applied to U.S. history. Adams, by the way, had also read Hegel. It's a theme I think about often and wish I had more time for book reading and study and opportunities to ponder this notion of chaos and order at greater length."

There you have it, as best I can reconstruct the monologue. It was a speech my boss could never have given in public—too brainy, utterly baffling to Joe Six-pack—and in the superficial manner in which journalists view things (sorry, Jill), threatening to define him as too hopeless an egghead.

I believe Duke had a vision. If he had lived and run for president, he would have articulated some of it, and still been elected and reelected. Besides, he was working on the book with which I was helping him—more ammunition for a national campaign. There was lots of stuff about Indians in it. They fascinated him. And he admitted one day, when once more we were discussing Nathaniel Bacon's Rebellion in Virginia in 1674, that the tyrannical English governor revolted against by Bacon had been trying to *protect* Indians and their land. Under Bacon, Democracy was employed to *despoil* Natives. How's that for a contradiction right at the start of the American experience?

All of a sudden, there, by myself in our kitchen alcove, I silently pictured the half a drawer full of files I had on Duke upstairs. CHILDHOOD, SCHOOLING, EARLY WRITINGS, BUSINESS CAREER, SELECTMAN, CONGRESS, GOVERNOR—they were tabbed and arranged in generalized sequence. Equally as quickly, I became antsy to go look at them. Later, I wondered if Jill, busy with her work, didn't find it odd how I abruptly gulped the remaining contents of my cup and bolted for the stairs. Oh, well, someday she might read this and maybe understand.

Can I ever explain to her the fascination that research often exerts? What I had compiled—although riddled with gaps—could have set me up to do several volumes on Duke alone. Yet, I now admit, such was not my aim. Why? Because, I'd finally told myself I would not write this opus for publication (who would print a bio of an obscure governor, even an assassinated one?), but for my own benefit—with my place at the center rather than as an occasional bystander.

Still, I had gathered all this material about Duke but I hadn't gone through it for probably several years.

Back in my office, I first picked out—perhaps logically—the file labeled EARLY WRITINGS. This was the voice of young Duke in his teens, so to speak, and a good way to begin, I thought, to refresh my memory.

Within this file was a large manila folder, stuffed with papers, whose exterior bore the title DIALOGUES. Along with other scattered typed memorabilia sent to me by Duke's half-sister Patricia, this one package had been included in toto and apparently kept so by Duke since he was fourteen or fifteen. The neat block letters of the title Duke had penned himself at that same age.

Before we delve into the one "dialogue" I most wanted to read, a few words are appropriate to introduce Duke's immediate family. Indeed, the interchange I particularly wished to bone up on again involved Duke's older brother Charles, whom Patricia, in her covering letter, referred to as "Bro." Nicknames did appear to flourish in the Ellery household. Patricia, the offspring Duke's father had had with his second wife, was "Paddy." Duke's *true* sister, Eleanor, two years younger than him, was "Sis." In point of fact, the passages I was planning to read anew dealt with Duke's own nickname and its origins.

Without further explanation, I will present Duke's own teenage version of a discussion with his oldest sibling, Bro, about whom I will solely suggest he was (and still is) the most reactionary snob I have ever encountered (but happily only through an uncomfortable telephone conversation) who, if Duke had run for president, would have organized "Ellery Family Members Against Ellery" (a committee of one, I'm sure). Oh, yes, he resides to this day at Helmwood, the family manor, which is in another state, not ours. Although *to the right of those to the right of Attila the Hun* sums up his political views, he never bestirred himself to sabotage his kid brother's career in our jurisdiction, but going national for president would have been a different matter.

Here's what Duke recorded when they were both under twenty years of age:

BRO: *Where did you get that silly nickname of Duke? You don't act anything like a real duke.*

D.: *How so?*

BRO: *I saw you laughing with Lonny.*

D.: *Right. Oops, I forgot—he's only a stablehand—and black, an almost purply black man* [underlined in the original, too].

BRO: *A real duke maintains dignity at all times. Remember, kid, a duke is just one step below a king.*

D.: *Oops, I forgot again. Had you been here at the time of the American Revolution, Bro, you would have been a Redcoat, a damn Lobsterback. You Tory, you still don't recognize our independence.*

BRO: *(negatively) Bad deal, all around. And don't call me Bro.*

D.: *Okay, Charles—Charles I. In the English Civil War, you would have lost your head. And in ours, you would have been rooting for the slave owners, wouldn't you?*

BRO: *(nodding) Now, you're talking about a way of life. Ducal. Absolutely ducal.*

Genealogy isn't exactly my schtik, as Miles taught me they say in Hollywood. I understand you can spend years tracing ancestors, and with Duke's bloodlines, you'd have to search way back in England and even Scandinavia. To spare myself and you, dear readers, I will simply parade the Ellery clan, those whom I encountered, in the guise of a dramatis personae, briefly on stage. I never got to meet the patriarch, Charles C. (for Chandler, his mother's surname) Ellery, still alive but in a fancy nursing home after a useful life as business tycoon, big-game fisherman, environmentalist, polo player, and philanthropist. Known apparently only by the appellation "Father," he had sired Bro, Duke, and Sis with his first wife, a Foxcroft; and thus Bro was Charles F. Ellery, instead of Charles C. Jr. With their mother deceased, the three children were then presented a half-sister whose nickname of Paddy had been Duke's teasing invention, to honor their Celtic stepmother, Moe, nee Maureen O'Donnell, a former maid in the Ellery household. Bro had been horrified, scandalized, utterly outraged by this marriage but had never dared to cross Father or criticize Moe until—under the old English tradition of primogeniture, he had inherited the entire Helmwood estate.

There. That's probably enough coats-of-arms chasing for now.

Paddy, who (no surprise) was Duke's favorite sibling, had salvaged those writings of Richard N. (for Nathaniel) Ellery, which, as she said in her note, "Bro would have had burned." She was putting them in my keeping, she indicated, because I seemed "the one person who gave a damn about my half-brother's legacy." I had met her once long ago, upon the occasion of a visit she made to the governor's office. I was asked to photograph this vivacious, more redheaded than blonde, charmer. Why she preferred to let *me* have Duke's papers instead of Madge is an explanation I've never sought. But I wasn't surprised when the material arrived.

Duke's blue-blooded ancestry was nothing he ever took seriously. (Madge, I believe, did.) He loved to tell about Franklin D. Roosevelt's opening address to the Daughters of the American Revolution that began "My fellow immigrants." A pet line of his own was "We Ellerys didn't get to these shores until 1632, more than 11,000 years after our Indian neighbors." For kicks, not because Duke requested it, I did do a traditional book search for him of the family tree, from Nathaniel Ellery, the earliest New World progenitor (b. 1601, d. 1653), and the succession of begats, numerous Richards, Charleses, and Nathaniels—and the female infusions through Chandlers, Foxcrofts, et al. Of this WASP horde, their geographical provenance in England, alone, interested Duke, due to its effect on American history. Especially East Anglia, birthplace of the first Nathaniel. My boss would talk about the *Danelaw,* installed by "an invasion of wild, tow-headed Scandinavians who, having descended upon that chunk of Great Britain's coast, raping and pillaging, grew gaga over the countryside and the allure of the local ladies and stayed." I remember him, too, regaling a group of English tourists in his office. Touching the gold of his hair, he'd declared, "Behold, evidence of the Danish gene pool." With a bold segue to what he called "the political gene pool," he'd also told this audience how his Puritan forebears had brought to Massachusetts a mode of handling public business, likewise transplanted from East Anglia: "Selectman and town meeting. They'd already invented those institutions. No other major part of England had them." And the final piece of this discourse involved the Native Americans with whom the early Ellerys had commingled, imbibing ideas of Indian democracy which collided with Anglo notions of monarchy and class structure.

Duke's preoccupation with our nation's tribes was, one might say, *intrinsic,* and certainly not smart politics. Or was it ultra-clever, really? The meeting in Colorado with the western Indian leaders—brief, low-key, no press, no staff except for Harry DeWitt—had been carefully prearranged, ostensibly to build support for the resolution we were presenting at the Governors' Conference. But rather, in truth, it was designed to head off opposition—western Indians versus eastern Indians, since Duke was proposing that *all* Indians be eligible for federal largesse and these westerners then had a monopoly. *Increase the pot* was Duke's intention, and he at least won the chiefs' neutrality while making superb contacts.

In the flow of my thoughts, as I sat with the portfolio of Duke's juvenile scribblings spread before me, I, too, wondered: Who first had called him Duke? Nothing in the old-fashioned typewritten pages provided an answer.

Should I go to press without that answer? As a conscientious historian, what should I do? Policy question. How essential is such a nugget of information? Absolutely critical, I suppose, were I to use DUKE as my title. Had I decided on a straight biography—third person stuff, footnotes, etc.—the Duke nickname mystery would need to be cleared right up front. Since, however, I'm creating this autobiography/biography for my own—well, not exactly amusement, but more like inner gratification and expiation—and not worrying about publication, I'm free at last, oh Lord, free to fart around literarily.

Still, one must remain accurate, thorough, and utterly factual.

Let me call my present excursion into Governor Richard N. Ellery's past a momentary digression. Others will occur inevitably, plumbed from all of my voluminous files—arbitrarily, too, but I assure you, I will try to keep injecting some method into my madness.

Very well, back to the National Governors Conference. I realize I brought you by plane to Los Angeles, and went swimming with my honey-to-be on the first day of the four-day event, then switched you unapologetically to the night of the second day and our end-of-the-evening coffee klatch with Duke.

The gap between those two events, separated in time and substance—splashing playfully versus listening to philosophy—is thus closed, and I hope from now on for a more concise, sequenced narrative.

14

To begin sensationally, at last here's the seduction scene!

Following our late afternoon dunk in the pool, a laze on beach chairs, another drink or two, Jill and I agreed to do supper together. It was hardly romantic in a massive hotel dining room full of boisterous pols, but we managed to end up by ourselves at a small corner table.

Her décolletage had set me a-buzz from the moment when, picking her up at her room (which she *occupied entirely alone*), I first beheld it. The blue dress had been replaced by a low-cut black sheath clinging to every silhouette of her softness. How my hands itched to feel yielding flesh and fabric, how my eyes kept wandering to those amazing orbs, her half-hidden breasts, those silk-clad legs, longing to touch them, too, to explore upward to unimaginable satiny pleasures hidden enticingly beneath the skirt of her garment. More sexy yet was the sense Jill somehow displayed that she wanted the same treatment from a reverse point of view, passive to my active, as soon as we finished wining and dining and could retire to appropriate privacy.

Unspoken decorum, subtly inculcated American Puritanism, I imagine, bade us not rush to her quarters and pop into bed right after dinner. Hand in hand or arm in arm, we essentially window-shopped in the hotel for more than an hour. An entire lower floor had been given over to glitzy stores. Neither of us could afford any of those goodies we saw on display and occasionally even examined inside, but it was fun pretending we were a couple of swells. Only in the inevitable sundries type of catchall boutique were the prices cut-rate enough for us, and I bought Jill her very first present from me—a stuffed, cuddly, German shepherd puppy. She had spied the appealing little creature, oohed and aahed, calling *him* "Rex," after a real live pet she'd had in her childhood, and we'd left it there—kind of too pricey. Not long afterward, while still on this same level, we had our initial kiss— just spontaneously, without words, ducking into the shadows under a staircase, a prolonged, passionate clinch accompanied by groping, stroking hands. Able to breathe finally, she asked huskily, mischievously, "What do you say, sailor? Shall we go up to my place?"

"I'd be deeply honored," I replied in a similar coy tone.

"No, I hope I will be," she whispered in my ear.

Her suggestive, naughty retort, besides inflaming my libido, endeared her to me in a way I can hardly explain. No doubt it helped account for the impulse I had, en route with her to the elevators, passing the "Sundries" sign, to say "Hold on a sec" so I could go and purchase the doggy. Everything about her reaction, her protest to save my money, her little girl delight when I returned and presented a package, her rapid opening of the box and instant embrace of the furry toy, tugged at my heartstrings. Who then should happen along at that very moment but my roomie Tim Lavery, out to buy a magazine.

"Look what Jonathan bought me," Jill exclaimed to Tim, holding up the stuffed German shepherd pup. "Now I've got a police dog. You guys can train him when he grows up."

Grim-lipped even in repose, the tough state trooper nodded. To my surprise, he also spoke. "If the mutt ever does grow up, send him over," he said in an effort at reciprocating humor. Again, as with his loan to me of his extra bathing trunks, this surly seeming cop had humanized himself.

The rest is an intimate, highly private slice of personal history. I don't remember reading in any biography of a famous public official any detailed description of his or her wedding night or first seduction. It's inconceivable for me to picture Duke and Madge "doing it" (they'd created two kids together) had I chosen a conventional approach to writing my late boss's life. Besides, I've gone titillatingly far already. So I might as well plunge on—no pun intended.

My career most likely is finished. No opponents, no ammunition for them. Jill? Well, I could keep this part out of the manuscript.

Why do I go on stalling?

Okay, we were not alone in the elevator, nor in the corridor leading to to her room. The best we could do for contact was snuggle together. Thus entwined, we entered the chamber, locked the door behind us, furiously embraced. One of my hands was immediately up under her dress, fulfilling my earlier fantasies of touch. My fingers stroked; then, it was breast time, both hands moving to both of hers, at the same time we were passionately French-kissing. We sank together to the soft rug. We were grappling like wrestlers. She removed the first pieces of clothing—mine: my jacket, my tie, my shirt, my undershirt. As if tit-for-tat, I pulled her dress way over her hips. The overhead light was shining. What a sexy spectacle—garter belt, stockings, sleek mauve panties, uplifted white half-slip against black interior cloth. Somehow, wiggling about, Jill managed to undo her zipper or whatever allowed her to raise her entire dress free of her body. Off with the bra (also white). I did it and the rest of the undies, with my help, followed. She, in turn, undressed my bottom parts, including shoes and socks.

On top of Jill, I was ready to thrust myself inside her when she gave me a gentle push away. Before I could utter *What?* she was saying, "Wait a second, darling," and wriggling out from under me. Savoring her word of endearment, I watched, more curious than worried, as she opened a drawer of her bureau and rummaged through it. What did she finally remove? Her lovely naked body headed into the bathroom. *Diaphragm*, I thought. A sound of running water, on, off, and she was back, soon sliding under me to her previous position.

We didn't need any words. Just kissed, while I "honored her deeply." Grunts, moans, sighs—a cacophony of low-volume sounds—did she cry out during the first of my ejaculations that first night? Or was it the second time, on the edge of the bed when I took her from the back? Or in the wee hours, after some sleep, throwing off the covers, with her sitting on top of me?

Hints of dawn were beyond the window at the end of this third climax.

"You know I really ought to get down to my room," I finally said to Jill.

She hugged me tightly. "I don't want you to go," she said.

"But you know I have to," I said. "All my stuff is there, things I need for work and to shave and—"

"Of course," Jill interrupted.

"You can sleep now, and you have work to do this morning, too," I told Jill, kissing her on the forehead.

"Mmmm," she made a cozy murmur.

"Maybe see you at breakfast?"

"Mmmm. . . ."

She was pulling the blanket up to her chin, turning on her side, a shadowy figure in the semidarkness, throughout my hurried dressing.

Outside, able to see my watch by the light in the hallway, I figured I could still get a couple of more hours sleep, myself. I'd let Tim rise ahead of me, occupy the bathroom, snooze as long as I could. I was dead beat, but exhilarated.

Our room was darker than Jill's had been. The drapes were pulled. I tiptoed carefully, making sure which of the twin beds was mine, undressing noiselessly, dumping my clothes on the floor, not bothering with brushing my teeth or washing my face. A gleam of white growing evident the moment my eyes adjusted to the blackness revealed that Tim had left me a note on a letter-sized sheet of paper. I folded it, left it on the bedside table, and dropped happily off to sleep.

Upon waking, the earliest conscious thoughts I had were of Jill and what we had done, and they were full of amorous emotion, too. Then I saw the note and opened it up.

Tim had written in his careful, almost printed, cursive script, "I need to tell you. Your friend Murray called."

A minute later, I realized what this meant.

"Oh, shit," I actually whispered aloud. "It's Miles, goddamn him!"

Cursing Miles was instinctual, while moments later, intellectual honesty had me admit I had no one to blame but myself. Hadn't I advised him I was coming to LA and when and why? Worse, I had really wanted to show off my attendance at the National Governors Conference. Yet also, at this pre-Jill juncture in time, hadn't I been sincere about getting together with my old buddy for old time's sake, weird as he'd been acting?

Not that I could afford to ruminate on the matter. Tim was out of the bathroom, almost wholly dressed, strapping on his holstered gun. I was already five minutes late if I were to try to meet Jill for breakfast and then reach the committee room by 9:00 A.M.

"You got my note, I see," Tim called to me, just before he left.

"Yup," I said as I went to shave and shower.

"How do you know this guy?" Tim asked. "Kinda pushy, isn't he?"

I stopped. "Friend from home," I said. "Since elementary school. For the moment, he's gone Hollywood."

"Well, tell Murray to call earlier in the future."

There it was again, "Murray," that silly pun of a name Miles had given himself—O. Murray Carr, our cutesy play on "America." Did he realize he was talking to a state trooper on the phone—while employing an alias? Part of my high dudgeon, I suppose, was fear—or rather, annoyance—of Miles causing complications for me, even trouble, with his antics.

It was theoretical fear. If I hunkered down, refused to call him back, I figured I could be free of the pest. So what if he kept on phoning me? This was a gated community, as full of security as any location in the U.S.—fifty contingents of state bodyguards and the Secret Service, too! Without credentials, Miles couldn't possibly set foot inside. No doubt I've taken it for granted you readers recognize I'm writing about a period prior to the invention of cell phones and minicams. High-tech security in those days, it seems to me in retrospect, was a sort of walkie-talkie arrangement.

The same morning, about to enter the committee room where I was supposed to be, I noticed a bunch of burly guys standing outside it. *The fuzz,* I thought automatically. Their haircuts, if nothing else, gave them away, and those enamel badges in their lapels, not to mention the guys who had plug-like buttons in their ears. Tim was standing among them and I got introduced and hung out for a few minutes. They were an affable, wisecracking group. I have always remembered the following joshing exchange, although at the time it was only offhand and rather sardonically funny.

"Okay, I need to go do a few errands," said a tall, brutish type as he turned to leave. "If some nut shoots my boss, please be sure to get his address and home telephone number."

"Sure thing, Sarge," the same wry cynicism answered him. "Count on us."

Gallows humor. But all those hard-faced cops were grinning. Clutching my briefcase, I proceeded into the committee room and realized belatedly that no one had checked me out for a weapon.

I wasn't late. Actually, I'd skipped breakfast after perusing the coffee shop and seeing no sign of Jill.

Here's a confession: I was secretly almost glad not to have to face her right away *the morning after*. Or I thought I was until I looked and saw her in the committee room. She was interviewing Duke. Her cameraman, whose back was to me, had his apparatus trained on the two of them while Jill held up a mike to my boss. As I watched, I was once more blown away by her beauty. I could hardly believe it had been me with her last night (nor could I tamp down a churning feeling stirring within my body once more).

The seating arrangements for the meeting had spaces for the committee chair, vice chair, and committee secretariat at one end, plus flanking rows to accommodate the rest of the governors and their accompanying entourages. At Duke's place were two chairs in addition to his. I took the nearest, sat, opened my briefcase, extracted a folder, glanced around, waited. I caught sight of George Everoff in the room. No sign of Harry DeWitt. So I surmised our fussy press secretary would be my staff companion for the morning. Sure enough, once Duke's interview with Jill ended, Georgie accompanied our boss to the assigned spot we had, which, incidentally, was marked by a miniature banner on a stand bearing the football colors of our state's leading team. A distraction I later allowed myself when the proceedings turned tedious was trying to guess each of the colleges or universities represented in the room, somewhat like the game I'd played with Jill.

My honey and her cameraman hadn't lingered after they'd done their job. I'd managed only to catch her eye for a quick exchange of smiles before the two went out the door. She'd turned for a final peek in my direction just prior to the arrival of

Duke and Georgie at my side. Thereafter, I had to give my attention principally to the governor. Did he need anything? "Talking points," for example? I knew he never brought documents with him; usually spoke off the cuff instead of using any set speech Harry or I had written. I was thanked, no, he was fine—and then Duke promptly got right back up again, going over to a governor he wanted to lobby—Tennessee, it looked like, from the single orange and white little triangular flag in front of the guy.

Government meetings rarely start on time. The committee chairman was in his seat, but blabbing away to people around him. George Everoff, sitting next to me, was showing a smirky, self-satisfied air, I thought. Suddenly, while I was impatiently watching the chairman converse, I felt Georgie tap my shoulder.

"See that bald guy wearing the red vest and green tie?"

"Talking to the chairman?"

"Do you know who he is?"

This small snatch of dialogue between us has been reconstructed. What it fails to convey is the press secretary's unctuous mannerisms. Shit-eating grin'll have to do it.

"I haven't the foggiest notion."

Georgie leaned forward, conspiratorial-style, and whispered a name to me.

I whistled. This was that famous columnist.

"Wants to interview the boss after the end of this meeting," Georgie told me, all puffed up as if he'd scored a coup.

I humored him. "Good work, Everoff," I said.

"I didn't *exactly* arrange it," he confessed. His pudgy, high-cheekboned face contained pale Slavic gray eyes, which blinked several times as he continued. "I couldn't believe it when the boss told me. He wants to write about the Indian thing."

I shook my head. "No, I'll bet he wants a promo on the *presidential* thing." My own eyes then went to the figure of Duke across the table, in earnest conversation with Governor Tennessee. "Just pray to God, my friend" I said, confronting Georgie again, "that the boss has got this whole *Indian thing* iced. I'd hate to see a line in that article saying, 'But failed to get a resolution passed in his own National Governors Conference committee.'"

Time to point out a few subtleties. I know it irritated Georgie for me to sometimes call him *Georgie.* But long ago he'd stopped correcting me. There wasn't a lot of fight in the guy, just a raft of pettiness and touches of paranoia. He came from a prominent political family in a heavily Polish/Slavic section of our state. Yet Duke, he knew, would never keep him on unless he handled his duties well, which he did. No matter how hard I tried, I could never quite convince him that I wasn't a rival for his job. So I thought now sadistically, *Why not sweat him with suspense, make him fear a loss in the committee vote, the specter of a great national article dampened if not ruined?*

Fat chance. Harry and I and Duke had carefully gone over the politics of the initiative. We'd counted noses, to be exact. Sometimes these resolutions, ephemeral as they might seem, were argued vociferously. Any trouble we could have would be with western governors—only one of whom was on the committee—and besides, we had covered all bases of opposition from the western tribes at the meeting of the chiefs in Colorado, where Duke had made a fantastic impression. In my mind, at least, the Indian thing seemed a *slam-dunk,* in today's parlance, but Georgie Everoff didn't know it.

Clairvoyant, I certainly was. Smug, too, as they called the roll of committee members. Duke didn't lose a single vote. The sole western governor issued a few tame remarks of "concern" and abstained. The resolution (word for word, as I'd written it) was soon on its way to enter the National Governors Conference's annals. Its adoption the next day at the plenary session would be a mere formality.

Well do I remember listening to therest of the debate in the committee room. It was hardly anything the governors said—I have a lifetime of memories of such banal, hortatory chitchat. The crux in this case was that Jill and her cameraman had returned and were filming the whole affair for a local audience back home.

Even had Demosthenes or Cicero been orating, I would have found it hard to concentrate. How often in the life of a man does he look at a woman and say to himself, *I want to marry that girl?* In my situation, only once, and it was right then, moments after she started working, directing what camera shots she wanted and from what angles. Whichever way I glanced, it seemed, she was in and out of my view. Breathtaking. Yet I tried to maintain my inner dignity. The phrase "lovesick puppy" was going round and round in my head. It implied surrender, weakness, passivity. But I swore I would never grovel to win her. Win her, though, I must. Unthinkable, now, suddenly, was the idea we'd be a one-night, two-night, even three-night stand, out in California, and then go our separate ways back on the other coast.

To a certain extent, the successful passage of the Indian resolution was a wrap-up to the four days and three nights of our convention activities. Tomorrow, there would be the opening plenary session during the day and a dinner and entertainment at night. Following another plenary session the next day, the president would address us in the evening, with a "gala" afterward. The big party was the climax. On the fourth day, Duke's committee had a breakfast meeting and then we were homeward bound—no stops, west to east, Harry had indicated; the *boss* (read Madge) was anxious to get home.

Since the taxpayers were footing the bill for this—well, quasi-junket—we couldn't duck out entirely with only one morning's worth of work accomplished. Attendance at those plenary sessions was obligatory (but they didn't last too long). Failing to hear the president would be an insult to his high office and no doubt a lost opportunity to bore my grandchildren by telling the story someday. Free food and booze even at an official speech-filled dinner was always stupid to pass up, leaving us still plenty of recreation time. Because the press goofed off, as well, we weren't at all concerned they might rat to their respective media outlets about our behavior.

I mean, how dare the public begrudge us a dip in the Pacific? Yes, swimming was possible. The beach to which our gang of young people was bused seemed full of surfers, most of whom wore wetsuits because they stayed in the water so long. The liquid temperature, while hardly tropical, was definitely tolerable for those of us used to the northern Atlantic. I believe, also, there had been an El Niño that year to warm up the West Coast seas.

No matter. Jill and I did venture in once. Mostly we lay on a blanket, side by side, wrapped in beach towels, aroused but content with a minimum of touching, talking a lot instead. Beyond just sex, which was good. We were getting to know each other, hopefully to love each other.

Whoever had arranged our outing had included food—a veritable barbecue—and music—several guitar players. Jill and I partook, like the others, in both these distractions. Wanna-bes, political guys and gals on the make, rising young professionals—whatever you wanted to call us—we were a bunch of American kids, blacks intermingled among the whites, Asians, too, having a good old-fashioned time together. Like their elders, American youngsters bond pretty easily, laugh generously, joke incessantly, sing songs they all know. Most of us had been strangers a few hours earlier. Some of us were political antagonists. Who cared?

It would have been a perfect afternoon in my estimation except for a certain nagging, sporadic tug at my conscience.

Miles Monahan, again. The sonofabitch had actually had me paged at the hotel. While I was standing at the entrance with Jill and George Everoff and a whole group waiting for the bus to the beach, one of the print media guys from our state came out and said they were calling my name inside.

At the concierge's desk, a phone was put at my disposal. I wasn't too worried the bus would leave without me. Jill and others would make sure I boarded, so I'd rushed back inside because I thought the summons might be from Duke. When I heard Miles's voice, I was—frankly—*bullshit*.

Worse, he opened with, "Jonathan Jackson, this is O. Murray Carr."

I almost slammed down the receiver. "Oh, crap, Miles—not now!" I fairly shrieked.

"I called yesterday," he shot back. "You never answered."

"I'm busy, Miles. I'm up to my eyeballs in work!"

It was the earliest of my fibs. The purpose of his call, which he soon blurted out, was that he planned to come to the hotel to see me. This very afternoon!

"Impossible!" I cried.

"Why?"

"I'm in meetings with my boss. Working on an important speech."

From fib to outright lie, I was aware. Miles argued. Didn't I have to take a break?

"Sorry." I noticed the bus had arrived. "Maybe tomorrow. I'll call you tomorrow."

And I hung up on him.

Theoretically, a kind of amnesia regarding my pest of an old hometown friend should have established itself for the rest of the visit. Amid the fun at the ocean, the infrequent splotches of guilt I experienced were weak enough; furthermore, they immediately turned into silent, outward-directed anger: *Damn you, Miles, you selfish bastard*, or *What do you want from me now, you prick?* or *Grow up, Mr. O. Murray Carr, ha, ha, ha.* In retrospect, I was being objectively unfair to Miles.

By the end of the afternoon, I'd simply forgotten about him. Returning to the hotel, Jill and I were heading to her room. Our hours of semi-chaste, half-naked proximity had both of us as horny as could be—our understanding, whispered in so many innuendoes, was that we were programmed for a "quickie" before needing to get ready for tonight's fancy dinner. In the lobby, however, to my surprise, I was approached by Tim Lavery, who had apparently been waiting for me.

"Jonathan, could I speak to you for a minute?"

His tone was so serious, his mien so solemn, that reluctant as I was, I had to say, "Sure."

Jill understood this was *business.* Her eyes told me she would meet me up at her room as soon as I could get away.

"What's up, Tim?" I asked, the moment she was out of earshot.

Until he spoke, I wasn't really baffled. Duke had sent him, I figured. Maybe some emergency piece of writing needed to be done.

But Tim said, "There's some guys here I want you to come and talk to."

Couched in the bland politeness of a state trooper asking to see your license and registration, those words sent a shiver through me.

The three men whom Tim took me to meet were quickly introduced. Agent This, Agent That—Secret Service, I gathered, although I never saw any badges. In my memory, they have remained a fused set of disembodied voices.

One of them startled me with the information that, in my absence, a Mr. Murray Carr had tried to enter the hotel compound, claiming he had an appointment with Jonathan Jackson of Governor Ellery's staff.

"It couldn't be confirmed and he was sent away."

"Kicked up quite a rumpus. Made threats. Used foul language."

"Jesus!" I erupted. "He *knew* I wasn't available! What a pain in the ass he can be! Doesn't listen! Just like when we were kids!"

All exclamations, my surprise and indignation were unfeigned. If any cunning existed in my diatribe, it was my failure fully to expose the little white lie I'd told Miles—how I was working at the hotel—thus tempting him to barge in on me. Had I dared, I would have asked if they'd told him I'd gone to the beach. I could simply hope Miles had been utterly stonewalled. And yet, so what if he learned I'd prevaricated? He was known to tell far more than a few whoppers himself.

On the other hand, my would-be inquisitors were semi-apologetic. The president was coming; they had to be extra careful; Tim had vouched for me, confirming that this guy Murray Carr had tried to reach me by phone. Anything else they should know about him?

Here was the dicey part—telling them he was using an alias. But, if nothing else, besides being pissed off, I felt I had to cover myself, be cooperative.

"One thing," I commenced, "is that Murray Carr, or O. Murray Carr, as he prefers, isn't his real name. He's an actor. I guess he uses it as his professional movie stage name now. Actually, his real name is Miles Monahan."

"A Hollywood actor?"

"Aspiring."

An exchange of looks and nods seemed to generate a lack of further interest. I was thanked for the information; in effect, dismissed.

"If you need his address in LA. . . ."

"We'll be in touch."

Walking away, I didn't know whether to focus my rage on Miles or myself. Probably Miles, for acting like Miles. Crossing the lobby, I was dredging up memories from our boyhood, incidents where he'd angered me and lied. I was almost at Jill's door when I recalled—for the first time, honestly—the nonsense this past summer with guns at the lake and the talk about presidential assassinations. *It would have served him right,* I thought, savoring the vicious idea, *to have told those G-men and gotten Miles into real trouble.*

What comforted me for a moment was the realization that I still could hold that weird business over Miles's head.

Jill's door opened to my special knock. The sight of the lovely lady in lingerie holding a stuffed-toy German shepherd puppy was more than ample reward for the aggravation I'd suffered. Instantly forgetting Miles, I hurried into her arms.

15

I SAT BACK. Again, it was like waking up—a sharp return to present reality. Everything I write nowadays, I do on the computer, word-processing as if in a trance, remembering, composing mentally, typing, saving, making hard copies. Hours can pass and the stack of printed pages on my desk will mount.

Home from long-ago California in my mind, affirming with a glance out the nearby window that the ocean was on *the correct side,* I temporarily wondered: Should I give memory a rest? Or what about switching to the file I had amassed on Miles, changing the focus to *his* perspective?

Question No. 1: How could I document that Miles, on his foray to the hotel, ostensibly to see me, was, in effect, intending to "case the joint"? His writings were seized following the killing of Duke and, frankly, I've never dared to ask for them. They had been packed in the trunk of his jalopy, in which he'd been living after leaving his apartment, an event estimated by police inspectors to have occurred two or three days *before* I arrived in LA.

Question No. 2: How could Miles, apparently homeless, expect I could ever phone him back? Answer: Easy. Like most aspiring actors, he had an answering service, so as not to miss the always anticipated "big break" news of stardom beckoning, and it was a luxury he hadn't canceled.

Question No. 3: Why was I still pussyfooting around in my own private inquiries regarding Miles Monahan? Understandably, immediately post-tragedy, I felt scared shitless I might be linked to him as a co-conspirator. Several years later, the GOP effort to smear me failed miserably. Okay, this may make you laugh. What if I do run for office again?

There is no fool like an old fool. Until now, this deep, dark secret thought of mine had never been revealed to a living soul. That included Ron Gordon—and Jill—and any invitation I might receive tonight to do so was pure speculation, if not utter fantasy.

With this thought in mind, I posited Question Nos. 4 and 5 to myself. *Do I really want to stick my neck out once more?* and *Is defeat, or rather, failure, un-American?*

I considered Miles Monahan a prime example on the latter score. The twerp had chosen to wrap himself in a name, "O. Murray Carr," as if in a star-spangled flag, his last-ditch pathetic gimmick for seeking success. The use of an Uncle Sam bit had no doubt seemed brilliant to him. *Yankee Doodle Dandy.* Jimmy Cagney as George M. Cohan. How Miles loved that movie. At the drop of a hat, when we were kids, he would do his Cagney song and dance imitation, ". . . a real live nephew of my Uncle Sam, born on the Fourth of July."

During my earlier trip to Los Angeles, just prior to meeting Duke, Miles had dragged me to a re-run theater because the Cagney film was playing. We had dates, a couple of bimbo starlets. What a night! My old pal had been irrepressible, performing nonstop, cracking jokes like a stand-up comic, quite manic. Even back at his apartment with the girls, he was on. Truthfully, I've always been grateful I never got the clap, or worse, from my visit. But what the hell, we were two young, lusty bachelors with no caution about possible dangers ahead.

Neither was good fortune foreseen. My pure dumb luck again. On the way home, I boarded an airplane and randomly, a certain politician sat beside me.

Or had the divergence between the two of us already been a long time in the making? A strong *maybe* was my answer so far.

Switching to childhood memories of Miles might help bring a bit more clarity, I considered.

My childhood home was on the same block as the Monahans'. We all had lawns, trees, flower gardens, presenting a budding suburbia. The Margolises were on the next street over. Out of the city ghettos, Jewish, Irish, Italian, Greek offspring were making it into a new world of their own creation. We WASPs were barely a majority so close to the urban center. Intermarriage was not uncommon, even in my family. A mixture of Huguenot and Scots-Irish on my father's side, plain English on my mother's, I had first cousins in Chicago whose mother was Croatian and they were being raised as Catholics. Then, too, in the neighborhood, we had the example of the Fineberg kids, Randy and Priscilla. Their mother was as Irish as the Monahans. Taken for Jewish, they weren't Jews, our friend Gerry Margolis explained. "You can't be Jewish if your mother isn't, unless you convert and they don't make it easy." Nor did their mother raise them Catholic. A new breed, so to speak. I had a crush on Prissy Fineberg in the seventh and eighth grades, but she liked Miles better.

"He's fun," Prissy once told me. I guessed I wasn't, which hurt. Before then, I'd excused her preference on some *Irish thing* they had through their mothers. But how could I be more like Miles? I couldn't act. I didn't sing. I lacked daring. My joke-telling was awful. To be sure, I was a better athlete. Girls were supposedly impressed by jocks. But was I too cerebral to play first-string varsity or ladykiller? I certainly envied my friend whatever secret knack he had with the opposite sex. I often put it down to the fact he had sisters, while I never had anyone to coach me, no older brother even.

My parents? In those days, you didn't talk about such matters with them. Probably kids still don't. I can't remember Jill and I ever having any intimate conversations with Ritchie. Like me, he grew up an only child.

I know it was fashionable during the era when Freudianism was riding high, to whipsaw parents, to visit the sins of the sons upon the fathers. Shall Michael and Bridget Monahan face indictment for the heinous crime Miles committed? Unwitting co-conspirators? Both, incidentally, were dead by the time of the shooting.

In retrospect, my images of Michael and Bridget are highly selective. It was from his mother that Miles derived his freckles. "Sandy Irish," he jokingly called her, not "Shanty Irish." The father was partly bald, thin, pale, bespectacled, witty and bright— a bank executive. They actually had *lace curtains* in their house. And crucified Christs on the walls.

My parents and the Monahans knew each other as neighbors. The same with the Margolises. None of these families socialized with each other. But there was no objection to their children's doing so. I'm told this is one of the cultural mores that makes America different from Europe and other places.

Here's my bias, then. I'm no Freudian. I'm more for *Nurture* than *Nature.* It was as if Miles had caught a germ from the very air of the USA. Why else did he call himself, as it were, "Mr. America"? Why morph into Uncle Sam? Crucified, not on a cross of gold, but of red, white, and blue. *I can't believe I'm going to fail. I'll show them—make a name for myself, no matter if it's in infamy.*

Was it combined with—perchance a stressed tilt of brain chemistry—a touch of temporary madness, manic exultation? But I don't mean to sound like a defense lawyer. The bastard knew he was doing wrong, including enmeshing me, whether by malevolent design or unthinking accident or both, into his web of fury.

Since, in my office, we were now into December, darkness came early. Without remembering doing so, I turned on the lights. Lo and behold, it was soon time for me to dress for dinner and decamp with my bride for the Swanstown Country Club.

Once upon a time, I must explain, this institution was really hoity-toity, exclusive as could be. Nowadays, it's still not easy to become a member, but not because of your pedigree. There's a mammoth waiting list for golf and a fairly robust one for tennis. Thanks to Ron, Jill and I belonged to the club, had for years. Occasionally, with the Gordons, we were a foursome at tennis. Jill and Mitzi were out on the links quite frequently; me, never, Ron at least twice a week with local guys. The wholly non-snooty part of the operation was the restaurant, open all year to everyone, but very pricey. When we ate there with the Gordons, not an uncommon occurrence, we always went Dutch. Except tonight, we were to be their guests—most unusual—on Ron's nickel.

As you know, my answer as to why had been instinctively: *That sonofabitch; he's going to try to get me to run for the state senate!*

Peg McEntee had announced her retirement several months ago. The Republicans already had a candidate. To my knowledge, the Democrats didn't.

An open seat! No incumbent!

I would never have considered for a fraction of a second running against my good friend Peggy, and not only because she would have beaten my ass. She truly was my *friend* (rather than simply in the anodyne way we pols often refer to each other), a pal who'd done legitimate favors for me, with whom I'd teamed up on bills we'd cosponsored to help our region. Ditto, even after I'd left the house and was up in the capital, helping out local groups.

With the path clear and a little-known Republican on their ticket, what should my response be?

Play hard to get? Openly question what was in it for me? A chance to serve in the so-called "Upper Body?" Big deal. But it *would* be a new experience, a new perspective on government, and I could continue to work on this quixotic book project of mine, too.

Jill would agree to my running again, I was almost sure.

However, on the ride to the country club, I had no plans to discuss anything with her. We went in Jill's car and I was pretty quiet. I'd told her how nice she looked, and that was about it. She had thanked me for the compliment and stayed mostly silent as she drove.

Her perfume smelled good, as it always did, exuding femininity. I knew I shouldn't stare at her. It made her self-conscious. She was always fussing about her appearance, hating the aging process, although it had really been quite kind to her. As I turned away to gaze out the car window on my side, I caught a jeweled glimmer—one of a pair of gold and diamond earrings I had given her on a certain occasion.

Was life just one memory after another? To be sure, this precise moment in Jill's Ford Taurus, plus this evening at the country club, would soon be among my remembrances, too. Was the amassing of recollections simply the essence of the aging process? Part of *entropy*, a breakdown of mind and body in a slow race to the final snuffing out?

We soon had headed away from the ocean and were traveling inland up Elm Street through the center of Swanstown. As my thoughts had grown unexpectedly morbid, I found I was gazing at the First Parish cemetery for the umpty-umpth time. The phrase was somehow itching me: old home week; also a remembered line from a hymn: "In the sweet by and by, we shall meet on that beautiful shore." Less darkly, I switched mentally to the Reunion Day we had each year at the legislature, followed immediately by the unspoken realization: *Good God, am I seriously considering going back to the capital full time?*

My wife, I swear, is an intuitive clairvoyant and has mystical mind-reading powers. Out of nowhere, she broke the silence by asking, "Are you actually making any significant progress on your book?"

I could suppose it was an idle, friendly inquiry. Then again, it could be a loaded question, a trap even. Was she privy, via Mitzi Gordon, to information I didn't know? If so, did she fear by my running again, that I might once more avoid the long-put-off pain of getting Duke out of my system?

"I'm making progress," I said, whatever that meant.

"Great," she said.

All further talk ceased until we reached the country club. And maybe this paradigm is the fate of every couple who ages together. There aren't a huge number of fresh things to say to each other.

From the center of town, we followed the road to the Interstate, my oh-so-familiar route to the capital. At Earl Johnson's farm, we veered off and, suddenly, we were in *sprawl* country. Earl, after his defeat, had sold big chunks of his family property to various developers. The old reprobate had died a pretty wealthy man—we think of cirrhosis of the liver. His two sons still farmed, but half a mile down Wing Road from them were clusters of tract houses and, except for the architecture, they could have been in California. I've always hated the sight. Yet campaigning among them might be fun—all new people, a challenge. Or possibly a disaster. Those yuppies could be 100 percent Republicans. Still, didn't John Harrison live there? No yuppie, either. A retired salesman. Lifelong Democratic Party worker. He'd attended some of our town committee meetings since he and his wife moved here. As Jill turned onto Country Club Road from this scene, I found myself warming to the idea of getting back on the campaign trail.

Sprawl hadn't reached the sylvan entranceway to our destination. Ron Gordon had seen to it that a mile-long border of magnificent evergreens and adjacent land had been preserved. With

Swanstown's "Establishment" behind him, it hadn't been hard to whip up extra zoning to make this greenbelt safe.

Local government again. *Ye gods*, I instantly speculated, first with a shudder, then an inward laugh, *maybe Ron wants to run me for selectman!*

More evergreens flanked the driveway to the clubhouse. They were venerable and majestic white pines and prepared you for the classy building soon in view. Built in the 1880s, it was all made of handsome, intricate, brownish stone construction, laced with ivy, the roof shingled with purplish-black slate. The new stuff, like tennis courts, golf cart spaces, and general parking, was in back, to maintain the immediate visual effect of antique swank. Evenings, for the dinner crowd, there was valet parking. We reached the front entrance, gave the Taurus to a parka-clad and bow-tie-wearing kid, and entered the august premises.

If I belabor you with certain extraneous details of this evening, it's because they illustrate my overarching theme—the role of the personal in public life, the play of human egos. For instance, the fact that Constance Hilton should have been at the club the same night with her husband, which leads me, pedantically, into yet another level of governmental activity—the *non-governmental* organizations—the NGOs—since Connie was still chair of Friends of the Ocean, and I had been a long-time member of her board.

We didn't see her at first because she and Jim were in the dining room, while the four of us, the Jacksons and the Gordons, commenced our evening with cocktails in the lounge.

Ron liked martinis. I am a Scotch-and-soda man. The "girls" (God, I can't believe I wrote that, but I swear it was Ron's un-PC term) sipped white wine. Even Mitzi said, I remember distinctly, they had to go to the "little girls" room. Anyhow, while the women were away, Ron chose the time for us to have our "talk."

He and Mitzi had been in Florida for Thanksgiving with one

of their kids, so he had a remarkably nice tan—you'd think he'd burn due to his light, freckled complexion. We'd heard all about Mark and Noni's house, the doll of a granddaughter, Clarice, age four, and the precious baby, Jason, eighteen months. Upon a lull in the conversation, Mitzi made her move and she and Jill disappeared. A setup, I thought.

Having downed his second martini, my redheaded friend, tanned as he was, seemed a bit flushed.

"It's not so bad getting old, is it?" he commenced blandly.

I nodded, raising my highball glass in agreement.

"You're keeping busy, I hear. Started a new book."

Again, I nodded, still silent, waiting.

"All those nonprofit boards you're on," Ron suddenly asked me, "do they take up a lot of your time?"

Suddenly, I knew, a response was demanded. I replied, "No, because I've cut back on them considerably."

Hearing myself, my next thought was, *Okay, there's your lead-in, Ronnie.*

Except Ron merely said redundantly, "Slowing down, huh?"

"To an extent," I said impatiently. "Like Friends of the Ocean. I'm just a trustee emeritus now."

"Me, too, I'm slowing down, also," Ron said. "Taking more vacations."

Immediately, then, he came right out with his intention, which seemingly underlaid all the folderol of this special invitation to dine tonight. Pure chutzpah.

"What would you say to taking over the chairmanship of the Democratic Town Committee from me?"

Such were Ron's precise words.

I'm not great at poker faces, but politics has taught me to mask my emotions. Secretly, I was indignant as hell. But to be honest, I had to admit I had set myself up. No fool like—well, you know the rest.

I bought time by taking a long, deep swallow of Scotch.

It was like a game of *gotcha*, I silently theorized. Except it was I who had played the trick on myself. State senator, indeed! I didn't blame Ron.

"It's not a light undertaking," I finally said, without a trace of irony.

"With everything else on my plate, I need out," the redhead retorted. "But the work isn't much, except in an election year and only if we can find good candidates for local state races."

His last remark, it occurred to me, did offer an opening.

"Speaking of which," I interjected coyly, "where do we stand? House. State senate—do we have the district covered?"

Ron made a face. "For the house, Dorothy's set on running again."

"She can't beat Bannister," I quickly said.

"She knows it. I know it. The whole world knows it," Ron said. He made an exaggerated, Jewish-seeming, helpless gesture with upraised hands.

"Don't look at me to challenge her."

Okay, I was venting a bit of my repressed anger. I knew Ron knew enough not to ask me. But the state senate? I *was* curious.

"Have they found anyone yet for Peg's seat?"

I tried not to appear hopeful they hadn't.

Yet they had. Ron smiled broadly. "Great candidate. Remember that three-star athlete from Tracy High School fifteen years ago? Jimmy Wright?"

"Yeah, I know Jimmy," I said. "He's on the Tracy Town Council."

"Very popular. A joy to work with. I doubt we'll have a primary."

"Good deal," I said simply. I thought to myself, *Jonathan, you're certainly not going to get into a contest with Jimmy Wright.*

Absolute end of all fantasy.

Moments later, the "girls" were back.

Had it not been for our chance encounter with the Hiltons, especially Connie, when we entered the dining room from the lounge, I might have ended my account of this misadventure right here. Oh yes, I did give Ron sort of an answer. Had he thought of John Harrison for town chair? No, he hadn't. Would Ron like me to talk to John? I knew him pretty well. No thanks. He'd do it himself. Finis to Ron's fantasy, too. He'd gotten the message and both of us and our wives could go on eating our dinner and chatting, mostly about old times.

As to how Connie Hilton enters the picture—she was, as the Honorable Matthew X. Drew once had quipped, "an attractive nuisance," and quite lovely, yes, particularly in her younger days when she first started visiting the legislature. Pesty? Let me use a less pejorative adjective, like *dogged*. It was hard to say no to her. I didn't try, mainly because I supported her cause fervently. She was all about protecting the oceans, or, mostly, our little corner of the Atlantic just off the coast of Swanstown and Tracy, the adjoining town where she lived—stuff like stopping pleasure boats from dumping excrement, policing oil leaks, cleaning up the harbors in general, saving wetlands. *Dedicated* and *tireless* were further descriptions of Connie, plus Matt's other term for her, *pain in the ass*, although I usually could get his vote on Friends of the Ocean issues.

"Oh look, Jim, there's Jonathan and Ron Gordon!" Connie's soprano voice rang out like a bell as our foursome appeared in the dining area. "And Mitzi and Jill," she continued, in sequence, since we males had unchivarously gone ahead of the ladies, both pairs of us jawing away. We looked up to see a handsome, be-gowned brunette waving. In any event, we would have gone over to say hello.

We men exchanged handshakes, cheek kisses for the women, and chaste hugs from Connie for Ron and myself. Chitchat followed about this or that. Connie admired Jill's earrings and I had to keep a straight face (more about that later). Just before we took leave, Connie said to me, "I'm going to give you a call, Jonathan. The Friends need to strategize. We'll set something up."

"Sure," I replied. Surreptitiously, however, I checked out Jill with a sneaky sidelong glance. I'm sure she heard the exchange. But she was expressionless.

Let me explain. Jill did not care for Connie, and vice versa. They had *hated* each other in the old days in the capital, prior to my appearance on the scene. Two ambitious knockout chicks in the same environs—that alone could have caused sparks. There may have been a guy involved. *Don't ask, don't tell,* has always been the policy on intimate matters in our household.

When an explosion did come, it was an unanticipated shock. Admittedly, until then, I'd been up in the "fleshpots" of the capital for at least a decade after our wedding, although Jill had been with me those months while I worked for Governor Big Bob and before we purchased our house in Swanstown. By myself, "batching" it post-election, I spent maybe half a year away from her. Nary a jealous peep from the missus, except some wisecracks about "your raunchy workplace" and how, before our marriage, we two hadn't exactly been angels.

At my bedside, whichever place I happened to be, was a framed photo of us leaving the church in a shower of rice. On my finger was a plain gold band, never removed, and every night, when absent from Jill, a phone call went to her and always ended with "I love you" out of both of us.

Eventually, such interchanges of endearment began to seem pro forma and, seemingly a bit grudging on her part, I started to think.

Consequently, I made a huge mistake. I decided to surprise my brave, selfless wife.

My heart was in the right place. I wasn't calculating, I swear.

As we cynically used to say around the Statehouse, "No good deed ever goes unpunished." The same holds true for good intentions, apparently.

Home one weekend evening, with Jill and I window-shopping in downtown Tracy following a movie, she paused at a certain jewelry store and tugged my arm.

"Ooh, look!" she exclaimed, another way of saying she would *love* the pair of exquisite earrings her pointing finger had indicated. It was all she said. No plea to buy them for her. We both saw the price and moved on.

God, the images that haunted me afterward. Home, in our bedroom, on a shelf among other stuffed animals, was the fuzzy miniature German shepherd puppy she'd transported from California. Staring at it nostalgically that Sunday night, about to leave again for the capital, I made a decision—damn the cost, I'd buy her those gorgeous earrings.

With what conspiratorial pleasure I left the capital earlier than usual on a Friday afternoon and detoured to Tracy. Well do I remember the saleswoman's oohing and aahing over this purchase. "Oh, she'll love it! Oh, this must be such a special occasion. . . ."

I can still picture my own smug half-smile in a mirrored wall of the store, inwardly contemplating Jill's delight opening the tastefully wrapped gift I would unexpectedly bestow upon her.

Ritchie had been put to bed. We were in our bedroom when I sprang the surprise. Oh God, I won't try to duplicate her language. A decade of pent-up feminine frustration burst forth as a cascade of banshee yells and truck-driver swear words. I was thunderstruck, hearing abuse upon abuse hurled at me—speechless, dumbfounded. And then, the earrings in their natty box were flung across the room.

"There, go pick 'em up," Jill shrieked. "Go give 'em to that bitch."

"What?" I couldn't believe my ears. "What the hell do you mean?"

"I know what you've been up to with Connie Hilton. You can't buy me!"

"Bullshit!" I screamed back. "Jill, you're absolutely nuts!"

Okay, folks, to make a long story short, I resolutely refused to retrieve my ill-received gift. How long the earrings remained on the floor in a corner, I have no idea. For the next several weeks, on weekends, I slept in a guest room on the third floor. Finally, I got lucky—not in the old sexual sense—but, would you believe it, in the media!

A sensational press was not the norm in our state. However, a prominent divorce *was* news and Peter Warner, Jr., always news, too, a top-flight lawyer, one-time Democratic state party chair, several times unsuccessful candidate for Congress, son of a governor, from Warnerstown, a city named for his ancestors. His wife's lawyers were only too happy to publicize Constance Hilton as the *corespondent*. Always arrogant, Pete merely slammed his ex-spouse-to-be back for her own infidelities. Connie kept quiet, even about a dalliance shown to have been going on over the past four or five years.

Can you guess how this affected me?

Jill was at first incredulous. Still, she could hardly say I had invented the story to cover my butt. Her TV reporter's background gave her friends in the capital who verified the Warner-Hilton trysts had never stopped—and that someone mistook me for Pete, thinking him a state legislator, which he never was (he lobbied in the Statehouse). Whether gradually or abruptly Jill accepted my innocence, I never knew. The first real sign I had of it was when—some months later—she wore those same earrings to a legislative reception we attended. At home, the very same night, I moved back into our bedroom.

During the return drive from the country club, all of this sad history was in my mind. The one earring I could see on my wife's ears as she handled the wheel made a constant, sparkling reminder of the incident. Ostensibly, since, everyone of note in the state had forgotten, if not forgiven, Pete and Connie's indiscretions. They both remained as much an accepted part of the capital scene as ever. Pete remarried; Connie's husband Jim had clung to her like a faithful puppy dog. And here was I, vindicated, alongside my bride, the two of us soon to celebrate an umpty-umpth anniversary as a happily married couple.

You will never read about such dramas should any future author attempt to chronicle this era in our state's immediate past. Duke's assasination, yes, possibly a comparison of his record with those of his successors and predecessors, nuts and bolts political science analysis. Dry, dry, dry, but accorded a place on the library shelves.

More than ever, there in the car, my own unorthodox approach to the human side of history seemed important and appropriate.

Tomorrow morning, I told myself, *back on the job first thing.*

Going into the house, I said to Jill, "Nice earrings, Mrs. Jackson."

So help me, she laughed.

16

To INTERTWINE A LOVE STORY (mine and Jill's) with a set of
political events probably does not do full justice to either genre.
But it happened. We basically met on the Air National Guard
coast-to-coast flight. We found each other attractive. We coupled.
That our romance ripened, survived the trauma of Duke's assassination, and has kept us wedded for decades, could form a narrative all its own. Forgive me, sweetheart, but I do have bigger fish
to fry than just you and I in this tome.

I might as well state now a suspicion I've hitherto always
kept to myself. Jill certainly didn't marry me for my money.
Admittedly, I had some and did offer some security, despite the
perilous profession of public life I had so tentatively entered. No,
I've always believed she saw something in me. This may be unfair
to her, intimating an expectation on her part that I was somehow
going to end up in the big-time, conceivably starting in D.C. if
Duke went to the White House. I know she was tired of slaving
in the provincial media. Could she not climb with me? My holding high office was not inconceivable. Ah, the daydreams of the
young. Or am I simply projecting onto her my private fantasies
of the era?

I might as easily argue Jill was eager to settle down, have
children, get out of the rat race, fulfill her feminine side—and
blind, emotional, nonrational feelings did have to figure in our
mix. Not to mention also we have become—well—friends.

While I'm into this spate of analysis, let me add another
notion. It's about the nature of evil. A big topic, but I'm narrow-

ing it down to Miles Monahan. Before we get into the events immediately surrounding Duke's assassination, a more modern consideration inserts itself. Could you call Miles a terrorist?

For example, what was the point of what he did? In the end, it was as random as a bomb thrown into an innocent crowd. His ostensible lack of any political cause may argue against use of the word. Yet is not terrorism merely the last resort of the weak, the means, when directed against authorities, intended to change history by a single violent act? Or to make history yourself, even if only a poof in the press, or as a footnote? All I have to go on concerning Miles is a guess. His writings, as I've said, are beyond my reach. I wonder if they have ever been read, except to seek links to a conspiracy. A couple of fanciful theories did bubble up in less responsible publications. The Irish Republican Army was cited, for heaven's sake. Officially, nothing but silence. I assume, like me, the security high muck-a-mucks took him for a lone-wolf wacko, the main difference being they didn't have the personal history angle I did, firsthand knowledge of that lifelong ache of his to see his name in lights.

But I'm getting way, way, ahead of myself.

So back to Gated America, back to the Summit of Power, back to the Conclave of Governors and the intersection of the states and the federal government. We, the "fifty American kings and their satraps" were doing our business and awaiting the arrival of the real "King of Kings," whose title had to be plain "Mr. President," in keeping with the U.S.'s sacred—and legally ordained—non-monarchical traditions. The chief executive's scheduled appearance, the night before we adjourned, was billed as the absolute highlight of this whole festival of federalized democracy.

These four days were, indeed, a *kermess*. The carnival costuming was interesting. Primarily suits, masculine and feminine, as working clothes. Navy blue pinstripes were popular (for both sexes) and old-fashioned charcoal gray, and probably the lightest color was a sleek gray worsted; red power ties were predominant on the men and blue cotton shirts for TV were likewise big. We lowlier staffers, with no prospects of appearing on the tube, mostly wore white shirts, while senior aides like Harry DeWitt could be rakish, sporting yellow or pink or pale orange button-downs. Cowboy boots—ultra-expensive ones—and Stetsons were de rigueur for many of the western attendees. Mind you, all this was during business hours. When relaxation time came, we did as we thought the Californians would: splashy, short-sleeved shirts, slacks, loafers, thin dresses or tight jeans for the ladies. Plus, interspersed among the sheep, you'd find quirky types. Like fans at a ballgame, they dressed up outlandishly, or it was their job to do so: such as "Cheesehead" from the Wisconsin Farm Promoters, and the California guy in the golden bear outfit, handing out tourist maps of the state.

Didn't we have a Miss Kentucky and a Miss Utah? In bathing suits, too, when they were by the pool? Not that I was looking at them a lot, given my involvement with Jill, but I distinctly do remember those two beauties.

One of them was black—er, African American. I doubt it was Miss Utah. But don't get me started on the historical digression needed to underline the *American* meaning of a black sister from Kentucky and a most-likely Mormon white sister from Utah, cheek by jowl, almost half-naked by a pool in California.

Realize, I didn't take sustained notes during the National Governors Conference. I couldn't foretell any future need to do so. I'm just going on scraps of memory.

Dreamlike, they tantalize me. Our Native Americans—the Indians— have their vision quests. Duke, who had a Seneca roommate at Harvard, spoke of young braves out in the woods, fasting and engendering hallucinations of an animal spirit to guide them as their private totem for life. The same air of unreality hung about the Los Angeles setting, except we didn't starve ourselves—just the opposite—and the animals we encountered were university symbols—the golden bear of California, the wolverine of Michigan, the longhorn steer of Texas.

True, these fleeting images conjured up a sense of the great diversity of nature in the U.S. If you found yourself humming "America the Beautiful" amid the bustling, advertisement-crowded hotel halls, it wasn't surprising: "amber waves of grain," okay, Kansas would throw that at you; "purple mountains' majesty," think of Colorado; "above the fruited plains . . . ," try Nebraska; "for spacious skies," which was anywhere, even Rhode Island. Following such stanzas, the haunting refrain, "America! America!" morphed in my own brain into "O. Murray Carr." Holy cow! Miles, again!

In a sense, here was my vision quest trophy—the figure on the posters that went up two days before the president's arrival. I did a double-take, walking by the initial one I saw, taking a few more steps, then whirling back for a sharp second gawk. It was Uncle Sam on the poster. The gaunt, goateed old guy was in his most famous pose, forefinger pointing straight out, with a caption of *I Want You*. It wasn't a drawing, either, but a photograph of a costumed actor in the well-known star-spangled-banner outfit. My carefully squinted scrutiny of the colorful broadside convinced me the model in the picture could be Miles!

It struck me exactly as the apparition of some ghostly bear or panther or rattlesnake must have startled a famished Indian youngster in his half-sleep. Only slowly did I understand what the actual message at the bottom of the poster was saying. For the entertainment following the president's speech, we would be regaled with a pageant of *Americana*.

Intrigued, I stopped to read the fine print. The Hollywood hype of the producing group's flack publicist has not stuck with me word for word. Red-white- and-blue rah-rah, most of it.

From the Pilgrims to the Moon Walk, with a nod to Native Americans, African Americans, ethno-Americans of every ilk, with the promise of plenty of traditional and patriotic music and chorus girls—"cheescake," "gorgeous gams" (they actually used those archaic slang terms), and in the background, a sketch conveyed the impression of a heterogeneous costumed ensemble sporting everything from Indian feathers to Amish bonnets to coonskin caps, and in its amorphous collectivity as a drawing, making the lone photograph of Uncle Sam, of Miles, if that, indeed, *was* he, stand out all the more.

"Kinda campy, huh?" I heard a voice next to me say.

Other people were studying the poster. The guy who spoke, I remembered. He had been across the room from me at our sub-committee meeting, a staffer to one of the governors (I can't remember which state to this day).

"Oh, hi," I said, and added, "Pure cornball, but always a surefire favorite."

With his forefinger stretched out like Uncle Sam's, he traced above some bold-faced letters and repeated the text aloud: "Don't miss it, folks. Be sure to stay. Dancing afterward." Then, he added, "I wonder which company's putting up the tab for this extravaganza."

I cast another long glance at the poster. "No sponsor mentioned," I said. "Maybe the Governors Conference is footing the bill."

"Are you kidding?" was the cynical retort. "There's more anonymous dough floating around here than you could shake a stick at."

"Most likely is," I agreed.

"And just think of it, all this hoopla needed just to get everyone to come to listen to that bozo."

Although I nodded, I realized immediately he was talking about the president of the United States. New food for thought.

Badmouthing the president was more American than anything in the poster. I looked around and noted the guy had left, but made a mental note to contact him at the forthcoming meeting of Duke's full committee, to which I was headed and assumed he was, too. I pegged him for a fellow Democrat and felt I could further the connection and maybe recruit a supporter if Duke, himself, did run to be Chief Bozo.

Alas, the staffer in question wasn't by his governor's side at any time during the full committee meeting. Incidentally, our Indian resolution was adopted unanimously here, as well, making it part of the final package the plenary session would rubber-stamp later this same afternoon.

Throughout the meeting, I debated to myself why I should go hear the real chief bozo the next evening. Harry had told us our attendance was optional. My chickenshit reason soon be-came: *It's to pay homage to the office, not the man.*

Or, rather, because Jill had to cover it for her station.

No, really, being intellectually honest, what American can resist any chance to see a president in person?

Still, the poster photograph was before my mind along with my wonderment that Miles appeared to have been the model for Uncle Sam, and maybe—logically—an Uncle Sam figure would take part in the pageantry and it *could* be played by Miles. Was that why he was trying so hard to contact me? For boasting, I suppose.

I ended up deciding I wouldn't snub Mr. President.

Let me now shift to some chronology. This was the second day of the conference. That afternoon was given over to finishing up the bulk of our work. From the different committees, ap-proved resolutions like Duke's Indian one were sent to the ple-nary session, which was a meeting of the entire assembly, where they had to be adopted. Only a handful were debated. Most—as we would say—went under the hammer. The chairman of the

National Governors Conference, who presided, would ask, "Do I hear any objection to Resolution X, coming from Committee Y, and recommended unanimously by said committee?" A pause, followed by only a few seconds, then, "Hearing none"—bang!—with a smack of his gavel, the said resolution would be included in the conference's final report.

Those rare instances where the solons weren't simply endorsing motherhood-and-apple-pie ideas drew discussion, and the sleepy atmosphere of droning voices would suddenly come alive with pithy, if not heated, speeches. These guys and gals loved to talk and here was their chance to orate—and orate, they did—but under time limits set by the chair. The most contentious issues were saved until last and the disputes handled beautifully by the presiding officer who was, I can't quite remember and am too lazy to go look up the governor of either Delaware or Maryland.

Thanks to him, we were all dismissed with plenty of time left for tennis, golf, swimming, and other forms of recreation before attendance at a banquet in the hotel's grand ballroom. The next evening, another banquet would feature the president and that theatrical Americana extravaganza.

One more detail I don't feel like chasing down is at which banquet we had the cutesy touch of specialty dishes from different states—pork rinds and peach cobbler from the South, lobster from the Northeast, Southwest barbecue, Wisconsin cheese, Idaho potatoes, California wine, etc. Most probably, such a treat was reserved for the presidential gala.

Okay, to continue the narrative flow. On our second night, after parting from Duke around midnight, my lady and I went to her room and enjoyed ourselves, fell asleep, and, awakening around 5:00 A.M., I decided again it would be prudent to return to my own quarters. Tim was still under the covers as I tiptoed past him to the bathroom and then back to my own bed, but he was gone when my alarm went off at 9:00 A.M.

I had to be at the next and last plenary session starting at 10:00 A.M. That is, no, I really didn't *have to* be there, except Duke was scheduled to speak. Boy, wouldn't my ass get fried if I skipped a momentous occasion like that for my boss!

There was a mystery, though, about the whole business— how Governor Ellery got invited to the podium. Nor was it my job to find out what strings were pulled. Ordinarily, I might have been asked to prepare a draft speech, or really, more an outline exposition of ideas. When I'd asked Harry DeWitt earlier whether the boss wanted something on paper, he shook his head but gave no explanation. Ordinarily, too, Georgie Everoff would have distributed advance copies to the media. Only there weren't any advance copies. At this plenary, once Duke delivered his remarks, Harry, who was sitting next to me, leaned over and whispered sardonically, "I heard he wrote it on the back of an envelope."

Surely, the allusion to Lincoln's Gettysburg Address was meant to be funny, but I could have pedantically responded by informing Harry that the famous story of Honest Abe's hurriedly scribbled masterpiece had been debunked by serious historians. Yet I shut up. On a piece of scrap paper, I jotted down some of Duke's key remarks. Now, those notations are before me as I struggle to resurrect what no one could dream then were to be Duke's last public words.

"Permit me to start with a joke," Duke began. "No, wait," he caught himself, "it's a true story, or it should be, and relates to my theme today, which is nothing less than what constitutes America, the land and idea we all love, spawned by us over the past 400 years." Almost immediately, I noticed, my boss had the room quieting. I took out my pen and began jotting as he told his tale of an incident during World War II when the Germans were infiltrating English-speaking spies through American lines.

An outpost at night heard sounds of men approaching.

"Who goes there?"

"Americans."

"Yeah, well, if you're Americans, sing the 'Star-Spangled Banner.'"

"We don't know the goddamn words."

"Okay, advance, you're Americans."

Duke's punch line elicited mixed reactions—laughs and gasps.

Utterly unperturbed if some conservatives were offended, the grinning speaker proceeded to make his first point. American irreverence was America's strength. "Winston Churchill was half American," he went on. "One of his sayings was that every Englishman had a duty once a day to tell his government to go to hell. For full-blooded Americans, shouldn't it be twice a day? In this case, let's examine what constitutes a full-blooded American."

His answer to his own rhetorical question wasn't put in words entirely. He made a gesture—I can still see it—in which he stretched out his arms, like a preacher blessing his flock. "I mean all of you," he explained, but adding, "Technically, juridically, I may not be exactly correct. Among you might be a few non-citizens, maybe on their way to becoming legalized. What matters is the potential. All the world can potentially join our American community."

In retrospect, it's much easier to tell where he was headed. A catchphase developed, a concept expressed by those two words of his, "American community," soon rhythmically inserted into the cadence of a political stump speech: *the American community is this, the American community is not that,* but intellectually embellished, too, with citations from U.S. history—stuff his audience wouldn't know. One example was the "hedge" of Duke's Puritan ancestors, the notion of a colony so tight-knit that no one was supposed to migrate beyond Boston's immediate pruned greenery, but the wide-open nature of surrounding wild forest land and their group's rising fecundity would not allow their being *hedged in* for very long.

Honestly, he really did use the word *fecundity*. I have it in my scrawls, accompanied by exclamation marks. "Pearls to swine," I had scrawled smugly.

His narrative line was about how the American community had grown from scattered seeds, from Boston, from Plymouth, from Jamestown, in the beginning. "Thus did we swell," Duke said. "Thus did we fill a continent," and like a coda, I remember his adding, "from sea to shining sea." He had started with the unsingable "Star-Spangled Banner" and gone next onto "America the Beautiful," the lyrics emphasizing his primary point of how God will "shed His grace on thee" only so long as we "crown thy good with brotherhood" within the immense, seemingly blest space between the two great oceans on either side of us.

The cadence of his speech was like the cadence of "America the Beautiful," that favorite patriotic song of mine. Some present (maybe in my imagination) actually hummed the refrain.

It seemed to me, also, there was a sort of silence once Duke finished, as allegedly happened to Lincoln at Gettysburg right after his "Address."

No, I'm certain I caught the sound of perfunctory applause, before other talks ensued, which were universally of the platitudinous variety.

The post mortem on Duke's performance, among our own staff, was mixed. Fussy as always, Georgie was upset Duke had used profanity at the outset, mild as it was: *goddamn* and *hell*. Can you top that for press corps superficiality? But Harry DeWitt had a much different reading. "They listened," he said. "Ordinarily, they don't even listen." And he meant the governors. Personally, I thought Duke was great, if unorthodox. It was his game plan, I calculated: showing himself to the Democrats present that he was *different* and would make an interesting national candidate. If so, I was soon to receive an inkling of the strategy's effect.

On the way out of the meeting, I was asked, "Is he gonna run?"

My interlocutor was yet another "suit" like myself, a well-dressed, clean-cut-looking young African American, another guy I'd noticed among the entourage of one of the Democratic governors. I answered with a big abashed smile, a shrug and a mutter of, "No official word yet."

"I'd encourage him" was the reply, in a distinctly Ivy League accent. "That was a damn fine speech."

"Thank you," I said.

In the jam-up by the exit, we were momentarily face-to-face. "Are you his speechwriter, by any chance?" my newfound companion inquired.

"Not for today's," I admitted. "Duke—Governor Ellery—did it entirely by himself, I'm told. He writes a lot of his stuff without any help, except research, and that's my department."

"Obviously the man's a thinker."

Had he not accompanied this approving remark by handing me his card, I might have come away feeling he was being no more than offhand friendly. Yet we suddenly had a recruit, it appeared: Dudley Montgomery, Special Assistant for Minority Relations. In those cultivated tones of his, I heard, "If Mr. Ellery decides to enter the primary, let me know. *My* governor likes him, too."

Montgomery and I separated then. Spying Harry DeWitt back in the crowd, I waited up and handed over the card, explaining why.

His eyes twinkled when he finally put the elegantly embossed square into his wallet. "By gum, we're gainin'," he declared in a fake back-country accent.

Duke was still in the meeting room, schmoozing with the governors.

It was a moment to be savored. Historic, conceivably. Had things turned out differently, the start of something big.

Did it matter, I asked myself, that Jill and Charley Fischer hadn't been there to capture Duke on video tape? Her boss at home had wanted a "color story," instead. She was off interviewing those two Miss Americas.

We had arranged to meet in the main lobby at a certain hour. The rest of the day would be ours until the president's wingding in the evening. I was a few minutes early and, you can imagine, in a damn good mood, contemplating my seeming good fortune in politics and, not insignificantly, the pleasure of my honey's company for the next X number of hours.

The fascination of watching the passing parade of all America kept me from fidgeting when I realized Jill was a tad late. Those faces, those skin hues, those hair tones, those varied styles of dress—what better illustrations of Duke's "American community?" You could pick out different types: the gaunt Puritans, the sunburned westerners, the high-cheekboned southerners, the golden-blonde Californian, the obvious black-haired Italian, a Jewish redhead (I had met Ron Gordon by then), several Hawaiians, Asians tall and short, an African American (light-pigmented), another (almost blue-black), and a Native American with a ponytail and string tie, wearing a pinstriped suit.

Were the strains of "America the Beautiful" playing in my head? *Ohmuhricar! Ohmuhricar . . . ?*

Who knows? I caught sight of Jill. My heart, as they say, went pitter-patter.

And yet—simultaneously, the damnedest thing happened.

Into the lobby from outside at the same precise instant came a rush of people. My first instinct was: *They're an athletic team.* Mostly young men and women, each carried a canvas bag, as if they had their uniforms and equipment in them. Only here it was costumes and props. These were the performers of the much-advertised pageant, arriving for a rehearsal of their show.

I had thought so, even before Jill confirmed who they were. Meanwhile, I gawked, especially when I spotted one guy carrying a pair of stilts, in addition to his duffel. My glimpse was in part obscured by another member of the entourage next to him, but I could have sworn I'd noticed Miles Monahan. There was a split second when the fellow lugging the stilts turned and glanced right at me. It *was* Miles—sandy hair, freckles, pug nose, green eyes, and all! I was about to raise my hand to wave, but no sign of recognition escaped him. Didn't he see me? Maybe not. But it struck me that his glazed look seemed to take in nothing any-where. It was so inwardly concentrated, so dead to anything external, I actually shivered. As if paralyzed, I stood flat-footed, open-mouthed, while my old boyhood pal, face thrust forward again, marched purposefully off with his troupe of thespians.

A kiss on the cheek from Jill the next moment brought me back from my surprise. Yet while laughingly wiping off the smear of lipstick she'd deliberately planted, I felt an undercurrent of consternation. *Damn you, Miles,* I swore for the umpteenth time, before giving my full attention to the lovely lady beside me.

17

SOME INTROSPECTION, I'm afraid, is necessary now. Much as I'd like to carry the narrative directly into an event as colorful as the presidential dinner at a National Governors Conference, an instinct has led me first to muse on the subject of male friendship and, naturally, mine with Miles Monahan. His appearance within the gates of my temporary California sanctuary was like a warning sign, I somehow felt.

What novel is it where a bunch of kids are roughhousing at a boys' prep school and the narrator, for no discernible reason, pushes his best friend so he falls off a tree limb and is badly injured? The image has remained with me ever since I read that book. And, subsequently, the question: *Did I push Miles?*

Was the author writing about suppressed homosexuality? This idea was once very fashionable in our literature. Actually, I'd bet more on an underlying rivalry between two pals for the smiles of our American success goddess—I mean like between Miles and myself, not those imaginary youngsters in the story.

Another literary allusion has been hinted at earlier. Joseph Conrad's work of fiction, *The Secret Sharer,* provides a different model—the Janus concept of good and evil in the same personality, each of us humans having a demonic shadow, always capable of bursting into—what else?—chaos.

One more bite at this introspective apple, and then I'm finished. Was Miles mentally ill? Did his behavior fit the manic-depressive syndrome (the more modern term is bipolar), an imbalance of chemicals in the brain ignited by stress and leading to unimaginable heights of grandiosity and depths of despair, in which murder or suicide is never to be ruled out?

I had a brief flash of thought in the hotel lobby, instants before Jill pecked my cheek. *Did Miles send me a message earlier today saying he'd be here?* Or had he given up on me, and thus his blank, possibly hate-filled expression, looking straight at me? Why not check at the desk to unearth any such notification and, if so, at least establish my old pal's rationality?

Except Jill was by my side and bubbling like a schoolgirl. We had originally planned to grab a bite of lunch in the coffee shop while deciding what to do for the afternoon. What she was telling me instead, in a gush of delight, was that she had signed us up for the conference-sponsored trip—to *Disneyland!*

That famous brand name had a freshness then that it doesn't have today; the first mammoth theme park of its glossy type had opened in nearby Anaheim not long before. Once we got there, Jill said, we'd grab our bite at one of the concession stands or restaurants. The drill now was to rush up to our respective rooms, change into casual clothes, and hurry back down. The buses were leaving in twenty minutes.

She who must be obeyed, I thought wryly, yet happily.

In my rush, I had no chance to go to the always-crowded desk and ask for messages. However, neither was any red light flashing on the phone in my room, nor had Tim left me a note.

Of course, always, when you're counting every second, interruptions pop up like dummies on an obstacle course. Initially, Tim was one. I was bolting out the door; he was heading toward the room.

"Hey, did I get a call from that guy, Miles, that old buddy of mine?" I yelled as soon as I saw my roomie.

"Miles?" Tim stopped and looked puzzled.

"Oh, hell," I banged my fist against my forehead. "Uh, the stage name. Okay, Murray. Did I get a phone call from Murray?"

"Not that I know of." Then, cop-like, Tim asked, "Why?"

"I gotta run," I blurted, passing him. "Nothing important," I said over my shoulder. "Just wondering."

It was like the final minutes of a sporting match with no time-outs left. Rushing out of the elevator I ran into a corridor that seemed especially crowded. Soon, I saw why. A figure on stilts was scattering brochures around, a figure in costume, Uncle Sam, and it *was* Miles! All I had time to do was pick up one of those handbills, move toward him and cry "Miles!" But he kept staring in another direction and it was very noisy. Did he hear me? I couldn't try again. Panicked about squeezing through the rush, I bulled my way and literally sprinted across the lobby in order to reach Jill before the buses started loading.

"What have you got there?" she asked, pointing to the piece of paper I still absentmindedly held.

I merely handed it to her to read, adding, "Some guy in an Uncle Sam suit was tossing these out—a promo for tonight's show."

Nary a whisper about Miles and certainly not about any queasiness I experienced, which slippery emotion was to lie dormant—but extant—during the next few hours of "fun and frolic" we all sincerely had on our excursion.

These many years later, it's possible to wax intellectual about Disneyland. Even while goofing off, I do have a habit of observing. We started on the rides, Jill and I; she shrieked and clung to me, whether we were in a spinning teacup or in a simulated free-fall down a mountain wall. Less frightening were the amiable ghosts and skeletons in a haunted mansion or comical pirates in the sack of a Caribbean treasure town. My favorite, actually, was *It's a Small World*—a touch of internationalism in the midst of rampant Americana, with one squeaky, catchy tune that reverberated long afterward in a mind as musically simplistic as mine. I enjoyed the Main Street parade and the old-fashioned music—

recalling the sights and sounds of an epoch long before Jill and I were born, yet which is still a part of us. These were fantasies of an American small-town child of the late nineteenth century, turned into cash, into entertainment having worldwide appeal, with a bow to good literature—Tom Sawyer Island—and a salute for American history's special message to humanity—Great Moments With Mr. Lincoln. This whole hodgepodge of cutesiness and sanitized adventure struck a chord in even a semi-sophisticated bloke like me.

And Mickey Mouse! What a phenomenon! They had actors and actresses dressed up in outfits to portray Disney's cartoon creations—Mickey and Minnie and Donald and Goofy and Snow White and Grumpy and Dopey, etc., etc. But it was Mickey on whom I fixated, watching the anonymous thespian who played him sticking out a gloved hand which excited children in the parade crowd hurried to shake, and meanwhile remembering an amazing story I'd been told about Mickey Mouse.

I don't know Mickey's birth date—sometime in the 1920s—but the incident I'm about to describe happened in 1936 and in Nazi Germany. How did I learn of it? I've mentioned my friend Gerry Margolis. Staying over at his house one night when we were kids, I listened during dinner to a man who fascinated me. He was a relative of Mrs. Margolis, born in Germany, Jewish, who had escaped the Holocaust by leaving Europe and going to America with his little sister Erma.

Thus, in 1936, two years before they were put on a *kindertransport* out of the Reich, Erma was about six years old. Hard times had already descended upon the German Jews. Among other restrictions, they were not allowed to attend movies. But Erma had been promised she could go see Mickey Mouse. So the family took a chance. In the darkness of the cinema, they hoped they would not be conspicuous. On came a newsreel to start the program. Featured were images of Joseph Goebbels, the dark-haired, gnome-like Nazi leader and chief propagandist, and while he strutted around on the screen, all of a sudden the wail of a child's voice cut across the soundtrack. It was poor little Erma bellowing out her disappointment: "Is *that* Mickey Mouse?"

This punch line was left to stand alone, I remember. No hint of the German audience's reaction. Obviously, Erma survived unscathed—to become a refugee with her brother. Of the parents, not a word; Mickey's reach, even then, was impressive. Next, I thought of Nikita Khruschev on his visit to the U.S., absolutely furious, throwing a veritable tantrum, because the Secret Service wouldn't let him enjoy Disneyland for alleged "security reasons." Just a big Russian boychik. *The global power of Hollywood* was another reflection.

Jill didn't notice how quiet I'd become as the Mickey replica reached our section of the parade watchers. Instead, among dozens of fans, mostly small fry, she rushed out to shake the surrogate movie star's hand. My own little groupie.

Later on, we—a bunch from the bus—got to pose for snapshots with a whole lineup of these costumed characters. I kept watching to make sure the guy in the Mickey suit didn't try to grope my girlfriend when they posed arm in arm.

Still, I had to admit that whoever in the National Governors Conference secretariat had arranged our trip did a terrific job. At the popular attractions, where there were always long lines, we were taken right past by representatives of the Disney management. We were let in "backstage" everywhere. All of us got free Mickey ears, too. I wouldn't wear them, but some of the fellows and gals on the bus did, the whole way back to the hotel and inside, as well. We were certainly a rowdy crowd on the ride home, cracking jokes, telling risqué stories, dancing in the aisles (the exhibitionists among us, that is), some community singing, a few of the tunes quite racy, and chorus after chorus of the

Mouseketeers song. Moreover, we were uniformly sober, as far as I knew. And to me this memory remains another tribute to the ease with which Americans of all types, political persuasions, and ethnic backgrounds can bond seemingly spontaneously. Years later, when I was a legislator, I went on a trip to the Soviet Union (sponsored by the legislative counterpart of the National Governors Conference) and our bus rides were similar—lots of carrying on, lots of hilarity—and we, politicians of every stripe, never forgot the parting words of one of our interpreters, supposedly a KGB agent, who told us, "It is not your wealth we Russians envy you Americans for. What we envy is your ability to laugh."

Lest it be thought I am being Pollyannish or sloppily patriotic, realize I am on the verge of unveiling the opposite side of the coin—the warts, the wormwood, the gnawing puzzle of our American spurts of violence despite unprecedented (when compared to the rest of the nations of the world) success and prosperity.

Once the bus dropped us off, the fun part was over for the day. Jill and I didn't even have time for our afternoon "quickie." She had to change clothes and do interviews surrounding the President's visit. I would have a bit of free time before the big dinner, so my plan was to get into my uniform of suit and tie and end up at the lobby bar to fortify myself against the onslaught of windbag oratory we would hear tonight and the lack of Jill's companionship. This was my intention, anyway.

And it happened, but not without some unexpected stress. In my room, I found Tim was also getting dressed for the evening. Nothing unusual there. But it was a tad surprising when the taciturn state trooper greeted me immediately.

"Oh, good, you're here" he said. "You received that message you were expecting from your friend Murray."

Following his pointing finger, I saw an envelope on my bed.

Dimly, I heard Tim say, "It was slipped under the door."

Engrossed in wanting to find out how my old friend would explain himself, I simply nodded. A moment later, I had the envelope ripped open and retrieved a single sheet of paper from inside. Instantly I knew the handwritten penmanship was Miles's.

His actual note, I still have, so I'll produce it now verbatim:

> Showtime tonight, Jonathan, old boy, eight-thirty curtain. Be in your seat. Because I'm going to bring you right to your feet. Hey, that rhymes. Maybe they'll consider me a poet, too. My extravaganza, you won't forget. You always were a teacher's pet. Iambic pentameter once more, eh wot? Remember, Buster, when it comes, don't use Miles, like you just did. My name is Murray, full name O. Murray Carr.

Two readings, three readings and then I heard Tim's voice again. "Is it news you were expecting?"

I knew I had to answer my roommate. Maybe I had five or ten seconds to think of what to tell a cop. Push Miles off the precipice? Follow through on my instinctive suspicion of something sinister? Or shut it all down, make an innocuous reply to Tim Lavery?

Dozens of angles could have been explored and I had no wiggle room.

Didn't I have a duty to let Tim see this incoherent message?

Suppose he had earlier steamed the letter open, read it, then resealed the envelope . . . sheer paranoia, but plausible.

All Miles's stuff from last summer about guns and presidential assassinations was back in my mind.

Was I overreacting to Miles's babble and hyperbole? Had Miles gone literally nuts, freaked out? One way or another, I had to act. Tim, I could feel, was impatiently awaiting an answer.

"No," I finally said. "This is really strange. Have you got a few moments to read this and tell me what you make of it?"

Admittedly, the contents might have struck any law officer as weird but harmless. Tim studied those lines and afterward wore a quizzical expression.

"Where do you see the problem?" he asked, handing the letter back. Then I launched into a description of our target shooting at the lake.

"Miles claimed he was rehearsing for a part in a movie where he plays a professional hit man, *hired to kill the president.*" I emphasized this last phrase.

Tim was being maddeningly dense. "He's an actor, isn't he? But do I now understand he's in the hotel with the group putting on the show tonight?"

"Right, I saw him twice," I said. "The second time dressed in an Uncle Sam suit. Handing out fliers."

"I guess I saw him, too," Tim volunteered. "The guy on stilts."

What happened next, seen in retrospect, might have resembled a mystery drama where a false clue is introduced. It had to do with Miles's note. I had, without thinking, stuck it in a side pocket of my suit coat.

When Tim, after quite a silence, suddenly said drily, "Very well, I'll have somebody check on it," I didn't think fast enough to give him the piece of paper.

Before I knew it, he had his own suit coat on over his holstered weapon and was out of the room. An audience might have concentrated on the seemingly important fact that he had left without taking prime evidence with him. *There'll be a screwup* would remain my thought. *We'll see.* At the moment, I merely felt I needed a drink—no, more than one, I promised myself.

Had I sat alone in the bar lounge, I might have fingered the incriminating document and revivified my odd feeling of having betrayed a buddy, so to speak. And why? Covering my ass, you bet. Yet no sooner had I plunked myself on a stool and ordered myself the usual Scotch and soda than a young man about my own age, attired pretty much the same as I was, took the seat next to me and started a conversation.

His name was Roger Robinson. If this means nothing to you, don't worry, a political groupie would instantly tag him as a one-time rising Republican star in one of the border states. Later, he made lieutenant governor, ran for U.S. Senate, lost, and never quite found electoral traction again. He'd lost to a Democratic incumbent and had had the *chutzpah* to hit me up for a contri-bution; I'd actually rewarded his audacity with a token gift, but one so small it didn't have to be reported publicly. However, at the time we met, Roger's position paralleled mine: ambitious, aspiring young gubernatorial assistant.

We had another thing in common, as well: double initials, RR and JJ. Ironically, after we introduced ourselves, my thought flashed immediately to Miles Monahan—MM—and how in the second grade, this inconsequential fact had helped in our form-ing a friendship. Perish any further thought of Miles at that moment, though. What a relief it was to plunge right into con-versation with this glib, well-spoken, friendly fellow who'd taken the stool next to me,

"Roger Robinson, Republican," was how he presented himself.

"Jonathan Jackson, Democrat," I countered, then added, "Also a double initial, but our alliteration ends there, I'm sure."

He smiled appreciatively and went on to say, "I noticed you're with Governor Ellery. What's the story? Are the rumors true?"

It was a frontal assault, seemingly ingenuous, but obviously a calculated question that had led him to me. "You mean about running for president?" I answered warily.

"Any inside dope?"

"Officially, no." We both had drinks by then. I took my ini-tial swallow.

"Unofficially?"

"I'm too junior to know anything."

"Welcome to the club."

Whereupon we exchanged a mock high-five.

I could well stop there. A bit of a rapport had been established and Roger and I continued conversing. The part of this talk I wish to reproduce follows strictly from memory, not from any notes. It was when we somehow got into a freewheeling discussion of Mark Twain's *Huckleberry Finn*.

Both of us agreed it was the quintessential American novel. This, despite our opposite political views. Frankly, I would have thought Roger identified more with Tom Sawyer than Huck— Sawyer, the entrepreneur, the incipient businessman, imaginative, an activist, a leader, a future captain of industry in the making, while his alter ego, so to speak, the kid from the other side of the tracks, was rootless and restless, adventurous, irresponsible, and, in later life, probably among the destitute whom bleeding hearts like me loved to succor.

I suddenly asked Roger, "If Tom and Huck had grown to manhood, what do you think their political affiliations might have been?"

To my surprise, he answered, "The two of them, Republicans." Surprise; I'd thought he would have branded Huck a nonvoter, too shiftless or drunk to ever register.

"How so?" I pressed him.

Roger produced an elaborate and thoughtful response. Tom Sawyer was a no-brainer. Although the lad chafed at Aunt Polly's discipline, Roger said, in later life, Tom would come to appreciate the need for order she had instilled in him. Being creative alone wasn't efficient. His tremendous energy, ability to manipulate and think outside the box had to be channeled. Organization skills would come, thanks to Aunt Polly's hectoring.

"In the pre-Gilded Age era," Roger went on to say, "America

was growing those kinds of people—John D. Rockefellers, Henry Fords, Fricks, and Mellons—Republicans all. As for Huck—"

"Yes, that's what I'd really like to hear," I interrupted more than a bit sarcastically. "Huckleberry Finn among the Fricks and Mellons."

Could I say his logic was tortured? Not exactly, due to my experience as a candidate. I'll never forget knocking on the door of what looked to me like the poorest home—literally a hovel— in my district. A woman in tatters with frazzled hair and a poverty-lined face answered. She could have been Huck Finn's mother. After I introduced myself, she asked suspiciously, "Are you a Republican?"

"No, Ma'am," I said, beaming, sure I had a supporter.

Guess at my astonishment when she handed me back my card with the words, "Sorry, young man, we've always been and always will be Republicans."

Roger also pointed out Huck's closeness to his raft companion, the Negro Jim, plus the boy's anti-slavery sentiments. The Grand Old Party, he reminded me, had emancipated the blacks.

"Not doing too well lately with them," I rejoined.

"All those Southern governors who stood in the schoolhouse doorways were Democrats," he shot back.

"They's switchin' over," I teased, using a touch of a drawl.

My cynicism was ignored. Dead serious, Roger launched into the dangerous topic of *gun control.* Huck was an outdoorsman: he fished; he most certainly hunted. No government he'd support would ever take away his guns, his Second Amendment rights, his freedom in the woods.

"C'mon, now," I cajoled. "Nobody's weapon has ever been confiscated." I had a momentary flash then of the arsenal of rifles and pistols in Miles's car last summer, and this image, coupled with my apprehension about my boyhood friend's behavior and mental state at the moment, sent a sharp shiver right through me.

But Roger was already leaving that angle. "Here's another salient point," he said. "Moral values. The sinner redeemed. Huck finds religion in his older years, repents his wastrel youth. Faith is important to the always-poor. They will receive their rewards in heaven, if only they will firmly believe."

"Letting the Fricks and Mellons have their jolly good time down here."

"You catch on quick for a Democrat," he smiled.

I was beginning to like the guy. We probably could have talked a lot longer, but a witching hour was soon upon us—time to go to the gala dinner. An exchange of cards ensued, those gold embossed squares bearing state seals and the words *Office of the Governor,* of which we were so proud. Roger and I promised to keep in touch and we have, tangentially, as I've indicated.

Oh, I should also include what happened a little later in the ballroom where they held the presidential affair. It was, in truth, entirely innocent on Roger's part. We had left the bar together and then split up once inside the vast multipurpose space, heading for tables set up all over the dance floor. A cash bar existed and as soon as I found my name card, I went to join one of the mobs crowding around to buy drinks, and, lo and behold, who did I see but Roger Robinson, bottled brew in hand, talking—nay, flirting—with my girl, with the beauteous Miss Jill McKenzie of Channel 7 News.

Now, she didn't know he had just met me; he, in turn, was just trying to hit on a good-looking chick he'd spied, having no means to know I was involved.

Well, let me put a stop to that right away, I told myself. *March right over to them. Don't even wait to order another Scotch.*

Wait a minute. How presumptuous of me to say she can't talk to any other guy. Just because we'd. . . . I suddenly had that tickling fear again that our little fling was destined to be short-lived. Tonight, would we even, shall we say, tango?

My strongest instinct then was to silently curse Miles once more. I glanced back toward our table, seeking in vain Tim Lavery's trim ramrod form. No, he was probably with Duke and they still hadn't arrived. Would he bring some news?

I hadn't left the booze line; nor had Jill and Roger Robinson stopped chatting. But suddenly the president and his entourage were entering and all heads turned and people applauded and Jill was instantly back directing her cameraman, Charley Fischer, to shoot footage. The president moved slowly, acknowledging the applause of the standing crowd, taking his seat. No noise like a backfire erupted. All was peaceful.

When Duke arrived, Tim Lavery wasn't with him—just Madge and their guests. It wasn't unheard of for my boss to dismiss his bodyguard. And here, Duke's logic would be that if anyplace in the country were safe, it would be in this ballroom. Secret Service security up the ying-yang, and these only the visible ones. Moreover, Tim's absence meant to me the business with Miles had proved a non-starter. Any hint of danger would have had Tim right by Duke's side. No, we all knew how Tim hated these rubber-chicken feasts and so the boss had taken pity on him and given him a night off.

I suspected somewhere in the vicinity you might find an undercover guy—maybe borrowed from our State of California host, detailed to keep an eye on Duke, an arrangement of Tim's to salve his conscience. Otherwise, banality soon ruled. I found myself directing a good deal of my gaze at the president. The head table wasn't too far away. Talk about banality! And this, before I heard him speak! He was Mr. Average American in looks, in manner, in everything except the expensive suit he was wearing. They had dressed him up *real nice.*

Harry DeWitt was sitting next to me. Catching him staring at the chief executive, too, I commented, "He photographs a lot better than he looks in real life."

"Don't let that carefully designed ordinariness mislead you," was Harry's response. "He's a formidably clever and slimy sonof-abitch."

"When Duke was in Congress, and you were staff, he was in the U.S. Senate, right? You had a chance to see Mr. Prez in action, right?"

"Chairman of Armed Services. Rode it right to the top."

"We sure underestimated him, huh?"

"Too many people have."

The president's eventual speech was duly recorded by the media (page five, below the fold, in the *New York Times* the next day). A bit of meat had been included among the platitudes, some itty-bitty movement on a weighty issue of the day, which the world has long since forgotten. And nowhere was the best part of the evening—the "show"—so much as mentioned.

This entertainment was not dissimilar to a "tired business-man's" preferred attraction on Broadway. The music consisted primarily of souped-up patriotic tunes—some George M. Cohan, some Irving Berlin, some John Philip Souza, some regional folk melodies, and, in keeping with the theme of the miniature table flags, a medley of football fight songs. No Woody Guthrie, nothing overtly political, except a nod to long-buried issues with a few bars of "Dixie" and "The Battle Hymn of the Republic." "Yankee Doodle" was a constant refrain, starting with the opening big Revolution number. Male dancers wore three-cornered hats, knee britches, et al., but the chorus cuties showed plenty of leg in their scanty buff and blue costumes, little colonialettes with stage muskets and sabers routing an equally underdressed line of beauties representing the hated redcoats. They had a guy dressed as George Washington, powdered wig and all, accepting Cornwallis's surrender, and to finish this boffo performance, a Fourth of July simulated fireworks to welcome the new nation.

Pageant—Americana—musicale—girly show—there was no

one way to peg this Hollywood potpourri of styles and formats. We had Lewis and Clark amid Sacajawea-clad dancing girls in tight, short buckskin dresses; antebellum belles whose crinolines were well above the knees; and Lincoln, both freeing the slaves and asking to have "Dixie" played, his "Malice toward none . . ." words projected orally and visually against the alternating strains of the "grand old" Southern anthem and the rousing Yankee battle hymn. We had Harlem flappers and "Take Me Out to the Ball Game" sandwiched between the football songs, and the astronauts posed against giant photo backdrops of the moon and the American flag. It was kitsch, it was cornball, it wasn't all quite politically correct, and the audience ate it up; they were giving standing ovations for practically every number.

Yes, I enjoyed it, too. I rose, applauding. I hurrahed. I sang along with everyone else. But, more than halfway through, I suddenly wondered, *Hey, where is Uncle Sam?*

Certainly he would have to appear sooner or later. They couldn't have brought Miles along just to distribute handbills. But as each scene went by without a single sign of the gaunt, goateed, star-spangled figure, on stilts or without them, I eventually reasoned how the symbolic personification of the U.S. was being saved for the finale.

I wasn't wrong.

My research on what exactly happened next has been pretty desultory over the years. I'd seen to it that Jill and I eschewed Los Angeles entirely—that is, until Ritchie ironically decided to go to college at UCLA. Our son had been after us to visit and we'd finally conceded; more than a bit of guilt had led me to contact people in LA connected to Miles with whom I'd hitherto only corresponded. I thought for a while I'd be able to see his former landlady in person, but she canceled before we arrived, due to a sister's illness. Anyway, she had already provided me the one possibly helpful fact she knew—the exact date Miles had piled his belongings into the jalopy and left for good, paying off his arrears of rent because of a new "gig" he'd gotten, he'd said.

Truthfully, during this later LA trip almost a decade ago, I made but one face-to-face connection, an interview with Jack Provost, a septuagenarian Hollywoodean, retired from show biz, and since deceased. He had been stage manager of the pageant troupe performing for the president at our gated Shangri La, although the president didn't stay to watch them, it developed. Very professionally, the prez had been ushered out once the house lights had dimmed—a Secret Service precaution, taken slickly without causing a stir.

While Jack Provost and I sat on the porch at his West Hollywood bungalow, we sought to piece together, backstage, on stage, and audience-wise, everything that had transpired. If an official, exhaustive report existed, it was Secret Service stuff and doubtless still classified. The media concentrated heavily on Duke's assassination and nearly completely neglected Miles's connection to the presidential dinner. No one played up the potential presidential assassination angle, except as rumor, and the most attention given Miles was the radical left murmurs that the prez had ordered him to rub Duke out.

Jack had much earlier received my written questions. He had the same list with him as we talked and drank beers—at least three apiece. I took fairly unreadable and sloppy notes. For example: one of my key inquiries dealt with timing. Some Secret Service guy, picking up on whatever Tim had said about Miles, went backstage to question the Uncle Sam impersonator.

"They didn't find him," Jack told me. He'd already written pretty much the same thing years before. "No, they didn't find him." Jack liked to repeat himself. "He flew the coop because he'd spotted them first and panicked."

Other artifacts Jack had brought out included a yellowing copy of the script the company was using for the pageant. He showed me stage directions where Uncle Sam originally had a significant role in the show.

"See here, opening number—then here—and here," he continued and finished up by commenting, "Only the sonofagun skedaddled and we had a helluva time, dressing up a guy to put into the finale. Good thing that—what the Christ was his name?—Murray Monahan dropped his costume on the dressing room floor."

"And you told me in your previous letter, he left the stilts, too," I volunteered.

"Yeah—it's where he hid his guns, those little peashooters—.22s. I saw 'em, well, I saw the one he left. He'd cut compartments into the foot blocks on those stilts. Clever—clever—fit in snug, and he opened one and grabbed that little pistol when he went on the lam."

"And no one really knows how he got away from backstage."

"Like Houdini. Or there might've been a window. I can't remember everything. Except the size of the tiny popgun they found. And the one he had with him was identical, too. How can you kill a man with an itty-bitty .22?"

"Bobby Kennedy was killed by a single shot from a .22."

"By God, you're correct, and right in this city, too."

From this sample dialogue, you can gauge how tough it was to keep Jack Provost focused. A moment later, he produced another artifact from his pocket. In a glassy envelope was a business card.

"After those G-men were gone, I found this on the floor near Murray Monahan's locker, which they'd emptied. I've kept it as a souvenir of a murderer." Through the transparency, he showed me the—to him, seemingly precious—and to me, morbid if not pathetic—item.

It was one of Miles's *O. Murray Carr* cards. At the bottom, in handwriting I recognized as his, had been written, obviously to be added to a future text, "Performed for the president" and the date.

Among Jack's paraphernalia was also a scrapbook, which he took up next.

"Well, that's that about Murray Monahan," he said. "I got other interesting stuff here to see. Mostly me, and some o' the stars I worked with. Even Cagney. You know that Monahan guy, he sure did a good Cagney."

Being as polite as possible, I looked at some photos, oohed and aahed, but carefully beat the hastiest retreat I could. In point of fact, I did have to get back to UCLA soon. Jill had gone with Ritchie (and Irene, too, who was in his class) for a tourist visit to Universal Studios and I was taking them all to supper. I thanked Jack for his help and, as he would have said, *that was that.*

Except for a description of my response when, at the end of the patriotic revue, an Uncle Sam appeared, not on stilts and doing nothing more than waving to the audience. I saw at a glance it wasn't Miles. Whereupon, touching the sheet of paper in my side pocket, I thought, *Now I understand. They detained him for questioning.* And I concluded uncharitably, *Serves him right, the bastard, for messing around the way he has.*

My own finale that night did turn out to be another "roll in the hay" with Miss Jill, who had been absent from all but the last few minutes of the show, doing interviews about the president's speech. Despite my incipient paranoia earlier in the evening, she was just as eager as I was. Our passion lasted almost until dawn. Returned to my own room, I went straight to sleep, not even bothering to reflect, seeing Tim's shadowy form asleep in the opposite bed, how I would have to remind myself to ask him about Miles later in the morning.

18

WELL, I DIDN'T GET MY QUESTION for Tim answered right away. Nor did I hear any rumblings from anyone about the previous evening. All of us were swept up into the hullabaloo of a final day at the conference. Even in the morning, when we had a farewell plenary session, people were running around with suitcases, preparing to dash to planes, in some cases their own (a few states had small jets) but mostly commercial carriers.

As you know, our state delegation had arrived on a less than comfortable aircraft—and if I may say so now without hurting the feelings of our faithful pilot and Air National Guard Commander at the time, General Bill Thompson—the kind of second-class transport that has long since been superseded by sleek, up-to-date giant jets. The plan had been, of course, to fly back cross-country in the same torturous manner, although without any stops, from west to east. However, midway through our droning last official National Governors Conference meeting, Tim Lavery came into the gathering, whispered something in Harry DeWitt's ear, and left before I could jump up and confront him with my smoldering curiosity concerning Miles. Besides, Duke was up on the podium, delivering a final report for his committee chairman and I sure didn't want to create any distractions. The moment Duke finished, Harry passed the word that our entire delegation would meet in Duke's suite once the meeting adjourned—everyone, including the media.

So I would see Tim there. No further prolonged delay.

When our whole bunch settled in Duke and Madge's spacious digs, none of us, except possibly myself, seemed in an apprehensive mood. A bit tired, perhaps. Glad the hoo-ha was over and happy to be homeward bound, but not looking forward to an interminable no-frills trip. Thus, actual cheers erupted when Harry DeWitt announced, "Folks, we need to move a little faster than we originally thought because we're flying home on a commercial flight."

That was that. Also, I did have a brief exchange with Tim. He was moving fast toward the door and I called to him, "Hey, Tim, did you ever get any response to the matter we spoke about?"

Over his shoulder, he replied, "Told them the things you told me. But this morning, I've been running around making arrangements for Harry. Got a quick briefing. Talk to you later."

Before we knew it, we were jammed into a pair of vans heading to LAX, the well-known abbreviation for our sprawling southern California host city's sprawling airport.

Jill was in the other vehicle, so I found myself sitting next to Harry DeWitt. In a low voice, as we sped along various freeways, he revealed in strict confidence the little drama that had led to our abrupt change of travel mode.

"Madge threw a tantrum" was the simplest explanation. Let me add that she and Duke and their guests were in a motorcycle-cop-escorted limo leading our cortege. Still, my immediate superior and I half-whispered as if the first lady were only a few seats away from us.

"When was that?" I asked.

"Last night," Harry answered.

The scene was described to me—the three of them, Duke, Madge, and Harry, by themselves in the gubernatorial suite, prior to leaving for the presidential dinner.

"She was hectoring poor Duke in front of me like a banshee," Harry said, or words to that effect, and he quoted her shouting, "The state won't go broke if you spring for a few airline tickets!

It's a legitimate expense. And who cares, anyway?"

Duke's rebuttal was the problem of needing to pay out of his executive budget for their guests and the press who'd come along.

"So what?" Madge kept crying, according to Harry. "So what? Find a way. Find a way."

Harry's final line was, "I knew from the boss's hangdog look how it was going to end." And Harry, who had good mimicking ability, mimed a clown-like expression, part funny, part piteous.

This is the closest approach to documentary evidence I am able to present. Madge—I have to tell you—later denied in toto that it had been her idea to change planes, asserting that Duke had arranged the whole thing, thinking to please her. Nonsense. It was early the next morning when Harry was called by Madge and told to make the change to a regular airline and he'd have Tim to help him.

Meanwhile, as we sped toward our *rendezvous with destiny,* what of the other side of the fatal equation—Miles Monahan? His movements have been roughly traced. Somehow, he made his escape across the hotel grounds without detection. Aware he was being hunted, he hadn't gone back to his conspicuous red-white-and-blue jalopy parked on a back street in Santa Monica. We don't know where he hid out until his arrival—coinciding incredibly with ours—late morning the next day at LAX.

Personally, I like to picture him hiding in a Catholic house of worship. As a matter of fact, I imagine him inside a replica in my mind of St. Patrick's, which was the parish church of our old neighborhood, with its weathered stone façade that reflected, at least in my eyes, a nostalgic sense of Ireland. Miles sometimes took me with him to the rectory next door, where I played Ping-Pong against the priest while he cheered me on. The awesome interior of the holy sanctuary, itself, witnessed on occasion (a wedding, a funeral, or waiting for Miles to confess) is mostly in my memory a pastiche of burning candles and gaudy stained glass windows, the bloody reds of their colors particularly. And thus I see Miles in a similar ambiance that night, the lone sinner, the would-be assassin, murder in his heart and a small pistol in his pocket, back to his deepest roots, seeking haven, full of fury, more than half-crazed and scared out of his wits. Confession? If so, no priest has ever been found to confirm one, so I can't possibly discover if my scenario has any validity in the first place.

How he got to LAX is a no-brainer. He had money for a cab. They found cash and an airline ticket on his body. Miles was headed to Sacramento. For this piece of information, I have only the word of Harry DeWitt, who heard it from someone else, maybe Tim Lavery. When I got questioned during the aftermath, no one brought this up, like asking me, *Why do you think Monahan was going to Sacramento?* Would I have answered what I had come to believe? *Probably planning to shoot the governor of California.* It seemed plain that once started down his crazy road, Miles was bound and determined to shoot somebody—a person of note, who could win him a substantial headline.

Or, and this has always bugged me as well, was he gunning for me?

What a shocking thought! Realistically, I had to tell myself there was no way on earth Miles could have known our transportation plans and the last-minute shift to LAX. Unless—suppose he'd phoned the hotel and disguised his voice, cleverly obtaining info on our departure destination? No, that was too far-fetched. He couldn't have been lying in wait, expecting to shoot *me* down.

Guilt has to be behind such maundering on my part. Maybe I get a secret masochistic pleasure out of torturing myself. Every time my mind wanders into the awful territory of the LAX scene, I'm haunted by an image. His O. Murray Carr business card—shown to me by Jack Provost—is the troubling ghost, the one Miles had annotated: "Performed for the president."

Now also let me explain why this intended piece of self-advertising had disturbed me so much. Maybe, on the very cusp of the abyss, about to plunge into chaos, my old buddy had decided to draw back and his note to me at the end was a desperate reaching out for help. All unconsciously, then, ever since my arrival in LA, I'd kept turning my back on him, totally absorbed in my own selfish needs, i.e., Jill, but not *only* her, the whole *success* thing, too.

Miles's final fatal note in its entirety lay before me on my desk now. Remember John Hinckley, Jr., who wounded Reagan, thinking to impress the movie star Jody Foster? I mean, we're talking mental illness here, a serious aberration of thinking. Right from the start, Miles's tone was exalted: *Showtime tonight, Jonathan old boy, eight-thirty curtain. Be in your seat*—followed by his giveaway rhyme: *Because I'm going to bring you to your feet.* Yes, he most certainly was planning to do something sensational. Then, a less gaudy assertion but absolutely sinister: *Maybe they'll consider me a poet, too.* Got that? —*a poet, too.* What else would they consider him? An assassin, naturally, after he'd shot the president. No doubt about the hint. *My extravaganza, you won't forget*—plain and simple, his boffo finale of pumping bullets from the stage, maybe jumping down from the proscenium and shouting "Sic semper tyrannis" as he had in our grammar-school play. His meaning seemed so plain in retrospect.

However, despite Miles's immersion in an airy dream world, he still had enough wits about him to flee, sensing danger, doffing his telltale costume (another act of rationality), and grabbing one of his pistols, which might not have seemed rational but merely preparation for a new act of madness, for example, like trying to settle for shooting the governor of California.

Instead, he killed a governor anyway, through sheer incomprehensible chance, and died doing it, too.

I have tried to examine this tragedy from Miles's point of

view. He surely felt I had squealed on him. Most assuredly, he wouldn't have sympathized with my argument that an American citizen, knowing the president was threatened, had a duty to inform the authorities. For all I know, there may be a law you must report. I regret nothing

Except, forever, the scene that ensued after our party entered the terminal at LAX.

At the time, I was walking alongside Jill, looking forward to the five- or six-hour ride back to the East Coast, being with her close to me the entire time (Harry DeWitt had seen to it that we were in adjoining seats).

Duke and Madge and—what-the-devil were their names?— the Leavitts, yes Leavitts, were up ahead in the hallway. Tim Lavery was next to Duke. Without being aware of it, we were approaching a set of public restrooms.

As in any fatal accident, everything happened too fast.

Gazillions of moments have I run that enduring picture in my mind. The ladies' room was closer to us than the men's room. I myself noticed a phenomenon I was to observe many times— males—husbands or boyfriends—standing outside and guarding luggage while wives or sweethearts were inside freshening up. I never had a chance to notice if just beyond, females were waiting by the men's room in a similar scenario. Duke and his immediate entourage were on the point of reaching the men's room entrance. Bringing up the rear behind me were Harry DeWitt, Georgie Everoff, those three print reporters, and Jill's cameraman.

A couple of guys were coming out of the men's room. Was Miles the third or the second?

At any rate, I saw him! I cried, "Miles!"

He saw me. I could see him see me.

And here's where it gets all kafoodled. Did I ever see the gun he pulled from his pants pocket? Did I ever see him take his eyes off me and spy Duke striding toward him?

All of a sudden, I heard the first gunshot. The sound was that low level *pop!* I don't believe I caught sight of Duke as he fell.

Then *blam!* the much louder blast of Tim's service revolver rent the air. Focusing my horrified gaze in the next few seconds, I discovered Miles was lying on his back, completely still, near the men's-room door. Blood was forming around him on the slick surface of the airport floor.

We all rushed forward. Tim, weapon in hand, waved us back. Duke was down. Leavitt and his wife were on their knees beside him. Madge was screaming.

There is always an aftermath and it was just beginning. I soon had a chance to verify that it was, indeed, Miles Monahan who had fired at my boss and been felled by Tim.

From where I observed Miles, I couldn't see his face the way his head had twisted, but the hair—the sandy shade of blond—that was surely his hair that I'd known since childhood. Usually, it was tousled, but occasionally spit-shined neat, when he was en route to church, looking like a little angel.

No angel now, with smears of blood staining his locks.

Once the nightmare had been absorbed and the dreadful news came back that Duke was dead, questions started raging, at least in my mind.

What was Miles doing at LAX? The obvious answer, which turned out to be correct, was to catch a plane. That ticket to Sacramento *was* found in one of his pockets. Another uncanny coincidence: the commuter puddle-jumper he planned to take was run by a subsidiary of the major commercial carrier flying us home, and the same terminal served both types of flights.

Why was Miles in the men's room? Silly question. Any answer would include an act of nature or maybe combing his hair, but a more cogent query would be: what was his mood, emerging out into the hallway? Was he furtive? Was he wound up tight as a drum from the tension of his fugitive status? He may have already had his hand on the .22 pistol in his pocket, as if to conceal any bulge. (All this was before the days of metal detectors.)

And the impulse, itself, that bade him shoot so spontaneously, what (no pun intended) *triggered* it?

I had yelled. He'd seen me. Why wasn't I gunned down instead of Duke?

Miles had met Duke, knew he was a governor—was this the motivation, his name in lights, headlines, a newsworthy trial? He probably never expected to be shot dead himself.

Something snapped, and the results were there before us, in the absolute—shall I call it chaos?—of crowds, police, and 911 responders that soon were swarming around the murder site.

Media, too, and the earliest recorders of the incident were Jill and her cameraman. Before I knew it, she had left my side and was directing Charley on what angles to use with his hand-held camera, providing coverage for her unbelievable *scoop*.

When I noticed such behavior, frankly I got very pissed off at her.

But before I go into that added complication, I need to impart one bit of information I already knew about my erratic chum Miles. I had received it earlier from Tim, as promised, back at the hotel while we all were waiting in the lobby for our transportation to the airport.

The state trooper, himself, initiated the conversation.

"Got a second?" he asked, taking me aside after he apparently saw a lull in my conversation with Jill.

"Sure," I said, and once we were out of earshot, I quickly added, "You know, last night my old schoolmate [an instinct told me not to say *buddy*] never appeared on stage."

I knew this would be an opening for him to provide me with some news. Instead, he inquired, "And you had another wild night with the TV lady?"

I could see her watching the two of us and answered sotto voce, "If you must know, yes."

"In her room?"

My response was, "Right after the show, practically. We didn't stay to do much dancing." Instead of asking, *Why do you want to know?*, I realized I was offering, at his invitation, an alibi of some sort.

"Good," Tim said.

Thus I realized I had correctly sensed some big problem with Miles.

Tim gave me one of his rare tight-lipped smiles, saying rather sardonically, "You may win a medal, Jonathan."

I kept myself from asking what exactly had happened.

"They're looking for him, Jonathan," Tim went on. "If you ever hear again from this Mr. O. Murray Carr, let me know real pronto."

"I can't believe I ever will," I said.

Those were my actual words, I swear. But not my actual thought. It was a sort of cover-up, if you must know. What I should write is, *I had a stab of fear.* Instinctive terror. Not aware then about Miles's hidden guns in the stilts, I nevertheless sensed he was dangerous, at large, and undoubtedly considered me responsible for having fingered him. I would be safe temporarily. But why couldn't he come after me at a later date? Maybe a year from now. It was like having the Mafia on your trail.

Consequently, one of my first emotions, seeing Miles stretched out and lying inert in his own blood, should have been relief, right?

No way.

Once the shock wore off, shouldn't I—rationally—have counted my blessings? Like with Gerry Margolis, following the horrendous accident that took his life and could easily have taken mine. I was in the back seat that night. Gerry was in the *death seat* up front, next to the driver, who was a guy named Parker Ingstrom. We were a bunch of high-spirited college kids on vacation, headed to pick up Miles, the four of us to go "cruising." Then, Jesus!

"Parker, you idiot, why didn't you stay on Scott Street?" Gerry and I were yelling at him in unison. Did we spook him? The pickup truck, which ran the red light on Carter Avenue would have hit us all the same. Smashed right into the side where Gerry sat. We rolled over at least once. I hit my head, was knocked cold, cut by flying glass. Parker walked away without a scratch. Gerry was DOA.

It happened. But it can't have happened. Yet you knew it did. Throughout the service in the synagogue, amid the wailing crowd at the gravesite, sitting *shiva* in the Margolis household, I kept mulling over this mystery. Why him, why not me? The rabbi's answer was cold comfort. Almighty God knows what He's doing. Bullshit. I could merely munch delicatessen, repeating thoughts of, *If only Parker hadn't*—or—*If only Parker had . . .* and, to be honest, feeling guiltily glad to be alive. Nor will I ever rid myself of a final image: Irish Miles Monahan wearing a black yarmulke and his tawny head resting on my shoulder, tears in his tough emerald eyes, while he whispered to me, his remaining All-American Patrol companion, "I miss that damn Hebe already."

Back to LAX. It was getting close to noon by then. Cell phones, as I've indicated, had not yet been invented or else we all would have been on them, but instead we were milling about, then waiting, waiting, until the bodies were removed.

The original plane we were planning to board, of course, left without us. Airline schedules don't stop for assassinations. But our journalists were soon ushered off to another flight and thus Jill and I were parted.

Our whole staff needed to stay, we were told. Jill had protested to Harry that she had wanted to contact her office to see if they would like her to remain and afford them coverage from Los Angeles. That little scene she had with Harry somehow angered me even more—she was just being a news hen—and Harry was saying if we, the state, were paying her airfare, she had to get her ass on that next plane. Then she dragged me into it, asking, "Can't you do anything with him?"—making me out as a wimp. I told her I didn't very much care for her taking advantage, and did she think she and her cameraman would be remembered like Zapruder, or win the Pulitzer Prize? I probably said some other stuff I shouldn't have.

So Jill went off in a fury. No tender farewell, no parting kiss, a huff to end all huffs. She was positively dry-eyed, too, not shedding a single tear, neither for Duke, nor for me, an iron maiden newswoman to the core.

Watching her walk away, my thought was: *Miles has fired his second bullet.* With the luck of the Irish, Miles has killed two birds with one stone.

One of them a single, lucky shot straight into Duke's heart.

And I had other things to worry about, as well. Tim, for example. Was he eyeing me with suspicion or was I just fantasizing? My yelling "Miles!" maybe meant something. But explainable as an exclamation of surprise. It so happened I did get questioned by various investigators of the crime, whose agencies ranged from federal to state to municipal and county. What weighed most heavily in my favor was Tim's avowal that I had tipped him off and that he had tipped off the Secret Service and the prez had been spirited away to safety. I never received a medal, needless to say, but Tim took the trouble to inform me I'd done well in my answers and that I had his full support in backing up my innocence and putting down this whole bizarre affair to sheer if mind-boggling fate.

Pondering the event afterward for all these years, I would always end with the conclusion that if the president had been shot and killed that night by Mr. O. Murray Carr, Uncle Sam impersonator, it would not have mattered a great deal. My decades-long study of presidential and other assassinations in the USA, or would-be attempts, has convinced me that no public figure's murder among us has ever fatally rocked the Republic. Lincoln's undoubtedly produced the most profound impact, but the intricate problems that his successors essentially blundered would have plagued him the same way and perhaps lessened his legacy. Kennedy's demise brought sharp, wholesale grief, as the death of any young god would do, perpetuating lingering melancholy for another would-be Arthurian golden age lost. The other two presidential killings—those of Garfield and McKinley—heck, they were sad and stupid, yet in the final analysis, inconsequential. Who else shot down might have had a countrywide effect? Huey Long? He could have given FDR a serious run for the Democratic nomination in 1936 and, if successful, provided us a tough dose of homegrown dictatorship, as he did in Louisiana. George Wallace? Just another would-be Fascist sidelined. Bobby? Would he have been elected president? Martin? Wouldn't we have gotten where we are, anyway, in race relations?

Duke's death provoked a handful of "what-might-have-been" columns in national newspapers and a brief flurry of coverage on the network news.

Almost before we realized it, Richard Nathaniel Ellery slid into history and left me, in particular, suffering sleepless nights, counting the what-ifs of my own life. Big shot in the White House? A star on the national stage? Cabinet officer? U.S. senator?

Also, the negative. I won't go into every what-if I used to torture myself with in Duke's case. For example, *What if I'd stayed home and never gone to California?*

But—I would end up arguing—*in that case, I might never have married Jill.*

You see, there's no drawn-out broken romance suspense here. She and I obviously did manage to get back together: the rocky road of true love and all such sob stuff. Outside events, I suppose, can only do so much mischief once a relationship seems preordained. Nevertheless, you must have realized by now, the assassination of Governor Duke Ellery, while only briefly noticed beyond the boundaries of our state, most certainly changed my life forever.

19

How long have I been writing? I ask the question not because I want to put down an answer, but as a rhetorical attempt to illustrate a truism. Time means nothing when you're at your keyboard. Neither does it count, really, when applied to the created product on the screen. An author might take a week of eight-hour workdays and fill up twenty pages to describe an event lasting forty minutes.

On second thought, before I go on, let me backtrack a bit, break down and succinctly fill out the love story from the time Jill and I had our epic spat.

Any reader who has been paying attention knows that while I am upstairs in my office within sight of the ocean, Jill Annette McKenzie Jackson is a second member of the household. If she is not physically present in the house at this moment, her clothes certainly are in her closet and her scent, her perfume, tinges the air inside to mingle with the briny smell off the nearby beach and its breakers. We married, had a child, have stuck together. Yet a fair question: How did we two get to the altar?

God knows, it's taken me long enough to finish the National Governors Conference story and its startling denouement. The love story has almost an equally full set of complications. But honestly, since I'm much more interested in the political story—a turn of events that affected the United States of America, no less—for me to switch into the soap opera mode of a male-female relationship, trite in its telling albeit the God's honest truth, was genuinely too scary. But then again, I have argued with myself that the backdrop to our reconciliation was directly linked to political events in the wake of Duke's death. As a favorite clichéd phrase often heard in our Statehouse debates expresses it, in this case, love and government were "inextricably intertwined."

A quick aside first: In ages past, I used to smoke. Jill didn't, never started. That she put up with my tobacco mouth and wreaths of secondhand bluish haze should have indicated to me the force of our kinetic attraction for each other. She was also amused by the silly habit I had of employing my pants cuffs as an ashtray when there was no other appropriate receptacle nearby. She called it *cute.* Later, once she took charge of my wardrobe, she wasn't so thrilled discovering the little holes I had burned in the cloth.

"You'll set yourself on fire one of these days if you don't quit," she nagged. Eventually, I gave up the nasty weed and that was still many years ago.

The transition from lover to housewife occurred gradually. Okay, but how about the complications of our courtship? We'd had a serious row. Stuck in California, feeling bad about our quarrel, I kept silently bringing up the question: *Will I call her when I get back?*

Three days of numbed, seemingly round-the-clock activity in LA were enough to fulfill our staff's responsibilities. While we—particularly Tim and myself—underwent various degrees of interrogation (and for Tim it was pro forma routine in any instance where a law officer has to shoot someone), an autopsy was performed on Duke's body and it was finally released to an undertaker for embalming and shipment home. Irony of ironies: we traveled with him on the same Air National Guard plane—Madge included.

I should have foreseen that Jill and her faithful cameraman would be among the media covering the landing at home and the slow, sad business of transferring the flag-draped casket to the hearse that would carry it to the capitol for the lying in state prior to the official funeral.

Big Bob Benton was now the governor. His jocular, hail-fellow-well-met presence at the airfield only added to our deep gloom as we alighted after a many-hour trip endured for the most part in silence. Politics too complicated to explain had led to Big Bob's lieutenant governor spot on Duke's ticket in the previous state election. I always remember Harry's remark when a member of our staff referred to Big Bob as "nothing but a damn ribbon-cutter."

"Yes," Harry agreed, "but, heaven be praised, he's *our* damn ribbon-cutter."

Standing on the tarmac while the coffin was being lowered, watching Big Bob approach Madge, who stood with those two family friends, the Leavitts, who had stayed in California and accompanied her back, his hands outstretched to enfold her hands in his, I thought to myself, *Oh, my Lord, he's our damn governor! God help us!*

In all honesty, I hadn't noticed Jill until the "press opportunity" commenced. Strange to say, I immediately focused on what she was wearing. The weather had turned cold, a nippy fall day, but sunny and bright, as if to mock all of the sorrow we felt. Her plaid wool skirt was visible where the unsecured bottom button of her topcoat let it peek out, and then, given the circumstances, ashamed that I was staring at her hem and legs, I lifted my eyes quickly to the woolen scarf of the same plaid draped around her neck and shoulders. A McKenzie tartan, I surmised.

Our eyes didn't meet during the speeches. There might have been only one talk—a pontifical set of platitudes from "Governor Bob," had not Madge stepped up to the microphone after he finished. The suspense was almost palpable. What would she say, the grieving widow dressed in black? We on the staff hadn't a clue. None of the three of us had been asked to prepare anything for her.

If she had intended to make the news—and I'm sure Madge did—her discourse was perfect. I know some of our crew had always considered her a spoiled, pretty woman, basically an airhead, who was a nice adornment for Duke, photogenic, great smile, whose celebrity looks complemented those of her husband. I was of a different opinion, suspecting although without any proof, that she was tough and brainy beneath her finishing-school exterior.

Right away, she opened up on a taboo subject. There was a brief preamble—a thank-you for all the expressions of support she had received—and then she went at it—gun control! Yikes, even Duke, politically courageous as he was, hadn't ever dared to touch that hornets' nest!

I was ungracious enough to be shocked and automatically, momentarily in a staffer's mode, worried about a political faux pas. My head cleared the next minute with the realization of where I was, what had happened. Ashamed, I forgot about Jill's fetching plaids, her silken legs, and listened to my late boss's widow.

Soon, my mind was drifting off. The core of my thinking derived from Madge's premise, which was logical enough, that the U.S. population was gun-crazy, and therefore tragedies such as the one that had just touched and ruined her life, could be averted with laws that clamped down on the sale and possession of weapons. It was an understandable syndrome. Do something! Devote yourself to a crusade! Thus assuage your grief.

But silently, I quite instinctively counter-argued with her, telling myself the problem was deeper. I had Miles Monahan to use as an example. It wasn't his ability to obtain handguns that had been his impetus. He'd told me his arsenal had been purchased legally, and I had no reason to doubt him. An inner motivation had detonated his act of madness, so where had that impulse come from?

Madge talked on and on. I caught snatches of what she said, phrases like: "End the climate of violence in America." And, "License the license to kill." Occasionally, there was some tepid applause.

Meanwhile, I pursued my own thoughts. They were not terribly original. Crucified on a cross of red, white, and blue was one image: *O. Murray Carr*—a dead giveaway of the pressures to succeed in our society and the ignominy of failure. Miles's very talent had brought him down in that it had never shown through enough. But, feisty kid, he wouldn't stay among the downtrodden. He would make a name for himself, for the history books, like John Wilkes Booth, for example.

Of course, there are millions of losers in the U.S. and only a few, but all too many, go on such rampages. What laws, what government, can prevent this? Madge was going down a road that made sense to her. But I was—honestly—genuinely skeptical.

I couldn't help but wonder what Miles would have thought of his "accomplishment." One bit of his thinking might have been that he was playing the *heavy*, the Hollywood slang for *villain*—and that *heavies*, if their performances were good enough, had been known to win Oscars. Had he not been unexpectedly shot down, had he been arrested, gone through a trial, what kind of bravura figure would he have made for the media and history? What defense would his lawyers present? Or would he have tried to dispense with legal counsel and stand in the spotlight alone, at last a star? Poor Miles. Boy, had he ever screwed up. But screwed me, too.

Yes, I could think bitterly, that's why he didn't shoot at me in the airport, why he turned his gun on Duke. He saw me forging ahead of him, entering the big time on the coattails of my boss. He'd show me.

Oh hell, I remember musing as I stood listening to our ex-first lady, what a mess.

I acknowledged the fact that I was now facing a potentially bleak future. *There's America for you,* I told myself, also bitterly. Quick, quick turns of fate.

Madge was finishing her talk. The applause at the end was still only polite.

Would I still have a job?

I stared in Jill's direction again. She was still directing Charley Fischer's camerawork. How could I even think about trying to get back with her? All of my fantasy—marriage, a family, apple pie, and red-white-and-blue America for Jonathan Jackson—all seemed to have come crashing down.

I watched Jill signal to Charley that they had enough footage of Madge Ellery, and then, like a stroke of lightning, she and I made eye contact.

I can hardly describe the feeling. Maybe *heart-pounding.* God, I had to see her again!

Once she smiled, I felt faint, but afraid to become elated—until her lips threw me a simulated kiss, followed by two words mouthed silently: *Call me.* Immediately afterward, turned around, facing the camera, she was the busy television anchor-woman once more, recording commentary into her portable microphone.

I might have sought Jill out except that Harry DeWitt was gesturing to me. The new governor wanted to see us. "Big Bob says to follow him as soon as he says goodbye to Madge," George Everoff and I were told. I reflected on two things then: 1) that previously Harry would have said "The Boss" and how he couldn't bring himself to use that term now; and 2) that I noticed a tall state trooper in civvies standing next to Big Bob as his bodyguard, not Tim, because Tim had stayed behind in LA, working with federal and California investigators on details of the shootings. My bet was that he would never regain his old assignment upon his return, which proved to be true.

Anyway, I stood with my colleagues, eyes on Governor Big Bob and Tim's replacement as they escorted Madge to the state limousine that had been arranged for her use. Only then did I realize I hadn't seen the two Ellery children. They had apparently been waiting, with a nanny, inside that sleek black vehicle and now rushed out, a girl and a boy, to hug their mother. It was a memorably touching moment. And what touched me even more was a silent bit of drama that I was perhaps the only one on that military airfield to note and appreciate. Charley Fischer, the cameraman, made a motion as if to go photograph the scene. But Jill, with quick, even angry, sign language, waved him away. Wow, was I ever glad to see her do so!

Eventually, we staffers moved to the same hangar where we'd started our flight to California. It felt like eons ago, but actually less than a week had passed. Our discussion with the new governor occurred in a quiet side room. The first words out of Big Bob's mouth were, "Well, boys, I want you guys to stay on . . ." and, right afterward, the rest of what he said became mostly mere noise. I do remember noting several things, however. He didn't set a time limit for us—no mention of "interim"—and I could say to myself, *Jeez, maybe now I can marry Jill,* and almost concurrently, *But Christ, how long will I be able to stand working for that bozo?*

Harry, Georgie, and I were given the rest of the day off to get resettled and were to report for work at the Statehouse the next day.

My own resettling in my bachelor pad took about five minutes. The rest of the time was spent fretfully waiting until I thought it opportune to phone Jill.

I reached her at the television station. We agreed to meet for drinks during the cocktail hour, then had dinner, went back to *my* digs (she shared an apartment with another girl), and within a week, my honey was moving in with me.

It was like a miracle. Neither of us so much as breathed a word about our quarrel and the huff with which we'd parted, or the reasons for it.

To be fair to Trudy (the roommate), Jill continued to pay her part of the rent until a suitable tenant was found. Soon, the two of us, quite imperceptibly, fell into a form of domestic routine. We each had different working hours. Most often, I was home by five or six in the evening (I wasn't going to break my neck, staying late for Big Bob Benton), and Jill, with the six o'clock news to do, would be lucky to arrive by eight. Then we would go into our EF/FF, private-joke game.

The inspiration was an actual joke I'd heard when I was a high-school kid. It goes like this: A sailor in the U.S. Navy is on a ship arriving in port after six months at sea. From the railing, he spots his girlfriend among the welcoming crowd on the pier below. He begins yelling down to her, "FF." She yells back, "EF." He shakes his head and calls out "FF" again. She shakes her head and replies, "EF." One of the sailor's buddies who'd been listening to this exchange, asks his pal, "What's all that about?" And he answers, "Oh, she wants to eat first."

Jill and I reversed these sex roles. Because I was usually hungry, I would call "EF" when she came in the door and she would ordinarily respond, "FF." The rule was that if we differed, we would have to play a round of charades and whoever won got to decide. If both of us concurred, it would be EF or FF, without the need for pantomime.

Silly, sexed-up youth. In love, too, no doubt of it, and no questioning or discussion of it. Grand passion, such as comes only once in a lifetime, if ever, to us mortals. Happily, our luck and satisfaction in each other has held, whatever waning of physical interest age and repeated usage has wrought.

Needless to say, we talked, as well.

We talked and talked and talked, when we weren't performing sex. I once rather cynically likened our conversations to the fiction in the *New Yorker* magazine—endless reminiscences. What we did in high school. Who our friends were. College days. The neighborhood. Going to summer camp. Trips abroad. Eccentric relatives. Escapades. I could go on and on, *ad nauseum*—but to each of us, it was fresh material, of interest because these anecdotes, as they unfolded, added up for each of us to a biography of our beloved. I saw Jill in pigtails playing touch football with her burly brothers, scoring the winning TD on a Statue of Liberty end-around. She saw me hiding under my covers when a cop came into my bedroom to take away my BB gun because I'd shot it at one of my playmates.

Who was that playmate? No surprise. The kid I had pinged in the leg was Miles Monahan, and the Monahans' well-justified complaint had brought the local constabulary to our house, and earned me a major scolding.

But—now here's the rub—in all these reminiscences of mine, I'd never mentioned Miles by name. I'd totally eschewed talking about the All-American Patrol for the same reason. You have to know that Miles Monahan, dubbed a *film actor*, had only been identified by some news sources reporting on the killing at the LAX airport. And it was not even until days later that his real identity had been bared, since the sole ID found on his body had been those O. Murray Carr business cards in his wallet—no driver's license, no credit cards, nothing else. Remember in his final note, how peeved he was that I'd called him Miles?

Even Jill, on the air, spoke of "Murray O'Carr," the way the Associated Press wire had listed Duke's killer, once she had started her broadcasts with the edited footage Charley had shot. Initially, anyway, she'd had no knowledge of "Miles Monahan" and no inkling of my involvement.

Disclosure was inevitable, but in my case, totally unpremeditated. Jill and I had finished a "quickie" on my living room couch early one evening several weeks after the assassination. My post-coital cigarette was already lit (I absolutely had to have a few drags following intercourse), disgorging its whitish-bluish smoke into the air. The piece of padded, pillowed furniture on which we'd thrashed and strained had turned into a love seat for the momentarily exhausted duo we'd become. Finally relaxed enough, our stories resumed, one from Jill, following which, from me, up popped the saga of the BB gun.

Next was my pause. I had described the big, burly cop standing by my bedside, but then I hesitated far too long.

The *secret!* One lover has kept information from the other. It's the suspense element, if not the core, of most romantic dramas—that is, its revelation determines the action, produces the circumstances for a denouement.

Jill was staring at me quizzically, while I remained as if frozen in open-mouthed midsentence.

"And?" she softly demanded.

Plunge right in, Jonathan. That was an instinct, not a command. *End the stupid fuss now.*

"Do you know who I shot, hit with that BB?" I asked rhetorically, and continued right straight on with, "My God, I really hadn't thought of the irony. Me shooting him! It was Miles Monahan, age eleven."

The puzzlement on Jill's pretty face was brief. "Why do I know that name?" she said.

My answer need not be reproduced here in its entirety. It was nothing less than the whole divulgence of what had transpired in Los Angeles, unbeknownst to her, as related to my childhood pal, complete with touches of guilt I hadn't worked out, namely how I somehow felt partly responsible for the tragedy, and a lot more besides, including the All-American Patrol, Miles and Gerry and myself, some of our escapades, Gerry's sudden tragic end, and now something similarly horrendous again, but no mere accident.

Jill listened, seemingly spellbound, not saying a word until I had apparently finished.

She nodded to herself a couple of times. "You yelled out something in the airport terminal," she stated. "I heard you yell out something that did sound like 'Miles,' which made no sense to me."

"But you never asked me anything."

"I didn't want to pry. I was afraid you might think, 'Oh, she's just after a story—just another pushy news bitch.'"

To say that I was deeply touched (emotionally) would be an understatement. I just looked at her and kept looking and I believe tears may have shown in my eyes. Gently, Jill took the remainder of the cigarette I'd been smoking from my grasp and stubbed it into an ashtray, then cradled my head in her lap, like a mother crooning to her child, comforting me, purring almost, over and over again, a murmur of "Poor poodle, poor poodle."

A long period of silence ensued, after our joint confessions, and then Jill moved to get her clothes, which had been tossed on the floor.

"Wow, you look good like that," I called from the cushion I was lolling on. "You should go on the air like that."

She shot me a look that seemed partly annoyance mixed with a sense of mischievous humor. "Why should I show the world what is only meant for your eyes, sailor?"

In the same vein and tone, I responded, "Well, it might improve your ratings."

"Fuck you," she said, and threw the garments she had picked up at me, followed by a physical attack, landing on my chest, kissing, kissing, and a lot more action over which I will draw a discreet veil.

This pre-marriage period of our lives—an idyll, you might

say—arrived at its foregone conclusion in another rather similar scene. On this occasion we were in bed, not in the living room, post-coital once again, and I had more than several butts in the ashtray on the end table next to my side.

It had struck me, as I gazed languidly around the bedroom and through an open door out to the rest of the apartment, that Jill had already partly domesticated these surroundings. Not just the dresses, et al., hanging in my closet and several drawers of my bureau given over to frilly things. I realized there was now a prettily patterned cloth on the previously bare wood surface of the kitchen table where we ate. The sofa's cold brown leather had an attractive spread on it. Curtains, for God's sake, were draped from our few windows; framed photos of Paris, France, were on the walls, and the one item of decoration she'd left me—the triangular college football banners of my childhood—had been permitted to remain.

"What do you think?" I suddenly said, apropos of nothing we had been saying earlier. "Should we get married?"

"What a charming way to propose?" Jill rejoined.

"Does that mean yes?"

She tenderly smacked me on the side of the head. "Clown!"

I began picking the cigarette butts out of the ashtray. "She loves me, she loves me not, she loves me . . . ," putting back each one as I chanted. It was obvious I would end with *she loves me not.*

Restraining my hand, Jill objected. "Can't you at least get down on one knee?"

"I'd have to get out of bed," I whined.

"Oh, all right. . . . Yes," she said.

Whereupon we both arose, unclothed, and jumped up and down on the mattress and squealed and hugged and kissed and squealed some more—my God how we squealed!

20

HERE'S AN INSIGHT into the secrets of a writer. I'm standing in my office, having had to get out of my chair to retrieve a sheet from my printer. It's the previous page of this manuscript and it has struck me that it should end the chapter. At such a juncture, however, art and real life clash. What better place—theatrically—to take a break. We're getting married! We're going to live happily ever after! End of a perfect story, right?

Like hell it is. Fiction can truncate wherever. Any reader worth his or her salt, though, will feel dissatisfied if left dangling like this. As I realize the problem, I've decided to keep the page break but go right into a chronological flow of what relevant details developed out of our momentous decision, mine and Jill's, to take the plunge.

For instance, the wedding. Everyone likes to know about such lacy hearts-and-flowers stuff. I can even tell you the outfit the bride wore. I believe it's called a "suit": a jacket and skirt, with silk blouse to match—absolutely stunning in pale, shimmering blue-green (none of this white virginity business for us). Actually, we were trying to save our money for a honeymoon trip to France (do you have any idea of the prices they want for those one-time-use gowns?). We had the ceremony performed, too, in the capital, where we were both working. Her folks flew up from Florida, to which they'd retired; her brothers came from scattered small-town locations in the Midwest. We even found a Presbyterian church nearby (they're rare in New England) in which to exchange our vows and have a nonalcoholic reception to please

"Mom" and "Pop," or Sandy (Alexander) and Penny, as I was instructed to call them.

Harry DeWitt was my best man and Georgie Everoff one of the ushers. Jill had a passel of bridesmaids from the TV station staff along with some of their other personnel like Charley Fischer. Guess who else came? Governor Big Bob Benton! I'd sent him an invite, strictly out of courtesy, and the big lug, large as life, ended up right in the front pew with his new bodyguard. (Tim had gone back to trooper status up north and couldn't attend.) Yet another pro forma request for the pleasure of her attendance had gone to Madge Ellery. We never heard back from her and I, for one, couldn't have cared less.

The honeymoon? Two weeks abroad. Jill had spent her junior year in Paris, so we decided to stick to France but also see something of the countryside. With her memories of the Left Bank surfeited (I'd never so much as been to Europe then, so I loved everything), we headed for Brittany and discovered Cancale on the Emerald Coast (*Cote Emeraude*), near St. Malo, and Mont St. Michel.

Did we ever slurp up oysters, wash down white wine, imbibe the smell of algae and the sight of sails on the horizon! And somewhere in this revel on the other Atlantic shore, I heard Jill say, "When we get home, we should think about living by the ocean someday."

And that, dear folks, brings us to Swanstown.

My first visit then to the historic seaside community had been with Duke. He'd been invited to address a Democratic supper held in the old Swanstown Grange Hall, which had long since been converted into an all-purpose, bipartisan meeting space for local events. It was a potluck affair entitled "Meet Your Governor," and Ron Gordon, its chief organizer, had put out fliers inviting any citizen regardless of party, without—I might add—indicating where the admission fees would go.

I'd heard a lot about Ron ahead of time, how smart he was, how aggressive in a hopelessly Republican climate on that stretch of wealthy and redneck coast, but that he was little by little making Democratic inroads and (from Harry DeWitt) how Duke wanted to give him every support.

To make a long story short, I met Ron, and we hit it off. We saw each other in the capital, at conventions, had drinks and dinner together on occasion—that is, all prior to the fateful trip to the West Coast.

Afterward, back home one spring weekend when Jill was off work, I had the bright idea of driving to Swanstown, called Ron, and he found us a nice bed and breakfast a block from the beach. Jill also met Mitzi and they instantly "bonded." Or should I say: became genial co-conspirators on a number of fronts.

The upshot, four months later, was a radical change in our lifestyle.

We're talking about September now. Approximately a year and three months remained of Duke's unexpired term, and Big Bob would then have to run that following November to keep his position. I knew he wanted to be reelected and I knew I didn't want to go on working for him, so I thought the decent thing would be to give what amounted to more than a year's notice.

Please don't get me wrong. I actually came to like Big Bob. No, certainly I didn't admire him, but he was a kindly guy who meant well. Most interesting to me about him was his ambition. He seemed to have none. Yet he had drifted—if that's the right word—with a minimum of effort into high places.

Under Big Bob, I was easily replaceable. Each day, the governor's office received hundreds of letters, mostly from constituents—voters—who had to be answered. During Duke's tenure, I had done some of that scut work, which everyone needed to do considering its overwhelming volume. On Big Bob's payroll, I answered letters and more letters, almost exclusively, until

I was ready to scream or run amok.

What I didn't know for some time was how frustrated Jill was with her anchorwoman's role.

One night, it just burst for both of us.

"Oh, for a smoky old bar lounge," I started off the complaining after we'd finished supper, sitting at the kitchen table, with the dirty dishes uncleared. This was a pet phrase of mine and Jill knew its origin: on one of the trips Miles and I had taken to Lake Edgeremet, we'd seen the phrase scribbled on a hut doorpost in the deep woods where some canoeists had been marooned for a week by rain. When exasperated by a boring task, I often let that expression fly willy-nilly.

"Well, you seem to be doing a good job of converting *these* premises," Jill remarked lightheartedly, pointing to the half-filled ashtray near me. But then, looking serious, she asked me, "Are you really so homesick for Manhattan?"

In our subsequent discussion, a major misunderstanding got ironed out, thank God. True, I had been making noises—like the cryptic comment cited above—regarding the lure of a city atmosphere. Yet, as I immediately explained, concerned over the worried frown on my wife's face, I had been thinking that's where *she* wanted to go in order to continue her career. It soon became clear to me that she felt as much at a standstill as I did.

Once we were both on the same page, essentially pooh-poohing any move to a major urban destination, we could plan much more easily what she—and the Gordons—already had in mind for the Jacksons.

We would give notice at work, move to Swanstown, buy a house. Jill (with Mitzi's help) had checked on one we could afford and Ron had reconnoitered a post for me teaching in the state university branch in nearby Tracy, the county seat. But Jill started blushing as I said, "So now you're going to be a lady of leisure. No Big Apple national network stardom for my gal."

"Who needs it?" she responded. Then, a sort of shy quality crept into her gaze and voice when she told me, "I've got better things to do."

Thus did I learn she was pregnant.

Also, little did I know that among the items on Ron Gordon's hidden agenda for luring us to his town was to induce me—after a few years of establishing myself—to run for office. His "invisible hand" in the community guided the trajectory of (Associate) Professor Jackson, generally in accordance with my predilections, to the Historical Society, the Environmental Watchdogs, Friends of the Ocean, and—just as important—the Swanstown Area Fish and Game Club.

Nor should I ignore Duke's unseen spirit. By the time Jill and I moved from the capital, he had been dead three-quarters of a year and people were forgetting him, even on "the Hill," as we, too, referred to *our* capitol-topped knoll. Our state government, like a mechanical behemoth, had merely clanked on.

We're all aware of what's known from its practice in Washington, D.C., as the "Inside the Beltway" syndrome. The capitals of the fifty states exert a similar parochial pressure on their political pros. Another name for it, usually applied to the self-centeredness of children, is "the illusion of central position." We spoke of an *-itis* appended to the name of our capital, much as you might have *Jefferson Cityitis* in Missouri or *Frankfortitis* in Kentucky. Okay, Governor Duke was dead; long live Governor Big Bob; and the public would genuflect to this quasimonarch, whoever he was, to whom they'd rendered fleeting power. I kid you not, you should have read some of the letters my bosses received, which began, "Your Excellency, please do this for me . . . ," but, reflecting our deep American sense of Democracy, they could as easily tell the chief executive, "You are a total jerk, you jerk"

It's a percentage game in the USA. You win some, you lose some. The idea is to go over 50 percent in favorability and, hopefully, much more. Duke was around 73 percent at the time he was slain and close to 84 percent right afterward.

No kidding again, he could have become president. I've never let myself doubt that fact, despite being the only guru to put such a prediction in print.

Madge undoubtedly thinks the same, but she has never expressed these feelings. Frankly, she might serve as a poster child for "illusion of central position" through her insistence that the only fitting memorial for her late husband would be a gun control bill passed by the legislature and signed into law. Nothing else will do, not even a good biography, as I learned the hard way.

One reason, to be frank, that I put off undertaking this work for so long was Madge's lack of cooperation. I've not been allowed to look at Duke's letters and private papers—at least those in her control. Fair enough, I thought, she's planning to give them over to an author with a national reputation and guarantee the maximum exposure possible. But nothing has ever appeared.

Therefore, despite my thick folder of research on Duke, I was hamstrung at the start in framing a conventional biography of the late Richard N. Ellery.

One of the things I did, for the fun of it, one particular afternoon, was to Google Governor Richard N. Ellery. A page full of entries had me busy for about half an hour—most of them pretty slim pickings, those online encyclopedia squibs that give you bare facts: birthplace, Hamilton, Massachusetts; descendant of early Puritans on both sides; Exeter and Harvard and Harvard Law for schools; Peace Corps in Micronesia; military service, captain U.S. Army; congressman, governor, assassinated (with the date); and a paragraph about his political career; mention of his GI Bill II state educational initiative and his work in D.C. for clean water and children's health programs; married to the former Marjorie Nesbitt Jones, whose father had been a CEO at . . . and so forth, incontrovertible bits of information and nothing else—resulting in a line drawing, a stick figure, hardly rising to a caricature.

A few of the Google offerings included Duke's photograph. He looked like what he was ethnically—an impeccable WASP, perhaps using the word *impeccable* in the French sense, which Jill has taught me means *terrific,* or as the Brits would say, *smashing,* not merely *neat* or *sleek.*

Unfortunately, no one had really posted any of those extemporaneous slugs of blog writing that crop up now and then on Google. I had high hopes for the sole maverick piece about Duke, written in French ("Needs to Be Translated") and Jill did the honors for me and said it was simply a crackpot delineation by some socialist of a plot involving "*Hellery*" [Ellery] and "*Moorie, le tueur* [Murray, the murderer]," who were contriving to do away with "*Monsieur le Président,* so "*Hellery*" could take his place, but that the scheme backfired and ended with both of them dead, so neither could talk.

Gimme a break!

And while engaged in playing the Internet, I likewise—less for fun than out of curiosity—Googled Miles Monahan. Nothing showed about him, the killer of a public person, though some other Miles Monahans appeared—the name is hardly unique. Therefore my poor old pal remains bereft, left out of today's virtual *Who's Who,* except for that one fleeting, incomprehensible reference by an unnamed French crackpot. The real big boys of assassination, I should add, like Charles Guiteau, who gunned down Garfield and whom I also looked up, are doing fine in their little corners of Internet-spawned history.

Irony was a thought. The shame of Miles's utter anonymity. Then a totally extraneous image flashed through my mind. A bunch of us kids were gathered at a neighborhood street corner, and Bobby Hanrahan was standing in the middle, bleeding from the nose. Next to him stood Miles, his fist clenched, ready to hit Bobby a second time. "You don't ever call me 'Milesy' again, pig face! Understand?" That scene, buried in my memory, had been retrieved unbidden. Oh, you can bet he was always *Miles* ever afterward around the neighborhood and nobody dared ask him why such rage and insistence over a trifle. I dwelled on this memory for a second. In the quiet of my study, catching sight of a memento I had tacked on the wall—a Christmas card from Duke and Madge—I had another idea. *Dredge from your own memory, Jonathan, your own "Google" of Richard N. Ellery, as well as that of Miles Monahan, and submit it to Wikipedia.*

Wow, what a tall order. The files I had on my desk were daunting enough. *God, I could be here for years* was the next thought I had.

"I need a break," I suddenly said aloud. The initial impulse I felt was to go take a walk. But first I halted by my single window and surveyed conditions outside. The ground in sight still had a dusting left by a mild snowfall several nights earlier. Just enough substance so I'd had to shovel our walks and snow-blow the driveway. The whitish stretches covering our lawn and filling the vacant lot across the street, and the icy-looking hot-top surface of that plowed side road below exuded a real shivery sense of chill, of winter that had come at last, although we were still a ways from its official start, December 21. *I'll take a relaxing drive, instead,* I silently decided.

Elbows still on the windowsill, I ended up peering, as I often did all through the year, at the empty, weed-covered plot of land opposite our house. Some accident of title problems had forbade its development, despite its choice location close to the ocean. In the colonial past, I understood, proximity to the water hadn't constituted a high-rent district. Farming had once gone on here. Stone boundary walls occurred amid the underbrush, which was like an impenetrable jungle three-quarters of the year. Among the animals I had observed from my perch were skunks, raccoons, a white-tailed deer or two on occasion, a single wild turkey in recent years (a flock of them had been introduced elsewhere in Swanstown by the state fish and game department—at my urging), rabbits, and various bird species. I always kept a pair of binoculars handy when I indulged in these temporary vacations from brainwork.

A *drive* was a more serious detour from duty. I could be away for several hours. In better birding season, I would always take my field glasses. Now I wondered if I should. Cardinals and chickadees and a few blue jays weren't much of an inducement. Oceanside, there were mostly herring gulls. Should I just cruise through a lot of open country, prettied by a coating of snow? The answer, a moment later, was, *You're not going anywhere, Jonathan. Not just yet.*

For what I saw was Jill's car approaching. Within range of my vision, she started her turn into our property. Ordinarily, I wouldn't let her arrival disrupt any of my plans, but I hadn't expected her so early. It was one of her shopping afternoons with her girlfriends.

Puzzled more than anything else, I decided to intercept her in the driveway, on the pretext of carrying whatever bundles she had inside the house.

There were two shopping bags with handles.

But something more noteworthy, as well—a kind of concentrated frown on her still beauteous face, as if she needed to tell me a burning secret. After all these years together, I was instinctive about reading her signs, her moods.

"Anything wrong?" I asked, taking those two loads of bundles from her.

"We have to talk, but I have to have some coffee first," she answered in a brisk, business-like manner.

Thus, she left me in suspense, ensconcing herself at a kitchen counter while I took her purchases up to the second floor and deposited them by her bed. Back downstairs, I waited quietly, seated in the breakfast nook, until my wife produced two cups of coffee for us. No initial hints were yet forthcoming as she deliberately sipped her brew and I tried again to read the latest expression she showed. To my surprise, the grimness, the curt air, gave way to an almost half-smiling, shiny-eyed display of introspection.

I'm not exactly putty in Jill's hands. Sometimes I think she would like me just to sit with my hands folded all day, awaiting her pleasure and her orders. It was now very plain she had a secret she wanted to share. But only on her terms.

Quite possibly next, another shift occurred, a sudden sense of her irritation, which I took to be aimed at me. That I hadn't pleaded for information and would only keep on drinking coffee.

At last, she blurted out, "I had a call on my cell phone from Irene."

Suddenly, it was my turn to become—temporarily, anyway—openly perturbed. "Oh no, not Ritchie again," I groaned. "What's the bad news?"

That woman of mine will drive me crazy. She laughed right out loud. "Well, *bad* news isn't quite it," she responded cryptically.

"What? C'mon!"

"Jonathan, dear, the news is you are going to be Grandpa Jonathan. And I'm going to be Granny Jill. And the little tyke is going to come into the world legitimately, since Irene and Ritchie are going to get married. Quite pronto."

"And you . . . you're bullshit?"

"Hardly. We two girls, sweet as pie, seriously, were on the phone for an hour, planning the wedding."

Was I missing something? Wasn't a glaring contradiction staring me in the face? The one fear I'd had was that Ritchie would descend into a Miles Monahan-type tailspin and tragedy; and Jill, hadn't she in the past shuddered at any thought that her baby boy would attach himself permanently to a dingbat woman unworthy of him? And here was my Jill like a Cheshire cat—

well, not exactly grinning from ear to ear, but visibly excited over the prospect.

After an extensive discussion until our coffee was quaffed, I finally divined what had turned her on—besides the Granny thing, the little "tyke" (I didn't ask if they knew the sex) would make his or her debut in maybe eight months. A quick rush to the altar—that was Jill and Irene's little ploy, and I saw them as two giggly co-conspirators, having to fool the latter's folks, who, like Jill's parents, were midwestern squares and hadn't a clue about their daughter's live-in arrangements on the West Coast. Consequently—in less than three weeks, I was informed—Jill and I would be on a plane heading to LA again.

The last of my coffee was downed as the last of this new development was being revealed.

"So what else is new?" I said facetiously.

To my amazement, she had an actually straight-faced, if baffling, answer: "Well, there's the swans."

"Swans?" I repeated incredulously. "What swans?"

"Two were spotted in Swanstown today," Jill said. "Wild swans."

"Jill," I replied, "we haven't had wild swans in Swanstown since 1630."

"Go see for yourself," she shot back. "They were swimming at Crockett Cove. Guess who told me? Mrs. Maurice Bilodeau—that's who. Maurice has been there since this morning, and his whole group of Environmental Watchdogs, and the local press. If you rush, you might still see them, the swans, that is."

"Mute swans?" I interrogated her. "Or are they tame escapees?"

"How the hell should I know?"

"Mute swans—wild ones—that would be something. There've been sightings in the past, supposedly—"

"Go get your binoculars," Jill interrupted. "And I'll have supper ready in about an hour and a half."

"Well, I was going to take a drive, anyhow," I said.

A ten-minute ride would get me to Crockett Cove. About forty-five minutes—max—remained of the dimming December light. I bundled up against the cold, grabbed gloves as well as field glasses, and hurried to my car.

On my ride that late afternoon, I kept fretting I might be too late, until a first glimpse of Crockett Cove's blue waters appeared.

Yes, the swans were still in the inlet. En route to the parking lot maintained by the Environmental Watchdogs, I caught a side glimpse out my driver's window of good-sized floating white birds. The view was cut off momentarily, but my excitement was mounting while negotiating the curve past the small Crockett Cove Park entrance sign.

Maurice Bilodeau was just about to enter his own vehicle as I pulled in and braked. He straightened, waved, and waited to talk to me.

We were old friends, even of fellow paternal French Huguenot origin, only his forefathers had never anglicized their surname. Tall, gawky, courtly, like an *ancien régime* aristocrat, he had the ruddy complexion of the outdoorsman he had become, the leading activist nature lover in our neck of the woods and also the minister of Swanstown's Second Parish Congregational Church.

"I was about to call it a day," he said when we shook hands. "I've been here ever since I got the phone call this morning. If you agree, I'll stay a bit longer and introduce you to these distinguished visitors."

"I'd be delighted," I told him.

Off we went, back in the direction from which he'd come, over a path through rock formations and down to the shore, a journey of, I'd say, a hundred yards.

Decked out with several slung sets of binoculars and cameras, Maurice moved with impressive speed for a white-haired gentleman clearly a decade, if not more, older than me.

As I adjusted my own binoculars and finally focused, we both gazed in silence. Maurice snapped another picture to add to dozens he'd undoubtedly already taken. The two swans, as if in response to our adulation, stayed beautifully posed for us. "Ah, the ladies," Maurice Swanson commented. "How they love to be admired."

"The ladies?" I said quizzically. "Aren't they a mated pair?"

"Mother and daughter, rather," Maurice said. "Tell me what you see, Jonathan. What do you remember from our EWD identification classes?"

"They're mute swans, right?" I glibly retorted. "The orange bill and—wait a minute . . ." my pause was like a double-take. "The other has a black bill."

Maurice nodded. "Juvenile," he said.

"But full size. Just as big as that big adult," I blurted.

What I meant to wonder at was how seemingly fast baby birds became equal in size to their parents, a matter of days almost, or with a cygnet, such as the one we were seeing, transforming its gray fuzz into fleecy plumage in possibly a matter of weeks. Neither Maurice nor I was a scientist, but we loved to talk about nature and its wondrous techniques. As befit his profession, Maurice also had a religious view. He brought moral values into evolution and evolution into God: "creationism" of his own invention, he boasted, with none of this nonsense about the Earth as 6,000 years old—*the Bible said it and that's it.* He'd been known to say that God created evolution and Darwin was his prophet.

We'd worked together, when I was in the legislature, to provide state funds for acquiring Crockett Cove and saving it from a rapacious developer.

After we'd feasted our eyes sufficiently on those two lovely avian visitors in the water, I said to the Reverend Mr. Bilodeau, a veteran birdwatcher, "Surely, between 1630 and now, swans have been here."

"But of course," said Maurice. "Yet this is a rare sighting. I know of none in recent times."

"Those earliest settlers took it for a sign of God's favor," I said and added, "Do you irreverently think our luck, as moderns, is changing?"

"Look around you. Look at all this beauty you helped rescue. That's why they've come."

"Well said," I remarked.

Indeed, the magnificence of the scene, in the approaching twilight, was fairly breathtaking. God's creation, unsullied, with nary a house nor telephone wire in sight, had remained preserved as "a jewel of a miniature fjord," to quote Maurice's words at the dedication ceremony for this mini-park natural wonder the Environmental Watchdogs had fought to keep in its pristine state.

Speaking a few moments later of the local organization he had founded and commanded for many years, Maurice then surprised me. "Jonathan," he suddenly said straight out, "would you take my place as chairman of the EWD?" and then, "It's more than accidental for us to meet like this, because I had actually intended to phone you today. Our Lord works in His own fashion, doesn't He?"

As if on cue, the swans started to move gracefully away from the vicinity of the land, leaving the two of us alone to confer on human matters.

I was stunned at first by his request. But on second thought, I admitted I knew Maurice had been talking about retirement. Seeing my hesitation, he quickly reinforced his rationale. "Fran isn't any better," he said. "We're leaving next week for the South and spending the rest of the winter. I have my replacement at the church. The EWD is my only hanging thread."

For a reply, I merely volunteered, "Jill heard about the swans from Fran at a store in Tracy today. She made me come. I'm so glad I did."

In an almost humorous vein, brown eyes twinkling, Maurice clasped his hands together, shot a glance skyward, and said, "Thank you, Father."

Except I hadn't said *yes*.

Nor did I initially think I would.

Yet I have to say there was a definite magic in the air, a palpable feel of the uncanny, of a preordained direction set for the future.

"I will stay on as vice-chair, " Maurice encouraged me, "and render every assistance I can. It's not an onerous job, Jonathan, which you know, being a faithful member, but it's of the utmost importance to have someone of your stature at the helm."

Well, it wasn't the flattery that changed my mind, I assure you. Nay, if you must know, it was kind of a nasty streak I once in a while exert. I'm referring to Ron Gordon's insulting offer of another pro bono task: chair of the local Democrats. Gleefully, I reflected, *If the redhead calls and tells me Johnny-boy Harrison said no, my perfectly proper answer can be: Sorry, Ronso, you're too late. I'm going to head up Maurice Bilodeau's outfit.*

"Okay. I don't see any reason why I shouldn't," I conceded.

"Do you need to talk to Jill first?" Maurice asked solicitously.

"Nope."

And I didn't. My life was mine; hers was hers. Thus our marriage thrived.

Maurice was overjoyed and effusive with his thanks. The pair of swans, in their unhurried fashion, had reached Crockett Cove's outlet to the sea. Like children, we two grown men bade them goodbye with friendly hand-waves.

I was literally stimulated driving home and silly enough to declaim aloud in the quiet, "Imagine being reprogrammed by a couple of wandering birds!"

21

MADGE ELLERY. I HAD BEEN WAITING to write more about her and now it suddenly seems time—a conjunction in my own mind—which I will proceed to explain. What, you may ask, links my just-finished meeting with Maurice Bilodeau and the almost spectral appearance of the swans, with the widow of my former boss and erstwhile hero? As I see it, simply this: By telling Maurice I would accept the responsibility he'd offered, I was, in effect, turning my back, arguably forever, on again running for or holding an elective office. Madge, if she knew, would be ecstatic. So it seems to me a fitting moment to bring her full center into the narrative and add another dimension, arising from the drama of Duke's assassination and its aftermath.

Until now, I have been alluding to Madge almost entirely in her role as Duke's consort—a pretty appendage, spoiled, and, on occasion, openly bitchy. Yet she had all the charm of a grande dame. She might have become first lady of the land. It is a realization that always takes my breath away.

I believe she would have made a very good first lady for our nation. As our governor's wife, she had had plenty of experience, and in the state, we did call her our first lady.

I'd been to events at the governor's mansion where she was the ever-smiling hostess, making everyone feel at home amid those intimidating surroundings. Like my friend Norman Page, Madge spoke with a type of New York City Brahmin accent we called "Park Avenue brogue." It was redolent of Miss Somebody's Finishing School, and, despite her best efforts at being friendly, could have an edge quite intimidating on its own.

I had watched her, too, at ribbon-cutting ceremonies. She did charity events all over the state and I helped write her speeches once in a while and went along as an aide, although she most often took one of her female staffers.

Some of *them* and some of us males in the governor's office referred to her secretly as "the queen" or "Her Majesty." Oddly enough, no one ever had thought to call her *Duchess*, to complement our *Duke*. And certainly, to her face, she was never anything but Mrs. Ellery for most of the Statehouse gang. Duke openly called her Madge. So did Harry DeWitt. I didn't—not until I got into the legislature, that is.

Finding myself "the Honorable Jonathan Jackson" put me into a whole different category. It started upon receipt of the Notification of Election from the secretary of state. One day, an official-looking envelope arrived and inside was a printed document confirming the final tally in such-and-such seat and instructing me to report on a certain day to be sworn in by the governor at the opening of the legislature. This final act made everything kosher. Under the state constitution, the legislature is the ultimate arbiter of who its members are. Once you take the oath, you are "in like Flynn," as the saying goes, unless you misbehave so badly they expel you (which *has* happened now and again).

Right now, in my memory, I was with all the others taking the oath that first time from Big Bob Benton, who read it haltingly, and in the crowded visitors' gallery were my invitees, including Jill, of course, and little Ritchie, and Ron and Mitzi Gordon and friends, key supporters, and former colleagues. Madge Ellery wasn't there, although I'd sent her an invitation at the suggestion of Harry DeWitt, who did attend.

It was not the first inaugural of the legislature since Duke had been assassinated. Big Bob had served out the rest of Duke's term and been reelected, mostly on a deliberately generated wave of nostalgia and sympathy for our late governor. Although I'd left his employ and become a "professor," I helped him with that endeavor and he was helpful to me when I did finally decide to run for office myself.

Okay, with that as background, let's now talk about the issue of *gun control*. Remember Madge's speech the day we came home with Duke's body?

Parenthetically, in a quasi-rural area like ours, it's not the only issue, but it's a biggie. I experienced this real quick during my maiden campaign when I spoke at a "Candidate's Night" sponsored by our local Swanstown Fish and Game Association.

On stage first, I gave my usual spiel about continuing Duke Ellery's heritage, while tailoring it, too, for a specific audience— how much we had done for fishing and hunting in the state, and the statistics that proved it. I didn't fail, either, to include general stuff on the environment, on habitat restoration, and the common-sense notions that you didn't have good, healthy deer herds unless you had plenty of undeveloped open space and forest cover and "edge," nor good, fish-packed trout streams if you let them get polluted or sprayed, killing off the insect life, or let loggers clog them up with silt.

I saw heads nodding in agreement. I felt I was making headway. And when the question period began, I was ready for the tough one.

It came, no surprise,simply as: "What about our guns?"

"I'm gonna stick with Duke on that one, too," I glibly answered. "He didn't see the need to put any restrictions on 'em."

This was precisely the answer my opponent, Earl Johnson, would have given (had he bothered to show up), albeit admittedly not in his salty language, although I did throw in a *gonna* and an *'em.*

I was silently congratulating myself that I might have picked up a few votes, when a "good ol' boy" in the crowd, whom I recognized as a friend of Earl's, raised his hand.

"Yes, Chuck," I said, tensing somewhat.

"Mist-ah Jack-son." He was a hard-eyed little man, bald as a billiard ball, with a pompous, bombastic manner, wearing overalls and a checkered lumberman's shirt—but in reality, a town merchant. "Puh-lease explain, sir. Mrs. Mar-jorie Ell'ry. Isn't she talkin' about takin' away our guns?"

"Maybe she is, Chuck," I responded without hesitation. "But Duke Ellery never did. And I don't aim to, either."

The applause I received probably had as much to do with pushing out a snappy answer to a guy they didn't all that much care for, as it did for what I said. Also, by God, I wasn't going to defend Madge. She certainly hadn't consulted me before she'd started her crusade.

In fact, one of the officers of the club stood up then and said, "Well, Mrs. Ellery's just trying to work out her grief, boys. We shouldn't be too harsh on her."

Instinctively, I followed advice Matt Drew later drilled into me: "First choice is always say nothing, if you can." Thus, I let that statement stand as the final word, kept my trap shut, and, as you all know, got elected. Quite honestly, when Madge Ellery failed to appear at my swearing-in, I was relieved, yet ego-wise, a tad miffed that she had snubbed me entirely.

About a month later, her bread-and-butter note apologizing for her absence and lag in writing me arrived and somewhat softened my pique.

Otherwise, for reasons best known to herself, Madge pretty much left me alone during my first year in the legislature. The sole exception occurred about a month after we were sworn in, when I received a message from one of our young pages that a "Mrs. Emory" had called and would I please call her back. "Mrs. Emory?" I said, wrinkling up my nose since the name meant nothing to me. "Did she say what she wanted?"

The boy shrugged his shoulders. "No, she just said you'd know her. You used to work for her husband."

Finally, it dawned on me there might have been a garbling of identities. "Are you sure it wasn't a Mrs. Ellery?"

"Might have been" was his unhelpful answer.

Lest you believe I'm as much of a scaredy-cat as many of my legislative colleagues, know that without more than a few moments of hesitation, I went straight to the Members' Retiring Lounge and telephoned (no cell phones in those days). Her voice at the other end sent a brief shiver through me. Yet I waited in vain for her to lobby me on the gun-control bill she was planning to have introduced. Would she ask me to sponsor or co-sponsor it? Would she say she at least expected me to speak for it on the floor and, needless to say, openly vote for it? We had some polite chitchat and that was all! The ostensible reason she had bothered to contact me was her wish to be sure I had received that note of apology for not having been able to attend the swearing-in ceremony.

"It was so sweet of you to think of me. But I was called away so suddenly. . . ." Those were her exact words, I remember.

"Don't worry about it, please. I know how busy you are, Madge." Such were mine and, see, I didn't shrink from calling her by her first name.

We talked less than two minutes. Throughout, I had an impression *she* was waiting for *me* to say something—and, after we both hung up, that she had had something she wanted to say to me but couldn't quite bring herself to broach the subject, which was undoubtedly the gun-control measure.

At this juncture, I'd been at my new job barely long enough to locate the men's room, as we liked to say. Close as I'd been to the legislature, working in the same building with those guys, I was finding practically everything a learning experience. The leadership put me on the Environment and Energy Committee.

Legislation had already been introduced and soon taught us that the small, easy stuff would be handled first, early in the session. Controversial bills were always held back, Matt Drew had explained, because—well, it had always been a disaster to try to run them before you got into "the rhythm of things." So we had really pressing matters like *naming the state insect* (brought by a bunch of fourth graders and providing a fun hearing) and *correcting the Charter of the Millersburg Light and Power Company*—fourteen nit-picky "conforming changes," presented by a pedantic lawyer who took an actual hour and twenty minutes to explain in excruciating detail each nuance of these utterly cosmetic alterations to a lot of boilerplate gibberish. Worse, the whole board had come to offer support and did so at fulsome length. Squaring such trivia with the lofty visions of Duke Ellery that Madge's call had reawakened was a chore,

One day, I remember, this dichotomy hit me real hard. I had gone into the library annex in the Statehouse to do research on one of my bills. It wasn't exactly déjà vu I experienced—not actually a "sense" of having been someplace before. I knew full well when I'd last been on these premises—doing research for Duke's book, to put it plainly.

If you detect a touch of diffidence, it's probably because I shouldn't admit having done personal work for a governor on state time. A really nasty opponent could holler foul, call the effort *an illegal campaign contribution from a public employee,* since Duke's publication would surely have appeared in conjunction with his running for president. As a defense, I could argue I was on my lunch break, although this delving into U.S. history had occurred in the late afternoon. Then, again, I could also claim—dishonestly but successfully—that I was gathering material for my boss's speeches.

Indeed, if a grand inquisitor confronted me, I would have argued how sticking my nose into the eighteenth-century diplomatic maneuvers of the pre-independence USA was hardly a sub-ject for a contemporary voting audience. John Jay, whose bio I was scanning, was not exactly a name you could toss out to a Rotary Club or chamber of commerce. Similarly, *The Diplomacy of the American Revolution* by Samuel Flagg Bemis, another book I was examining that day, might not seem to lend itself to the repertoire of a modern pol.

What Duke wanted to get at was the vulnerability of the embryonic Republic about to be born through the negotiations taking place in Paris in the 1780s. The French acted the role of a midwife to the infant United States, but did so only to jab a stick into Great Britain's eye. Neither did the French want too lusty a child growing up in North America. The Comte de Vergennes was their foreign minister. Jay, Franklin, and John Adams, the chief members of the American team, had been instructed to defer to him in their talks with the British. Vergennes, an untrustworthy sly boots if ever there was one, would have final approval of the terms, and what this French nobleman most wanted consisted of a mini-United States of America, hemmed in along the Atlantic coast and extending no farther west than the Appalachians.

The key moment, conceivably, of all subsequent American history occurred there in Paris when the three Americans said the equivalent of "Screw that," got the Brits to accept our "going west," didn't tell Vergennes (thus disobeying orders), and signed our Treaty of Independence in a modest building still standing on the Rue Jacob on the Left Bank, a few blocks from the Seine. Vergennes, no doubt, was bullshit, but helpless, and the infant kingless nation across the seas grew into a colossus as a conse-quence.

I have to add I took an extra special pleasure in doing this specific research in that my family had always boasted we were distantly related to John Jay. We had common Huguenot ties, if nothing else—a surname, *notre nomme de famille*, back in France, becoming *Jackson* for us in honor of the hero of the battle of New Orleans, or so the story goes.

I have always deeply regretted that Duke was never able to write his book of *Americana* (the working title). Ever since, I still experience spasms of wanting to finish it myself. Carbons of the research I did for him are among my files; and should gaps exist for me to fill on my own, I would need Madge's permission, I suppose—a deal-breaker in any case. Then, too, the legality of my present book, this unauthorized biography disguised as an autobiography, is something I haven't checked with any lawyer yet—I *will* touch base with Ron Gordon in the event of publication—but I'm absolutely positive Madge would never find grounds to sue me and win.

Knowing her anger at me, she still might try, though.

To be perfectly open, it's no fun to confess the bad blood between us. I'm sure that Madge Ellery, in her heart of hearts, has convinced herself I was part of a conspiracy with Miles Monahan to murder her husband, despite knowing she could never prove it. However, had I joined her crusade for gun-control legislation, as she later begged me to do, no emotional accusation so atrocious would have stayed in her mind.

Nevertheless, I must forthwith offer the whole sad story in its entirety—capsule form—Madge and me, clashing repeatedly.

As I've said, she left me alone during my first term; in fact, no gun-control bill was proposed at all throughout those two years. When subsequently running for reelection, I got a check from Madge, totally unsolicited. *Scary*, I thought. And I knew why I felt queasy. *She's going to come after me big time if I win.*

Wrong. Before the campaign ended, I received a questionnaire from her organization to fill out: half a dozen killer inquiries as to my positions on guns. A week earlier, I'd completed one for the gun-nut crowd.

That sort of Hobson's choice dilemma was an occupational hazard of getting elected, but in most controversies I knew which side I was on. When it came to weapons, I had no particular axe to grind except for those guys at the Swanstown Fish and Game Club who'd befriended me when I needed them. I'd answered every query of the state sportsmen's group the way they would have wanted, saying yes to everything, or rather, no, when it came to gun control. The letter they would send out to their members just prior to the voting would put me in their A-OK column. Provided I didn't double-cross them.

For several days, I recall, I stared at the letterhead of "The Coalition to End Gun Violence," agonizing over what response, if any, I should make. She had written a note under her signature: "Jonathan, we're counting on you to be a leader on this vital issue. Will you please sponsor our bill or at least cosponsor it?" Every day I stalled, I expected the phone to ring. I was too gutless to tell Jill, "If Madge Ellery is on the line, I'm not at home." It was the tail end of my campaign. I was out every day knocking on doors. Victory seemed certain this second time around. And every night, I almost dreaded going home.

Day in and day out, I damned Madge Ellery for spoiling my expected triumph. I had dozens of imaginary conversations with her, justifying my course of action (or non-action, as she would see it). "What law could ever have stopped Miles Monohan?" was my habitual key response. "His weapons were all purchased legally." Since that didn't sound convincing enough, I would add, "You'll never get a gun registration bill through. Never! Believe me. Even Duke didn't attempt it." Did I dare in reality to breathe a word of that last sentence? And I most likely would shy away, too, from an allied argument that "I can do so much more for his [Duke's] legacy if I'm up here, but if I touch your bill, I'm a dead duck in my district."

A standard technique in those dicey situations is to do nothing and hope your trouble will go away. Or wait for an opportunity to escape the problem because of a new development. Election Day came and went and I still hadn't heard from Madge the dreaded "You never returned your questionnaire." I'd been prepared to lie, to say it had been lost in the mail, seeing that it hadn't been sent registered. But the opportunity to perjure myself failed to arise. Instead, as soon as we were back in the capital, starting our session, I heard a nasty rumor.

It was Matt Drew who stopped me in the hall by the Members' Retiring Lounge and said abruptly, "The bitch, do you know what she's saying?"

Mystified, I asked, "Who's saying what?"

"Her Majesty. Queen Marjorie, the First," said Matt. "Come inside and sit down with me. You've got a problem, boy."

The lounge in those days was also Matt's "office," a favorite place for private conversations. Since Matt was seldom without a cigarillo and he could puff away in that sanctuary, this was his only Statehouse venue for nicotine and talk when the weather was too cold outdoors (how he griped that in the "good old past," you could sit in your seat and smoke in the house chamber, in and out of session).

He had grabbed me by the lounge entrance and we went in and quickly settled in a corner.

I know I've partly described Matt before. That he was truly huge, nearly 300 pounds, and, as he liked to say, "Irish as Paddy's pig." His china-blue eyes twinkled or glared intelligently in a face the color of rare roast beef, and while he looked like a stevedore, tough as nails, he was fatherly to us "young Democrats," i.e., those of us who weren't veterans, no matter how old we were.

"What's my problem with Madge?" I asked, after letting him take several drags of that quasi-cigar smoke he actually inhaled.

"I assume you want to be reelected in the future," he countered.

Whether I did or not, I knew I had to answer *yes*. For Matt, it was inconceivable that anyone, once sent to the legislature, would want to do anything else until the day he or she died. You could go from the house to the state senate here, or the governorship or to Congress, but to give up this form of public service was in his eyes a *venal*, if not a *mortal*, sin.

Besides, having been reelected, I assuredly did plan to run and win again.

"Is Madge going to come out publicly against me or something?" I asked, feeling more than a touch of alarm. "Because I didn't answer her damn questionnaire or wouldn't agree to sponsor her bill?"

Before he responded, Matt had a sudden small fit of coughing. These paroxysms, "smoker's hack," he called them, had seemed to become more frequent recently. Even now, however, he kept on smoking as he spoke. "Listen, Jonathan," he said, "I don't know if she can hurt you in your own district, but she is badmouthing you big time. I don't know if you plan someday to go higher, like Congress. That's where most certainly she could have an effect. Now, tell me about this guy Monahan."

"Miles Monahan!" I felt somewhat flabbergasted. "Where does he fit in?"

"She's saying you were in with him."

"Oh, Christ, no!" Then, I was *really* flabbergasted.

"That's what I hear," Matt said, "from an utterly reliable source."

Then I was really *angry*. I actually stood, as if going to bolt, as if it had been Matt who'd insulted me. "Goddamn it!" I swore. "They tried that against me in my first election. It backfired. Those frigging Republicans did. What the Christ is the matter with that woman? The Secret Service agents at the scene told me I should get a medal for what I did, helping save the president. They cleared me, absolutely cleared me. It's on the record!"

Matt motioned me to sit down. A few others in the lounge had turned to look in our direction.

Once I'd reseated myself, he said, "So what's with this Monahan, this Celtic *luntzman* of mine? You knew him when you were a kid. He had mental problems, right?"

Like myself and other goys who had Jewish friends, Matt liked to use a Yiddish phrase on occasion. I answered him back with one. "*Meschugener,* from the second grade on."

Yes, it did occur to me I was speaking like a cheap politician, simplifying, exaggerating, distorting. Miles hadn't been nuttier than any of us at the Edward W. Foster Elementary School. Tantrums didn't count and he threw his share of them, maybe a tad more. Seriously, it wasn't until that business with the guns in the canoe and the "O. Murray Carr"–Uncle Sam stuff that I began to have doubts about him; only then had I rummaged mentally back into our past and dredged up incidents that made me think him potentially unhinged. Beforehand, in my mind, he'd simply been an immensely talented, high-strung guy of the *wild Irish* variety, who hadn't gotten his big break yet. It would come, I kept hoping—or rather, frankly, hoping it wouldn't come before I had my own success nailed down.

But sharing my intellectual integrity with Matt Drew wasn't called for at the moment. We had a spate of silence as he inhaled and exhaled more smoke. "What do you think, Captain?" I suddenly said to him. "Should I go and pop her one on the nose?"

"Keep your mitts to yourself, verbal or otherwise," Matt cautioned me. After butting out his fourth cigarillo since we'd sat down, he instantly brightened, as if with an idea. "Support her bill," he blurted. "Hell, offer at least to sign on and cosponsor the goddamn thing. It's going nowhere, anyway."

"Shit on her bill," I spat. "Frig her."

"Then go to the hearing and oppose it. That'll get you some press."

I stared at Matt for a full ten seconds, while a batch of thoughts raced through my brain. "Maybe I'll do just that," I grimly said.

Every bill in our legislature must have a hearing. I understand it's not the same in some other states where the leadership can pick and choose those they wish to address. Consequently, with us, hearings are mostly small, held in the committee rooms in the Statehouse. If we need a bigger space, there's Room 270 in the state office building, which holds about 300. And if it's a real biggie, an issue that excites everybody and draws lots of media, we rent a hall seating 1,200.

Madge Ellery's bill to register all weapons drew standing room only in this humongous auditorium.

For anyone who hasn't been to a legislative hearing, here is how it works—at least in our state. Unlike the U.S. Congress, we have joint committees, the house and senate combined, dealing with whatever subjects fall within each assigned jurisdiction. Logically, the gun registration bill had been sent to the Fish and Game Committee—although not a happy prospect for Madge, since most of its members were hunters. The presiding officer for all hearings was usually the state senate chair, and the committee, seated on a raised dais, flanked him or her, while directly below was a microphone on a stand from which those wishing to give testimony could speak to the lawmakers and be heard by the rest of the hall.

Sometimes, we did get *real testimony*. More often than not, though, we were subjected to bombast, propaganda, super-prejudiced opinion, yet still somehow received a general idea of what people were feeling. When it was an explosive issue like gun control, the place might turn into a circus.

Except that my friend, the Honorable Peggy McEnte,e would be in charge and that experienced, charming, steel-nerved senator ran a tight ship. No demonstrations. No applause. No long-winded exhortations, either. She wasn't afraid to rap her gavel, and like a domineering schoolmarm, she soon cowed everyone, including those hordes of flannel-shirted rednecks who had come to shout down the hated measure.

I could hardly believe I was planning to testify on *their* behalf.

The protocol at a hearing follows an age-old pattern. The *proponents* speak first. Leading off is the chief sponsor of the bill, and next are the cosponsors, if any, who wish to add their voices and support, and finally the public. In the latter category, if there are lots of would-be testifiers, the managers of the bill might submit a list to the committee clerk of those they want to be heard before it's thrown open to anyone. Or sometimes there's a sign-up sheet, first come, first serve. The same procedure applies to the *opponents*, who come next. And the whole operation, which can take hours, is rounded off when there is a call for those who "wish to speak neither for nor against," and sometimes there are plenty of these neutrals.

I came late and stayed at the back of the auditorium. In the interests of full disclosure, let me flatly state I was trying to hide from Madge. For two reasons. Cowardice was one. I couldn't bear to have her see me and think I was on hand to support her bill and greet me with a pretty smile. And the other was my anger, if it were true she was telling those stories about me. I feared I might accost her, create a scene. The mere fact of my testifying as I did would send a message, I reasoned.

Rather, I mostly hoped Madge would leave before I had to speak. Under ideal conditions, my "treason," as I'm sure she would have put it, would only have been related to her by those of her followers who had stayed until the bitter end. Alas, Madge herself sat rooted in her front-row seat, having helped to lead the debate for the proponents, and remained tight-lipped to listen to the opponents, who outnumbered her pitiful handful of adherents by probably ten to one.

By the time I appeared, the last of Madge's hardy band was speaking. I heard some words about "the epidemic of violence in this country." I heard the same man say, for it was an elderly gent with silvery hair, "Listen to the wisdom of Mrs. Ellery. She knows from indescribably painful experience the horrific consequences of letting gun traffic in the United States go unchecked." I sensed the restlessness of the vast majority of the crowd, wanting to boo and hiss, but held back in awe of Peg's gavel and leadership. Then, with only silence greeting the chair's inquiry of "Are there any further proponents?" and her subsequent statement of "We will now hear from the opponents," the circus began.

I do not mean to imply there was disorder. Instead, despite a brief spattering of applause after the first negative speaker, which Peg quenched with a mere frown, the hortatory play of rhetoric from those aroused "gunners" went unsaluted, withal it had the tinny, colorful quality of noise and bustle under the big top. These guys' expressions, uttered with absolute sincerity, were not so much quaint and repetitive, but seemingly like folk gospel. "God-given right to bear arms." How many times did we hear that bromide? "Fired the shot heard 'round the world." The 1776 Minutemen were evoked more than once. True enough, the first spokesman of theirs, slick representative of a national anti-gun-control organization, had sounded like a shill for those who sold weapons *(every household should have one or more firearms, preferably automatic types)*; still, most of the fellows who came out of the audience to vent their emotions were like my pals at home in the Swanstown Fish and Game Club—good citizens, patriotic Americans, outdoorsmen, decent, hardworking men and women, too, not stupid. However, after about thirty of them had spoken, there didn't seem much else to say, and I hadn't taken my turn, either, concentrating on trying to wait out Madge.

Once more, Peg was repeating her formulaic "Are there any further opponents?"

At last, I raised my hand and stood. Walking to the front of the hall, I was aware of all the heads swiveled to glance in my direction, all the gaping faces. The hubbub of whispered conversations had ceased. Even before Peg welcomed "Representative Jackson" by name, there had seemed a clear indication that a fresh element of interest had entered the debate, commanding attention. Unfortunately, such feeling also spread to Madge Ellery, who was already staring daggers at me.

My speech was in my mind. I had written it out at home, then memorized the exact language I had devised to explain my gist. Not for posterity nor the press was I being so careful. For myself, rather—I had to convince myself.

I noticed the guys and gals at the press table picking up their pens and Jill's old TV cameraman, Charley Fischer, training his instrument at the microphone behind which I stood.

The time-honored salutation of "Madame Chair, members of the Fish and Game Committee . . ." flowed easily enough and, surprisingly, so did the rest of my peroration. Here are the key passages:

> If, for one moment, I thought that the passage of Legislative Document One Hundred and Twelve, An Act to Restrict Gun Violence, could have prevented the image of horror in Los Angeles that I will carry with me to my grave, then I would support it. I'll tell you what I saw with my own eyes, what I can never get out of my thoughts. I saw a madman emerging from a men's room and drawing a small pistol from his pocket. Yes, I knew him, I had grown up with him. But at the same time, I didn't know him. He was wild-eyed, delirious, twisted beyond recognition. Twisted by what? Some would say by America, the burdens our way of life places on us, the drive for success, the shame of failure. Or was it his own

genetic makeup, incipient mental illness, fueled to a white-hot fury by stress? Or was it some moral flaw in his character that he, Miles Monahan, had let overcome him? At any rate, on a crazy impulse, he pulled the pistol's trigger and I saw my Governor Ellery, my boss, my friend, my political idol, crumple to the airport terminal floor in a pool of blood. No legislation on earth could have averted that inexpressible, almost Greek, tragedy. . . .

That's one segment. Here's another:

As an historian, let me remind this hearing of another fact. During the years of Governor Ellery's administration, he did not once address the issue we are debating today. Why not? At one of our staff meetings, I once asked him, 'What about gun control?' His answer: 'This is a law-abiding state. Our people, yes, many of them own firearms. They use them mostly for hunting, far more than any need for protection, since we are essentially rural folks, even in our cities. We know our neighbors. We know how to handle weapons responsibly. We don't need nanny laws and our criminal statistics are among the lowest, if not *the* lowest, in the land. Maybe in New York City or Los Angeles, but not here.' That is an exact quote, taken from my notes and kept in my records.

It was true. I was honest enough not to make up or embellish any words of Duke's, although there was no one really to challenge me. Maybe Harry DeWitt had heard him say something else privately, but Harry had been at that staff meeting and so had others and no contradictions were ever extant, as far as I could discover. Behind me, after I recited Duke's statement, applause did break out. They were saluting his memory, it seemed, which was why, I guessed, that Peg allowed them some seconds of leeway before bringing down her gavel.

When I finished and turned to go back to my seat, I didn't dare to look in Madge's direction—not so much as a peek.

Once the hearing was over, I was mobbed by fish-and-game-type guys. They shook my hand, pounded me on the back, thanked me profusely, and one of them actually said, "We're gonna run you for governor, Jonathan."

At just about that moment, Madge walked by, leaving the hall. I've always thought she heard what my admirer said.

At home afterward, Jill and I were watching the early evening news on her old station. Throughout my presentation, I'd been conscious of Charley Fischer's lens trained at me. A politician's vanity isn't entirely the egoism of wanting to see yourself on the TV screen; it's a bread-and-butter issue, too, because every exposure adds to your recognition—and in my case, dreams of eventual glory. Charley showed me being cheered and there was footage of yours truly being surrounded by loads of gun lovers.

The commentator's voice-over mentioned my especially electrifying effect in this debate as a former aide to Governor Ellery.

Naturally, no reporter had captured those random words about a future *Governor Jackson* someday. So I sort of boasted to Jill how "there'd been talk" about running me for chief executive. "It's not beyond the realm of possibility," I added seriously.

Her reaction was amazing. Never have I seen her blue eyes so adamantly marble-hard. Unsmiling, even openly scornful and hostile, Jill spat out her words in a mean-sounding, snappish response to make sure I got the point.

"No way, José."

22

Fast forward about half a decade. The same setting. It can be described as "the domestic hearth" (i.e., living room) of Representative Jonathan Jackson and his lovely wife, where the two are observed while watching the news on their state-of-the art television set. This modern piece of technology is not the only difference from the previous five years. Thanks to our son, who is now too much of a handful to be put to bed right after the supper hour, we find ourselves viewing a later broadcast.

So at last Jill and I are alone. Oh, we're no longer sitting cuddly side by side on the sofa, but in separate comfy chairs. Nothing dire has happened between us—simply we've both gotten older. And ever since that "No way, José" of the past, I've never offered another word about running for a major office.

You will see, in a moment, why I have brought back this obdurate comment of Jill's.

There we were, in separate armchairs, our eyes glued on the screen, seeing Jill's old news station airing an interview of the human-interest variety. I commented afterward, "God, what a bore. The kid gets back his stolen bicycle. Who cares?"

Jill just grunted.

Yet it was a story right afterward that grabbed our attention. *Real* hard news, and where *my interests* were possibly concerned. A bit of background: We had a congressman from our district, a Republican, who was as unbeatable as Peg McEntee. The state Democratic Party was forever seeking a "sacrificial lamb" candidate to run against him and I had once been approached.

"Sorry, boys, I'd love to offer myself," I told them with utter dishonesty, "but my wife has ruled it out and it's no use talking to her," the latter statement containing, as I thought, God's own complete truth.

Okay, the breaking story that evening was how the honorable gentleman in question had announced his sudden, totally unforeseen retirement. Under no circumstances would he seek reelection.

To illustrate how Mickey-Mouse an outfit Jill had worked for, there wasn't a single film clip from the GOP congressman's press conference in Washington, briefing the media. Jill's replacement merely read excerpts from a release the station had received. Mr. Unbeatable was stepping down, he declared without the slightest trace of originality, for "health and family concerns."

"Do you think they're going to indict him?" was my joking response.

"Shh, let me hear the rest of this," was Jill's rejoinder, which surprised me, but I did shut up and turned my semi-smirk into an expression of rapt interest. For twenty more seconds, that is, until the piece came to a close.

Once more, Jill did something I didn't expect. Grabbing the remote, she shut off the set.

"You ought to run," she said.

If I had been puzzled previously, now I was stunned. "Enter a p-p-primary?" I literally stuttered.

"You'd win it," she said.

"But. . . ." This time, I didn't stutter; just repeated myself. "But, but Jesus, don't you remember a conversation in this very location when I hinted—merely *hinted*—something about a run someday for governor and you bit my head off."

"That was governor," she said. "This is Congress."

"What's the difference?"

"Washington, D.C."

As best I now recall, the above conversation flowed in the

direction of an internalized secret Jill had kept hidden from me for years. Possibly I felt a pang in thinking it may well have accounted for our marriage in the first place—that she had set her cap for me on the plane ride to California because she saw me taking her out of the humdrum provincial boondocks of this state and into the glamorous hotshot world of the nation's capital, and that she would climb in her profession alongside me, her "comer" husband, the rising aide to President Ellery. Remember, she was positive he would run.

Therefore, she was suddenly telling me flat out the ballgame was not over. *Her* game plan, anyway. Was it mine? As I reflected on what I had gleaned of Jill's intentions for me, some familiar feelings returned, a surge of excited ambition and, for that matter, an injection of youthful idealism predicated on following in Duke's footsteps and carrying on his legacy. Notwithstanding which, showing my age and maturity, I was more cautious than five years earlier.

"You really would like to live inside the Beltway?" I asked Jill eventually.

Her answer was, "Ritchie's the right age to start a new school. We could live in Arlington or Fairfax or Chevy Chase. They have good systems."

Should I have probed further? Asked her how long she had been carrying these thoughts in her mind? Was she hopelessly fed up with our life here? Frankly, I didn't want to know.

My own response came a moment later. It had all the hallmarks of a calculating politico's reaction to an unexpected question.

"Well, okay, I'll explore the feasibility," I said—in other words, a *very strong maybe* in our cynical Statehouse lingo.

What this hesitation of mine showed was not that I was getting smarter or less ambitious or middle-age pusillanimous, but mainly that I had more experience under my belt. I could not say to myself as blithely as Jill had said to me, "You'd win it," meaning the primary and, by logical deduction, the general election in the fall. For one thing, an open race without an incumbent would bring on a swarm of candidates—like insects to a light after all those years of pent-up waiting among us toilers in the minor leagues. I could see at least two guys ahead of me in my own party—Pete Warner, Jr., and Ted Alexander. The former you may remember as the hotshot lawyer-lobbyist, one-time state committee chair and unsuccessful congressional candidate, who'd been caught cheating on his wife and was now remarried to a woman of significant means. The latter personage, a charming older man, owned Alexander Industries, had been a president of the state senate and our Democratic national committeeman in D.C. for many years. If I'd had to pick between the two, I'd choose Ted, but if I were running against them both, I'd have to emphasize my independence from the Establishment, my idealism and ideas, my ties to Duke, plus a record of accomplishment during my years in the legislature.

And then, it goes without saying, I had to worry about how I was going to raise several hundred thousand dollars.

I caught Jill staring at me in a demanding, silent, dissatisfied manner, as if awaiting a far more positive response from me.

"Well, I'm not going to mortgage the house," I said to her.

"Don't worry, I'll break open my piggybank," she shot back.

"Okay, but before I do anything else, I'm going to talk to Ron," I replied. "Ask him to head up my finance committee."

"He owes you," she said.

"Let's see."

Avoiding a footnote here, I will say quickly that Jill's remark in no way implied any impropriety, i.e., that I had used my position to aid Ron illegitimately. For the last two sessions, I had been on the all-important Appropriations Committee. With Ron's full acquiescence, I had recused myself from several votes that might have had the appearance of a conflict of interest in regard to clients of his. So one could say if he owed me anything, it was just his being, in a general sense, a constituent of mine, as well as my personal attorney.

I phoned Ron at home a few minutes after my exchange with Jill and secured an appointment at his office the next day.

It's needless for me to report our entire conversation. The canny redhead had guessed why I wanted to see him and was prepared to answer just as soon as the words were out of my mouth.

We sat in his elegant, oak-paneled quarters, Ron in a swivel chair while I occupied what he jokingly referred to as the "witness seat" on the other side of the desk. He was wearing glasses now (I, too, needed them for reading) and he took off those wire-rimmed spectacles to study me thoughtfully. "I suspect you're already determined to run and want my advice," he ultimately said.

"More than simply advice," I responded.

"I thought as much."

The tone of his last remark was immediately unsettling. There was nothing welcoming about it. I braced myself for the bad news I expected to follow.

Ron's *advice* was not to run. His conventional wisdom was that, to quote him, "You still haven't been around long enough to pay your dues in entering a primary that will have Pete Warner and Ted Alexander sucking up most of the money that's around."

"Suppose I could make it through the primary on my own dough?" was my comeback—a hypothetical question, if there ever was one, but testing Ron, to see if he'd help me raise funds in the general election.

"Can you?"

I should have expected that prosecutorial type of inquiry.

"In truth, Counselor, I've promised Jill I won't mortgage my house, but I've got a few shekels of my own to spare. And if I get through the primary—"

"Whoa. Stop there," Ron broke in.

In the ensuing conversation, some things became clear. Actually, how much I was not in the loop of party affairs was brought home to me. Rumors of a vacancy in Congress had been bruited about for weeks. My putative finance manager had since been contacted by the Warner and Alexander camps and by several other possible contenders, as well. It became obvious that Ron, although silent on the subject, had made a choice—I guessed Ted Alexander.

"Who do you think will be the strongest in the fall?" I asked, testing again.

"Frankly, you might be," was his totally unexpected reply.

"Then, why not—?"

But Ron didn't let me finish. "Don't imagine I haven't tossed your name into the pot," he said. "Yet you have an overwhelming obstacle, I have to tell you—at least for winning an election *within* our party."

"An enemy?" I asked.

"Big time."

"Madge?" I queried.

"She would gladly break your balls, my friend. Gun control. Gun control."

"Hell, I'll take her on!" I exclaimed pugnaciously.

"Sure," Ron said, "your position on the issue would be strong in the general election. The trouble is, with her against you in the primary, screaming like a banshee, you're toast, Jonathan. I kid you not."

I still said nothing, admitting to myself that he was probably, if not undoubtedly, right.

Ron went on: "Hell hath no fury, as you certainly know the old saying. She'll never forgive you, Jonathan—never—and

Christ, in her half-madness, she still holds *you* responsible."

Nodding sadly, tacitly acknowledging his superior wisdom, I did think to ask, "So do you believe I'll ever be able to run for major office in this state with that witch against me?"

"Maybe she'll get married and move away," was Ron Gordon's hardly satisfactory answer.

"Fat chance."

I prophesied correctly, Madge Ellery never vanished from the state's political scene; she remains with us to this day, somewhat muted, and avoiding being a ridiculous harpy by toning down her rhetoric and rationing her appearances on the public stage. There were rumors she might run for governor herself, and if they were a trial balloon on her part, Madge did not wait long to disavow them. And that was a number of years ago. However, she would back candidates—in primaries especially—with money and endorsements, while on occasion in a general election making her displeasure evident if the Democrats put up someone she didn't like.

Pardon my digression. One more bit of drama still seemed left for me to face after I departed Ron Gordon's snazzy office that day, a crestfallen figure, emerging into the lawyer's private parking lot. All around me was the center of Swanstown, its stores, its commercial buildings and bits of nature, too, the newly leafed maples that had been planted to replace the elms on Elm Street killed by Dutch Elm disease, the just-started grass of Bannister Park, the near-distant smell of the sea. There was an overall aroma of spring's having arrived, a time when I should have been joyful, opening my lungs, full of fresh juices and energy.

If I seemed to mope on the way to my car, it was with good reason. I had to confront Jill and tell her the unpleasant results of my quest.

It's amazing how banal such moments can be. I took a walk

on the beach, rehearsed my little speech, prepared to counter Jill's arguments, and went home. Her car was in the garage. But she wasn't in the kitchen as I entered through the back door. Presently, I heard noises. She was in Ritchie's bedroom upstairs.

The two of them were playing catch with a tennis ball. As I entered, my son let fly with a wild pitch that Jill lunged for, sprawling on the floor while the fuzzy yellow projectile bounced against a wall, two feet from a window.

"God, you're gonna break the glass!" I cried.

Jill was laughing over her mishap and slow to get to her feet. "Old worrywart," she called me. "We were working on Ritchie's no-hitter."

"Yeah, great," I commented, as Ritchie came running up to hug me.

Jill stared intently at me, watched as I lifted the boy. God, was she perceptive and intuitive. "You, on the other hand," she said, "definitely struck out, didn't you?"

"Definitely," I said, nodding.

"Tell me about it later," she said, going after the tennis ball and resuming their game once I lowered Ritchie down.

There was no push-back when, following supper, after Ritchie had been put to bed, we discussed the matter. If Jill had had her heart set on my success in Washington, D.C., no one would have known it. "You have to do what you think is best" was the sum and substance of her reaction.

By the way, Ted Alexander won that primary election, beating Pete Warner and several other aspirants. Jill and I ended up supporting Ted—that is, sending him a little money and adding our names to an endorsement ad. To my surprise, Ron backed Pete. Trying to fathom the Machiavellian mind beneath that carrot-top head of his, I originally thought he might have *wanted* me in the race to take votes from Ted, but on second thought, I saw his scheme of discouraging me as a subtle, never-stated means of hurting his fellow lawyer, Pete, whom he only *seemed* to support. Did I have hope then that maybe he'd been exaggerating about Madge and I could count on another try for the congressional seat? Well, there was one small problem. Ted Alexander beat the Republican and we were entering a period when incumbents barely ever lost.

Meanwhile, I did rise in the ranks at home. We had no term limits in that era, so my people kept sending me back to the capitol. Under its (still ungilded) dome, I rose to the awesome position of house chair of the Appropriations Committee, a wielder of real power. Consequently a good question would be: Why wasn't I satisfied to stay on "the Hill" for a lifetime, like my pal Matt Drew, and actually die in the saddle as he did, collapsing out on that Statehouse balcony while enjoying a smoke?

It's not easy to explain my motivation, even to myself. All of a sudden, I was tired. That's one angle—you awaken one morning in a hotel room in the capital and you've simply had it. Your day will be filled with an endless parade of humanity and everyone is beseeching you for money, for those finite appropriations it's your job to dispense. Was this the idealism of Duke Ellery that I had sought to follow, support, and re-create? Maybe, I thought unexpectedly, I should go back to writing books full-time and teaching on the side.

At that time, Ritchie would be going off to college after the present session ended and I had to face preparing myself once again for the campaign trail. What if I simply said, "Screw it"? Jill and I could take more vacations. Matt Drew was dead. His scolding, which I could only imagine, wouldn't threaten to make me change my mind.

Jill agreed. Or at least there was no attempt by her to dissuade me.

The Democratic State Committee made a feeble effort. They offered me a chance to run for U.S. senator. Yeah, as a "sacrificial lamb" against an unbeatable Republican.

"You'll get enough name recognition statewide to run for anything you ever want to and we'll help you raise money" was their pathetic promise.

"Sorry, boys," and Jill helped, reinforcing my irreversible *nay*.

But for all my bravado, I'd caught the bug. One year, Peg McEntee made signals she was retiring. A state senate seat, as you've seen, continues to be a temptation to me. Too late, alas, she now finally does seem to be letting go (poor dear, she has breast cancer), and I'm an old has-been and the party has other talent.

Fate, Mike Fishman, and my perspicacious wife have led me to this latest project—this odd new book of mine, the biography that's an autobiography, the history that's been lived, and yet an effort, which if it isn't a purge of all my feelings, allows me to review the past as it has unfolded in the political life of one of the fifty building blocks of our nation.

I could swear I'm now ready for a last chapter, or two.

23

LET ME END, THEN, where I started. I'm talking about the Statehouse building, the capitol, with an *ol*. The legislature holds a yearly event there called Reunion Day. If you remember when last I drove into that extensive parking lot, it was neither quite autumn nor quite winter. Now I was back at another season of, so to speak, indeterminate sex, neither quite spring nor yet summer. The legislative session was pretty much finished. The guys and gals had lots of time on their hands. This was the traditional moment for us all, past and present members, living and healthy, presumably of sound mind and body, to get together for half a day of speeches, lunch, reminiscing, and schmoozing.

On this occasion, the leadership, God bless them, had had the foresight to rope off a section of the parking lot for the returnees' vehicles. Thus, without benefit of an elected mandate, old-timers like me temporarily could assume a privileged role once again and the swagger that went with it. Once again, we were among the little tin gods who held at least a modicum of power in the state and exercised it beneath the watchful but still ungilded figure of Minerva.

It struck me now, as it often did, that the governmental complex where we had all worked was not unlike a large sprawling factory. Churning out paper. Laws, the ultimate product. Yet since these were always changeable through amendment, repeal, tweak, correction—it was an eternal round by which a herd of humans in the state continually strove to bring some order into a basic Homo sapiens disposition toward chaos.

Also often, when I drive up here, my first thought is of the old joke: Why are there no one-armed politicians? Answer: Because how can they say, with accompanying gestures, "on the one hand" and "on the other hand"?

Actually, when I was in the legislature, we did have a member with only one arm. Major Tom Randlett—a combat vet, lost his limb at Omaha Beach, a decent, garrulous old fellow, full of war stories, and a fair-minded conservative. He died while we were in session and lots of us, even Democrats, went to his funeral, which was complete with color guard and burial in the veterans cemetery his bill had established in the state (we'd all helped Tom on that one).

As you can see, my mind was primed for reminiscences—a wealth of individual histories that never would be written. On the way to the capital city, I had started off wondering: *Who will be there today?* Then I would conjure up a face, a name, and supply each with an anecdote or two. It wasn't exactly déjà vu, more like a stream of consciousness. I was parking when my train of thought brought me to Major Randlett, and my next question to myself was, recalling my last visit and Mike Fishman: *Who'll be the first person I run into that I know?*

In a million years, I couldn't have guessed correctly.

Across from my parking space was the egress from one of the state office buildings. Who should be coming out just as I was about to shove the lever into Park but Tim Lavery! It had been literally years since I'd seen him. Somewhere along the line, I'd heard he'd retired from the state police and opened a private security agency. Seeing that slim, erect, dark-complexioned figure, I immediately swung open my car door and yelled, "Hey, Tim! Tim!" waving vigorously.

He spied me, paused, and waved back in his controlled, low-key way.

I hurried over and we shook hands. Words gushed out of me.

"Jesus, Tim, it's been a month of Sundays. How've you been? You look great, not much older, not like me. What brings you up to the funny farm? I'm back for our Reunion Day in the legislature."

I'd noticed his leather briefcase and three-piece suit, and it was no surprise to hear, "Been to the attorney general's office, looking up records on a case."

"Of course," I blurted. "I guess I knew you'd started your own business."

"Sold it," he said in his usual laconic style. "Doing freelance stuff now." I was about to respond, *Well, that's great,* or something equally fatuous, when I sensed that Tim seemed to have another thought to verbalize. He prefaced it with a quick half-smile, which was rare for him. "You made me remember," he said. "You called this place the funny farm. The Boss always called it that, too."

"I guess I picked up the habit subconsciously," I replied, with a half-grin of my own. "From Duke. I picked up a lot from him."

Our next few moments of shared silence were not so much to honor Duke's memory, I felt, as to reflect on his loss.

"Things sure would've been a lot different," Tim finally commented.

"That sure is for sure," I agreed.

As I uttered those words, I was instantly reminded of a war movie I'd seen as a kid in which one of the GIs, a Southerner, would always say: *That's for danged sure,* and so when another bout of silence followed between Tim and myself, I actually said, "Yes, that's for danged sure."

Tim looked up at me—he was almost a head shorter—and with his small, dark eyes veiled in memory, solemnly repeated, "Yes, that *is* for danged sure."

Well, this last exchange just about exhausted our conversation. Here at the funny farm, there seems to be a rhythm to all discussions. Both parties in a chitchat have an instinct about when to break off, of having to rush away to the next person or next thing to do. Tim and I said our goodbyes. He walked into the parking lot, headed for his car, and I remained in place, watching him go.

I don't think he had wanted to schmooze about old times. For me, the mere sight of him disappearing flashed a mental image of him from the back firing his service revolver at Miles, bringing once more the sniff of cordite, the screams of women, those visions of blood spreading at our feet. Two seconds of violence! My world forever changed. Tim's world forever changed—for *danged* sure.

But had the world's world actually been transformed?

Entering the Hall of Portraits, this perennial question assailed me again. The reunion registration desk was there. Around it, the first contact with former colleagues was made, the handshakes, the pats on the back or shoulders, the exchange of civilities, up-to-date curricula vitae, and in a number of cases, quips, witticisms and even an off-color joke. "You old sonofagun, how are you?" That was for times you didn't remember a name. Thank God for ID tags with big print, which we soon were all wearing. Hugs from the women. I even got one from Helen Bailey Pratt, the Republican's Republican, that nice little ditsy old lady. And all along, Duke was watching from his canvas perch on the wall, while despite the hubbub, I continued to have thoughts of him.

When I could, too, I would sneak glances up at that oil painting.

Because he had died in office, Duke could not have sat for the artist, who had had to work from a photograph. As you know, it's not a portrait of him that I like. Madge had chosen as a model what she called her "favorite snapshot" of him. Seated at his desk in the corner office, formal, unsmiling, "gubernatorial," even "presidential," he hardly seemed like a man who would refer to this whole crazy atmosphere on our "Hill" as the *funny farm*.

In other words, where was his humor, his ease, his empathy with humanity? And furthermore, I wondered about such elements of his character and personality, and the inner glow that attracted so many of us—were they missing as much from his legacy as they were from his likeness?

Still, the artist had caught something: his handsome, patrician features, the incredible intelligence behind those dazzling blue eyes, a sense of style, of grace, of America's best.

Soon enough—maybe all too soon—we "reunionites" were being ushered upstairs into the house chamber for the pre-lunch ceremonies.

I sat in the house gallery and listened once more—as I had for a gazillion hours—to speech after speech after speech.

From that vantage, I suddenly conceived a notion of the world bound together by an endless tape made of words. The verbal glue of civilization. Of democracy, at any rate, and of our own "Omurraycarr," with a sardonic nod to Miles—our good ol' USA, anyhow—where in our chambers of government, we bear aloft methods of maintaining order, justice, and fair play upon a huge, ever-filling balloon of talk.

Other societies use guns a lot more for those purposes than we do.

Then why did we have our Charles E. Guiteaus and Leon Czolgoszes and Lee Harvey Oswalds and John Wilkes Booths and Miles Monahans?

Even the very idea of such misfits, dissidents, soreheads, nut cakes, madmen, murderers, call them what you will, seemed utterly absent from Reunion Day activities. How much more foreign was my thought, focused briefly on Miles Monahan, so hung up—in my mind—by the essence of America that he could commit such a desperate, senseless act. The whole Uncle Sam bit, the O. Murray Carr bit—and I couldn't get that crap out of my

mind and totally enjoy what should have been a pure fun time—
one big happy family of big shots, past and present, getting
together without any responsibilities or partisan rancor, merely to
reminisce and eat a copious free lunch.

The get-together in the house chamber was what we called a
"joint session." The senate, much smaller in numbers, came over
from the other side of the capitol and took special seats set out
for them down front. According to ancient protocol, the senate
president presided. In this case, in this legislature, the senate
president was a woman. That had never happened in my day,
although we'd had a goodly number of female members. I
recalled my surprise one day during a discussion of the gentler
sex's future roles when Helen Bailey Pratt said she hoped women
would never be in any leadership positions.

"Including arch-conservative ones?" I asked teasingly. She
ignored my irony.

"The Bible says women should be subservient to men," she
replied instead.

Someone else attacked her with, "Do you think women
shouldn't have been given the vote?"

"We don't need it," she answered. "Big mistake."

"So are you a mistake, Helen?" was my follow-up query.
"Why did you run?"

And then, still remembering that impromptu bull session,
I realized I'd forgotten her answer or even if there had been one.
Smiling to myself mischievously, I thought: *I'll see her at lunch,
see whether I can get her to say "on the one hand" and "on the other
hand."*

For the record, the female senate president I was watching
preside had the reputation of being among the most conservative
members. She ran the proceedings as slickly as I'd seen any man
do it. Kind of a bittersweet sense of progress, to my way of
thinking. But a breakthrough is a breakthrough. And there were

others. Two African American members were plainly visible. There hadn't been a one in my day. I also picked out several legislators seated below whom I knew to be openly gay, of both sexes. In the past, if present, they'd have stayed in the closet. Poring over the little booklet that had come in our registration packets, which listed the names and addresses and CVs of all the members, I continued my search for diversity. There was a Native American, there was an Hispanic—at least the name was Gomez—and a whole raft of ethnic surnames: Slavic, Italian, Franco-American, Irish, Jewish. Completing my digression from the blah-blah-blah continuing below, I reflected that in another generation, we would undoubtedly have descendants of the newest immigrants to the United States who are even now reaching our out-of-the-way part of the country: Somalis, Ugandans, Brazilians, Cambodians, mainland Chinese, Bulgarians.

Midway through the speechifying period of these morning activities, the governor came to speak. There was always a bit of a rigmarole about this act in the show. He—(it was a *he*)—had to be invited. In fact, he had to be escorted. A committee of members, senators and representatives both, was appointed "to attend upon His Excellency the Governor." The group assembled, marched off, and about ten minutes later, there was a commotion out in the hall. The doors of the chamber were flung open and the governor's military aide, wearing the uniform of a National Guard officer, preceded the entourage, shouting like a town crier, "Make way, make way for His Excellency, the Governor of the State!" Flanked by the Committee to Attend, the governor arrived to instantaneous applause—everyone rising— *everyone*, me, too, although I couldn't stand the guy. The tribute was to the office, I always told myself on similar occasions. Not until that pompous, pinstriped figure reached the dais did we sit again.

Throughout his oration, which was as banal as I thought it

would be, I dwelt inwardly on remembering previous governors.

They do come and go. We give them two consecutive four-year terms, like the president of the United States. But unlike an occupant of the White House, they can run again after sitting out four years. No one yet has. This twerp below, in his last term, had been making noise about doing so in the future. It galled me, you can well imagine, that he had achieved a certain popularity. Anyone can in public life when all you do is talk about cutting taxes.

Was there a pattern, I wondered, mood swings among the electorate, that those chief executives reflected—Duke at one extreme and this doofus below at the other? Or did personalities alone make the difference? I had to remind myself that Big Bob Benton, may he rest in peace, had been an accident. Was it his ineptitude that had frittered away all the gains made during Duke's administration, or was it a reaction against so much positive action—or both? As I've mentioned, after filling out Duke's unfinished term, that good ol' boy had won another four years on a wave of sentiment. Yikes! His pals then talked him into running for what the GOP crowd called a "third term" and he got trounced and we ended up with a guy named R. J. Coleman. We said of him he "never met a tree he didn't want to cut down, a lake he didn't want to pollute, or a beautiful vista he didn't want to despoil." We creamed old R. J. on the environment when he ran for reelection. How many followed after that? An interspersal of D*s* and R*s*—so-so types—economic times were rough . . . hold the line . . . and Mr. Rollback, whose speech was just about finished, had succeeded them, and we all stood again and applauded when he left.

The activity that was the "funnest" (as my Ritchie used to say) immediately commenced.

This was the highlight of Reunion Day. It was a *count-off*, in reverse order. The senate president, who was acting as master (mistress?) of ceremonies, asked for all the members of the present legislature to stand. Then, those who had been in the immediate past legislature. The spectacle thus became to see who still stood, who sat and who rose as each preceding legislature's number was called. It wasn't exactly a game, but there was a winner. The last person left standing was the oldest member and received a standing ovation, thunderous, prolonged applause and an opportunity to address the gathering.

This day, we had a special treat. The ninety-year-old man who was led up onto the stage was carrying what looked like an instrument case of some sort. When people saw that, particularly the older folks in the audience, they went wild, screaming out his name—"Steve! Steve!"—and stomping their feet. The elderly gentleman, once he was at the rostrum, held up his hand for silence and when he got it, delivered a short, graceful speech in a pleasant down-home accent.

"Heavens t' Betsy," he started off. "Ain't you a fine lookin' bunch o' men an' women. You mostly all know that I been comin' back year after year, hopin' I'd win the big prize. But that Richard Sargent who got elected two years afore I did, he kept beatin' me out—an' he just wouldn't die [laughter]. So I fixed him. I got his wife t' take him t' Florida an' keep him there [more laughter]. Waill, finally I triumphed and yer gonna have t' listen t' me." At that point, he opened his case and took out a clarinet (great cheers) and began assembling it. A moment later, he was playing and for the next twenty minutes or so, we had a concert. In his youth, he'd been part of a jazz band and he soon had us clapping in rhythm and roaring for encores. His finale was again that old favorite "America the Beautiful" and we all stood and sang, as if it really were the national anthem.

I timed the ovation for him—five full minutes of delirious applause and chanting of "Steve! Steve!"—and after he was loaded up with presents, another three minutes of noisy appreciation followed him back to his seat. The fellow sitting next to me, a Republican I knew slightly, gave me a nudge in the ribs and said provocatively, "Yeah, well, he's one of ours," and I answered him in the same vein, "Yeah, well, you had to have a *few* good ones." With that spirit of non-serious camaraderie spread among us and cemented by Steve's performance, we all finally went to lunch.

Traditionally, the meal is prepared by a state-run cooking school, which does vocational training for the restaurant industry. It's all buffet style. The kids in their white outfits stand behind the tables and dish the food to us as we pass by with our trays. If the line is slow, which it always is, we have a chance to talk to some of these youngsters. We see our state tax dollars at work, providing worthy youth with a future. They speak to us of their hopes, their plans, of how valuable their school experience has been. I stood in line with my Republican friend from upstairs and we talked to a young couple handing out portions of chicken breast. Upon graduation, they told us, they would get married and start a restaurant in a small town upstate.

"Good program," my GOP companion commented as we moved on. I nodded in agreement, then couldn't help adding, "And Governor Slash-and-Burn wants to cut their funding." He simply rolled his eyes.

I saw Helen Bailey Pratt, her tray full, heading for a table to sit down. What was I going to ask her? Oh, yes, her answer to me why she'd run since she didn't believe women should vote. But when the time came and I was searching for a place myself, I dropped the impulse. Instead, I remembered Matt Drew's saying that we should gild Helen and replace the statue of Minerva with her. I figured I'd leave Helen alone and concentrate on thinking of people who weren't here, who'd passed on, like Matt, and whom I keenly missed.

Thus, I chose a seat where I sat alone, at least temporarily.

Matt, had he remained alive, would have taken one of the prizes of the day—most consecutive terms for a still-serving member. He never would have retired and he never would have been beaten in his district. The legislature was his life—and his death. He never stopped working, never stopped politicking, never stopped drinking or smoking or eating heavy meals, and as you already know, the big lug dropped dead one crisp winter afternoon, standing out in the cold, puffing on a cigarillo.

Suddenly, I felt a pang of regret. I missed Matt and I wished I hadn't come to this event.

Rather wildly, I glanced around at the jam-packed tables. Who did I see who had served with Matt? There should have been dozens of people. Yet I really wanted one of the "gang," those young guys like me, all Democrats, who had hung around with Matt in the days when you could smoke in the Retiring Lounge.

Names came back to me: the Honorable Walter Parmalee, the Honorable Todd Phelps, the Honorable Mary Heffernan, and—

I was interrupted. First, there was the sensation of someone arriving at my table, taking one of the seats. Then I heard my name spoken. "Representative Jackson?" The intonation was that of an inquiry.

I looked up to see a young man, as young as we were in those days when those guys and gals I was seeking to remember had crowded around Matt Drew. Like us then, this fellow wore the identification badge of a freshman member of the house. He hadn't set his tray down yet.

"Okay if I join you?"

Indicating it was fine, I noticed his features: a nice-looking kid, blondish, intelligent pale blue eyes behind glasses, and, most striking, his high cheekbones, denoting a Slavic background. After he settled himself, he stuck out his hand and said, "Representative Jackson, you won't remember me. I met you at my house when I was a little kid. I'm Jimmy Dudzik."

Whoa! This *was* like déjà vu, but attended by knowledge, not vagueness. I at once pictured a wooden three-decker apartment house on a side street in an industrial section of one of our communities. There was a porch on the ground floor where the kid and his family lived. He must have been eight or nine. The tyke—there he was, holding a football in his hands, watching the limousine in which we were riding pull up in front of his dwelling. Three of us got out—myself, Tim Lavery, and Governor Richard N. Ellery—and started up the walk. Instinctively, it seemed, this kid knew who was the person in charge, for he turned to Duke and asked, "Hey, Mister, where'd you get that funny license plate?" We all turned and stared back at the long black car in which sat a uniformed state trooper at the wheel, and focused on the rear plate that was in full view. Number 1.

Duke turned to the boy and answered him, "Well, I guess I know some important people," Then he asked, "What's your name, son?"

"Jimmy" was the answer. "Jimmy Dudzik. And you say it like Howdy Doody—dood-zik."

We three smiled at the child's apparent precociousness.

"We've come to see your father, Jimmy," Duke said.

"Yeah, I know," was his response. "You're the grubbinor, aint'cha?"

Our smiles became a collective laugh. Duke, especially, seemed tickled. "That's right, Jimmy. I *grubbin* the state."

Perhaps my memory of the incident remained so sharp due to this incident. It became a standard joke in the corner office: *Grubbinor* Ellery and how well or ill he *grubbinned.*

Another clear image was of Duke telling Jimmy, "Okay, I'm going out for a pass. Throw me the ball," and the handsome man in the elegant business suit and highly polished shoes ran out on the muddy grass of the tenement lawn, catching the toss from the towhead on the steps and flipping it back in a lateral, which Jimmy grabbed and fired again, and Duke snagged it. In the middle of all this, Jimmy's dad, the leader of the union local at the mill, arrived on the porch, A burly blond man of about forty, he had a phalanx of similar muscular fellows, and all paused to watch the pitch and catch in open-mouthed amazement.

We had arrived in the midst of a serious strike there in Warnerstown and I'll go into that whole story later, since the *grubbinor's* intervention, in which I played an active role, is also well etched in my mind.

But for the moment, I wish to direct my attention to the young man opposite me at the table.

"You know I do remember you, Jimmy," I said to him.

"Gosh, I'm flattered," he said. "I know my dad, if he knew I was seeing you, would want me to say hello for him."

"Your dad—what a great guy! Pug, we called him. But that couldn't have been his real name."

"Paul—Pavel, in our language. He's retired now. Pension from the union. He and Mom live in Florida."

"God bless America."

"You're not kidding."

We chattered on, genuinely pleased to have connected again. I did say I was surprised we hadn't met earlier at Democratic Party events, but Jimmy told me he'd only recently come home to the state after college, grad school, and a few years of work and had gotten into politics and been elected on his first try. "Like you," he said.

"Wow, you've done some homework," I said.

For a reason, I soon learned. He wanted my input on a bill he had introduced in this session. It seems I had put in a similar bill in the past and it hadn't passed. Such a very bright young man was conscientiously touching all bases on what was essentially a rather minor item of legislation.

I was impressed with his sincerity and flattered, myself, to be taken into his confidence and treated like an elder statesman as we huddled over our lunch trays and *conspired,* you might say, as if I had returned to the funny farm as a member in full standing.

24

Two things were at work simultaneously. I will leave aside
for the moment my working and plotting with the Honorable
James Dudzik on his proposed legislation and finish the memory
of the Warnerstown strike. Young Jimmy had his football back
and watched all of us adults troop into his house and maybe he
peeked from the porch through the family's parlor window while
we grownups talked.

Pug Dudzik's home had been the first stop on our visit. The
next was the Warnerstown mill itself. A TV news crew filmed our
arrival at the main gate. Up to forty or fifty strikers, men and
women both, were on the picket line outside, waving their
homemade signs and chanting slogans, but as we drove in they
stepped aside and cheered. It was no secret where Duke's sympa-
thies lay, although he didn't wave back to the crowd, trying to
appear solemn, gubernatorial, and, above all, impartial. We were
paying a "fact-finding courtesy call" to the management side, just
as we had stopped to say hello and listen to Pug Dudzik and the
union guys.

The plush offices housing the top brass of the mill, I have to
admit, did not provide a congenial atmosphere, but Duke
received what I would call a bunch of diatribes from them with
perfect equanimity. Some of these well-dressed, well-manicured
big shots of industry were used to dictating to governors. They
didn't forget to remind us how much they contributed to the
state's economy. They wanted our intervention to force their
employees back to work and to accept the offer the company had

tried to dictate. They threatened to bring in strikebreakers. They wanted the leaders of the strike arrested. One guy hollered that we should bring in the National Guard and "teach those lefty agitators a thing or two."

Duke sat in his chair, not saying very much, and nodding when he could find something reasonable in what they said.

Finally, he rose and declared, "Okay, we'll be meeting tonight at the high school. My job, fellas, is to get this thing settled and with no more violence. See you then."

"Wait a minute, Governor," the most vociferous of the company hierarchy cried. "Does that mean you're not going to call out the National Guard?"

"'Fraid not, Mr. Templeton," Duke replied. "We've got a state policeman here . . ." he pointed to Tim, "and another in the car. They'll be sufficient to maintain order."

All I remember from then on was a masterful performance by Duke, how we had labor in one high-school classroom and management across the hall and he crisscrossed from one place to the other, back and forth, back and forth, until the wee hours when somehow an agreement was reached. Then Duke put me to work, along with the company's PR man, and we drafted a joint statement, approved by both parties, for Georgie Everoff to include the next day in a press release and arrange for all sides to appear before the media.

No National Guard. No tear gas grenades. No strikebreakers. End of work stoppages. Tensions defused. Governor Richard Nathaniel Ellery earned his salary that night.

How many years ago had that been? Jimmy, I figured, was undoubtedly in his thirties now—so it was a quarter of a century, quite possibly.

Back discussing his bill, we were also descending into the past. Jimmy said to me, "One thing I couldn't find in the records was where you got the idea for this legislation."

I thought for a moment, and finally answered, "It's too bad they can't afford to have a stenographer take down oral testimony at a hearing. I did report to the committee that one of my constituents gave me the idea. He was a trucker, went all over the U.S., and it was one state—Ohio, or possibly Indiana, some midwestern state in any case—where they'd made it a law. When your windshield wipers were on, you had to turn on your headlights. A pure safety measure."

"But the Transportation Committee killed the bill on you," Jimmy said. "Unanimously opposed."

"Yes, those old codgers just laughed at it."

"Did you know that in Denmark," Jimmy said, "you have to drive with your headlights on at all times, night and day, rain or shine."

"You *are* thorough," I commented.

How thorough I soon discovered when he told me he had sewed up all but one vote on the committee. The actual hearing was scheduled for the following week and he didn't think it necessary for me to be there, but if he could have a note from me to read on the floor of the house when he presented the committee report, it would be a nice touch to credit me as the pioneer since I still had a lot of friends in office who'd appreciate it.

What a smart cookie, I kept thinking to myself. *He's going to have a helluva career.*

Before long, the dining area had pretty much emptied out, the old-timers leaving and the present-day members whose committees hadn't finished their work going off to hearings or to those activities we called "work sessions" where you discussed and argued and formulated the final legislative document to present to the entire body. There were also, this far into the legislative year, afternoon sessions in both chambers to try to get rid of the pile of work that still needed to be done.

"Okay, Jimmy, I'll see that you get some remarks from me

that you can read into the record, and I know you've got plenty of other stuff to do now. And what a pleasure to have run into you like this."

"Let's not be strangers," he said.

And we shook hands and formally took leave of each other. "Please give Pug and your mother my very best regards," I said as we went our separate ways.

I also had a quick reflection as I was leaving him. A phrase we often used in the legislature was: "an idea whose time has come." In other words, conditions have to be right for legislation to pass, and bills are defeated and resubmitted again and again until they ultimately are accepted. Some are big deals like abolishing slavery or attaining civil rights; others are just small items, like what Jimmy Dudzik was doing. The zeitgeist changes. But even those changes of attitude are slow and thus help provide us governmental stability in the USA.

To exit the Statehouse, I had to go down from the third floor, the heartland of the legislative process, containing the house and senate chambers where all debate and voting took place and the leadership and staff offices were located, as well as the Retiring Lounge and other perquisites available to the elected few. One floor farther down was the headquarters of the executive process, i.e., the governor's office and the rabbit warren of cubicles that housed his staff and a humongous conference room adjoining His Excellency's private quarters. It might seem logical then to expect that on the bottom floor you would find the judicial process enthroned, only to learn that the judges—the state supreme court, that is—and those who serviced our entire legal system throughout our state, had their own separate building in the capital.

I entered an elevator on the legislative floor and discovered to my surprise that I had it entirely to myself. For a fleeting moment, I considered disembarking at the second floor, going to the governor's office and telling the receptionist I had once worked there and wanted to stop in for old time's sake. But the occupants were now all Republicans, all strangers, so why waste my time? Consequently, I was at the first floor and the elevator door was opening before I'd had more than a moment of superficial thought about our American tri-partite system of legislative, executive, and judicial processes and how they intermeshed.

Needless to say, this was ground I've plowed mentally for years and even had formulated for one of my lectures at the college. I would base the talk on an obviously hypothetical instance of a bill passed by the legislature requiring all citizens of our state to dye their hair blue by a certain date. Opponents naturally screamed how it was unconstitutional. Yet the executive branch approved, via the governor's signature, and prepared to put this bizarre measure into effect. Not surprisingly, a citizens' group took the matter to court and the state supreme court ruled as might be expected, deeming such an imposition in violation of our state constitution. The proponents could have appealed to the U.S. Supreme Court, but to end this fairly sophomoric run-through of "how a bill becomes a law" and what can happen on the way, I said that cooler heads prevailed and its principal backers—a blue dye company—let it perish.

Smiling a bit as I silently reminisced about all this folderol, I decided that before I left the building, I would pause briefly in the Hall of Portraits for a last look at the painting of Duke on the wall.

Someone was there ahead of me, I noticed, as soon as I entered, and my smile suddenly became broader. Ironies of coincidence are not infrequent in the political world. The gentleman staring up at Duke's likeness was none other than—can you believe it?—the chief justice of the state supreme court!

His name was Leonard Verne Follansbee. He had served in the house with me and I *had* noticed him at the Reunion Day festivities; we'd waved to each other but hadn't gotten a chance to talk. Not that we were close buddies. He was a staunch Republican, a partner in one of the state's biggest law firms before running for office, easily elected, and then picked for the bench by a GOP governor and moved up by other chief executives in his party to the top judicial post. Although conservative to the core, he and I had always enjoyed a friendly relationship due to our shared interest in American history.

He was in profile as I approached, a short, portly, dapper figure in an expensive pinstriped suit, still wearing his Reunion Day name tag, who became aware of my presence when I was only a few steps away.

"Brother Jonathan," he greeted me.

"Mr. Chief Justice," I said.

"How about just plain Len?" he replied.

"Good to see you, Len. I had hoped we'd have a chance to meet." We shook hands like warm old friends, genuinely glad to encounter one another.

Forgive me, but I must interject at this moment what would be an explanatory footnote of the type I've tried so hard to avoid: Len's use of *Brother Jonathan*. History buffs would know it as a nickname for the symbolic American of the Revolutionary period; its counterpart *John Bull* for the British. Also, lawyers call each other *Brother*—although as I like to say jokingly, I am not a lawyer, and my other habits are also good.

At any rate, Len and I met there by Duke's portrait, gazed up at him, exchanged our admiration for him, and finally moved on together, prompted by Len's remark that he liked to "make the rounds here" and had only just started with Duke.

We were an appropriate combo, I had to think, the two of us going around the spacious room as if on an inspection tour of this array of commemorative artistry from different eras, done in the styles of their epochs. For Len and I had teamed together—

he, the Republican floor leader, and me, a Democrat on the Appropriations Committee—to arrange funding for nameplates and plaques that identified these fellows (universally males) with mini-bios and historical facts about their administrations. Most of these ex-govs were obscure, and the hall for years had been ignored and merely considered the last resting place of a bunch of bearded, mutton-chop-whiskered and mustachioed old geezers. Thanks to Len and myself, they now received a lot more attention.

Only a handful of them were really well known, starting with our "George Washington," or rather, the post-Revolutionary figure who had led us to statehood. Our Civil War governor was to make his national mark afterward in the U.S. Senate. One man had been U.S. secretary of commerce, another the Speaker of the House in Congress, and finally the ex-congressman who might have become president, although this conjecture had been left off the info about him—Governor Richard N. Ellery.

Len and I made our tour and ended back in front of Duke.

Whoever had written those extended captions beneath the frames had also, in Duke's case, left out his nickname. I mentioned this to Len, who had apparently noticed the other unspoken omission, as well, and remarked, "Jonathan, you and I know, I'm sure, that Duke was planning to run for the White House."

"Well, he never *exactly* told me," I had to admit, although my tone definitely declared that I agreed with him.

"Well, he did tell me," said Len.

"Really?" If I sounded incredulous, I genuinely couldn't totally disguise my sense of doubt.

"I was planning to support him," Len quickly volunteered.

"Wow!"

My exclamation reverberated, causing me to glance around furtively to see if anyone had heard me. A few individuals had since come into the gallery, but no one that we knew. Nevertheless, Len kept his voice low while telling me about a secret meeting he'd had with Duke a week or so prior to the fateful trip to California. Having wrung an admission from Duke that there was a good chance he would go for the Democratic nomination, Len said he had told him, "Governor if you're the nominee, I will be with you—openly—in the general election and, if you wish, head up Republicans for Ellery." It was an offer gratefully accepted, I was told. Then Len gave his reasons. They boiled down to Duke's character, which overrode his positions on issues. The cynic in me thought momentarily: *Len was betting on a winning horse.* But the supreme court chief justice really seemed much too sincere to have been pursuing politics as usual.

No matter. It was never to be.

While we were having this discussion and Duke, above us, was, as it were, listening in, we became aware of protracted noise in our vicinity, a bubbling of children's voices, and discovered a troupe of school kids with their teacher and a Statehouse guide viewing portraits nearby and asking questions when they weren't horsing around and poking each other and wisecracking.

Len had a pleased look on his face as he stated, "That's how I began my career, Brother Jonathan, among a busload from our junior high and right here in this room, especially, seeing these ancient worthies before we had any identifications for them. You and I done good, Brother."

"Thank you, Brother Follansbee. Democrats do sometimes have their uses."

"Alas, yes."

Interrupting our mutual chuckling was the arrival in our immediate vicinity of that parade of youngsters following the two adults accompanying them. The guide, after nodding to us, pointed out to his audience that they were now in the more modern section of governors. He indicated several of the portraits. "That's Governor Benton. . . . That's Governor R. J.

Coleman . . ." before turning back to Duke: "And here's Governor Ellery." The guide drew their attention to the informative placard. "Read about him. He was murdered."

That stark statement quieted the group immediately. The teacher thereupon chimed in, "When a public figure is killed," he said pedantically, "we call that an assassination. Governor Ellery was shot in California, on his way home from a governors conference."

"Why?" asked one of the boys.

"A crazy man did it" was the answer from the uniformed guide. "No one knows his motive. He was killed, too, by a policeman. The mystery remains." Acknowledging our presence finally, this longtime employee of the state added, "These two gentlemen worked here when Governor Ellery was in office."

All those kids shot us a once-over expression of interest that soon faded. The next minute, they were off to see another part of the Statehouse.

Len and I parted. My last words to him were like a feed-in from the scene we had just witnessed: "Brother Follansbee, you've spent a good deal of your life dealing with crime and criminals. Why do *you* think Duke was shot? Can you clarify the mystery?"

"Brother Jonathan," he responded after a bit of thought, "it could have been a full moon for all I know."

"Conceivably," I conceded, although remembering quite clearly a crescent moon during our stay at that glitzy hotel spread in Los Angeles.

The ride back to Swansville was like hundreds of others I'd taken. Down from "the Hill," descending Government Street, into the business and shopping center along the riverfront, over the Governor Richard N. Ellery Bridge, off to the Interstate. Clear of the city, of the dominating Statehouse shadow, of poor Minerva, still her pukey green color, I started to sing aloud, despite knowing how ridiculous I would appear to any passing motorist.

"Oh, beautiful, for spacious skies, for amber waves of grain. . . ."

My favorite of favorites.

When I reached the chorus, I was suddenly aware that my voice had morphed into those "O. Murray Carr" sounds.

"Quit that," I commanded.

Consequently, the refrain became distinctly: "Am-er-ri-ca! Am-er-ri-ca!"

Several more verses, several more refrains, and pretty soon, I grew tired of my silliness and traveled a few more miles in utter silence. But all of a sudden, a thought—at once disturbing and even eerie—hit me. *Brother Jonathan!* The personified symbol representative of the thirteen colonies, a simple lad toting a musket, a patriot, if also a rebel, building a nation and exemplifying the old-fashioned "virtue" praised so significantly by Duke— and what symbol had taken his place since? I hadn't realized its significance until now.

Uncle Sam!

I want you. . . . That pointing finger.

Taking a deep breath, I eradicated the mental image of a goateed man in a gaudy costume striding on stilts, then reached for the car radio knob, twisted it to tune in to the afternoon news, and settled back, driving leisurely home to the still lovely grandmother-to-be awaiting my return.

Quite possibly tonight, we would start planning our imminent trip to Los Angeles, to Ritchie and Irene's wedding, the impending birth, and a whole different era in our American lives.